THE
HIDDEN
RELIC

The Evermen Saga, Book 2

OTHER TITLES IN THE EVERMEN SAGA:

Text copyright © 2014 James Maxwell

Published by 47North, Seattle

www.apub.com

Amazon, the Amazon logo, and 47North are trademarks of Amazon.com, Inc., or its affiliates.

ISBN-13: 9781477823811
ISBN-10: 1477823816

Cover design by Mecob

Library of Congress Control Number: 2014930972

Printed in the United States of America

THE HIDDEN RELIC

The Evermen Saga, Book 2

JAMES MAXWELL

47NORTH

This book is for my wife,
Alicia,
the jewel of my life.

THE TINGARAN EMPIRE

IN THE YEAR OF THE EVERMEN 542

PROLOGUE

Evrin Evenstar had given Killian a quest, and now he would see to his own vital task. If Killian succeeded in destroying Stonewater's magical machines—the harvesting plant, the extraction system, and the refinery—Evrin would have to work to ensure that the greatest relic of all remained hidden.

Evrin followed Killian with his eyes until the younger man disappeared from view, vanishing along the pilgrim's trail, heading for Stonewater's heart.

Evrin had done his best: He'd imbued Killian with as much power as he could, considering the young man's lack of knowledge about the runes, and armed him with the destructive cubes. The lad's fate was now out of his hands.

Yet he couldn't help worrying. Killian would face perils within Stonewater, and Evrin wished he could do more. He wished the young man good fortune and prayed they would soon be reunited at the appointed place, the sky temple in Salvation.

The old man rubbed at his eyes, looking up the mountain, his gaze finally resting on his destination—the very summit of Stonewater, the place they called the Pinnacle.

Evrin began to climb, his joints creaking as he placed one foot in front of the other, the path becoming steeper. Soon, Evrin knew, there would be a fork in the path. The left fork led to the workrooms of the senior priests and templars. It was the right fork Evrin was interested in.

Taking a series of winding stairs, Evrin paused for breath, leaning on the stone wall for support. He could remember a time when the scenes carved into the stone were fresh and crisp, the steps sturdy and new. Now each step was cracked and worn, and he could barely make out the whorls and lines that had once created an image on the wall.

What was it a picture of? Surely he had once known.

As he waited for his strength to return, Evrin looked out at the vista below. The wind buffeted him, and he again clutched the stone for support. He was high, so high that even the buildings of Salvation were tiny, the people like ants.

Evrin thought of the primate. What it must do for a man's sense of hubris to live up here at the top of this mountain.

Killian would be inside now. Evrin resumed his climb; he couldn't afford any more pauses. He came to the fork and took the right-hand path, bearing upward. The pilgrims who took these same steps would be flushed with excitement, about to reach their destination—the place they had journeyed across the world and faced the hardship of travel to see. The Pinnacle.

Evrin increased his speed, but the next stage was a long set of steps without a break, and soon his breath ran ragged, the muscles in his legs burning. He kept his head down, his hands on his knees, taking one step after another, counting them. It frightened him, how hard he now found this path compared to days gone by.

Evrin heard a rumble from within the belly of the mountain and smiled to himself at the sound of the explosion; Killian was doing well. Evrin had been searching for Killian for an eternity, and although he knew the questions Killian was burning to have answered, first he must—

Some loose gravel rolled under Evrin's foot, and the wind twisted the robe around his ankles. With a cry the old man's muscles gave out, and he tripped, falling to the ground and smashing his knees on the hard stone. When Evrin was able to think, he realized he was on the ground, sprawled across the steps. He clutched at the wall, but pain shot through his ankle, sending stars bursting inside his head. He looked down at his sandaled foot. The ankle was twisted, and already his foot was beginning to swell, the flesh white and puffy.

Evrin probed it with his hands, and the pain made him gasp. He shook his head ruefully.

"In the name of all that's holy," Evrin said. He almost smiled, realizing how fitting the words were, given where he was, but the smile came out as a grimace.

The sharp pain settled to a regular throb, timed to the beating of his heart. Evrin needed to get to the Pinnacle before the next explosion. It wouldn't take Killian long to find the extraction system and then the refinery. He wondered what surprises the primate had in store for the young man, whether there were templars defending the relics—or something even worse. Nothing the lad couldn't handle, he hoped.

Evrin winced as he tried to stand. Once, he would have been able to heal himself, and the pain would have vanished, the tendons knitting together until he was again whole and undamaged. It was an ability he no longer had.

Evrin finally used a mental trick to ignore the pain in his ankle and continue up the endless steps. He had been counting, hadn't he?

"What's the point?" he muttered. Yet for some reason Evrin again found himself counting from one.

"One."

Groan. Step. Drag. Pause. Deep breath.

"Two."

Evrin wondered if he would make it before the extraction system blew. He listened intently for the rumbling sound of another explosion. The pain of his twisted ankle was a constant distraction, occupying his mind when what he needed most was to plan what he would do when he reached the Pinnacle.

It was just ahead.

The stone wall fell away as Evrin approached the summit of the mountain. The howling wind blew with power, gusting at his body, causing the pilgrim's robe to whip against his legs. With no hand-holds and a sheer drop to either side of the stairs, Evrin resisted the urge to look down. He'd never had a head for heights.

The summit of Stonewater, the very peak of the mountain, was a circular space a hundred paces in diameter. Located in the center of that space, the Pinnacle was the holiest, most renowned place in the Tingaran Empire. The Pinnacle shone on the world, and from here the light of the Evermen could be felt from anywhere, or so the priests said.

The Pinnacle was undeniably a work of great power. It was a hemisphere of light, as tall as a tree and wide as a palace, shining with golden radiance day and night. The glowing nimbus of the Pinnacle wasn't too bright to look at, yet its sparkle could be seen for leagues in all directions.

Stepping into the light was an experience the pilgrims said had to be felt in order to be appreciated. First came a feeling of warmth, and a soft buzzing sounded in the ears. Closer still and nothing but light could be seen in all directions—said to provide a feeling of the utmost peace. A few more steps, and the buzzing became a crackle. Every pilgrim tried to approach still further before he or she was pushed away.

The light simply repelled the visitor, and then the pilgrim was back where he or she had started. People from all nations of the

Tingaran Empire speculated about whether anyone would one day penetrate deeper inside and whether what was inside was simply more of the light or a grand secret of the Evermen, hidden within its confines.

Evrin knew the truth. He gazed steadily at the Pinnacle as he crested the steps, limping toward it. The light shone back at him, impassive and unchanging. Evrin knew the truth, and he also knew he would have only this one opportunity and that what he was doing was perhaps the most important task of his life.

Five pilgrims clustered around the light, staring at it in awe.

Evrin raised his voice as he approached. "There is danger here. Be gone, all of you."

A voice came from close behind him. "You don't give the orders here, pilgrim. I do."

Turning, Evrin saw a man with the sword and uniform of a templar. Evrin noted the yellow eyes. The templar had the taint.

"The danger," Evrin said, "is from me."

Evrin spoke three words and opened the palm of his right hand. A bronze bracelet appeared at Evrin's wrist and a matching ring at his index finger. Silver symbols decorated the edge of the bracelet, and as Evrin spoke two more sequences, the bracelet and ring flared red.

As Evrin raised his arm the templar stepped back. A circle of pure light came from Evrin's bracelet, traveling along his wrist. The circle grew tighter and smaller as it approached the ring, finally condensing to a tiny disk of energy too bright to look at.

The light left the ring with incredible speed, too fast for the eye to see.

The templar looked down at the hole in his chest, an expression of surprise and disbelief on his face. His breath rattled, and he crumpled to the stone.

The pilgrims fled, and Evrin turned back to the Pinnacle, thinking about what it actually was.

A barrier.

The Evermen once met here at the summit of Stonewater to discuss the issues and plans that affected them all. Their greatest works of lore, from mighty weapons to complex machines, were conceived at the structure now hidden by the light.

In days long gone, the chamber at the summit of the mountain was open to the sky. Only later was the barrier conceived, activated to repel any unwelcome visitors and keep the chamber concealed.

Evrin was here now because the barrier was about to vanish. Before today, he'd always been confident that the secrets preserved within its confines could never be discovered, especially by a man like Primate Melovar Aspen. Evrin himself could not break through to the chamber hidden within the light.

But the barrier had a weakness: It was powered by the refinery, deep in the bowels of the mountain.

The refinery Evrin had just asked Killian to destroy.

Evrin dragged himself closer to the light. He cocked his head to the side as he listened.

The explosion was bigger than he had imagined it would be. When he felt it, Evrin's first thought was relief that Killian had come this far. He'd destroyed the extraction system, and only the refinery remained. The rumble grew in intensity, becoming a series of explosions as each part of the massive system caused the next to detonate, while the ground trembled under Evrin's feet and dust rose into the air. The noise was deafening, and Evrin put his hands to his ears. If the templars didn't know about Killian's intrusion before, they would now.

The barrier still held. It wouldn't be until the destruction of the refinery that the light would fade, revealing the secret chamber within.

Evrin withdrew a destructive cube from his pocket. When the device was unleashed, it would feed on other magic, increasing the cube's destructive power while devouring anything it encountered that was built with essence.

The moment the barrier came down, Evrin planned to destroy the chamber at the Pinnacle. The last great project of the Evermen would remain secret for all time.

Evrin took a shaky step forward into the light, waiting for the final explosion, yet when it came, the destruction of the refinery still took him by surprise. The quake threw him to his knees, the pain from his ankle shooting through his leg. Even here, at the top of the mountain, the sound of falling rock was deafening. Evrin tried to stand, but the quakes grew in strength, and it wasn't until the shaking subsided that he finally struggled to his feet.

The hemisphere of light surrounding the chamber was gone. Where it had been was a level space, and in the middle of that space stood a solitary structure, the highest building in the world.

As the ground continued to tremble, Evrin limped forward. Killian had done it—that much was clear—but whether the boy was alive and unharmed by the explosion was an unanswered question. Evrin prayed he would be well. They still had much to discuss.

The low structure had four arched entrances, one at each of the cardinal points. A myriad of symbols decorated each arch, appearing untouched by the centuries. Evrin limped forward, for the first time seeing it as a temple with dramatic entrances and intricate stonework. This was where the Evermen came to acknowledge their own magnificence.

The mountain rumbled again. The explosion must have been immense. How could Killian survive such a thing? With an effort, Evrin pushed thoughts of the boy out of his mind. Killian had achieved his objectives. Now Evrin needed to complete his.

He walked forward and entered the structure. It was laid out as two concentric squares: an outer chamber where glorious artwork described the wondrous feats performed here and an inner chamber where the actual work was done. Mosaics decorated the floor of the outer room, scenes of the Evermen working in concert, creating works of lore that none of them could ever have made on his own. The walls burst with color: golden suns shining on green fields; silver stars sparkling from a midnight-blue sky; a tall mountain that could only be Stonewater, looming over a crowd of men and women.

Evrin gripped the destructive cube tightly in his fist, surprised at his reaction after so long. Emotion gripped him, and he suddenly felt alone, more alone than he'd felt in an age. He'd thought himself accustomed to his place in the world, but it seemed his heart knew better.

Evrin reached the inner chamber and stepped forward, his heart hammering and the pain in his ankle momentarily forgotten. Diagrams and symbols were everywhere, etched into the marble with veins of gold. Runes covered the floor and the ceiling, matrices and patterns too complex even for Evrin to grasp alone.

In the middle of the room was a raised series of steps. On the highest tier stood a pedestal, and on the pedestal lay a closed book.

Made of the same metallic fabric the Evermen used in all their works, the book was as thick as the span of a man's hand. On the cover was an androgynous figure wearing a crown, head tilted, looking up at the sky.

The skin rose on the back of Evrin's neck; the room fairly reeked of power, and even through the urgency of his task, Evrin couldn't help himself.

"Tuh-ruk. Suh-ran. Tuk-ruk Evrin Evenstar," he spoke without thinking.

The room came to life. Soft music sounded, fluting and triumphant. The runes on the walls, floor, and ceiling shone in a multitude of colors. The Evermen's final plan was revealed in all its glory, and with a word or a gesture Evrin could call forth any detail, examine any aspect of the project. For a moment he was filled with awe at the magnificence of it; this was the greatest work of lore the world had ever seen.

With a sigh, Evrin spoke the words, and the room became empty once more. He reminded himself that the relic must be kept from the templars at all costs. Destroying the chamber filled him with sadness, but the risk was too great not to.

Evrin climbed the steps up to the pedestal, placing the destructive cube on top of the book. *"Lot-har,"* he said, activating the device and turning away. There, it was done. He had several seconds to depart.

The ground trembled again. Evrin stumbled as he stepped off the last step, and his ankle turned, pain driving up his foot and through his leg in waves. He fell to the floor.

As the mountain heaved, Evrin looked back at the pedestal and the book that sat atop it, seeing the cube fall from the book and land on the topmost step. The mountain shuddered again, and the cube fell down to the next step with a tinkle.

The device had been activated. It would explode at any instant. More than anything, the book must not escape.

Evrin launched himself at the cube, but it was just out of reach. Ignoring the pain in his ankle, he reached for it, but it moved away from him, tinkling as it rolled along the floor, gathering momentum as it left the inner chamber completely.

Evrin realized he wouldn't make it.

He rolled onto his stomach and covered his head with his arms.

The cube exploded.

Far below, in the town of Salvation, people looked up in awe as smoke billowed from Stonewater like a volcano.

1

Miro deployed more troops to the northern regions of Halaran. Immediately, the weakness in his eastern defenses became apparent: The Black Army would push through all the way to Sarostar. He rubbed at his eyes and reset the simulator.

The simulator was the size of a large table and occupied a special room inside the Crystal Palace. Miro ran his dark eyes over the lands of the former Tingaran Empire, represented in incredible detail, suffused with the color that thousands of tiny runes projected onto its surface.

To the extreme west was Altura, bordered by the Dunwood in the north and the land of Vezna farther still to the north and east. In Altura's west, the Great Western Sea stretched endlessly. Some said the world of Merralya ended here, although a minority said no sea was endless. Only the Buchalanti could know, but the sailmasters of House Buchalantas weren't known for being informative.

Bordering Altura in the east was the land of Halaran, now occupied by the enemy. Miro could only wonder at the horrors Altura's traditional allies must be enduring.

South of Altura, across the blocked Wondhip Pass, was the homeland of House Petrya. Miro never stopped fearing an attack from that direction, though he knew of only the one route, and passage that way was barred by massive blocks of stone.

Farther south, past Petrya, was the great Hazara Desert. Never part of the Tingaran Empire, the tribes had hitherto kept to themselves. In this war, that was no longer an option.

To the east of Halaran was the heartland of the enemy: Torakon, the homeland of the builders; Loua Louna, where the Black Army had driven through in a surprise attack; Aynar, where Stonewater formed the spiritual heart of the empire; and Tingara itself, where the late emperor had ruled his dominion from the city of Seranthia.

Each land's borders were shown, but all lands except Altura were darkened, under the dominion of the enemy. Two dots still glowed on Altura's southern coast: the free cities of Castlemere and Schalberg. Another region, the Hazara Desert, was also free from the enemy's grip, but who could say what occurred in the yellow sands of the far south?

Miro thought about the fierce tribes of the desert lands. What game would they play? How would the Hazarans and this new lore they were said to possess influence the war?

"Look at you. You haven't shaved in days. Are you even sleeping properly?"

As Miro looked up, his black hair fell in front of his eyes, and he impatiently pushed it away.

Marshal Beorn stood across from Miro, both palms resting on the simulator's edge. "How long have you been here?" Beorn asked. "Get some rest, Lord Marshal."

Miro wiped at his eyes; they felt grainy and heavy, and for a moment Beorn's face wavered in his vision. The marshal's face was marked by his age, weathered and worn, but far from old. Beorn's hair and beard were gray, but his eyes were sharp, and he and Miro shared a bond of mutual respect that could only be formed on the battlefield.

Beorn's steadiness was the counterpoint to Miro's daring, and Miro knew that some of his bolder ideas had gone forward solely due to the veteran officer's support. If Beorn said no, Miro knew an idea had little merit; but if the marshal wavered, then perhaps a plan had potential, with a little more thought.

"I told you to call me Miro. What time is it?"

"It's two hours past daybreak."

Miro grinned. "Then it's morning. Time to wake up, isn't it?"

Beorn gave Miro a wry smile, shaking his head. "What have you learned?"

Miro turned back to the simulator, his expression again grim. "Halaran is the answer. See?" His fingers touched some of the runes, lighting up various elements of his units as he spoke about them. "We're wasting valuable men defending our southern regions from a Petryan attack that may never come."

"Surely you aren't advocating pulling them out. The Wondhip Pass could be cleared, or the Petryans could find another way in."

"I'm just hypothesizing." Miro activated some more sequences. "Look, here are the constructs we left behind at the ruins of the Bridge of Sutanesta. They aren't far away, just inside Halrana lands."

"Territory held firmly by the enemy," Beorn said.

"But if we take it, we not only get a foothold in Halaran, but we can add the salvageable constructs to our forces." Miro moved all of the allied units to the proposed area. At first glance, there were enough to win the region, but with a slim margin that could swing either way.

"And who would defend our north?" Beorn persisted.

"The Dunfolk," Miro said.

"I'll leave that argument for another day. And our south?"

Miro sighed. "That's where the plan falls down. The Petryans are simply too much of an unknown. Yet winter is nearly over, and with the spring bringing more battles, the one thing we can't do is sit back and let the enemy devour Altura a bite at a time. In fact, I keep asking myself, why haven't they attacked yet?"

"We broke their army," said Beorn.

"Yes, but they've had time to reform. Ella thinks it's something to do with essence, that we aren't the only ones running low."

"Miro, I trust your sister, but the primate of the Assembly of Templars—low on essence?"

Miro shrugged. "I know. The essence we depend on for all our lore comes from Stonewater in the first place. But that's where the signs are pointing."

"Lord Marshal," a voice called, echoing in the high-ceilinged room.

Miro turned. Many people disliked the Crystal Palace, with its arches instead of doorways, strange echoes, and scattered shadows, but Miro had already become fond of it in the short time he'd called the palace home. The Crystal Palace said something about the uniqueness of Altura.

An Alturan in the *raj hada* of a courier stood at the arched entrance to the room.

"What is it?" Beorn said.

"The emissary from House Hazara, Jehral of Tarn Teharan, has presented himself. With him is the trader from Castlemere, Hermen Tosch. They wish to see you."

Miro shared a glance with Beorn. He still didn't know what to make of this desert warrior and his new nation, House Hazara.

Jehral had arrived in Sarostar the previous day, claiming to represent his leader, a prince whose name Miro couldn't remember. Jehral had said House Hazara was not a new house, but rather a fallen house that had been reborn. Miro wasn't sure what to believe.

Miro cursed himself; he'd meant to speak with Ella about this man, but instead he'd stayed here, forming battle strategies with the simulator. *Tiredness leads to regret,* Miro reminded himself.

"First, please summon High Lord Rorelan, and then show them in," Miro said.

Miro spoke some words to deactivate the simulator and return it to the state where it was no more than a map. He heard footsteps and looked up as two men entered the room.

The two newcomers were as alike as night and day. Jehral was beardless, with long dark hair held back by a circlet of silver. His loose clothing of black silk was bound by a sash of yellow, and combined with his sharp features and olive skin, the garments made him look unmistakably foreign.

Hermen Tosch had the broad build of the Buchalanti, or someone of Buchalanti stock, which meant a denizen of the free cities, Castlemere and Schalberg. His hair was cut short, and he appeared to be a man who rarely smiled. He seldom spoke, but when he did it was with a thick, guttural accent.

Surprisingly, it was Hermen who spoke first. "We were told to wait, but Jehral is not used to waiting. Apologies, Lord Marshal."

Miro smiled tightly. "The high lord is on his way. He wishes to meet with you both."

"This high lord," Jehral said, his voice smooth and flowing, "he is your prince?"

Miro paused for a moment. "Yes, he is," he finally said. "High Lord Rorelan rules Altura, and I follow where he leads."

After the battle at the Bridge of Sutanesta, Rorelan had been made high lord, although he had made it clear to his supporters among the nobility that his acceptance was conditional on Miro's confirmation as lord marshal. Both Miro and the new high lord were happy—Rorelan was pleased to have a more experienced soldier lead the war effort, and Miro was content to leave the leadership of his homeland to a capable administrator.

"You'll remember Marshal Beorn?" Miro said.

Jehral executed a brief bow, culminating in a flourish, and Miro recognized that the desert warrior possessed grace. Beorn nodded.

"Can I offer you refreshment?" Miro asked. "The high lord will be along shortly."

"Actually, it is you I wish to speak with, Lord Marshal Miro Torresante," Jehral said.

"Apologies, Jehral of Tarn Teharan, and I realize it may work differently in your land, but we should wait for the high lord before discussing matters of . . . political importance," Miro said. Lord of the Sky, he was tired. Where was High Lord Rorelan?

"It's about your sister," Jehral said.

"My sister?" Miro started. "What about her?"

"My prince is very interested by her. She is a mighty enchantress, is she not?"

"Yes, I suppose she is."

"And it is true that she built the bridge that saved your people at the Battle of Sutanesta? That she crossed a great chasm with nothing but lore?"

Miro tried to make sense of the Hazaran emissary's words. There was a subtext here that he didn't understand. He could tell when a topic was being spoken around rather than about. But in the Skylord's name, he couldn't figure out what Jehral was getting at.

Beorn grinned at Miro's discomfort. "Yes, it's true," he answered for him.

"And she created an illusion that sent many of this Black Army to their maker?"

"Yes, she did." Miro rubbed at his eyes again. Where was the high lord?

"Incredible," Jehral said. "Tell me, Lord Marshal Miro, what is her name again?"

"Ella," Miro said. "Her name is Ella."

"Ella," Jehral repeated.

As Jehral finished speaking, High Lord Rorelan entered the room. The recent battle had aged the late Lord Devon's son; his complexion was pallid at the best of times, and lately his skin was gray and drawn. But today his patrician features were set in a scowl, and he stormed into the room without even noticing the two visitors.

"Miro, I need to speak with you," Rorelan said. "It's about your sister."

Miro and Beorn bowed their heads, placing their fingers over their lips and then touching their foreheads, and Jehral and Hermen hesitantly followed suit.

"High Lord," Miro said, "this is Jehral of Tarn Teharan, emissary of House Hazara, and Hermen Tosch of Castlemere. There is a great deal for us all to speak about. The Hazarans share a border with Petrya,"—Miro glanced significantly at Rorelan—"and much of our trade is dependent on the free cities."

"Please, High Lord, we can see that we are interrupting," Jehral said. "We are presently lodging in your beautiful city, and we can discuss these matters at a time more convenient."

Jehral and Hermen Tosch bowed and withdrew, leaving the three Alturans watching them depart.

"What was that about?" Beorn said. "First they storm in here without so much as a by-your-leave, and then when we make time for them, they go."

Miro sighed. "I fear there's a lot about these people that we don't understand." He turned to Rorelan. "Apologies, High Lord, they were supposed to wait while I sent a courier for you. It's probably for the best that we speak with them another time. I need to ask my sister about this Jehral and his people. She said she spent some time with them, and we should properly formulate a response before negotiating with them. I take it something else brought you here?" Miro stifled a yawn, and his jaw cracked. "You mentioned my sister?"

Rorelan's scowl returned. "I've just come from a meeting with High Enchanter Merlon. Miro, do you have any idea how low our supplies of essence are? We can't afford these experiments of hers. The High Enchanter says she won't listen to reason. And this new companion of hers . . . let's just say the Lord Marshal's sister needs to consider the company she keeps."

"I'll speak with her," Miro said. "Where can I find her?"

A great boom sounded from somewhere, followed by a whoosh that made the ground rumble. If they had been anywhere except the Crystal Palace, dust would have fallen from the ceiling.

High Lord Rorelan leveled Miro with a frown. "I don't think you'll have any trouble finding her."

2

Tapel was always finding strange things, but this was certainly the strangest. He regarded the man, as always trying not to stare too hard at the bandages around the man's throat, while the man regarded him back with coal-dark eyes. The man tried to sit up, and when Tapel pushed him back down as his mother had instructed, the stranger was too weak to protest.

Tapel's mother was always telling Tapel what to do and what not to do when it came to the stranger. She was out a lot of the time, so it was often Tapel who took care of him.

It was only fair, Tapel supposed. It was he who had found the stranger, after all.

———◆———

The armies of Altura and Halaran met the Black Army just outside Ralanast, in a great collision of men and steel in the now-ravaged land that had once been low farmland, gentle hillocks, and forested copses.

Like so many others, Tapel and his mother, Amelia, prayed for their countrymen and their Alturan allies. Ralanast had been occupied for weeks, and all knew the attempt to liberate the Halrana capital from the ruthless soldiers of the Black Army was a desperate gamble.

The explosions and screams could be heard throughout the day from all quarters of Ralanast, from the dusty masons' enclave to the deserted market district. The Halrana who'd stayed in their capital, rather than attempt the frantic flight to Altura, gathered in front of the Terra Cathedral, old men and women with small children peacefully demonstrating their wish for their occupiers to leave. The legionnaires dispersed the crowd with pikes.

Legasa Telmarran, high lord of Halaran, and Prince Leopold of Altura fought bravely. Then, in the afternoon, word arrived that the army of Alturans and Halrana was surrounded. High Lord Legasa asked for quarter, but none was given. The encirclement grew tighter, and the butchery began.

Tapel's mother cried, and Tapel held her hand, not sure what else to do. By nightfall, the battle was over. Some soldiers had escaped, bursting out of the enemy's net in leaderless groups, but Ralanast's last chance at freedom was over. High Lord Legasa was dead, killed in battle. Prince Leopold had fled the field.

The Black Army was here to stay.

Tapel's mother was starving, her arms growing thin, and the skin of her cheeks tight like a drum. Tapel could encircle her waist with one arm when he hugged her, and her golden hair, usually the color of wheat in the summer, was showing more than a little gray. Tapel hadn't eaten a proper meal in as long as he could remember, and the gnawing in his stomach was becoming truly painful. He and his mother had long ago sold every item of jewelry, traded every last winter coat and pair of boots. Tapel knew Amelia was feeding him more than she took herself, but he couldn't help eating the food she put in front of him, and he felt guilt every time his stomach rumbled.

So, the day after the battle, Tapel did what all the other boys were doing: He went to the battlefield to search the corpses of the dead.

It was worse than he could ever have imagined. Much, much worse.

Bodies littered the field, interspersed with the familiar shapes of constructs, from rows of charred woodmen to a shattered colossus, dwarfing the hill it had made its final resting place.

Tingaran legionnaires in black lay entangled with brown-clad Halrana pikemen. The green of the Alturan dead spotted the land-scape like withered plants. All shared the color red, although expo-sure to the air had oxidized the blood to a dark, evil shade.

The field stank—the worst smell Tapel had ever encountered. Men had voided their bowels and had their guts ripped open by swords, their heads smashed, and their bodies broken. The carrion birds had started to feast, and as Tapel picked his way through the carnage, he disturbed a crow as it consumed the matter in a Halrana soldier's skull.

Tapel wondered if the young man had left a family behind, and suddenly he was sick, falling to the earth and heaving up the contents of his stomach violently and painfully. He closed his eyes as his throat constricted, trying to use the darkness to blot out the visions of death and macabre destruction.

When the retching ceased and his body again came under his control, Tapel climbed back to his feet. He put his hand to his forehead, momentarily light-headed. He breathed slowly in, then out. He fixed his mind on his mother, and his face set with determination, deliberately walked toward the next dead soldier he saw.

The dead legionnaire stared at Tapel with glazed eyes. The sol-dier's head was shaved, and his face was flat and round. A tattoo decorated his cheek: the sun and star *raj hada* of Tingara.

Tapel squatted by the soldier's side and examined him in more detail. He had been killed by a pike—no question of that; the long haft still jutted from the center of the legionnaire's chest. The body of the Halrana pikeman who had killed him was nearby, and he still clutched his weapon with both hands, a red slash across his throat and an expression of surprise on his face.

Tapel tried not to think of the priests at the earth temple and their sermons about respect for the dead. This man was the enemy, he reminded himself. Somehow it felt better to search the enemy dead.

The legionnaire was a big man and wore a padded vest of scaled armor. The battle had taken its toll, and several of the scales were missing. If they hadn't been, he probably would have survived the thrust that ended his life.

Breathing slowly and evenly to suppress his revulsion, Tapel began to feel inside the armor where two of the metal scales had opened up a hole. The legionnaire wore a simple jerkin underneath the armor; Tapel felt up and down, using his thin arms and small hands to advantage. Finally, he gave up; there was nothing there. Where would the man keep his gilden when he headed into battle? He probably wouldn't take it with him in the first place.

Jewelry. He should look for jewelry. He decided to quickly and speedily search for rings, necklaces, earrings, fancy scabbards, anything that looked valuable. This strategy had the added benefit that Tapel wouldn't have to spend too much time touching the dead.

Scanning swiftly, Tapel immediately found a bronze ring on the longest finger of the legionnaire's left hand, and a small gold hoop around the lobe of his left ear.

The sooner he could work, the faster he would be finished. Tapel took the jewelry, then left the body and continued his search.

Some great explosion had left a huge gouge in the earth up ahead. With horror, Tapel realized that the lumps he had taken for clods of dirt scattered about were the pieces of bodies. He promptly left the scene behind and came to a group of Black Army regulars, motley soldiers whose luck had run out when they encountered a group of ironmen. The constructs had run through them like a scythe through wheat. Some twisted pieces of metal could be seen here and there, but scores of bodies in black tabards proved who had been the victor in that particular encounter. The Black Army regulars were laid out in an almost orderly fashion, limbs akimbo and flesh torn.

Tapel moved quickly from corpse to corpse, keeping his mind carefully blank. He picked up mostly cheap metal jewelry but also found a gilt scabbard and a gold ring set with a purple stone.

Tapel crested a hill, jumping when he startled a flock of crows gorging on the dead. They settled again, farther ahead, their beady eyes regarding him as they tilted their heads, hopping from one place to another and cawing to each other. A nearby sound caught his attention, and he looked down; at his feet a crow glared up at him, blood dripping from its beak. Tapel kicked at it with his foot.

It was growing dark. Looking around the battlefield, Tapel realized he was the last of the youths still out. If he came home too late, his mother would ask questions, questions he knew he wouldn't want to answer.

The shortest path back to the city was through yet another group of the dead, where it appeared a tremendous swordfight had taken place. As Tapel came closer, he realized that there were only black-clad legionnaires here; where were the Halrana dead or the Alturans? Perhaps some constructs had been the cause of this destruction?

But there were only dead legionnaires. And these bodies weren't burnt; there hadn't been an explosion; these were sword wounds. An epic battle had been fought here, a battle that had taken the lives of at least a hundred—no, perhaps two hundred legionnaires.

Tapel moved among the bodies, trying to keep his distance, anxiously looking back at the setting sun. He no longer looked for jewelry; he just wanted to get out of this terrible place and go home to his mother.

Then Tapel's heart stopped and his blood ran cold. Something had grabbed hold of his ankle; a hand was wrapped around his foot, and try as he might, Tapel couldn't move. Despite himself, a whimper came from his throat and he nearly voided his bowels.

He looked down.

A soldier lay by Tapel's feet, an Alturan by the color of his clothing and the sword and flower of his *raj hada*, but this man wore no armor, instead his body was covered in light, reflective green fabric. Silk? A sword lay by the Alturan soldier's side, a long, slightly curved blade, free from dent or scratch, and inscribed with arcane symbols. Symbols also covered the Alturan's clothing.

Tapel realized that this was the man who had left behind so many of the enemy dead, at the same time also realizing what he was. A bladesinger.

But he was old, with dark hair turning gray and faded scars on his face mingling with new wounds. He clutched Tapel's ankle in a grip of iron and his other hand held his throat, where fresh red blood welled out from between his fingers.

"Agh . . ." the Alturan looked up at Tapel, and tried to speak.

Tapel realized he was going to have to answer his mother's questions about where he had been, whether he liked it or not.

That had been many weeks ago, and as they nursed him back to health, Tapel and his mother still wondered who the stranger was. The jewelry Tapel had found paid for food—the Alturan was a ravenous eater—and day by day the Alturan's color slowly returned.

He couldn't speak, though both Tapel and Amelia knew he was desperate to. They had never seen him try as hard as he had when word arrived about the great battle that was fought at the Bridge of Sutanesta and the miraculous events that led to the rescue of the Halrana refugees and the salvation of what was left of the allied army.

It was a victory, clawed back from the jaws of defeat. The Alturan tried time and again to express himself, gripping Tapel's hand inside his huge one, squeezing until it hurt. Finally, the Alturan gave up, and tears came out of his eyes, spilling down his cheeks.

Not knowing what to do, Tapel had looked away.

Now, for the hundredth time, Tapel wondered who he was.

"Try again," Tapel said to him. "No, don't try to rise. Just try to speak."

The Alturan opened his mouth, but nothing came out except a ragged croak.

"I know you can do it," Tapel said. "Your name. Start with your name."

"Stop it, Tapel," his mother's voice sounded from behind him. "I've told you. He'll speak when he's ready."

"What if he never talks?"

Amelia came and sat by her son on the bed, where the Alturan lay, watching them soberly. "Perhaps he won't. But he fought to free us and our people, and we'll help him nonetheless."

"Can he write?" Tapel asked.

Amelia sighed. "I've tried, but his fingers shake too much. He can grip my hand, but he can't hold the chalk."

The Alturan's face contorted as he tried to speak. Amelia made soothing motions, but he kept trying, his forehead creasing into lines and the breath popping from his mouth in little gasps.

"You can do it," Tapel said. "I know you can!"

"Shhh, Tapel," Amelia said. "Let the poor man be."

"Your name—what's your name?" Tapel went over and knelt beside the bed, his ear close to the Alturan's lips.

"Tapel, stop it!"

"He's speaking!"

"He can't speak!"

Tapel moved his head closer to the Alturan's mouth.

"Rogan," the Alturan whispered. "My . . . name . . . is Rogan." He gulped and spoke again. "Rogan . . . Jarvish."

Tapel looked at his mother and wondered if she knew who Rogan Jarvish was.

3

Primate Melovar Aspen's home was in ruins. While far from his homeland, fighting those who would do anything to prevent peace, his home had been attacked in a cowardly, cruel manner.

His mouth set in a thin line, the primate kept his face impassive as Moragon made the report. He hardly needed his second-in-command to summarize what had been lost—he could see for himself—but he let the man continue. Somehow, reducing the damage to words had a soothing effect, implying there was something he could do about it.

"You saw the blast area at the foot of the mountain," Moragon said in his deep voice. "That was the largest of the explosions, where he destroyed the refinery."

They were walking through the corridors inside Stonewater. Primate Melovar looked at Moragon to gauge his reaction; did this attack affect the melding as much as it did himself? No, Moragon was a Tingaran; he wouldn't feel the same violation that the primate himself felt.

Moragon betrayed no emotion. Tall and commanding, the man who had once been the emperor's executioner had proven himself to be a capable leader, but more importantly, he shared the primate's vision of a world united under a single rule.

After the death of the emperor, Primate Melovar Aspen had made Moragon the high lord of House Tingara, and by agreement, in the event of his death, Moragon would lead the army that carried the banner of the black sun, and the unified nation the fragmented Tingaran Empire would become. Moragon's legionnaires and avengers were utterly loyal to him—he was a melding himself, with a right arm of lore-enhanced metal. And like the primate, Moragon had the taint.

Primate Melovar could feel it now, the hunger, never far from his mind. It took less than an hour now before the pain was so great, he could stand it no longer. At the end of this tour, he would give himself surcease—a sip of black elixir from a golden goblet—but for now, the pain kept him sharp.

With no more essence to come out of Stonewater, the primate knew he would soon run out of the elixir. The liquid, made from the further refinement of essence, gave incredible powers of longevity and rejuvenation, but the price was the addiction. For the first time, the primate felt a sensation he hadn't felt at any of the battles: not at Ralanast and not even at the Bridge of Sutanesta.

For the first time, the primate felt fear.

Ahead the stone was blackened, and the roof of the cavern had partly caved in.

"This was the harvesting plant," Moragon said. He pointed to the swaths of dried blood on the floor. "The templars tell me they left these here in case you wished to investigate further, but the bodies have been removed. When the explosion came, it caught a dozen templars."

"And no one caught sight of him?" the primate asked again.

"He was wearing some kind of cloak and couldn't be seen. The Alturan bladesingers do this. They call it shadow."

"Alturans," Primate Melovar spat. "It must have been them."

"Do you wish to see the remains of the extraction system?" Moragon asked.

"Is it in the same state as this?"

"Worse. There must have been a series of explosions. Each part of the extraction system detonated with greater force, causing a major cave-in."

"Saryah was here," the primate said.

"She was,"—Moragon looked at him—"and I have no doubt they fought. Yet the intruder was the victor."

Melovar Aspen shook his head. "I thought she was unbeatable. Did you know she killed several bladesingers as well as the Alturan high enchantress? Not a mark on her. If a bladesinger did this, he must have skill beyond the best of Altura's swordsmen."

"What about Templar Zavros? Have you spoken with him?"

"Not yet," the primate said. "I wanted to see this for myself before hearing his account. Clever as he is, he sometimes misses the bigger picture."

"I'll take you to the extraction system then." Moragon turned when he noticed the primate had stopped in his tracks. "What is it?"

The primate put his fingers to his temples. "I will see the extraction system—or what's left of it—later. Take me instead to the Pinnacle."

Melovar Aspen climbed the stairs with complete disregard for the height and the gusting wind that pushed relentlessly against his thin frame. He was barely out of breath; he had tasted the bitter sweetness of the elixir on his way and could feel the strength it gave him. He might still look an old man, but he felt as good as he had when he was a young priest.

Ahead of him Moragon turned, no longer surprised at the primate's progression from frailty to vitality.

"Here, Primate. This is where the fourth and final explosion occurred."

The summit of the mountain was once a pure place. The gentle glow of the Pinnacle was all that decorated the level area, and even the primate himself came here when the trials of the world imposed some much-needed time to think.

The pilgrims came from far and wide to see the Pinnacle, and many of Aynar saw the light from Stonewater's summit and felt in awe of the templars and priests who lived here. Much of the Tingaran Empire's reverence for the Assembly of Templars stemmed from the wonders of Stonewater.

And now the Pinnacle was gone, the mystery of the light solved once and for all.

The light had guarded a building. Whatever it had been, it was now in rubble, the broken blocks covered in dust.

"You say this was where the fourth explosion occurred. How much time passed between this and the explosion at the refinery?" Melovar asked.

"The templars thought it as strange as you do, Primate. Apparently, they occurred close together."

"How do you think he made his way from the foot of the mountain, the very base of the vault, to the summit of Stonewater in such a short span of time?"

"I don't know," Moragon said.

"Speculate," said the primate, raising an eyebrow at the melding.

"My thinking, Your Grace, is that this is completely different. The first three acts shared a combined purpose. The desired outcome was to prevent our production of more essence and more elixir, and the perpetrator was successful. I'm no loremaster, but it seems to me that one machine might be replaced, but three, including the refinery, would be difficult, if not impossible."

Primate Melovar's expression blackened at the mention of the intruder's success. "Go on."

"What happened here was a separate event, executed by someone else. He may have been allied with the first intruder, but he came here with his own purpose, and what was destroyed here was not related to our production of either essence or elixir."

Moragon's words stayed with the primate as he went back into the mountain and surveyed the destruction at the extraction system. He pondered as he frowned at the scorch marks and debris, seething with anger. It was impossible for him to reach the refinery; the broken stone would need clearing, a process that would take months.

The Tingaran Empire's supply of essence was gone.

Primate Melovar Aspen's role was to process and allocate essence, but no templar had ever understood the relics, not even Templar Zavros, the man most knowledgeable about the world's most valuable substance. It was Zavros who had perfected the elixir, a process still within the primate's grasp. Yet essence was needed to create elixir; only a small amount of *raj nilas* could be extracted and processed from a larger amount of essence.

It always came back to essence.

As leader of the Assembly of Templars, Melovar knew the age-old process as well as any. The energy of the sun, the water, the earth, and the air was absorbed by plants. Grasses, bushes, trees, mosses— they all held this energy, and it was only when they died that it could be regained. As the vegetation rotted, it condensed, and over millions of years it formed lignite. Any decomposed plant material could be used at the harvesting plant, but lignite offered the best reclamation potential and led to the largest extraction of essence.

With the relics now destroyed beyond repair, and even the wonder that had been the Pinnacle gone as if it had never been, Melovar had nothing left but to look forward to the pain of withdrawal from the elixir, leading to inevitable death.

Nothing left but anger.

As the primate walked back to his chambers, up endless stairways and through dimly lit corridors, he leveled his gaze at one of the templars guarding his workroom.

"Fetch me someone who was here during the attack. Now."

The primate entered the room and gazed around him, finally looking out of the large window, where at Melovar's request the panes could be opened. Living in a mountain as he did, the primate had always had a head for heights, and he took pleasure in the discomfort it brought visitors when he opened the glass wide, exposing the void. He walked over now and opened the latch, pinning the window open. The howling wind hit his face with a blast. Down below, he could see the town of Salvation, and he imagined the little people, squabbling and scraping together whatever existence they could.

This view always made him think about the people below. Melovar knew within his soul that their governing system of houses was wrong. What real advances had been made in the centuries of the Tingaran Empire's existence? Was lore a tool or a crutch?

The Assembly had no lore, no Lexicon, no market house in Seranthia. The templars were the best placed to lead the world in this brave, new direction, and with no more essence, change would be inevitable. But would it be a uniting of peoples, or would it be the change that came through squabbling, fighting, and rebellion?

The Tingaran Empire was dead, the emperor was gone, and what came next could either be a hundred years of chaos or an eternity of unity.

The primate turned away from the window. A templar and a priest stood silently just inside the entrance to his workroom. The anger returned.

"Why are there two of you?"

The templar, a tall man with a sword at his side, spoke first. "Your Grace, we weren't sure what you would ask. Father Pristin here was closer to the refinery. I'm in charge of the Pinnacle, and I was one of the first on the scene there."

"You," the primate said, looking at the templar, "what did you see when you arrived at the Pinnacle?"

"It was as you see it now, Your Grace," the templar said evenly.

"No different? So you saw nothing."

"The pilgrims who were there fled, most likely when they heard the first explosions. One old pilgrim was crushed beneath some stones."

"If only he had survived to talk," Melovar muttered.

The templar opened his mouth and then closed it. "Your . . . Your Grace. The pilgrim—he did survive."

Primate Melovar's eyebrows shot up. "Why am I only hearing this now?"

"He's old, and he was injured, but he survived." The templar began to sweat. Even the priest looked fearful. "But . . . Your Grace, he's mad. You know how they can be. He speaks no sense. At any rate, I can take you to him. I didn't let him go; I sent him to one of the dungeons in Salvation."

Melovar felt the elixir flowing through his veins and the blood throbbing in his head. He reached out and with his right hand took the templar by the neck.

As the rage took hold, Melovar began to squeeze. "If you'd let him go, I would have made your death slow. As it is, I'm merely disappointed." The templar made a choking sound. "Very disappointed." Melovar increased the pressure and felt the windpipe under his thumb give under the pressure. A gurgle sounded from the templar's chest, and a faint crack could be heard before the primate removed his grip and let the templar's body fall to the floor.

"Fetch me a guard detachment," Melovar said to the priest. "I'm going to Salvation."

Father Pristin nodded dumbly.

"Quickly!" the primate said, and the priest fled from the room.

———————◆◆———————

The dungeons at Salvation were more for drunks and petty thieves than for serious miscreants. The blood-streaked cells in Stonewater were much more suited to murderers, rapists, and subversives.

The last thing the lazing guards in white tabards expected was a visit from the primate.

"Your Grace, I didn't know you were visiting. Today is . . . today is . . . one of the guards is getting married, and so he brought the wine in. It's not usual, Your Grace, not at all."

"Be still, and be quiet," Melovar said. The guard's mouth shut with a snap.

"The primate is here to see a prisoner," one of the templars flanking the primate spoke. "The old pilgrim brought in the day after the attacks—is he well? Are we able to speak with him?"

The guard tugged at his collar. "Well, it's been a few weeks. We send in a bucket of water every now and then, but food's hard to come by, what with the war." He inadvertently looked at the primate. "I imply no criticism, Your Grace." He cringed.

"Take me to him," Melovar said.

Doors clanged, keys jangled, and guards returned to life, tabards straightened and hair hurriedly combed.

A guard led Primate Melovar into darkness. It took time for his eyes to adjust, but eventually he saw a long corridor, flanked on both sides with barred cells. He wrinkled his nose at the smell of stale urine, and the slumped occupants of the cells were strangely still, as if to move or make a sound would sap what little energy they possessed.

The guard stopped outside a cell no different from the others. His hand shook as he fumbled with the keys, but finally he turned the correct key in the lock, and the barred door opened inward.

Melovar stepped forward.

"Please, Your Grace," another of the templars flanking him said. "Let us check first." He held out a nightlamp. *"Tish-tassine,"* the templar spoke. A soft white glow came from the device.

The primate waited patiently until they had finished. With the elixir's powers of regeneration, there was little in this world that could harm him, but he'd lost the patience for argument.

Finally the templars withdrew, and the primate entered the cell.

It appeared the templar from the Pinnacle had been accurate in his judgment of the old man's mental state. He was hunched in a corner of the cell, cowering awkwardly. Drool ran down the pilgrim's chin, and a feeble grin tugged at the corners of his lips. He had intense blue eyes, eyes that now squinted against the shine of the nightlamp. Ragged white hair tufted from the top of his head, and a scraggly gray beard flecked with ginger covered his chin.

He looked quite mad.

"You," Primate Melovar Aspen said to the old man, "answer my questions, or you will die a slow death."

The pilgrim looked up at him and then hurriedly looked away. "Salvation," he muttered.

"You're from Salvation?" the primate asked.

"Salvation. When you die. That's what you say."

"That's correct, old man. Yet answer my questions, or the Evermen will grant you no peace, I assure you. What happened when you were at the Pinnacle?"

"Came to see the light. Heard rumbling sounds."

"Did you see anyone?"

"Saw a shape, like the shimmer of a hot day. A cloaked shadow. Primate, what was it?"

Melovar clenched his jaw as he grew increasingly frustrated. If the second intruder was also cloaked, there was little the old pilgrim could know. About to turn away, the primate saw something hidden by the old man's body.

"What are you hiding there?"

The old man cowered farther into his corner, but the prison guard came forward and kicked him until the pilgrim took the thing he was hiding and scampered along the wall, holding it in his hands.

"He had it with him when we brought him in," the guard said. "He won't let it go, and it doesn't look like much, so we left it with him."

The old pilgrim once more tried to hide the object with his body.

"Bring it to me," the primate said.

After some scuffling with the pilgrim, one of the primate's templars brought Melovar the object. It was mostly destroyed, curled at the edges and withered like a flower left in the sun, but Melovar immediately recognized the metallic fabric.

It was a book of the Evermen. The pilgrim must have found it in the wreckage at the Pinnacle.

Primate Melovar Aspen took the book in his hands, cursing that it was so badly damaged, but fascinated nonetheless.

"Keep the old man here, and see that he's fed. I don't care when I come back—or if I never do. I want him here in this cell."

"Yes, Your Grace," the guard said.

Melovar would see what Templar Zavros had to say about this.

As soon as he was alone again, Evrin put his head in his hands. The act had been hard to keep up, as weak and in pain as he was, yet it had come to nothing.

The knowledge he had been trying to destroy, or at the very least protect, was now in the very hands he had tried to keep it from.

The book was partly destroyed. Yet what was left might be enough.

The primate didn't know it, but the scraps of metallic fabric he held in his hands were the key to the most powerful relic the world had ever known.

A relic Evrin had to protect at all costs.

4

Ella stood by the bank of the Sarsen, upriver from the Crystal Palace, soot on her cheeks and an expression of concentration on her face.

"Don't bring your wrists so close together," a woman in a rust-colored robe admonished her. "Slowly condense the flame until you can feel it coiled tight. Then bring your elbows together. No—your *elbows*."

Sweat broke out on Ella's brow. She wore a red cuff on each wrist, and the pulsing colors on both cuffs indicated they had been activated. Between her wrists was a ball of fire, red with fiery heat and writhing as if possessed of a life of its own. It was strangely heavy, and Ella's arms ached with the effort.

"Get down!" Ella cried. The ball of flame shot out from between her wrists, fortunately away from her body or she wouldn't have been alive to warn the two onlookers.

The woman in the red robe dove to the side, while the other onlooker, Bartolo, fell off his seat, the fireball barely missing him. The ball of energy hit the river with a sound like a crashing wave, and water shot up into the sky in a cloud of steam.

Once again, she had lost it.

"You're hopeless," said Shani, the woman in red, shaking her head.

Bartolo picked himself up off the ground, making a show of dusting himself off.

"Don't worry, bladesinger, your pretty silk blouse is still nice enough to wear to the dance," Shani said.

Bartolo paused, midway through pushing back his curly dark locks and smoothing his tiny moustache. He opened his mouth to retort, when Ella interjected.

"What am I doing wrong?" Ella asked.

Shani came over and looked the young enchantress up and down. Ella wore her green silk dress, and she was slimmer and slightly shorter than the woman in red.

"You're too weak," Shani said, squeezing Ella's upper arms. "You're too accustomed to having big burly men like this oaf here do your dirty work for you. You make the zenblades and give them to others to wield for you—that's the enchanter's way, isn't it?"

"That isn't fair," Ella said.

"Well, let me tell you, being an elementalist isn't like that. Blessings, girl, I don't know why I'm bothering with you."

"Perhaps because she's the only one preventing them from locking you up for the duration of the war," Bartolo said. He'd taken his zenblade out of its scabbard and was looking down its length, examining it for marks.

Shani had arrived the previous week; the scouts had found her in Altura's south, scratched and starving, her dark skin instantly giving her away as a Petryan.

Her arrival had caused consternation among the commanders. With Wondhip Pass blocked, the Petryans weren't supposed to be able to cross over into Altura. Yet Shani had surprised them, for she was happy to show them the precarious mountain path she'd taken, and yet another way between the two lands was made impassable.

High Lord Rorelan didn't trust the elementalist and had wanted to keep her under guard for the duration of the war. The last thing the high lord wanted was someone who could control water, air, and fire loose in Sarostar. But Miro had wanted to give Shani a chance and found surprising support from his sister.

Ella had to be honest with herself: She had never met an elementalist and was eager to discover more about their lore. Rorelan didn't seem to agree, but Ella knew that with essence running desperately low, it would take more than conventional warfare to defeat the Black Army. They would need to be creative rather than rely on force alone. She had so many ideas, but convincing High Enchanter Merlon, the master who had replaced Evora Guinestor, to allow her to test them was proving to be more difficult than the lore itself.

At least Ella could learn something about House Petrya's lore, and she had been surprised to discover that her quest for knowledge had led to the growth of a real friendship.

"Bartolo," Ella said. "Shani has joined our cause. She's unhappy with the direction her house is taking, and—"

"Listen to you," Shani snorted. "'Unhappy with the direction her house is taking,'" she mimicked. "You mean my brother and my nephew were murdered in front of my eyes—tortured to death. My high lord confiscated the gilden I've saved over the last ten years, for 'war funds.' Oh, and my high lord's also a sadistic warmonger. Yes, Ella, I'm 'unhappy.'"

Bartolo looked away, and Ella placed her hand on Shani's arm, but the Petryan shrugged it off. "I don't need your pity," Shani said. "I just want to help my people. And kill my enemies. It pays to be strong."

Ella frowned when she thought about Shani's comments. Was she really weak? She and the Petryan were certainly as different from one another as two women could be. Where Ella was slight, Shani was statuesque, her red robe belted with a white rope and filled out with the curves of her breasts and hips. Ella's eyes were a startling green, her skin pale, and her hair a light gold, the color of sunshine. In contrast, Shani's skin was the hue of amber, her hair wild and dark, and her eyes smoky and intense. The Petryan lined her eyes with some kind of coal-colored paste, giving her an undeniably exotic appearance. Ella thought Shani was beautiful, but she would never say that to her friend's face.

"I'll try to save you some to kill," Bartolo said. "Enemies, that is."

"The way you handle that sword, perhaps you'd better leave it to me," Shani said. "You're far too pretty to be waving something so sharp around. Who knows what could happen?"

Bartolo opened his mouth and then closed it again. Shani usually got the best of their exchanges.

Miro may have been opposed to locking Shani away, but that didn't mean he was going to take a risk with his sister. He'd admonished Ella to keep an eye on the elementalist, and then assigned Bartolo to keep an eye on them both. High Lord Rorelan was content with the arrangement. Bartolo was a bladesinger, one of their best, and even an elementalist was no match for a bladesinger, so they said. Ella wondered how true that was.

Shani turned to Ella again. "Let's start again, shall we?"

Ella nodded.

"There are two cuffs, one for each wrist. They aren't the same, and it's very important that you put the correct cuff on the correct wrist."

"Or?" Bartolo asked.

"Or you're dead."

"And you think I'm the one waving something dangerous around?"

Ella glared at Bartolo. "Go on, Shani."

"My robe has runes that protect me from the elements, but only from the lightest touch. A direct fireball will kill me just as easily as it will kill anyone else. Are you sure your dress is as protective as you say it is? I can lend you my robe."

Ella smiled. "It is. It's what we do best."

"Ignore what she says," Bartolo said. "Lend Ella your robe, Shani. Don't mind me. I'll just sit here and watch."

"Bartolo." Ella glowered. "Shut up."

Paying no attention, Shani went on. "The cuffs, when activated, can be made to draw moisture or heat from your surroundings. How depleted the cuffs then become, and how successful you are, depends on three things. First, there's obviously the scale of the magic you're trying to perform. A wall of fire requires more energy and more control than a tiny flame. Then there's the amount of control the elementalist has. A small spot of heat is more easily controlled than a wave of water, and more control not only requires more physical strength but also more judgment and activation sequences to shape the outcome."

Ella listened to Shani intently, digesting the information and storing it alongside what she had learned about enchantment, animation, and illusion.

"Finally, one of the biggest factors is how much heat is in the air or how much moisture is nearby. Sometimes an elementalist builds a fire or goes near water to make the lore more effective."

"Is that why we're doing this here?" Ella gestured.

The place where they worked was close to the river, located in a path of direct sunshine, near a bower of weeping trees. Shani didn't know it, but she had chosen the place where Ella's friend Amber had married Igor Samson, one of the Academy masters, with Ella standing at her side.

Thinking about Amber always made Ella feel sad, and then she thought about her brother. Miro's experiences in the war had changed him. When he'd first realized how Amber felt, he wasn't ready to prevent her marriage, not when he still had to find his place in the world. Now Miro knew who their parents were, and he had grown on his journey from a warrior to a leader. At the end of his personal journey, he'd finally realized he loved Ella's friend. Miro tried to convince himself she was dead and there was nothing he could do. But Ella sometimes saw him staring into the east, his fists clenched at his sides, and she knew he was thinking about Amber.

"That's right." Shani removed the cuffs from Ella's wrists and confidently attached them to her own. "We've chosen this place because it's warm and because there's water nearby. It's cold at the moment, and there's still ice melting in the Sarsen, but . . ."

The elementalist spoke some words, and a tight ball of flame appeared between her wrists. Where Ella's flame had been wild and unruly, the fire Shani had called forth was controlled and almost perfectly spherical.

"Try to hit this with your sword, bladesinger," Shani said.

A lone hawk wheeled in the distance, scanning the earth for prey. With a flick of her wrists and a pushing motion from her body, Shani released the fireball toward the bird. Like a small, fiery sun it flew through the air, searing it with a sound like paper being torn, before colliding with the hawk in a burst of sparks and cloud of ash.

Little flickers of residue fell slowly through the sky, and Ella looked for the remains of the bird to plummet to the ground, but there was nothing left of it.

"Shani, that was cruel," Ella said.

Shani shrugged. "You should see what they use in Petrya for target practice."

"Birds don't fight back," Bartolo said, "and you overcooked it. You'll never get a man at this rate. I think we've found something you really do need to work at."

Shani looked at Bartolo and smiled, giving him her full attention for the first time.

She walked toward him, swaying her hips and dipping her hand in the cool river water. Then Shani suddenly stopped, and Ella heard her chant under her breath, before the elementalist made a sweeping motion with her arms.

A wave of water leapt from the river, higher than Ella's head, before coming down to fall with a mighty splash.

Directly on top of Bartolo.

Immediately, the bladesinger was drenched to the bone, and with winter barely over, the water was freezing.

"You were saying, Bladesinger?"

Bartolo was up like lightning, his armorsilk blazing. The water fell away from him, and he placed a hand on the hilt of his zenblade.

"Bah," Bartolo said.

His expression black, the bladesinger stormed away.

Ella watched his departing back as Shani chuckled and shook her head. Ella thought she saw something in Shani's eyes when she looked at Bartolo, but the feeling soon left as Shani turned away, with Ella wondering if she'd imagined it.

Not for the first time, Ella looked at the runes on the red cuffs Shani wore on her wrists. Ella felt that with time she could decipher them and truly understand how House Petrya's lore functioned.

Ella's quest for knowledge had a purpose. The war had changed everything. They were now saying that the Tingaran Empire was no more, but Ella knew that what came next would be up to people like Miro, Rorelan, and Shani. What came next could be centuries of chaos, or some good could come of it all, and the system of the world could be replaced with something new, something that allowed the houses to preserve their culture, but inside a greater framework of trade, peace, and unity. It wouldn't be easy, but Ella wanted to try.

Life in Altura had changed forever, but it had changed even more for the people of Halaran and Petrya, Vezna, and Torakon—all the common people whose lives had been destroyed and were even now oppressed under the weight of the Black Army. Ella had to help, in any way she could.

Ella had traveled more than most, and she knew that although cultures across the world were certainly different, at heart, people were essentially decent. Most people simply wanted to prosper, to enjoy both the routine and the variety of life, and to raise a family in peace and love.

In her quest for the Alturan Lexicon, Ella had been to Altura's south and crossed the Wondhip Pass into Petrya. She'd been to the trade town of Torlac and gazed out at the tiered city of Tlaxor, centered in a volcanic lake. She'd met Petryans and the desert warriors of the Hazara, and she even knew someone from Aynar, the land of the templars.

Killian.

Ella fingered the small pendant on a chain that she wore around her neck. A pattern of runes had been inscribed on the back of the pendant. Once, when the correct words were spoken, the pendant had been able to vanish and then reappear—a lovers' trick, designed to give the gift an element of surprise. Now, the pendant was simply a piece of jewelry. It was all she had to remind herself of him.

Not for the first time, Ella wondered if Killian was the reason for the primate's apparent inability to launch a full-scale assault on Altura. She knew in her heart that he'd gone to confront his past, but what he had found in Aynar was a mystery.

"Come on," Shani's voice brought Ella back to the moment, her hand jerking away from the pendant. "Let's go find something to eat at one of the taverns. Or," she grinned, "we could go and see what they're serving at the Academy. You might even run into High Enchanter Merlon. You know, is it just me, or is he not used to being argued with?"

"He's a fool," Ella said, frowning.

"He's just accustomed to the old ways. My teachers in Petrya were exactly the same."

"How about we see what they're serving in the Poloplats?"

"Ella, you know what they're serving—same as they're serving everywhere else: a large bowl of wartime rations."

"Do you think Bartolo will come back?"

"He'll find us. He's loyal to your brother, that one, and he won't let you out of his sight for long, no matter how much his pride's been hurt. He won't leave you alone with the dangerous Petryan spy," she said wryly.

As Ella and Shani walked through a grove of the weeping trees that lined the riverbank, Ella thought again about Killian. A breeze rose, and Ella caught the incongruous scent of jasmine, reminding her of the desert, and her mind turned to another, different man.

Tall and handsome, considerate yet ruthless, a prince of his people and a born warrior—he knew Ella by another name, and he thought she was dead. The two men cycled through Ella's consciousness, completely different and yet both fascinating her in his own way.

The scent of jasmine grew stronger, and Ella suddenly stopped, gripping Shani's arm.

"How long have we been walking through this grove?" Ella said.

Shani frowned. "It does seem like a long time."

"That tree, I've seen it before." Ella pointed. "Perhaps more than once. Something's happening."

"What do you mean? Is there danger?"

The floral aroma grew stronger.

"Jerune. Jera-mah. Ruran-muh-rah," Shani chanted a series of runes in quick succession. Sparks formed between her wrists, and a miniscule flame grew into a ball.

Then Ella turned, and all she could see was green; her vision was a patchwork of trees and leaves. She turned again; where was Shani?

Ella heard a woman's scream. "Shani?" she cried.

The colors in Ella's vision wavered, like a mirage over the desert.

Ella opened her mouth to speak the words and then hesitated. What if she activated the sequence that projected a destructive wave of heat from her enchantress's dress and hurt Shani? She couldn't rely on her vision. Where was her friend?

Ella spun around, trying to get her bearings. She turned to the left, and the vision of tree branches shattered.

A figure in black clothing, his dark hair held back by a circlet, came out of the green.

Ella opened her mouth, but before she could speak, something hit the back of her head, and her vision burst with stars.

A cloth was held to her mouth, reeking of spices, and involuntarily Ella inhaled.

All became darkness.

5

Miro's thoughts were sluggish and beset by doubt. Acting on Marshal Beorn's advice, he turned to sleep, after a grueling session trying to explain his plan to High Lord Rorelan. The high lord simply refused to take any more strength away from the border with Petrya in the south. All three men saw that an alliance with this new nation, House Hazara, must be attained at all costs.

Miro decided to get a few hours' rest before speaking again with the glib-tongued Jehral of Tarn Teharan.

Miro's eyes shut before his head hit the pillow. There was something he needed to do. It came to him as he drifted off. Ella could tell him about these strange desert folk; she might even know this Jehral personally. He would . . . he would . . .

A heavy knock sounded at Miro's door, and his eyes shot open. He leapt out of bed, his zenblade activated and fiery in his hand before whoever it was even had a chance to make a second knock.

As the fog of sleep gave way to awareness, Miro realized that whatever the cause of the commotion was, it didn't herald immediate danger. He looked to the window, where oblique rays of sunshine poured in. Early afternoon, he guessed.

Miro deactivated the zenblade and returned it to the scabbard by his bedside, then reached forward and opened the door.

High Lord Rorelan stood outside the door with Bartolo, the high lord's hand poised to knock again.

"What is it? Just come in next time," Miro said.

Rorelan smiled and looked pointedly at the zenblade. "With a twitchy bladesinger inside? I think I'll knock every time."

"Miro, I'm sorry," Bartolo said.

Miro had fought by Bartolo's side countless times. They had suffered through the same pains, and Miro had never seen his friend so distraught.

"What is it?"

"It's about the Hazarans," Rorelan said.

At the same time Bartolo spoke: "It's about Ella."

Miro looked from one face to the next. "What about her?"

"She's gone, Miro," Bartolo said. "I'm sorry. It's my fault. I know I was supposed to be looking after her."

"Jehral and Hermen Tosch are also gone," Rorelan said. "The courier I sent to issue a summons discovered they left their lodgings not long after speaking with us this morning."

"There are signs of a struggle near where your sister and the elementalist were working," Bartolo said.

"Is it just Ella or is the Petryan gone too?"

"Shani's gone too," said Bartolo. "I'm such a fool," he muttered and punched the crystal wall. Bartolo winced and looked at his red knuckles.

◆

Miro was furious with himself. He paced the length of the simulator, one hand formed into a fist that he smashed into his palm with every second step while Bartolo and the high lord looked on.

After the battle at the Bridge of Sutanesta Ella had attracted a lot of attention, and he should have done more to look out for her safety. The survivors called it the Deliverance, and Miro knew the news had traveled farther afield than Altura. Miro's head throbbed, and he rubbed at his temples as he shook his head, grinning without humor. Protect Ella? Control her? He'd like to meet the man who could do that.

Miro cursed himself for not seeing the truth behind Jehral's questions. He hadn't been interested in an alliance at all. It was Ella the desert warrior was interested in. How could he not have seen it?

What would the men of House Hazara want with his sister? Was it something to do with the lore she'd helped them redis-cover? Did they simply want someone with her skill to help them further? How worried should he be?

Miro tried to tell himself the Hazarans just wanted more of Ella's help, but he knew so little about them. Jehral and his friend Hermen Tosch had evidently managed to capture an elementalist and a skilled enchantress. Whatever else, they were dangerous men.

Miro paced as he wondered what to do. He had vowed to never again let those close to him fall into the hands of his enemies.

Like a dog scratching at a wound, Miro's mind returned to the battle at the Bridge of Sutanesta and the last time he'd seen Amber. He had nightmares about it, dreams where he was cutting through the press of the enemy, slashing through warrior after warrior, see-ing her auburn hair and green dress vanishing into the endless ranks of the Black Army. No matter what he did, he couldn't get closer to her. He screamed her name, but she never turned around. And she was always going in the wrong direction, away from safety.

Away from him.

Miro knew now that she'd loved him as long as she'd known him, and he'd been too blind to see it until it was too late. It was a cruel twist of fate that only when far from home had he real-ized why his thoughts kept returning to the smiling face of Ella's childhood friend. He'd desperately wanted to find his place in the world, when she was waiting for him all along.

He'd lost so many friends in the war: Blademaster Rogan, the man who'd taught Miro to fight; Tuok, the soldier who'd taught Miro the ways of the world; Ronell, the bladesinger who'd finally conquered his fears, fighting to his last breath; Varana, the gentle Halrana woman who'd only wanted to be loved and whom Miro had left behind in the doomed town of Sallat.

Miro had promised himself that the next time he saw Primate Melovar Aspen, it would be at his enemy's demise. He had promised himself that never again would he leave someone he loved to face his enemies without his protection.

Miro stopped his pacing. "I'm going after them."

"Miro, let me go," Bartolo said.

"You are not going," Rorelan said. "Miro, you know you have responsibilities here," he continued, "and we have—what?—four bladesingers left besides the two of you? Bladesinger Bartolo, I forbid you to go also. You will be needed for the war effort."

"High Lord, it was my fault," Bartolo bristled.

Marshal Beorn rushed into the room, stopping when he saw Miro. "Lord Marshal, we're under attack! A force is testing our defenses in the woodland to the east, near the Halrana border. We need you."

Miro turned to High Lord Rorelan and then to Bartolo. He threw up his hands. "Bartolo, go after them. Look after my sister."

"Lord Marshal, I forbid . . ." Rorelan began.

Miro fixed Rorelan with a stare. The Alturan high lord met his gaze and then faltered. "He's going," Miro said.

Bartolo put out his hand, and Miro gripped it in his own. "I'll find her," Bartolo said. "I won't let you down."

Miro nodded, at a loss for words. He watched his friend dash out of the room and then grimly followed Beorn, to discover what the enemy was up to this time.

6

No man or woman without desperate business wandered the corridors of Stonewater during solace. In these two darkest hours of the night, farthest from both dusk and dawn, the priests were silent, noise was forbidden, and even the patrolling templar guards halted their pacing, standing still and meditative during this time of contemplation and prayer.

The stationary nature of the guards made Sabithe's task that much easier. He crept along the gallery, moving from column to column, using them to hide his form, and fought to keep his breath even and quell the raucous beating of his heart.

Sabithe was a priest, and had little experience of danger. He'd grown up in a sleepy village in the south of Aynar, sheltered by the loving care of his parents, both tailors and regular attendees at the temple. When Sabithe had reached the age where he started to attend, and saw the way the priest earned the respect of the townsfolk—no matter their age or station—he had instantly known what he wanted to be.

He had scored high marks in all of the temple's examinations, from arithmetic to grammar, but where he had most excelled was in theology. Sabithe didn't exactly understand how all the events in the

Evermen Cycles could be related to the simple life of the townsfolk, but he had a strong sense of morals and a deft mind that could change a man's thinking without him realizing he had ever thought differently.

The priest of Sabithe's village had sent him to Salvation, in Stonewater's shadow, to study under the wisest men and women of the Assembly of Templars, drawn from all over the Tingaran Empire. The young priest thrived in the competitive environment—the late-night discussions of free will versus destiny, or when it's right to lay down the sword and when it's right to fight. He was destined for great things, they said, maybe even for the senior echelons of the templars. But then the philosophy of the Assembly changed, and Sabithe refused to change along with it.

Sabithe believed there were times when it was right to pick up a sword, and he knew in his heart when those times were: in the defense of one's self, or one who could not defend themselves; to protect the flow of goods from marauders, so that there was more wealth in the land and fewer went hungry; to keep more swords out of the hands of those who would put them to evil ends; and to put the sword back down, just to show it could be done.

One day, Sabithe woke up and realized there were more templars wearing swords. It was a right that templars—not priests—had, but with the exception of templar guards and soldiers, few exercised. Sabithe looked on as the people of Salvation's respect for the Assembly turned from awe to fear. The sermons of Melovar Aspen, Primate of the Assembly of Templars, changed.

Before, the primate had preached the maintenance of peace, even to the detriment of those such as the people of Petrya, who lived under oppressive leaders, or Tingara, who valued wealth too much and life too little.

At the time, Sabithe understood the primate's argument. Change came about with time, and in this troubled age the inhabitants of the Tingaran Empire were still living better than their fathers. It might take time, but the world would get there. Picking up a sword could be justified, but only the most extreme of circumstances called for war. An uneasy peace was better than no peace at all. This was logic Sabithe could agree with.

Then the primate's words changed.

Melovar Aspen began to speak out more against the great wealth divide in Tingara, particularly in Seranthia, where the poor were rounded up and cast out of the city, sometimes from the towering heights of the Wall, the bodies forming little holes in the dust when they hit the ground.

He raved at the terrible weapons the Alturan enchanters made, fit only for war, and the exploding devices of the Louan artificers. He spoke of an eventual end to the houses, of a new world of unity, without lore, without borders, without tyrannical high lords and an economy based on essence. At first, Sabithe agreed, such problems needed to be spoken out against, but then he saw the meaning inside the primate's words.

The primate wanted to change the world, and he didn't mean to wait. He wanted to change it now.

Sabithe knew what the words meant. There was only one way to bring about such wholesale change.

War.

When he heard about the annexation of Torakon, Sabithe knew it had begun. The lightning fast attack through Loua Louna only confirmed it. He heard about the depredations of the Black Army in Halaran, and the butchery at the Battle for Ralanast that the templars were calling a great victory.

All in the name of the Evermen.

When he heard about the intentional destruction of the Bridge of Sutanesta, the only escape route to Altura, and the Black Army's pinning of the refugees against the Sarsen, Sabithe wept.

Many escaped that day, thank the Evermen, but there were many who didn't: helpless people, ordinary people, not only from Halaran but from Torakon and from Loua Louna. Children with their mothers, husbands with their wives, the elderly and the infantile; they all died together.

Sabithe decided it was time to pick up a sword.

He was forced to wait, but when the attacks on Stonewater came, when some desperate warrior sought his revenge on the Assembly, Sabithe knew it was just a matter of time before the primate returned.

Now the primate was back, and Sabithe was ready.

He listened intently, waiting in the shadows of a stairway, but could hear nothing. Sabithe tried to slow his breathing and still his racing heart. He closed his eyes, and swiftly prayed to the Evermen for success this night. Sabithe opened his eyes again, looking up. Solace would finish soon, and the guards would once again be pacing the corridors of Stonewater. He had best be quick.

As Sabithe crept up the stairway, keeping a constant lookout for the guards he knew would be hard to hear in their stillness, he could feel the weight in his cassock. The prismatic orb was heavy, much heavier than he had expected it to be, but he knew how to activate it—such things were never complicated; the army was rarely the first option for the educated—and he had been told the orb would be more than sufficient for what he intended.

"Who's there?" a voice sounded.

Sabithe hadn't seen the guard, motionless as the man was, far from the soft light of the corridor's nightlamps. Earlier, he had made it past a guard simply by nodding, but he knew that as close as he was to the primate's chambers, this time it wouldn't suffice.

"I was told you'd know I was coming," Sabithe said, stepping close to the guard. Against the wall as he was, the man had nowhere to draw back to.

"By who?" the guard challenged.

"It doesn't matter," Sabithe said. Stepping forward, he thrust the stiletto deep into the guard's heart. He withdrew the knife and stabbed again, this time pushing hard, trying to reach through to the lungs.

Sabithe could see from the guard's yellowed eyes, now wide and filled with fear, that he had the taint. Sabithe didn't know what the taint was exactly, but he'd overheard it being discussed. Apparently it was a reward, a potion given to the warriors most dedicated to the primate's cause. Some magic that gave a man powers of regeneration and vitality.

Sabithe stabbed one last time; he wasn't sure how powerful the regeneration was. A gurgling sound came from the guard's throat, and he slumped against the wall. As the body began to slide down, it left a smear of red.

Sabithe was shocked as the guard struggled to stand back up again. As he watched, the templar's strength appeared to return to him.

"In the name of the Evermen," Sabithe whispered to himself. "This is not natural."

He grabbed at the base of the guard's throat and pushed until the man's head was back against the wall. Sabithe took a deep breath, and then plunged the stiletto into the guard's eye with as much strength as he possessed.

The guard kicked once, twice, and then was still.

Sabithe dropped the knife, barely cognizant of the clatter it made against the floor. He felt like weeping, but he knew this was a time when he needed to be strong. If anyone else was out at this hour—a likely event, given the war going on—they would immediately sound the alarm, and it would all be for nothing.

Summoning his strength, Sabithe straightened, looking up and down the corridor. Ahead there was an archway leading to one final set of steps, curving as they ascended. At the summit of the steps two guards would be waiting in an antechamber, behind them would be a heavy door of oak, and behind the door would be the primate's living chamber.

For good or ill, it would end here and now.

Sabithe took a deep breath, and then began to run.

"We're being attacked. There are dead guards everywhere!" Sabithe cried as he ran through the archway and dashed up the steps. With his white priest's cassock covered in blood, he knew he would make a believable impression.

Both guards instantly drew their swords and faced up to the priest.

"Get back, priest," one of them said.

"They could be right behind me!" Sabithe said.

Sabithe moved to where he was motioned and waited for what he knew would come next. The moments dragged by—the absolute silence of solace—and the two templar guards, standing with swords drawn, began to get nervous. Sabithe stayed silent, knowing one of them needed to be the first to speak. The air was filled with the hoarse sound of breathing.

Finally, one of the guards, a burly man with a high-forehead, cracked. "What did you see?" he addressed Sabithe.

"Dead, they're all dead. I came from three floors down, and every guard I passed was dead. We need to wake the primate."

"Quiet," said the other guard, a slim templar, lithe as a cat, with close-cropped black hair. "I need to think."

"I'll go down," said the burly guard. "If you get my confirmation, wake the primate."

"All right," the slim guard nodded.

Sabithe knew he needed one of the guards to open the primate's locked door, or he would never succeed in his mission.

The burly guard disappeared down the steps.

"He's right," called up the burly guard a moment later. "There's a dead man here. Wake the primate. I'll stay here and call out if I see anything."

The slim guard looked nervous, evidently torn between facing whatever may come and waking the primate.

Sabithe could see the brass keys at the guard's belt, and wondered whether he could take him, if it came to that. But this man was trained, and alert, with his sword drawn. Sabithe was no warrior; he would never succeed.

"I can do it," Sabithe said. "Give me the keys."

The slim guard looked relieved. "Come here," he said.

Sabithe came closer and the guard handed him the keys, keeping one eye on the stairs and the other on the priest.

Sabithe turned to open the door.

"Wait," said the slim guard. "Let me quickly search you first."

The guard began to hastily pat him down. "Stop moving," the slim guard said as Sabithe tried to draw away.

The priest desperately thought of an argument he could provide, a way to get into the primate's chamber before he was found out. There was nothing.

As soon as the guard found the prismatic orb, Sabithe knew he was a dead man. The greater tragedy was that he could have ended the war, here and now.

Then a clanging sound came from the heavy door, following by a creaking. The door opened, and a thin figure emerged, clad in a simple white robe. He had a feverish yellow glow in his eyes and the look of the fanatic in his sunken face.

"What is it?" the primate asked.

As the guard reached the pocket of Sabithe's cassock, and found the heavy roundness of the prismatic orb, Sabithe darted his hand into the opening. His finger found the lever, triggering the mechanism.

The orb exploded in a violent detonation of heat and energy.

Sabithe's last thoughts were triumphant.

7

The primate tried to open his eyes. The first sensation he experienced when consciousness returned was incredible pain, like nothing he had ever experienced. His body was on fire, burning as if a thousand red hot pokers pressed into his flesh. If he was flayed, his skin sliced and pulled roughly away from his body, and the raw pulp underneath whipped and then scraped with rough stones, it wouldn't come close to the pain he felt now.

He opened his mouth to scream, feeling his lips split and warm blood seep out, suddenly realizing he was unable to make a sound. His lungs were filled with liquid; he was drowning in his own blood! Melovar tried again to open his eyes, but they were covered by something moist. Bandages?

"Shh," a calm voice said. "Try not to move. I know you can't breathe, but you can last another moment. Your lungs are filled with elixir—it's the only thing keeping you alive. Don't worry; I've done this several times already. This is the first time you've been conscious for it. I know it's very uncomfortable, but trust me, Primate."

There was a pause, as if the owner of the voice was counting, and then he spoke again, urgently and forcefully. "Now, quick. Cough. Get all the liquid out."

Melovar tried to cough, but his body was too weak, the pain too great. He gulped, like a fish flopping on a beach, but with his lungs filled with liquid he wasn't able to take air in. After so long without breathing, starved of air, he felt the walls of his consciousness close in. It was all going to end here.

Melovar felt the pain fade, and as he fell into darkness he was suddenly at peace. A soft circle of light appeared in the distance, growing closer and closer as he approached. Melovar was with the Evermen, truly content for the first time in his life, and he knew that what he had done was right. Now that he had served his purpose, and the Evermen had no more worldly demands to make of him, others would take up his mission.

Or perhaps the Evermen had further use for him after all.

An intense sensation of bursting pain punched into Melovar's ebbing consciousness, taking away the light like a soap bubble being popped. It came again. In complete disregard for his ruined flesh, something was pounding on his back, slapping at it with strong, regular strokes.

Melovar opened his mouth and coughed. Liquid poured out his lips, and he retched at the foul, oily taste of the elixir, his body using the last of its strength to purge itself of the foreign substance.

When the liquid was all gone, Melovar choked and spluttered, drawing in lungfuls of precious air. Finally, normal breathing returned, at least as normal as it could be with the searing pain at the front of his consciousness.

The voice spoke again. "Open your mouth. I'm going to insert a funnel. It's time to do this again."

The next time Melovar woke, he could see. He tried to sit up, and the voice spoke, "Slow down. You're lucky to be alive. You need to rest, Primate."

Melovar ignored the voice and sat up. The pain was excruciating, indescribable, but with a great strength of will the primate put it to the back of his mind. The Evermen had spoken with him. He had been entrusted to see this thing through.

Melovar turned as he heard the scraping sound of a chair being pulled closer. A templar in the white robe and black stripes of the upper echelons sat watching. Plump and squat, he wore a frame of circular lenses around his eyes, a contraption he had made himself to improve his vision. The eyes behind the glass were small but intelligent, and the hands he held clasped on his lap were surprisingly large for his body, with long, delicate fingers.

"Zavros, it's you," the primate said. He vaguely remembered hearing a voice giving him instructions; this was the owner of the voice.

Zavros nodded slowly, a strange expression on his face.

"What is it?" Melovar said.

"I can't believe you're alive," Zavros said. "Anyone else . . . The only thing that saved you is you've had so much of the elixir that your body was able to repair much of the damage, even as it occurred."

"What do you mean, 'much of the damage'?"

"A prismatic orb detonated not two paces from you, Primate." Zavros shook his head. "It's . . . incredible. Three others died in the blast. One was coming up the stairs to your chambers—he was killed by shrapnel—but the other two were as close as you were. And Primate . . . there's barely anything left of them."

Melovar put his hand to his face, feeling bumps and crevices in his cheek where there never were before. "Bring me a mirror."

Zavros tilted his head to someone outside the primate's vision. A moment later a templar entered, a silver mirror with gilt edging held in his hands. The newcomer looked terrified.

"Hold it up," Melovar said.

Zavros nodded to the templar, who hoisted the mirror, and Melovar regarded his new self.

Everything was where it should be, at least he had that much. But it was as if Melovar was made of wax and had been held too close to a flame. His nose had sunk, and was now barely more than two holes in the center of his face. His cheeks and his chin were withered, lined with deep crevices, and his eyes were little more than almond slits. Melovar's lips were cracked and thin; they bled when he parted them, and they pulled in toward his mouth.

The primate looked down at his hands and the flesh of his forearms. He still had the complete use of his fingers. In fact aside from the pain, his body felt quite functional. He turned his hand over to display the palm, confirming that the fissures covered every surface of his skin.

Melovar chuckled.

"You can leave," Zavros said to the shaking templar. He waited until the templar had left, and then turned to the primate. "Primate, what are you doing?"

"I'm standing."

"But the pain!" Zavros said. "Primate, the fluid in your veins is like acid right now. Look." Zavros held up a bandage. Where the fabric was bloodied it was eaten away.

Melovar felt the fire pulsing through his body, regenerating the tissue, feeding him strength even as it sent waves of agony coursing through his veins. He shook his head. "What do I care? My work is unfinished, and my body might have little time left in this world. And Templar Zavros, pain is ethereal. The Evermen Cycles—perhaps you should read them sometime."

———————◆———————

Moragon made his report in his usual dispassionate tone. The newly-made Tingaran high lord, commander of the Black Army, had shown no reaction at all when he saw the primate's disfigurement.

Perhaps life as a melding had made him less shocked by what could be done with the human form.

The two stood high on the summit of Stonewater, where previously they would have been bathed in the light of the Pinnacle. The cool wind soothed the primate's constantly burning skin, and he sipped from a golden goblet, feeling the bitter liquid slide down the back of his throat.

"Go on," the primate said.

"Altura is bottled up, but with essence running so low it's proving difficult to take the battle to them. If we had more support from the Petryans I'm confident we could establish a stronger front and drive through to Sarostar, but there are rumors that Petrya's patrols in the south are being harried by the desert tribes, which is tying up more of their strength than we think High Lord Haptut Alwar is admitting."

"The desert tribes? What business do they have in Petrya? They're generally too busy fighting each other to be a threat."

"They've always harried the southern trade routes, taking caravans and stealing from villagers, but this is something different. I'm getting reports that they have a new leader, and a new lore."

"A new lore?"

"These are just tales really, told secondhand. Warriors, riding out of sandstorms on those beasts they call horses. That sort of thing."

Melovar snorted, a strange sound coming from his ruined nose. "There's no new lore. And it's barbaric, using animals like that. What of this leader?"

"He is a prince, they say, and with his father, the kalif, he has united the tribes. They have taken a name, House Hazara, and the color yellow, like the sand of their home. Their *raj hada* is the symbol of a desert rose. They're a warlike people, and this prince is their leader in war."

"It sounds like you're giving this more credence than I'd originally thought," Melovar said.

"The tribes are fierce, and this man must be a strong leader to unite them. They even say these Hazarans are building a city in the desert, but these are all rumors, remember."

"It comes down to the question of their lore. Without a Lexicon, they can't call themselves a house. House Hazara indeed. I'm sure the Petryans can handle them. What else?" the primate asked.

"In Halaran the people are getting restless, particularly in Ralanast. I want your permission to go to Halaran and take control of the capital. We've established a camp for the prisoners now, just outside the city, so quelling the Halrana should be no problem, provided the correct methods are applied."

"Good, good."

"But we still need a plan for the conquest of Altura. With the enchanters out of the picture, the resistance in Halaran, Vezna, Loua Louna, and Torakon will crumble. We can finally bring about the new order."

"Never fear, High Lord Moragon, I have a plan," Melovar said, gazing out from the mountain top. "I will share it with you in time."

"There is one more thing," Moragon said, licking his lips.

Primate Melovar turned, assessing the tall man with the shaved head and the arm of metal. He hadn't heard the melding use this tone before. "What is it?"

"The elixir," Moragon said carefully. "Have you spoken with Templar Zavros? How much remains?"

The primate smiled and his lips cracked, blood dripping down his chin. Where the fluid touched his skin he felt it sting as it trickled down. "I understand, my friend. Never fear. Every crisis is an opportunity."

Moragon grinned without mirth. "If you see the opportunity here, Primate, you are more clever than I."

"I was always more clever than you," the primate said. "There has just been an attempt on my life. Supplies of elixir are low, but not exhausted. And why are we running so low? Why, because of the many dependent on us to stave off the pain of withdrawal. Am I correct?"

"Yes . . ." Moragon said slowly.

"So let them feel the pain. Let them vie with each other to show their loyalty. I will start by purging the Assembly of Templars of any who knew this priest, Sabithe. Any templar who even spoke with him, who even knew his name, we will send to the prison camps. Those dependent on the elixir will die, and those who aren't, well, they'll die soon enough anyway. I'll have my templars compete for my favor. After a few days without the elixir, they'll be falling over each other to denounce those whose hearts aren't fully behind our cause. The most loyal, the fiercest fighters, the most influential, we'll let live. I will purge the Assembly, Moragon. And like the honing of a blunt edge, what is left will be stronger, sharper, than ever before."

Moragon bowed his head. "This is why I follow you, Primate. And then?"

"When we are done purging the Assembly, we will move onto the houses. There are those, even in Tingara, who are dependent on the elixir but whose loyalty might be in question. There are those like Tessolar, the former high lord of Altura, who once we had plans for but are now next to useless. We will purge, Moragon."

Moragon nodded. "It is a good plan."

"And when the time comes," the primate said, "I will reveal my greater plan. The Evermen have shown me a way, Moragon, a way for us to get more essence, more elixir, and to crush Altura once and for all."

8

Amber held the child's emaciated body close to her breast as the boy's lips turned blue and his shivering subsided. His eyes glazed, and then he was completely still.

She didn't cry; all her tears had long ago been cried out. Huddled in her group of about twenty prisoners, she just continued to stroke back the boy's hair in the same way she had when he was alive. It was all she could do.

"Give him to me," Lorenzo said. Amber turned dull eyes on the stocky Halrana. Who had he been in his former life? Did it even matter? "Here, yes, that's it. Let go. Give him to me."

Lorenzo took the child away, and Amber looked around her little group. Finally she stood, shakily, feeling light-headed with hunger and privation. Amber looked around the prison camp and wondered how she was going to get out. Would she be walking? Smiling and laughing as the camp was liberated? Or would she be on her back, carried like a sack of grain, yet another casualty of the conditions? Yet even with their losses, more prisoners arrived, always more than were taken by sickness and starvation.

Amber put her hand over her belly. She was more than a month pregnant, and there was only the tiniest of bumps on her abdomen, but it served as a constant reminder. She couldn't afford to die. She owed her unborn child that much. She needed to live.

Amber again cast her eyes over the camp. Without shelter, the prisoners had formed groups, most consisting of a dozen men, women, and children, but sometimes more. In the distance she could see the steel fence that bordered the camp on four sides. Between Amber and the fence huddled group after group, with barely space among them to walk to the latrines. Some had erected makeshift shelters from a blanket and a few sticks. Others had formed a circle of warmth, with the weakest of their group in the middle.

There were so many of the groups, she couldn't even begin to count them.

Not far away, Amber saw a pair, just two people, and she frowned with distaste. They sat a little farther away from everyone else, and one, an old man, had his head resting in the other's lap.

The younger man, Prince Leopold, former commander of the armies of Altura and Halaran, was in a world of his own. Leopold had been here since the beginning. He had arrived with Amber when the camp was built, not long after the battle at the Bridge of Sutanesta.

As Amber heard it, he had fled before the battle even began, looking for his uncle, Tessolar. Like Amber, he had been rounded up in the aftermath of the battle, and here they were.

The prisoners despised Leopold even more than the prison guards. He'd led the allies to defeat and then left them at their hour of greatest need. Occasionally, the Torak and Louan prisoners spoke with him, but all the Alturans and Halrana shunned him. Amber was almost surprised he hadn't been murdered in the night, another body with few questions asked, but who here had the weapon or the strength? It was hard enough staying alive. Looking at Leopold, Amber remembered the handsome face and flaxen hair of the dashing prince. Now, he was just another sad man.

Having left the battle at the Bridge of Sutanesta to find his uncle, Leopold's desire was granted when, just the previous day, Tessolar arrived at the camp.

Amber barely recognized the man who'd once been high lord of Altura. Tessolar was a broken man, shrunken and withered, with most of his hair fallen out and eyes sunken into his skull. The two legionnaires who brought him in dumped him unceremoniously with the other prisoners and then left without a word.

Leopold had immediately gone to his uncle's side. Tessolar appeared to have some strange disease; his eyes were yellowed, and froth sputtered from his mouth. Amber had watched Leopold try to speak with his uncle, but Tessolar was past communication.

Now Amber looked on as Leopold sat disconsolately, his uncle's head in his lap. Tessolar moaned and writhed, but none of the prisoners paid any attention. They could see and hear him, but they had their own problems, and in any case the two traitors deserved each other.

Amber's gaze returned to her own cluster of prisoners, and her eyes met Beatta's. The Halrana woman stared intently back, and Amber knew that here was a will that matched her own. Beatta's hair was darker than Amber's, brown to Amber's auburn, but like Amber, she would do anything to escape.

The two had formed a bond one night when Amber saw Beatta smile coyly at one of the prison guards, a nasty Tingaran named Hugo. Hugo was a bully, but Beatta was attractive, and he wasn't immune to her touch when she laid a hand on his bicep. Beatta ate well that night, and Amber's respect for her grew. This was a woman who had the strength to survive.

Her mind on her unborn child, Amber resolved to try herself, and after discovering Amber's state, Beatta felt for the younger woman and gave her some tips. She first asked Amber if she were prepared to do whatever it took, if it came to it. Trepidation sat like a stone in Amber's belly, but she assented, and Beatta told her what she needed to know.

Amber had lost some weight, but if anything her slim waist emphasized her hips, and with her soft brown eyes and full lips, she knew she was considered pretty. Her first time, she didn't even have to let herself be touched; she simply smiled at the guard, a young Tingaran growing his first stubble.

She received frowns from some of the other women, but that night she ate better than she had in weeks. Amber didn't care. She wasn't doing it for herself. She was doing it for her child.

Beatta had her own reason to live. The Halrana woman had been separated from her husband and child at the battle at the Bridge of Sutanesta and was desperate to be reunited with them. She spoke constantly about her son, and Amber reassured Beatta that her family would be waiting when they both escaped to Altura. Amber didn't feel bad about giving Beatta what might be only false hope; determination had to come from somewhere.

Amber now knew that Miro was alive and had been in command at the Bridge of Sutanesta. Amber had also heard that an enchantress, a young woman barely out of the Academy, had created the bridge of light that saved so many lives. It was the last time Amber could remember smiling. It could only be Ella.

She pictured Miro and Ella now, remembering the last time the three of them had been together, the day Amber and Ella had graduated from the Academy of Enchanters. Amber remembered sitting close to Miro, their legs touching, both aware of it, but neither moving away.

Thinking of Miro helped keep Amber going. In the darkest days, when hope was at its lowest, she would remember his face and the things he used to say.

"Mistakes are there to teach you," she could almost hear his voice saying. "You learn from them, and you move on."

Amber had made many mistakes in her life. But by far her greatest regret of all was never telling Miro she loved him.

Amber knew it was absurd to think about it, with life in the prison camp as precarious as it was, but still she couldn't help herself. If she ever saw Miro again and told him how she felt, how would he react?

Igor Samson, Amber's husband, was dead, and she supposed that like so many of the women here, she was now a widow, but did she really have a chance with Miro? Had he found some other woman by now and forgotten her altogether? Even if Miro felt the same way, would Amber and Igor's baby come between them?

Unless Amber could escape, there was no use thinking about it.

Gazing around the camp, Amber looked again at the metal fence, memorizing the layout of the guard stations, running the plan again through her mind.

Finally she sat back down, and once more her eyes met Beatta's.

Soon, they would be free.

It was another two weeks before the time was right. In early evening, when the camp was a scene of chaos as the prisoners fought each other to get their one meal for the day, Amber saw an older woman stumble into one of the guards near the eastern side of the fence.

It was the signal.

Amber nodded to Beatta, and the brown-haired Halrana nodded back. Immediately, both women began to walk briskly away from the commotion, toward where a storage hut screened part of the fence's western side.

Amber risked a glance over her shoulder. In the distance she saw the older woman—Ness, her name was—take a knife from her ragged clothing and plunge it into a guard's chest. There was instant pandemonium, drawing guards from all over the camp.

Amber thought about what Beatta had told her about Ness, and prayed that the old woman's sacrifice wouldn't be in vain. Ness was a distant relative of Beatta's, and she had the plague. The spots had appeared in a ring around her neck the day before. No woman over forty had survived the camp plague, and Ness was closer to sixty. But Beatta said Ness was strong and would rather give her life to help them escape than watch as her body wasted away.

With a knife in her hand, Ness would make a definite diversion, but she wouldn't take long to subdue. Amber and Beatta needed to move quickly.

The two women reached the fence, and for a moment the storage hut screened them from the other guards.

"Hurry, hurry!" Beatta urged, jumping from one foot to the next.

Amber knelt at the foot of the fence and reached into her tattered tunic. She withdrew the nightlamp she'd stolen and modified, and checked again where she'd scratched out some of the runes, creating new shapes out of the old. She didn't need essence: all she'd needed was to corrupt the matrix for slowing the nightlamp's release of energy.

"I hope this works," Amber said.

"Lord of the Earth, they've seen us—hurry!" Beatta whispered.

Amber could hear the shouts of the guards and involuntarily turned to check how far they were away. Ness had been dealt with— the old woman's crumpled body was already being dragged away— and now six guards were running toward them and had already reached the storage hut.

"Look away," Amber said. She placed the device at the base of the fence and spoke the activation sequence. *"Tish-tassine."*

The nightlamp flared up, bright as a thousand suns. Amber could feel the heat pouring from it as all of its energy was expended in one great burst. But would it be enough to damage the fence?

Amber looked back at the guards, feeling relief when she saw that all of them were in varying stages of blindness, their hands held to their eyes, though their shouts were bringing even more guards.

"Amber, come on!" Beatta said.

Amber saw the metal at the base of the fence glowing red. The Halrana woman kicked at the steel, and Amber breathed a sigh of relief when Beatta swiftly opened up a small hole.

Amber ran forward and kicked at the hot metal, further enlarging the hole. "You go first," she said to Beatta.

Beatta wormed her way through the fence, and then it was Amber's turn. Beatta held out her hand for her friend, helping Amber get to her feet, and then they were both running.

"We're free!" Beatta turned and called to Amber, a broad smile on her face.

The ground fell away from Beatta's feet, and an expression of astonishment crossed her face as the woman vanished into the earth.

Amber suddenly teetered on the edge of a wide ditch, waving her arms to regain her balance and halt her momentum. She looked down, and Beatta looked up at her with eyes wide with pain.

The trap was lined with jagged wooden spikes, scores of them now piercing Beatta's body. Amber watched as Beatta coughed, blood spluttering from her mouth, and her friend died.

Amber felt the rough hands of the guards grab her wrists, forcing her to the ground. She tried to look away, but Beatta still stared up at her.

9

Ella woke, and at first she didn't know where she was. Then it returned to her: the green of the trees, the confusion and the panic, Shani's scream, the figure in black lunging from the illusion.

She had been captured.

The covered wagon rocked and tilted, jolting and bumping as it moved along, and Ella winced. Her head still ached, and her mind was thick and slow.

"Looks like you got knocked on the head pretty thoroughly," Shani's voice broke the silence. "All you've done is sleep."

"Where am I?"

Shani snorted. "What kind of a question is that? Let's see. You're in a dark wagon, so dark you can barely see. Your legs are tied, but your arms are free. Problem is, if you move too close to the edge of the wagon, some kind of magic kicks in, and your vision goes black until you move back to the center. You're somewhere. Does that answer your question?"

"How . . . long?"

As Ella's eyes adjusted to the darkness, she saw Shani sitting cross-legged a couple of paces from her. The Petryan put a hand to her head. "This is the third time we've had this conversation. And the last time, all right? This time, the answer is that it's now been about four days."

Ella rubbed the back of her head, pulling away and wincing as she felt the large bump on her skull. Her mind was clearing now, and as the fog lifted, she felt it slowly replaced with anger.

"They drugged us," Shani said. "If it's any solace, this is now the longest conversation we've had."

"Has anyone spoken to us?"

"No." Shani shook her head. "Although I think someone's popped their head in a few times. We've been given food and drink." Ella could vaguely remember cold stew and brackish water. "And we've been taken outside to get some fresh air. They can make the dark cloud stay with you. You can hear, but you can't see a thing."

"I know who it is," Ella said. "Or at least, I know who they represent."

"Who?" Shani said. "I need to know so I can add them to the long list of people I'm going to kill once we get out of here."

"What do you know about the Hazara Desert?"

Shani snorted again. "Ella, I'm Petryan. Our southern border is the Hazara Desert."

"Then you know about the tribes."

"Those barbarians? They steal from my people, the way a flea bites at a dog. They raid our trade caravans and butcher our villagers. You're saying some men of the tribes traveled all the way to Altura and captured an enchantress and an elementalist? I don't think so, Ella."

Ella wondered if their captors would have been as bold if Bartolo had been with them. "I know it without a doubt."

"How?" the elementalist demanded.

"To start with, their lore. They can make illusions, impressions of light and sound that aren't actually there. Visions, like the mirages in the desert."

"I'll agree with you, that sounds like what's happened to us," Shani said. "I thought I was going mad for a moment there. What else?"

"Second, because I think I recognized the man who came out of the illusion and attacked me. His name is Jehral, and he serves one of their leaders, a prince named Ilathor Shanti, of Tarn Teharan."

"How do you know these people?" Shani pointed at Ella's chest. "How do you know so much about their lore? What interest do they have in you?"

"I know them because they held me prisoner for a time. We need to be careful, Shani. These men are ruthless."

"You haven't answered all of my questions."

"I know about their lore because I helped them regain it." Ella hesitated. "In return, they let me go."

"Ella," Shani said. "If we're going to trust one another, you need to be more honest with me."

Ella started to speak and then closed her mouth. After a pause, she tried again. "Well, perhaps they didn't let me go," she said wryly. "Perhaps . . . I escaped."

Suddenly, Ella cocked her head. She could hear unmistakable chanting, the throaty voice of an old woman.

Complete darkness clouded Ella's vision. "I can't see," she said.

"I can't either," she heard Shani's voice. "It's the dark cloud I told you about."

Ella felt a jolt as someone entered the covered wagon, and her heart began to race. How many were there? What were they planning to do with her?

She listened and caught the sound of a single newcomer, a man's heavy breathing.

"Remove this darkness, Jehral," Ella said. "I know you're there."

Ella heard more movement accompanied by another jolt and then a voice spoke outside. Moments later the sound of breathing came again, and Ella tensed.

Then she could see. The relief was intense, but Ella tried not to display any emotion, recalling the desert warriors' disdain for weakness.

As Ella's eyes again adjusted to the low light, she saw Jehral crouching just inside the covered area of the wagon. Ella thought they had once been friends, of a kind, but now Jehral regarded her with an expression close to anger.

"Ah, you are awake and feeling better, I see," he said. "It is good to see you again, High Enchantress Evora. Or should I say . . . Enchantress Ella?"

Ella caught a frown from Shani.

Jehral had changed subtly since Ella last saw him. The metal circlet he wore at his brow now appeared to be made of solid silver, and he wore a sash of yellow over his black clothing. In the manner of a *raj hada*, the sash was decorated with a stylized desert rose.

"You look well, Jehral. It's good to see you again too. Now," Ella said, color coming to her cheeks, "let me go. There's a war going on. Let me return to my people."

Ella prepared to activate some of the sequences in her dress. The words on the tip of her tongue, she looked down, and then she realized: Her green silk enchantress's dress was gone, and in its place she wore a plain yellow tunic. Looking at Shani, she saw that the elementalist's red robe was also gone, and her friend now wore a faded brown smock. Shani's red cuffs were nowhere to be seen.

"Where's my dress?" Ella said.

"They took everything," Shani said, sighing.

Ella glared at Jehral. "Who, exactly, took my dress?"

Jehral actually blushed, the first time Ella had seen the desert warrior anything but poised. "Not I. We have an elder with us."

"But you looked, didn't you?" Shani challenged.

Jehral raised his chin. "I have taken a wife, Petryan. No, I did not."

"Will you let us go?" Ella asked.

Jehral looked puzzled. "Why would I let you go when I have gone to such lengths to get you to come with me?"

"No one asked you to," Ella said.

"Ah, but someone did. My prince asks, and I obey."

"What does he want with me?"

"That, Ella, he will tell you himself."

"And why is Shani here?"

"Because it was easier to take her too and because I suspect, Ella, that you may cause trouble."

"I'm never easy, barbarian," Shani growled.

Jehral ignored her and addressed Ella. "I'm pleased to see that you have recovered." He prepared to depart.

"Jehral, will you at least tell us where we are?" Ella asked.

"We're halfway to Castlemere, on the Basch Coast. Contrary to what you may believe, no one will find you, Ella. This wagon is one of forty in the train, and thirty-nine of the forty are legitimate traders."

"Jehral," Ella said, "we used to be friends. Must it be like this?"

Jehral came forward, his eyes blazing, and Ella shrank back. "You lied to me, to my prince, to all of us. You took our knowledge, and then you left us."

"I had to help my people," Ella spluttered.

"Your name was a lie, and so was your position. You stole a great deal of essence from my prince's tent."

Jehral turned and exited the wagon, but not before making one last statement.

"And one more thing," he said, sealing the wagon shut behind him with angry tugs at the material. "You owe me a horse."

Then he was gone.

"Jehral," Ella cried after him.

She'd been taken from her brother after they'd only just been reunited. Every second took Ella farther and farther from where she wanted to be.

"He sounds angry," Shani said, "and I'll bet this prince he cares so much about is even madder."

"Shani, I have to get back to Altura," Ella said.

"Why?"

"Because there's a war going on!"

"And you want to fight?"

"Yes!"

"Think, Ella. Whatever this prince wants from you, do you think it might have something to do with the war?"

Ella thought about what Shani had said for a moment. Could she help Miro by aiding the prince? She then noticed that the Petryan woman was creeping steadily toward her.

"What are you doing?" Ella asked.

Shani darted forward and yanked several threads of golden hair from Ella's head. Ella yelped.

"Your hair stands out better than any signpost," Shani said. "Next chance we get, I'm leaving this on the trail."

"Who for?"

"For whoever your brother has sent after us."

10

The enemy came in a wave of soundless black shapes, pouring over the ridge and down to the wide, shallow river. Against the stormy night sky, Miro struggled to estimate their strength.

"It's a full attack," Beorn whispered hoarsely in his ear.

The black shapes hit the river where the enemy had discovered the Sarsen was shallow enough to be forded. They were immediately slowed by the water as they began to wade toward where Miro and his men sat in hiding, protected by the thick trees that lined the Alturan side of the border.

It was only the second night attack they'd faced. The enemy commanders were trying new tricks, some that worked and some that didn't. Miro wondered if night attacks would now be the norm.

For the hundredth time, Miro wished he could use the shadow effect of his armorsilk, but he knew it was more important to his men that they see their leader, fighting wherever the battle was thickest. At least he would be able to call forth the armorsilk's full strength.

He did have one surprise of his own in store for the warriors of the Black Army. Hidden in the forest were the four other bladesingers who had survived the battle at the Bridge of Sutanesta. The world's finest swordsmen had activated the cloaking effect, the low tones of their sonorous chanting unheard against the gurgling of the river.

Miro scanned the black dots in the river. There were too many to count, but he needed to get an overall feel for their numbers in order to determine how many precious prismatic orbs he should expend. So much of the fighting was like this now, assessing the enemy's strength before draining enchanted armor and swords to repel them.

"Every fourth man to throw a prismatic orb," Miro whispered to Marshal Beorn.

"Every fourth? It's a full attack, not a probe. I'd say at least every third."

"Every fourth," Miro said firmly. He agreed with Beorn, but there were no more orbs in their stockpiles. Each man here carried three, and that was all, for the duration of the war.

Beorn passed down the order while Miro watched more and more of the enemy enter the water, each soldier's sword held above his head, with the water reaching to his waist. Miro reached over his shoulder and drew his zenblade.

As much as Miro would have liked to wait until the enemy reached the bank and then fight them from the height of land as they emerged tired and wet from the river, he knew he couldn't afford the risk. This was where the darkness gave the enemy extra protection, for there was too great a chance that some would slip through Miro's thin defenses and regroup on the Alturan side. Miro knew his men wouldn't survive an attack from the front and the rear, and these men were the only protection Sarostar had.

Beorn was good, and Miro didn't even hear the command for the men to throw their orbs. He saw the tiny specks fly through the air and caught the shouts of the enemy as their fear and surprise carried across the water. They knew their crossing had been detected, and the black specks could only be one thing.

The prismatic orbs fell into the water and detonated with devastating force.

Miro almost felt sorry for his enemy. An underwater explosion sent bigger shockwaves over a longer distance than one in the air, and the pandemonium was instant as men screamed in pain. Water fountained high and body parts flew in all directions.

But any sympathy Miro felt was short-lived. His homeland was under attack, and these men either mindlessly followed the orders of their leaders or were attracted to the carnage by nature.

"Attack!" Miro cried, hearing his men take up the shout.

Even as the Alturans and the exiled Halrana who made up Miro's army surged up and out of the protective forest, the enemy launched their own volley of prismatic orbs.

Miro ran forward and commenced his song, feeling the armorsilk come alive around his body, hardening and settling tightly around his skin. A detached part of his mind noted that the enemy's volley was no greater than his own, lending credibility to Ella's theory; the Alturans weren't the only ones running short of essence. The rest of his mind recoiled in horror as the land erupted around him, flame and earth rising high above their heads, detonations tearing men limb from limb. The lightning-like flashes lit up the scene, banishing the darkness. An Alturan soldier to Miro's right flew down the bank to the river, screaming and snarling when a small sphere hit the ground at his feet. The soldier wore enchanted armor, but its protection still wasn't enough, and the explosion tore him apart. The snarl was still on his face as he died.

Miro concentrated on the task at hand as he plunged into the river, his momentum slowing as the waist-deep water took hold. He heard the splashing sounds of his men behind him, and looking ahead, Miro saw he would be the first to meet the enemy. With his lighter armor and long legs he was more agile in the water than the other soldiers, an advantage he hoped to press against his opponents.

Miro added more of his song to his zenblade, the symbols on the weapon illuminated with blue fire. The chanting formed a regular rhythm, the rising and falling of his voice a soft melody as he activated more of the sequences built into his weapon and armor. He was the leader of his men, and the more courage he showed, the more they would feel. Rather than using any shadow, Miro made his armorsilk bright, as bright as he could make it. The Black Army would know he was here; Miro planned to make sure of it.

The first legionnaire thrust a spear at Miro's unprotected face. Miro swerved and feinted at the warrior's armored chest before smashing into him with his shoulder. With the spear overextended and the legionnaire off balance, Miro swung from overhead, hitting his enemy's neck and continuing through his body as the zenblade met little resistance.

Another Tingaran, a huge, growling man with a two-handed sword, chopped down at Miro as he turned from the dead legionnaire. Miro blocked the sword with the zenblade, shearing it through, then thrust into the Tingaran's chest. Blood gushed out in a fountain as Miro withdrew his sword.

Three of them hit Miro at once, and all he could do was concentrate on his song, keeping his motions economical to conserve his strength. He dispatched the middle warrior with a thrust to the neck; then the swordsman to the right with a feint and a slice that opened up the surprised man's chest; and then the legionnaire to the left with three quick cuts.

They kept coming. It was going to be a long night.

The waist-deep river made the enemy sluggish, and it was simple for Miro to read their actions and dance around them, darting to the left and the right, his zenblade rising and falling as the blood mingled with the water. But Miro was beginning to tire. He was accustomed to covering a lot of ground when he fought— often when a battle ended, he was surprised to discover he'd traveled several hundred paces from where he'd started—but here, fighting in the river, the water dragged at his legs.

Bodies floated past, some in black and some in green, many mangled by the explosions of the orbs, others showing the deep gashes of swords.

Miro tripped on a log buried beneath the water and fell. A black figure above thrust down at him, and as water filled Miro's mouth, he knew he was dead. Then an orb flashed in the distance, and in the snapshot of light Miro saw the figure above him wore Alturan green. The warrior was holding out a hand to help him up.

As Miro regained his footing, he heard shouts. "Altura! Regroup!"

Miro looked around, given a moment's respite by the late arrival of a fresh band of his men. The battle raged, but the sheer numbers of the enemy pushed the defenders closer to the Alturan bank, and Miro saw the situation was dire.

Then Miro saw a shadow flicker and a line of light sliced through the air. A legionnaire went down, swiftly followed by another. A second shadow took down three soldiers in quick succession. Water dripped down the lines of a silhouetted form, and for an instant Miro saw the shape of a zenblade and the flickering symbols covering a man's armorsilk before he became a shadow again. Miro's brothers were out there.

Miro raised his zenblade above his head. "Altura!" he shouted.

The roar of his men echoed his cry.

Miro reactivated his zenblade and armorsilk, chanting the runes in quick succession. He blazed like a vengeful spirit as, with his men rallied behind him, he once more took the fight to the enemy.

⸻

Miro returned alone from the border, perhaps three hours before dawn. He'd left Marshal Beorn in charge, for with the situation growing desperate, Miro knew he needed to return to Sarostar, where he could press the case for diverting some men from the Petryan border to where they were needed most.

The fighting had continued for most of the night—vicious hand-to-hand combat in the river, on the banks, and finally on the enemy side—before Miro called back his men to avoid the trenches and towers on the Halrana side. The only blessing was that the enemy's use of avengers, dirigibles, and prismatic orbs was now as rare as Miro's. Either the enemy commander was a fool, or like the Alturans, they were pitifully short of essence.

As he crossed the Runebridge, heading for the Crystal Palace, Miro felt fatigue set in. He could still remember the moment when tiredness had led him to trip on a log and fall in the river. What if he fell just when he was needed the most? A bladesinger had never been lord marshal—was it too much for him?

The doubts were just a result of the fatigue, he assured himself. After some rest he would feel more like his usual self.

Miro's eyelids dragged down, and when he reached his soft bed, he fell instantly asleep, fully clothed and with his boots still on. Bloody footprints showed where he'd made his way through the Crystal Palace and straight for his bed.

Must talk to Rorelan in the morning. Must hold in the east, he thought and then sank into unconsciousness.

———◆———

Miro's respite was short-lived.

A hand was shaking him, first gently, then with greater insistence.

Miro opened his eyes. It was light, so it must be morning. Had someone been shaking him? He must have been dreaming.

Miro rolled over, and shouted with surprise. "Ah!"

A small woman stood beside his bed. She was young and pretty, in a manner, with ruddy features and eyes green as grass. Perhaps she wasn't young; perhaps it was just her size.

"Layla," Miro said her name.

The Dunfolk healer usually wore a mantle of fur on her shoulders, but ever since her people had joined the war effort, she carried a short hunter's bow and wore a curved knife at her hip instead.

Miro cursed himself inwardly. The Dunfolk were one of the main reasons for the change of fortune at the Bridge of Sutanesta. He'd meant to travel to Dunholme and see how they were faring, but in the time since the battle, the opportunity simply hadn't come.

"How did you get in here?" Miro asked. Layla simply regarded him inscrutably. He realized he'd never get an answer. When it came to tracking and stealth, none were as gifted as the ancient people who lived in the forests of Altura. "It doesn't matter. Are you well?"

"My people are dying," Layla said. "The Tartana did not send me; he is too proud to ask your help. Yet it is your help that we need."

Miro sat up, looking for clothing, and then realized he still wore his armorsilk. The blood from the previous night had stained his sheets.

He went to the basin near the bed and washed his face and neck, finally pausing and looking at Layla. "Of course I'll help. Come with me."

Miro found High Lord Rorelan discussing food stores with three solemn men from the granaries.

Rorelan exclaimed when he saw Miro. "Is everything all right, Lord Marshal?"

"We held," Miro said, realizing how he must look. "I left Marshal Beorn at the border." He glanced at the high lord's attendees. "May I speak with you, High Lord?"

"Of course. Please wait here," Rorelan said to the three men.

Rorelan led Miro into the next room, a grand hall of high ceilings, where the crystal was a soft rose color and paintings of historic events lined the walls. Layla followed.

"The situation at the Halrana border grows desperate, High Lord," Miro said. "We must divert some men from the Petryan border to where they're needed most."

"Yet you held," Rorelan said, "and I'm assuming it's safe to discuss this in front of your guest?"

Miro reddened. "Yes, of course. High Lord, this is Layla of the Dunfolk."

"The Loralayalanasa," Layla said primly.

"It is a pleasure, Layla of the Loralayalanasa." Rorelan smiled down at her.

"Yes, High Lord, we held, but the enemy's numbers grow greater just as ours are falling. The prisoners we've taken say they're sending still more men here in a constant stream. When that stream becomes a river, they will push straight through to Sarostar."

High Lord Rorelan sighed. "I hear you, Miro, but it's a matter of balancing risks. When that stream becomes a river, let me know, and I will listen."

"By then it will be too late!"

"Marshal Scola has two divisions in the south, you have ten divisions in the east, and that's how it will stay until something drastically changes . . ."

"What about the north?" Layla asked.

High Lord Rorelan turned to Layla. "I'm sorry?"

"These men in black, we can hold them back," Layla said, "and those in orange also. But there are two demons that fight with them, like living trees. Our arrows do nothing against trees. We have lost many of my people to these demons."

"The Veznans are moving south," Miro said. "Orange is their color."

"Which means the demons can only be nightshades," Rorelan said. "Scratch it, yet another thing for us to worry about. The cultivators have been quiet since the Sutanesta. I was beginning to hope House Vezna's part in this war was done, and perhaps Dimitri Corizon had learnt some restraint. They've always kept to themselves in the past."

"Their high lord has the taint," Miro said. "I saw Dimitri Corizon turned with my own eyes."

"Will you help us?" Layla asked.

"Of course," Miro said.

"And how do you intend to do that?" Rorelan demanded. "You'll never get men from the south here in time, and you told me yourself that the east is barely holding."

"High Lord, Layla's people saved us. Now they need our help."

"I know that! But like Beorn, they're just going to have to hold."

Miro pictured the small Dunfolk, gentle in nature, hunters who hid in the forest. Nightshades would tear them to pieces.

"I'll go myself."

"Miro, no," High Lord Rorelan said flatly.

"Beorn is an able commander, and he has four bladesingers with him."

"You're needed here. Your position takes precedence, Miro. People always say bladesingers enjoy too much freedom to make good soldiers. Free will is the last trait a commander can have. Do you hear me? You are confusing your responsibilities."

Miro turned his dark eyes on Rorelan. "We owe the Dunfolk a debt. I'm going." He followed Layla from the room, turning and speaking one last time over his shoulder. "But I'll be back."

11

Miro sat still and silent, once more looking over water and waiting for the enemy to arrive. Yet this time was different: Where before the river had been wide, with earthen banks to either side, this tributary of the Sarsen was narrower, and on both sides thick bushes grew all the way to the water's edge. And rather than night, it was early afternoon. This time Miro would see his enemy.

Next to him, Layla sat with her eyes closed, resting in the bushes, her bow across her lap. There was a time when Miro would have marveled at her ability to sleep when in the next hour her life might be taken from her, but that was long past, and Miro knew the value of snatched sleep.

He considered trying to rest himself, but his nerves were taut and his senses heightened by fear. Fighting legionnaires was one thing, but nightshades were altogether different.

Miro had never actually fought one, but he'd seen two bladesingers take on a single nightshade at the battle at the Bridge of Sutanesta. The living tree easily triumphed, tearing the first bladesinger in half before reaching for the second. Only the intervention of a Halrana colossus had saved the second warrior in green.

And Miro planned to take on two nightshades.

House Vezna's masters of lore were called cultivators for a reason. Where the animators of House Halaran built creatures of wood, iron, or bone, and required a controller to manipulate their movements with skilled activation of the runes, the cultivators applied their lore to the living trees and vines that inhabited their forest home. Of course, the essence inevitably worked its way into the veins of the plant and killed it, but the creations of the cultivators were capable of some truly impressive feats.

An iron golem required a controller, but it would continue the fight until its runes faded and the essence was depleted, and if renewed, it could fight again. The creatures brought to life by the cultivators required no controller; they were given a life of their own, but the plant would eventually die, to rot and feed other plants. The Veznans called it the cycle of renewal.

"You smell," Layla said, her eyes now open as she sat up.

"Thanks," Miro said with a wry grin.

"You smell like the town and the sweat of a man. It is important to adjust your scent to your environment."

Layla came over to Miro. Standing, she was only a little taller than he was seated.

"When stalking a deer, a hunter spreads the dung of deer on the skin of his arms and legs. The deer is then tricked by its senses into thinking the hunter is another deer."

Miro was mildly repulsed, but he could see the logic.

"We're not fighting deer, though," Layla said. "We're fighting men."

Layla leaned forward, and Miro wondered what she was doing, before he felt something soft and squishy being pushed into the hair on the back of his head. It felt like mud.

"We're fighting men," she repeated.

Miro's eyes widened, and he opened his mouth. Her expression was serious, but there was a twinkle in her eye. Surely it was just mud?

"The enemy approaches," a voice called softly.

Miro looked out over the narrow river but could see nothing. He turned back to Layla, but she was gone, vanished into the undergrowth. Quickly clawing his fingers through his hair, Miro did his best to imitate the Dunfolk. At least his armorsilk was green.

Miro felt his fear rise as he waited. Just as he was starting to wonder if the enemy was approaching after all, he saw the flicker of black against the trees on the other side of the river. A single man stepped out, a tattooed legionnaire clad in the scaled armor common among his kind.

A second legionnaire emerged from the undergrowth and conferred with the first. The first legionnaire then plunged a long stick into the water and, seeing that it wasn't too deep, said something to his fellow.

Miro wondered if this was going to be a repeat of the battle he had fought just the night before—hand-to-hand combat made clumsy and sluggish by the dragging water.

The first legionnaire jumped into the water and was soon followed by the second. A third soldier in black came out of the undergrowth, and then more appeared from all directions, taking quick stock before jumping down into the shallow river.

Miro heard a creaking sound and caught movement to his right. Turning, he saw Layla standing with her bow held in front of her, the string pulled to her ear, her arm trembling with effort. Wondering how many of the Dunfolk were here, Miro rested his right hand on his zenblade and waited for Layla to release.

More of the enemy plunged into the water, with those in front now halfway across the river. They walked forward in a broad line, more of their number joining them with every moment that passed.

When was Layla going to let go?

A muscled Tingaran with an arm made of metal—a melding—stepped forward, his eyes scanning ahead as he reached the bank where Miro sat waiting. The Tingaran's eyes met Miro's and suddenly widened with surprise. Miro's heart skipped a beat when he realized he'd been seen. The Tingaran opened his mouth to shout, but before any sound could escape, Layla released.

The arrow sped through the air with no more noise than the flight of a bird. In an instant it jutted from the Tingaran's throat, red feathers bristling. As blood gushed from the warrior's mouth, he placed his hands at his neck, then collapsed into the water.

Barely a breath later, arrows filled the air. Miro had never seen them used like this; it was like a flashing horizontal rain. One after another, the soldiers of the enemy were peppered with the razor-sharp steel of the arrowheads, the shafts jutting out at all angles. In just a few moments hundreds of the enemy were killed. Miro had only seen greater destruction from runebombs and prismatic orbs.

There was no lore involved at all.

As they became aware of the danger, the soldiers wearing enchanted armor hurriedly activated, and the glow of runes separated them from their fellows so that Miro could pick them out like sunflowers in a bed of nightblooms. The arrows bounced off their armor, but even so the Dunfolk persisted, and their marksmen found the small, unprotected places: the joints, neck, and eyes.

Before Miro could enter the fray, they were all gone.

Then the next wave came, a hundred more men plunging into the river, and the slaughter commenced again.

Just as Miro began to wonder whether he was needed at all, the enemy's numbers started to tell. As the soldiers reached the bank where the Dunfolk lay in hiding and the bowmen became embroiled in close combat, Miro saw that hand-to-hand fighting was the archers' weakness. The rate of fire dropped significantly and more of the Black Army's soldiers gained the bank.

Miro's moment had come. The symbols that covered his armor-silk blazed with sudden power as he called on one sequence after another. His zenblade came alive in his hands, lit up with red fire.

Layla stood at his side, arrows flying from her bow. A legionnaire crested the bank, lunging at the Dunfolk healer with his sword raised, but Miro leapt forward to run the warrior through, spinning on his heel and then blocking the cut of a second warrior attacking Layla from behind. As the enemy turned their attention to this new danger, Miro scanned the bank, and seeing it was clear, he jumped into the river.

Miro slashed in a sweeping arc at another melding, a black-clad Tingaran with a rune-covered arm of metal. Miro's stroke was blocked by the warrior's enchanted sword. As the melding countered, Miro raised his zenblade and blocked his opponent's weapon. He realized too late that the melding held his sword one-handed, before his vision went black as the melding's metal fist smashed into his chin.

As Miro fell back, the melding spoke some words, and the runes on his arm blazed red and purple. Miro's vision wavered and then stabilized; he knew another blow would kill him. He now had to watch both the melding's arm and his sword.

Miro narrowly dodged another punch, and his song fell short. His enemy chose that instant to launch a series of blows at Miro's head and body, alternating sword strokes with jabs and uppercuts. A sword thrust caught Miro's chest, turned by his armorsilk, and was swiftly followed by a straight punch at Miro's head with all the melding's formidable strength behind it. Miro ducked and weaved, the water dragging at his limbs as he concentrated on regaining his song.

Finally, Miro blocked an overhead blow with his zenblade and then crouched and hacked at the melding's legs. Miro's weapon encountered no resistance, slicing through one leg and continuing through the next.

The melding screamed and fell. Instantly, Miro was fighting yet another warrior, this time a flaxen-haired swordsman in the orange tabard of Vezna, his house confirmed by the sprouting seed *raj hada*. Veznans were not known for their swordsmanship, and Miro took him with a classic feint and thrust.

Miro dispatched his enemies, one by one, taking the battle to where he was needed, fighting from one bank to the other until the river was a sea of bodies. He was distantly aware of arrows flying through the air, sinking into tree trunks or plunging into bodies, the screams of men signaling a strike.

The river once again cleared of the enemy, and Miro returned to Layla, his chest heaving, feeling as if he'd run from one end of Altura to the other.

As Layla regarded Miro, he prepared to brush away her thanks. "Don't waste your energy," she said instead. "Trust me; you will need it."

Miro opened his mouth to respond, but stilled as Layla pinched his arm. "Here they come," she said, pointing.

At first all Miro noticed was the sound, like the breaking of tree trunks as they were snapped off at the stem—which was likely what it was. He exchanged glances with Layla as she pinched him harder, and for the first time he saw fear cross her inscrutable exterior.

Miro turned back to the trees on the opposite bank, his jaw clenched and muscles tensed. Across the river trees began to topple, falling into the water along with the vines and bushes tangled up with them. Soon the river became jumbled with a mess of tree trunks and branches. Fighting here would be treacherous.

Then one of the creatures that had knocked the trees over appeared, and Miro looked up at the nightshade in awe. Gnarled and knotted, vines covered its limbs so that it was hard to see the nightshade's body through the ropelike entanglement. Its torso stood tall and thick, as round as a large table and covered in gray-brown bark. High on the trunk two sunken pits enclosed malevolent brown orbs, the nightshade's equivalent to eyes. It moved across the ground with a sliding motion as the roots in front took hold of new earth and those in back withdrew. Across the nightshade's trunk and on its limbs, Miro saw runes carved into the bark with essence. The symbols glowed with colors of orange and soft green, barely visible against the creature's skin.

The nightshade paused as it reached the riverbank. Miro felt his heart race, and for the first time in an age he rehearsed the song in his mind before commencing his chant, suddenly fearful and unsure of himself. The second nightshade appeared, and if anything. it was larger than the first, a different breed of tree, an oak beside a cedar.

Miro wondered how he had ever thought he could defeat them.

"How did you defeat them the last time?" Miro asked Layla. He was shocked to hear his own shaking voice.

"We didn't," Layla said. "The land across there," she pointed, "used to be part of Loralayalana."

"Oh."

Miro took a deep breath as the two nightshades paused, just fifty paces away, directly across the river. He rehearsed his strategy. He only hoped it would work.

"Go, Layla," Miro said. "Tell your people to concentrate on the smaller nightshade. Keep it engaged, but draw away from it; make it chase you. If you can, your best plan is to tangle it with ropes and vines. Try bringing down bigger trees in front of it. Who knows, you might even pin it down with a heavier tree. Do you understand?"

"Yes," Layla said. "What about you?"

Miro took a second deep breath, slowly releasing it. "I'll take the big one."

Layla nodded and vanished. Miro stood, looking at the zen-blade in his hands, realizing that only if he gave it as much power as possible could he hope to damage the nightshade.

The smaller nightshade lumbered forward, making slow progress as it hit the tangle of logs and branches strewn across the river. Arrows began to fly through the air, sinking into the gray-brown skin of the creature's torso. A limb appeared out of the vines and creepers to the left of the nightshade's body, a bushy branch that swiped across its trunk, knocking the arrows away as if they'd never been there. The glaring eyes shifted, and the nightshade turned, moving across the river in the direction from where the arrows had come.

"No." Miro shook his head as one of the Dunfolk ran out of the trees, a long hunting knife in his hand. The small man reached the nightshade and started to hack at the creepers at its base. Faster than Miro had thought it could move, the arm-like branch at the nightshade's side shot out as it picked the hunter up around the waist with hooked wooden fingers. A second arm appeared and grabbed hold of the hunter's lower half, the two limbs pulling until Miro heard a tearing sound and the nightshade ripped the screaming warrior in two. The nightmare creature threw the two pieces into the river and continued forward, arrows hitting it in a continuous hail.

Once the way forward was clear, the second, larger nightshade followed, the great trunk swaying as it moved across the scattered trees and branches, water streaming from its base as it moved through the river.

Miro looked again at his zenblade. The slightly curved sword shone silver in the afternoon sunlight. He held the hilt in both hands and ran his eyes across the symbols that covered it from one end to the other.

Ella had made this zenblade, just as she had made Miro's armorsilk, soon after the battle at the Sutanesta. There was no one Miro would trust more with his life.

And Ella being Ella, she'd added some new matrices, giving Miro's zenblade and armorsilk new properties. A bladesinger's song was complex, and Miro had been fearful to add so many activations, but he knew he would now need the new abilities.

Miro opened his mouth and started his chant. Rather than building up to it, he pushed himself to direct his song straight to the most powerful sequences of all, where he would turn the zenblade blue and his armorsilk would blaze like lightning.

As the light of the runes lit up the forest, the bigger nightshade's malevolent eyes turned. The creature's arms came out, the fingers clacking together, and Miro knew the nightshade had seen him.

Fear hit him with sudden force. Miro's voice shook, and his song faltered until with a croak he stopped, and it was gone altogether.

The armorsilk went dead, leaving Miro defenseless. With the zenblade now just a sharp sword, it would be like chopping wood with a bread knife.

The nightshade moved forward, reaching the bank where Miro stood paralyzed. The creature rose to its full height, towering over Miro even as its base stood in the water below him. An arm came at him, faster than he would have thought possible, and Miro ducked and rolled, feeling the horrible fingers pluck at his armorsilk and tear at his long hair.

The movement kicked Miro into action. Suddenly he remembered the basic song of his zenblade, the core activations of his armorsilk. Ella's complex sequences were beyond him, but the next time the nightshade came at him, he swung at one of the fingers, taking it off halfway.

The nightshade reared up, and for the first time Miro saw the appendages at its base leave the ground, water spilling and the ground heaving as it smashed back to the ground with the force of an earthquake.

Miro decided to buy himself some time and jumped onto a fallen trunk, leaping to a second log and then a third, heading deeper into the thick forest. He finally paused in the crook of a huge tree to look back.

The great arm came at him and Miro dropped, the nightshade's hand smashing into where he had been just a moment before. He fell heavily to the ground, rolling onto his back.

The nightshade loomed over him, the creature moving with a speed that belied its size. Miro picked himself up and for the first time faced up to the massive living tree. He added to the song of his zenblade, leaving only lightness and agility in the armorsilk, and the shining sword shifted hue from red to violet. Miro sang as he leapt forward, dodging another swipe to jump up and climb the creepers surrounding the nightshade.

The zenblade turned blue as Miro held onto a vine with one hand. He sensed the nightshade's clawing hands coming at him and knew he had just this one stroke. He held his zenblade with the other hand and thrust at the torso with all his strength.

The zenblade bit into the bark, piercing no more than a few inches into the trunk. The blow was inconsequential, and Miro knew he was going to die.

The two gnarled hands wrapped around him, yanking Miro away from the nightshade's body and holding him high in the air while the glaring eyes regarded him. Miro felt the hands begin to squeeze as the nightshade crushed the life from him.

Miro's song faltered and then stopped, the light of the armorsilk's runes slowly fading. He had never felt such unbelievable strength. The nightshade squeezed at his body with a grip of iron, crushing his ribs and robbing him of breath.

Miro thought of his sister, and of Amber, both somewhere far from home. Ella had always told him he was too reckless.

Suddenly, Miro remembered.

"O-lunara-o-sumara. Na-tumara-kan," he chanted, choking out the new sequence his sister had built into his armorsilk.

Miro's green armorsilk lit up with shimmering blue lines, sizzling with lightning. Even insulated as he was, he felt the numbing jolt, and his teeth smashed together, biting through his lip. The metallic taste of blood suffused his mouth.

What the nightshade felt would be much, much worse.

The charge seared the bark of the nightshade's hands black. Smoke rose in a thick cloud, and the nightshade screamed, a terrible sound that reverberated throughout the forest.

In an instant it let Miro go, dropping him to the earth.

Gasping, Miro checked his body for broken bones, but aside from the pain in his chest, he still seemed to be in one piece. Miro picked himself up and looked up at the nightshade, lurching from side to side in anguish.

Miro checked his armorsilk. Using the lightning effect had taken much of its power. He looked for his zenblade and found it a few paces away.

Miro was ready, and he now had a plan.

He commenced his song, ignoring the pain of his body, adding the core sequences to both his armorsilk and his zenblade. Again he leapt at the nightshade, climbing up its body, but this time he kept a closer eye out for the sweeping arms. When a limb came at him, Miro was ready, and he put his whole song into the zenblade, turning the blade blue, giving his weapon an incredible searing sharpness.

Miro swung at the arm with all his strength and cut the hand off at the wrist.

As the creature tossed and turned with pain, Miro held on tightly. The other arm came at him, and this time Miro cut the limb off at the elbow. He continued higher, clambering up the vines until he was high enough to see where the limbs branched at the trunk. Miro roared as he cut the nightshade's left arm off, and then the right, before letting go and dropping to the ground.

The nightshade raised a root-covered appendage to stamp on the bladesinger, but Miro cut again, this time at the legs, leaving the nightshade unstable and filled with pain.

With a mighty crash, the nightshade fell to the earth.

Miro leapt atop the trunk and stood with his legs apart, his face grim as he stared down into the dark sunken eyes. He held up his zenblade and activated the new sequence Ella had built into it.

The blade flamed like a burning torch. There was no enhancement of its strength, or its lightness, or its sharpness; this was only heat.

Miro looked at the burning blade and touched it to the thick trunk, between the creature's eyes. He held the weapon to the bark long enough to set it afire before continuing further, slowly moving down the nightshade's body, running the blade along its length to the base of its torso. As the creature blazed, the runes on its surface turned black.

The nightshade writhed and twitched, hissing and screaming, and then the creature was still.

Miro turned away from the burning hulk. Over the crackle of the flames, he heard screams and the sound of breaking branches.

Layla! The thought of her fighting one of these creatures sent chills through Miro's battered body. He began to run.

Miro followed a trail of dead hunters, their small bodies torn limb from limb or crushed into unrecognizable lumps of red flesh. His rage grew. What chance did the hunters' arrows have against a nightshade? Miro's anger was directed at his own people. They'd neglected to give the Dunfolk any help, and this massacre was the result.

Miro's legs stretched as he jumped over logs and bushes. He commenced his song as he reached the scene of the battle.

Ahead, the nightshade faced hundreds of the Dunfolk. Arrows stuck out from it in all directions. It was enraged but far from crippled. Even as Miro watched, it picked one of the young hunters up and dashed her against a tree.

Another young hunter climbed up the vines on the nightshade's body, hacking at the limb underneath. A heartbeat later the creature plucked him off and threw him hard against the ground before smashing him with its gnarled hand again and again.

Near breathless from running, Miro's song almost faltered when he saw Layla step forward, a look of determination on her face and a bow in her hands. The Dunfolk healer took careful aim, heedless to the danger. She released her feathered arrow and true to her aim it flew through the air to lodge in the nightshade's right eye.

The creature roared and reared back, before dashing forward and picking Layla up in its right hand. It started to squeeze. In a moment blood would gush forth from the healer's mouth.

Miro jumped atop a log and leapt high as he could, launching off a branch to fly through the air. With his zenblade held at full extension, he swung down.

Miro took the nightshade's arm off at the shoulder, then fell heavily to the earth.

Still in the grip of the gnarled fingers Layla landed in a tangle, but in a moment Miro saw her crawling away, apparently unharmed. Miro noticed the nightshade's senses appeared to be impaired and called out to the hunters. "The eye! Aim for the eye!"

A moment later dozens of arrows sprouted from the upper region of the trunk. Finally an arrow hit the sunken area of the nightshade's other eye, the strike accompanied by a second great roar of pain.

Miro took advantage of the nightshade's distraction to climb its body and hack away its other arm. He dropped back down and cut at the creepers at its base, taking its appendages off root by root. When the nightshade fell to the ground, Dunfolk swarmed to cover it. The small warriors hacked the vines from the nightshade's body until they revealed the last of its sprouting appendages, trimming it down to nothing more than a trunk.

"Leave it," Miro said. "The essence will kill it."

Soberly, the Dunfolk gathered their dead. Some of the hunters returned to the river to watch for more of the enemy, but Miro could see this day's fighting was over.

Miro thought again about the deadliness of the Dunfolk's bows. He'd seen them hold off a horde of the enemy, the sharp arrows thinning their numbers better than any volley of prismatic orbs. Only the nightshades proved too much for the Dunfolk, but the hunters had learned today that the creatures could indeed be killed.

If Miro could combine the ranged attack of bowmen with the close-quarters strength of infantry, what an army he would have!

Essence supplies were low; only Rorelan and Miro knew how low they were . . .

"Layla." Miro saw the Dunfolk healer, pleased she had escaped her encounter with little more than scrapes and bruises. "Would you do something for me?"

Layla frowned and looked at Miro. "What is it?"

"Could you take me to your leader, the Tartana? I want to speak with him about your bows."

Layla thought for a moment. "I will take you to see him. And Lord Marshal Miro . . . ?"

"What is it?"

"Just this once, you do not have to worry about the customary gift."

Miro left Dunholme pleased with himself and the agreement he'd made with the Tartana.

The Alturans would provide two bladesingers to fight with the Dunfolk on the northern border for as long as they were needed. By protecting Dunholme from nightshades, the bladesingers would also be protecting Altura.

In return the Tartana would provide two hunters, Prayan and Aglaran, men he assured Miro were the two best bowmakers and archers in their nation.

The two hunters, father and son, now walked at Miro's side as he headed back to Sarostar. Prayan had small features, wizened with age, and he bore a tattoo of a sparrow on his cheek. According to the Tartana, Prayan could hit a sparrow on the wing from three hundred paces as a younger man. Now the old hunter was the most skilled maker of bows and teacher of young hunters among his people.

Prayan was grooming his son to follow in his stead, and Aglaran's muscles bunched even on his small frame. Aglaran carried the largest bow Miro had yet seen, and Prayan said he would be useful at teaching the taller Alturans. Aglaran wore his hair in a topknot, and around his neck was a wolf's tooth on a thong.

Prayan was the more talkative of the two, and Miro wasn't sure whether the younger man was simply shy or was perhaps deferring to his father.

Miro grinned, imagining the look High Lord Rorelan would give him when he revealed that he'd exchanged two bladesingers for two Dunfolk hunters.

It was an argument Miro looked forward to having. He'd seen too many of his men die at the eastern border clashes, men who could have been saved with the decisive advantage bows could give them.

This wasn't a time to be immersed in the past. The Tingaran Empire was no more. The world had changed.

Miro planned to change with it.

12

Blademaster Rogan Jarvish wandered the streets of occupied Ralanast. He supposed he couldn't call himself blademaster anymore. What was he? For now he was just Rogan.

He hobbled as he walked, and his throat felt tight and sore, but thoughts of complaint never crossed his mind; he knew he was lucky to be alive.

Rogan had always loved Ralanast, with its grand façades and warm, generous people. The capital of Halaran was a place of culture and learning, and a renowned center for trade, where merchants bought and sold the produce of Halaran's numerous farms, orchards, and workshops. Drudges always crammed the city from one end to the other, pulling cart after cart of goods, and the hearty people celebrated life with festivals and dancing, their food and drink shared among neighbors and strangers alike.

As with the builders of Torakon, the Halrana's favorite deity was the Lord of the Earth, but to them this was no distant being. He was present in the fruits of the trees, beloved in the sun's shine on a field of wheat. Before the war, the Halrana had been a happy, prosperous people, proud of their culture and their great city, Ralanast, where the spires of the famous Terra Cathedral could be seen for miles around.

But the city Rogan walked was now a different place from the Ralanast he remembered from before the war.

The cathedral still stood, but many of the stately old buildings were in ruins, the victims of dirigible bombing in the days before the Black Army's conquest of the city. Ralanast's residents walked with a defeated air, heads down and shoulders slumped. Many were starving, the Halrana far down the list of those their occupiers wanted fed first. Worst of all, any who resisted; who spoke out against the Black Army or those of their own people who'd gone over to the enemy's side; any who complained about the thieving of his goods or the rape of his wife simply disappeared.

Rogan had heard about the prison camp half a day's journey from Ralanast. It was a crafty insurance policy, for who would organize a resistance when they had loved ones in the camp?

As he walked the streets, exercising his injured leg and thinking about the future, Rogan glanced at the boy, Tapel, walking by his side, and wondered what he should do.

A stone turned under Rogan's foot, and he tripped, only saved by the walking stick in his hand.

"Are you all right?" Tapel asked quickly.

"I'm fine," Rogan said. What use could he be anyway?

The lad gazed at him with worship in his eyes, and Rogan sighed. Tapel was young, perhaps only eleven or twelve, and the brave boy who'd found him alive on the battlefield outside Ralanast several weeks ago obviously looked up to him. He'd questioned Rogan endlessly about the bodies of the enemy Tapel found littered in a circle around where Rogan had fallen. Had he really defeated that many men?

He was a bladesinger, Rogan had said. He was the blademaster. He was the man who had instructed and led the bladesingers. "I was," he had said, not: "I am."

Rogan leaned on his walking stick and looked around him, at the crumbling stone of a once beautiful fountain. He was as broken as the city itself, once strong and proud, now just a relic of the past.

He now knew all about the battle at the Bridge of Sutanesta. When he'd heard it was Miro, the son of the old high lord, Serosa, who led the Alturans to victory, he'd wept. Actually wept! He was proud of the lad he'd once taught swordsmanship at the Pens, and who now commanded the allied forces, the last bastion against the evil of the primate and his Black Army. Could the lad, now a grown man, have use for him now?

Rogan saw Tapel's mother, Amelia, up ahead, and for a time his thoughts shifted away from blood and warfare. Now there was a beautiful woman, still handsome in spite of the hardships of war, still determined despite the occupation of her city. The late afternoon sun shone on her gold-streaked hair, and she pushed the fringe away from her eyes in a girlish gesture, squinting as she glanced to the right and the left. The years had given Amelia a face of strength and wisdom, with more smile lines than wrinkles, and deep brown eyes.

Rogan had to be honest with himself—he knew what he'd stayed here for. He tousled Tapel's hair. "There's your mother, lad. Let's say hello."

Before Rogan could get Amelia's attention, she darted into the door of a terraced house, quickly entering the building and shutting the door after her. She was only gone a moment, and when she emerged, Rogan was surprised to see a basket in her hands, covered in a cloth of patterned red and white squares.

Amelia glanced around her again, but she didn't look behind her and so didn't notice Rogan and her son. She walked a dozen paces and then took a hard right turn into an alley.

Rogan's heart sank when he saw two Tingaran legionnaires in black uniforms follow her in. He didn't know what Amelia was up to, but he knew it was something dangerous.

"Stay here, Tapel. And lad, this time I mean it," Rogan said.

Rogan started to walk as fast as he could with his gammy leg, hobbling along with his stick out and sandals slapping against the cobbled stones. "Scratch you, boy," Rogan cursed when he saw Tapel following behind him. "Just stay back and stay out of sight, all right?"

Tapel nodded, his eyes wide with fear.

Rogan reached the alley and turned in. Amelia stood terrified, her face white as the two legionnaires talked to her.

"What's in the basket?" a thin Tingaran with a sibilant voice said.

"Medicines," Amelia said, her voice shaking. "Woman's things. You don't need to see them."

"Actually, we do," the thin man said. "C'mon, let's see 'em."

His companion, a shorter man with a hooked nose, said, "Heard of the prison camp? You want to go there?"

The thin man spoke again, his voice wheedling. "You can keep your basket secret, and we'll take you to the camp, so they can question you there. Or you can show us, and we'll decide how bad it is. Maybe it's just some liquor you're trying to keep from us, eh? That what it is? Maybe some valuables you're trying to smuggle out? Maybe—"

The thin man's voice cut off as the blow hit his head with a crack, splitting the skull with a precision strike. The legionnaire crumpled to the ground without a sound.

The warrior with the hooked nose turned in surprise. "Wha—"

Rogan's eyes blazed as he stood with his stick held out like a sword. On the other side of the legionnaire, Amelia drew back, one hand at her mouth and her eyes staring with shock.

"Defend yourself," Rogan said.

The hook-nosed legionnaire drew his sword in one swift move, the steel gleaming wicked and sharp. The legionnaire came forward, but rather than drawing back, Rogan came in to meet him, knowing that his leg gave him a disadvantage in a moving dance of weapons.

They collided in a crash, but Rogan had shifted, turning his body side-on to present a smaller target, and the legionnaire's sword thrust at empty space. With Rogan in a different place than his opponent expected him to be, and the legionnaire off balance, Rogan easily smashed his forehead into the legionnaire's nose before moving himself behind his opponent's back. The legionnaire fell away, staggering. Rogan swung his walking stick at the legionnaire's kidney, gut, and knee. Changing tactic, Rogan then thrust as if it were a sword he carried, rather than a stick, punching into his opponent's throat.

The legionnaire fell to the ground, instantly still, the breath gurgling in his chest and his sword jangling to the stone.

Shouts sounded in the square outside the alley.

"Leave him," Amelia said. "We need to get out of here."

"We can't leave him," Rogan said, panting. "He's seen us."

Rogan handed Tapel his walking stick and then bent down and picked up the discarded sword, testing its weight in his hand. It was a fine sword, he decided, light enough to use with one hand or two. "This is war," Rogan said.

He sliced at the legionnaire's exposed neck, and as the blood rushed out, it was over. Rogan glanced at Amelia, who looked at him as if seeing him for the first time. "This is war," he repeated.

Amelia nodded. "This way," she said.

Amelia led Rogan and her son down a series of alleys, quickly leaving the commotion behind, not stopping until they reached a fountain in a quiet part of town.

Rogan washed the blood from the blade. "I need to hide this somewhere," he said. "Good swords are hard to come by."

"I'll take it!" Tapel said.

"No, you won't," Amelia said. "Here, put it half in the basket, and I'll cover it with the cloth, as best I can."

Amelia pulled the cloth away from the basket, revealing what lay inside. Rogan whistled.

The basket was filled with prismatic orbs, the symbols decorating them still fresh and new. Rogan put his sword in the basket, and Amelia arranged the cover. More slowly this time, they left the fountain, to all outward appearances just a small family on their way home from the market.

"Now," Rogan said. "How about you tell me what you're up to?"

"You can trust him, Mama," Tapel said.

Amelia looked into Rogan's eyes. He met her gaze, unflinching. "I suppose I can," she said.

Rogan entered the designated storehouse, Tapel at his side. The heavy doors swung shut behind him, and he heard the sound of bolts being thrown. The darkness was absolute, and all he could hear was the sound of his and Tapel's breathing. Rogan caught the smell of sawdust and old foodstuffs. He hadn't wanted to bring Amelia's son, but it was one of the conditions of the meeting.

"Quit the theatrics," Rogan said. "How about some light over here?"

A light came on, blinding him.

Rogan felt Tapel grasp his hand. "Don't worry, lad," Rogan said. "If they wanted to harm us, they would have done so."

After a moment, Rogan's eyes adjusted, and he could see the area lit up by the glow of the nightlamp. A long table of polished wood stood on carved legs in the empty space, four chairs around it. The nightlamp rested in the center of the table, but outside the circle of light Rogan could see nothing.

"Come out," Rogan growled. "You're fools, do you know that? If you don't trust someone, then don't invite them to your lair."

"Why would this be our lair?" a voice spoke out of the darkness.

"The storehouse is in a disused part of town, yet the hinges on the door are well oiled. The table is heavy and expensive, as are the chairs, and there'd be marks in the dust if they'd been brought here recently."

"Anything else to add?" the voice asked.

"Finally, you're fools because you're wasting your time when your people need you," Rogan said.

A figure stepped out of the shadows. He was a young man, well dressed in clothing the son of a prosperous merchant might wear, but his boots were those of a soldier, and at his side he carried a worn scabbard that had seen some use, the hilt of his sword polished from handling.

"Who are you, to dictate to us, Alturan?" the young man said.

"He's—"

Rogan silenced Tapel with a squeeze of his hand. "Surely there are more of you? I expected to find some resistance, not a couple of bravos hiding out in a barn."

A second man walked forward, older than the first, with a receding hairline and neatly trimmed moustache. "The two of us are all there are, Alturan."

"That's not true!" the younger Halrana said.

"Hush, Marcus," the older man said. "Yes, there are farmers and wives, craftsmen and priests, all working for our cause."

"But no soldiers?" Rogan said. "No warriors?"

"We are still in the process of . . . recruitment," the older man said. "Now, I think we are long overdue for some introductions."

"I think I know who you are," Rogan said. "You have the look of a Telmarran about you."

"He is High Lord Tiesto Telmarran, Alturan," the younger man said, "Legasa Telmarran's nephew and heir to House Halaran. My name is Marcus. Marcus Toscan." He raised his chin with pride. "I'm the one who got him out of Rialan Palace before the Black Army arrived. And you are . . . ?"

"For now, he's the heir," Rogan said. "When Ralanast is back in Halrana hands, then he can call himself high lord. But to do that, you're going to need my help."

"Who are you?" Marcus demanded.

"My name is Rogan. Rogan Jarvish. Nearly twenty years ago I fought in the Western Rebellion at my High Lord Serosa's side, fighting with your people against the emperor." Rogan's voice was grim. "Prince Tiesto, I fought with your uncle, Legasa, in the great battle to try to free this city." He took a deep breath. "I was a blade-singer of Altura, and then I was the leader of all the bladesingers. I've led the world's finest swordsmen in too many battles to count, and in addition to the bladesingers, I've trained more soldiers than there are stars in the sky."

Prince Tiesto and Marcus exchanged glances.

"It's true," Tapel piped. "I found him on the battlefield. He has a zenblade. I can show you!"

"I can help you liberate this city," Rogan said. "There will be those among the townsfolk who know how to fight. Some will be old men, veterans of the Rebellion like me, but they will be dependable, and they can help the younger men. And . . ."—Rogan paused—"the one who commands the forces in Altura was one of my students. Let me help your resistance. When I tell him we're ready, he will come."

Prince Tiesto looked at Rogan's scars and then at Marcus, evidently contrasting the two men. "How will you know?" Tiesto asked.

Rogan grinned. "Trust me. When we're ready, you'll know it too."

13

The primate pored over the book the old pilgrim had rescued from the destruction at the Pinnacle. He'd locked himself in his study, examining the damaged pages, desperate to unlock the secrets within. The only people he allowed to see him were Moragon and Zavros, the former to discuss the war, the latter to discuss the mystery of the book.

Primate Melovar knew, deep inside, that the book offered him the potential to turn his fortunes and salvage his dream to unite the peoples of the world, if he could only discover its secrets.

His withered and emaciated frame was thinner than ever from lack of food and drink. The thirst for the knowledge burned within him, and he translated day and night, working with the unstoppable energy of the fanatic. He'd learned to live with the pain of his wounds now. If anything, the remorseless agony of his burned flesh drove him on, the fire in his blood reminding him he might not have much time left.

Now Melovar Aspen was coming close to the truth.

"Primate," a deep voice spoke, "you asked to see me?"

Primate Melovar tore his gaze away from the silvery writing of the Evermen and the strange drawings and diagrams. Their rune-based writing was so fresh in his mind that he was having difficulty reading the dispatches his second-in-command brought him.

"Moragon, please come in," the primate said. He noticed Moragon's gaze flicker to the book. "Let me share some of what I've learned with you."

Moragon came to stand beside the primate's desk and looked askance at the book of the Evermen. The primate could almost see the thoughts crossing the melding's face. They had replaced many of the templar leaders with those more malleable, and now those who depended on the elixir were fewer in number. The *raj nilas*, that incredible substance that extended the lifespan and bestowed powers of regeneration, would last a small time longer, but it would still run out. The primate had promised Moragon a plan, yet here he was instead, obsessed with this book. What of the plan Moragon had been promised?

The primate opened the burned and withered pages of the ancient book and pointed to a diagram, the lines shining silver. "See? It's some kind of structure, built into a strange shape. There's a pool in it. And that symbol on the pool? That's the symbol of essence. The Evermen used essence just like we do."

"A pool of essence?" Moragon raised an eyebrow. "I've never heard of so much in one place. It would take centuries to accumulate."

Primate Melovar smiled with thin, broken lips, and as he did, they cracked and bled over his teeth, the acid sizzling on his tongue before, as always, his body repaired itself. "Nor have I. The dimensions . . . this isn't a small pool, Moragon. It's dozens of paces wide. This is more essence in one place than anyone living has ever seen."

"But why?"

"To provide energy for the relic, of course." Melovar's eyes gleamed. He turned past four pages too damaged to read, stopping where there were some lines of legible symbols. "See this text here?

It describes 'the most powerful lore ever devised.' Moragon, think about it—and all we could do if that power were ours."

"So what is it then? Some great plan of the Evermen that was never fulfilled?" Moragon asked.

"I need to learn more to be sure, but it looks like it wasn't just a plan; it was actually built. It's out there, Moragon, hidden somewhere in Merralya. If we could find it . . ."

"This is your plan?" Moragon growled, his nostrils flaring. The primate hadn't seen the melding like this before—not with him at least. The fear of elixir withdrawal had to be powerful in Moragon's mind. Hearing the screams of those they'd purged must have shaken the melding. "You don't know *what* it is or *where* it is."

"That's true," the primate soothed. "There are sections I need to spend more time on. Zavros will be able to help."

"Then, Primate, what is your plan? There's a war going on out there. This could all be a waste of time."

"Yes, it could," the primate said, surprising the Tingaran. "It makes for tempting bait, though."

"Bait? For who?"

Melovar smiled. "For the Akari."

For a moment Moragon was too stunned to speak. Melovar had uttered a name that hadn't been spoken in many years. "No, Primate," Moragon said. The tall man shook his head. "Not the Akari." He looked away as the realization came to him. "So that's your plan."

"Think about it," the primate said. "They never needed the machines to produce their essence. It's perfect. With this as bait, we can make a deal, and with their help, we'll be unbeatable."

Moragon again shook his head. "Not the Akari. The first Tingaran emperor banished them for a reason."

"The Akari have a way of producing essence, Moragon. With essence, we can produce elixir. With more *raj nilas*, we can go on to convert them to our cause, or we can use this relic against them, if we can find it."

Moragon was pensive for a long moment before he finally nodded. "You've thought it through. What happens next?"

"I have a plan, Moragon, but I need your help. I will grant you your wish to go to Halaran, to Ralanast, where your task is to keep Altura at bay, but more importantly, to keep the people under your control. When the time comes, the prison camp will become very important. Keep the prisoners close, my friend."

"I can do that."

"The Akari must not find out about the elixir. The fact of its existence must be protected at all costs. They are powerful, Moragon, and they may see our current weakness. The elixir is our secret weapon."

"And you, Your Grace?" Moragon asked.

"I will go to the north and meet with the Akari. And if this hidden relic of the Evermen exists, I will find it."

The primate turned to the melding, locking the Tingaran's eyes with his burning, yellow gaze. "I may not be much longer for this world, Moragon, and when I'm gone, it will be you who rules not just the lands of the Tingaran Empire, but all of Merralya."

"The Akari," Moragon said, "don't trust them."

"Never fear, my friend. Now go. I will send word to you when I return from the north."

Moragon left the primate's study, leaving Melovar wondering when next they would meet.

The primate called for a guard. "Prepare me a carriage to go north—far north, into the cold. Then bring me the old man, the pilgrim we left in the dungeons of Salvation. Take him to the interrogation rooms here in Stonewater. He may be crazed and know nothing, or it may be an elaborate ruse. Either way, we will find out." Melovar licked his lips. "And either way the old man will die."

14

Killian sighed and placed yet another gold dinar on the growing pile. He knew he was doing the right thing, but Lord of the Sun, did it have to cost so much?

The stocky man seated across from him frowned. Killian groaned and added yet another coin; he only had four left.

They were in The Light Shines Above, a tavern in Salvation. It was a little . . . clean for Killian's taste, but he could see why his companion had chosen it to do this business. In this part of town, the templars would come at a moment's notice at any sign of trouble. In fact, many of the clientele were from the Assembly. Two men exchanging a large amount of gilden would be safe here, and Killian knew it was the last place the templars would expect to find him.

Sitting across from Killian was one of the Buchalanti, an imposing man named Scherlic, a blue-eyed sailor, weathered by the elements, with a broad build and a thick accent. Not for the first time, Killian wondered if he could trust Sailmaster Scherlic, but everyone said that to the Buchalanti, a deal, once made, was unbreakable, and there was no reason for the freedom-loving sailors of House Buchalantas to bear any love for the primate.

Killian added one more coin to the pile, and still Scherlic waited. Killian had thieved on six separate occasions to get this much gilden together, climbing across roofs, prying open windows, and stealing from temple coffers.

"Why do you not take the Halrana Lexicon yourself?" Sailmaster Scherlic asked, seeing Killian's reluctance.

"There are some things I need to do here," Killian said. "Someone I need to find."

Scherlic nodded. "This war has separated many from their loved ones."

Killian thought about Evrin, the mysterious old man who had the answers he needed but who had vanished after the destruction at Stonewater. "Yes," Killian said slowly. "Loved ones."

Killian added one more coin to the pile, and finally Scherlic nodded, taking the pile and pulling it toward him, counting the gold coins into a pouch. "You have my word. We will take the Halrana Lexicon to the high lord in Altura."

Killian lifted the object and placed it on the table between them, quickly pushing it in Scherlic's direction. Killian looked one last time at the Halrana Lexicon, praying it would reach safety, out of the primate's hands. The rune on its cover glowed softly, still bright from when the strange device Killian had found in the refinery had struck it with a burst of energy.

"Please take it," Killian said, glancing around the tavern.

He felt torn in two different directions. Killian knew he should take the Halrana Lexicon to Altura himself, and find Ella, but the hunger to find out who he really was burned inside him. First he had to get the Lexicon to safety—the knowledge belonged to the Halrana and their loremasters would need to keep it renewed— and then he could find the old man. Only Evrin knew about the strange power he possessed. Not only could Killian survive the touch of essence, but runes drawn on his skin enhanced him in the same way they enhanced a zenblade, or a set of armor. What was he?

"It must go to Altura, to Sarostar, to the Crystal Palace. Give it to the Alturan high lord and no one else," Killian said.

"You said, young man." Scherlic frowned.

The temptation to go to Altura himself still pulled at Killian. He knew it wasn't because of any altruistic desire to see the Halrana Lexicon to safety. Sailmaster Scherlic here probably stood a better chance at getting it to Altura safely than he did. A pair of green eyes and a soft smile hovered at the edge of his vision, framed by hair the color of sunlight. Killian pictured a body slim but curved, her fair skin blossoming with youth. Ella.

Sailmaster Scherlic suddenly stood, the pouch jangling at his belt and the Halrana Lexicon now covered with oilcloth in his arms. Salvation was rife with thievery, but Killian knew the Buchalanti had nothing to fear; his brother thieves would stay clear of this one.

Killian watched the sailmaster leave and realized he now didn't know what his next step should be. What could have happened to Evrin Evenstar? The old man never told him anything. Anything! Killian knew nothing to explain what his body was capable of, or about Evrin's own incredible skills with rune making.

Killian looked out of the tavern's window and up at the mountain of Stonewater, looming over the town below, still visible in the afternoon light. He thought about the tavern's name, The Light Shines Above, obviously a reference to the Pinnacle.

The Pinnacle was gone now. Killian wondered if the tavern would change its name.

Killian tried to think about what could have happened to Evrin. The old man whose piercing blue eyes matched Killian's own had sent Killian into the templars' home alone. Evrin had said Killian's task was important, the greatest blow that could be made against the primate's evil. Yet he had sent the younger man in alone, and they had made a plan to meet at the Temple of the Sky in Salvation.

But Evrin Evenstar never arrived.

When, bruised and battered, Killian had limped down from the mountain and made his way to their rendezvous, the old man was nowhere to be seen.

What had taken Evrin away? What was more important than Killian's own quest? While Killian had been deep in the mountain, fighting for his life against Saryah—the twisted creature that had once been the High Templar, changed by the primate's elixir— where had Evrin been?

Killian ran his hands through the fiery red hair that curled to the base of his neck and glared up at Stonewater. There was something here, he knew. The mountain held the secret.

Killian paid his bill and left the tavern, grimacing at the few coins he received in change. Of course Sailmaster Scherlic had left him to pick up the bill.

Killian squinted up at the mountain, trying to see to the top. The mountain had billowed smoke like a volcano, people said.

He suddenly stopped. How could it have? What exactly had caused the light to stop shining?

Killian's brow furrowed. He could climb to the top, following the pilgrim's trail, although there was a chance the trail had been blocked off, and the last people Killian wanted to see were templars. There was an easier way.

"Good day, sir," the shopkeeper said. As he took notice of Killian's clothing, his expression turned to one of distaste. "Ah . . . perhaps you'd like to try one of our sister stores near the temple district. Our prices might not suit what you're after."

"My master sent me to buy a looking glass," Killian said, his voice gruff. "One of those seeing devices the artificers of Loua Louna make. Here." Killian flicked a silver coin, his last, in the shopkeeper's direction. "I have more."

The shopkeeper's expression smoothed. "Of course." He opened a glass cabinet and withdrew a thin disk about the size of Killian's hand. "Is this the kind of device you're after?"

Runes covered the edges of the disk, while the center was blank and shone like a mirror.

"How do I know if it works?" Killian said.

The shopkeeper frowned and then looked at the window. "I can demonstrate it here?"

"That works," Killian said, "but not that window. Can we look out this one, up at the mountain?"

"Of course," the shopkeeper said. He led Killian to the window and showed the younger man how to position the seeing device in front of his eyes. "To activate it, you say *'semara-sulara.'*"

At the shopkeeper's words, the symbols around the rim of the disk Killian held in his hands lit up with alternating colors of blue and green. The mirrored surface at its center showed brown rock, dust, and rubble.

"That's the mountain," the shopkeeper said.

"Hmm," Killian said. He tilted the device, and suddenly he was looking at the sky. This was harder than he had thought it would be.

"I'll have to ask you to give it back now."

"Just a moment," Killian said. He moved the device, but now it was pointing too low.

"Please, sir, give it back now."

"Just a moment!" Killian growled. He glared at the shopkeeper, and the man backed away.

There. Just a little bit back down. Ah, there it was.

Killian looked at the place where once the Pinnacle had been: a beacon to the faithful of the Tingaran Empire and a source of pilgrims bringing wealth to the Assembly of Templars.

Where the light had been, there was now nothing, but Killian already knew that. What drew his attention was the mound of rubble on Stonewater's summit. Something had happened here, and it had nothing to do with the destruction that had followed in Killian's wake. What if Evrin Evenstar's disappearance had something to do with the Pinnacle, the most famous relic in a place known for its mysteries?

Killian absently handed the seeing device back to the shopkeeper and walked out of the shop, his gaze captive to the mountain's peak, unaware of the shopkeeper's words following him out. How could he find out more? Who would have answers?

Killian thought again about how he had first found out he was different. The templars had taken him, just another orphan and thief, and given him the strange liquid. They had been amazed at his body's lack of response, although at the time Killian hadn't known it was death or addiction they were expecting.

There was one templar, in particular, leading them, a man who was knowledgeable about the relics and their powers. A templar who valued knowledge above all else, with a fanaticism Killian could only now appreciate.

Zavros.

Killian decided he needed to pay Templar Zavros a visit.

Zavros stood, silently regarding the destruction of the refinery, deep in the bowels of Stonewater, at the foot of the great shaft that ran the height of the mountain.

The explosion blew outward, opening a seam into the open air, through which the intruder had probably escaped. Saryah had met her end here; they'd found her broken body in the rubble. Both Zavros and the primate once thought nothing in this world could kill Saryah.

Like Melovar Aspen, High Templar Saryah took too much of the elixir, but it affected her differently. For both, it took their humanity, but where Melovar became senseless to pain, whether his own or another's, Saryah became warped and twisted, a snarling, howling creature, part human and part beast. The elixir gave her incredible strength and speed as well as regenerative abilities that the primate was only now coming close to.

At any rate, she was dead now, and Zavros would never be able to study her further.

Zavros wondered about himself. Some of the prisoners had called him inhuman. That, and names much worse. Zavros wasn't inhuman; it was simply that he knew the truth: Nothing was more important than knowledge.

Knowledge had led to the foundation of this great civilization. Knowledge separated people from the beasts, and knowledge lasted forever. It grew like a mighty tree, passing from generation to generation like a seed that became a stem, a trunk that branched and took it in unexpected directions. A mathematical novelty could become a weapon of war; a sundial could improve crop rotation. Even so-called lore paled beside the wonders of the physical universe. Zavros shared the primate's vision for a world that had thrown off the shackles of magic. A world of libraries and universities, where the mysteries of the heavens were unraveled, and people were given an equal opportunity to learn rather than follow some archaic system of enchantment academies and builders' guilds.

Zavros wanted to know why blood could fill a human with life, yet if the blood were taken away, the person would die. Why did a babe die if it was never held?—something Zavros had tested himself. Why did a man's temperament change when he was wounded in the head? And if more of his brain was taken out, how is it he could sometimes talk, but not move his hands; or could move his hands, but not talk?

As for lore, why was essence a poison, the deadliest poison imaginable, yet a substance that could fill objects with life? Did no one ask? And how could elixir rejuvenate a man's vitality and heal his wounds? What strange fluid now flowed through the primate's veins?

Zavros burned to find out. Any more experiments, though, would require more essence. Essence that Moragon needed for the war effort. Essence he did not have.

"Destroyed." Zavros sighed, looking at where the refinery used to be. "Completely destroyed."

"Good to hear," a voice said. "That was my objective."

Before Zavros could react, a hand curled around his neck, twisting him and shoving him back against the wall.

Zavros looked through his oculars, down the length of his nose at the blue eyes that blazed in front of him. "You," Zavros said. "The one who is unharmed by essence." He nodded, looking pleased, even in the position he was in. "Ah, it all makes sense."

"I'm glad you remember me," Killian said. "I would say it's good to see you, Zavros, but I would be lying. Tell me, how many did you kill before you got the elixir right?"

"Killian, Killian," Zavros tut-tutted, "what lies have you been listening to? Once we were friends, and you shared our vision for the world."

"Not any more," Killian said. "I stole for the primate . . . I even killed for your cause. Not any more. Answer my question. How many have you used for your experiments? How many died for the knowledge?"

Zavros shrugged. "I keep only the statistics that are of interest to me. I can tell you percentages—but numbers . . . ?"

"I should kill you now," Killian said.

"Why don't you?" Zavros asked, raising an eyebrow. He sneered, even as he felt the grip around his throat tighten. Zavros wasn't an old man, but Killian was strong, with the lean body of a dancer or an acrobat. Zavros was no fighter.

"There's something I want from you first," Killian said.

Zavros tried to laugh, but with the squeeze on his neck it came out more like a choking sound. "Why should I tell you anything? I have no fear of death."

Killian snatched the oculars from Zavros's face and threw them to the ground. Zavros blinked and tried to focus on the man in front of him.

Killian pulled something out of a pocket, a small white stone, vaguely cube shaped and drawn over with black squiggles.

"What's that?" Zavros asked.

"It's one of the devices that caused the destruction you see here."

"Do your worst."

"Your library isn't far from here. Just two floors up, isn't it?"

Zavros felt a chill. Knowledge was forever and could last beyond the lifespan of any man, but books could be destroyed, and the knowledge could be destroyed with them.

"You wouldn't." Zavros knew fear was written across his face.

"Why wouldn't I?" Killian said. "Will you answer my questions?"

"No."

Killian's shoulders moved with what Zavros's blurred vision said was a shrug. "You've seen what this can do. I'll go activate this now in your library, and then we can see what effect pain has on one such as you."

"What do you want to know?" Zavros stalled.

"The Pinnacle . . . Did you find anything? Anything . . . or anyone?"

"What are you looking for?" Zavros was surprised. Killian had admitted to destroying the machines yet was seeking information about the Pinnacle. The primate would be interested to know about this.

"Just tell me what you know."

"The light guarded a building, but it was destroyed in an explosion like the one here. We found some runes on the blocks of stone and a mad pilgrim in the rubble. That's all."

Zavros felt he hadn't given away anything compromising. His mind worked furiously. What was Killian looking for? Killian must know something about the book. This young man had information the primate needed.

"You know, don't you?" Zavros said. "About the book. Tell me, Killian. Tell me how to unlock its secret."

Killian's hand closed tighter around Zavros's neck. He hesitated and then shook Zavros harder. "Of course I know about the book. Where is it?"

"Where do you think it is? The primate has it," Zavros said. "But you'll never find him. He's left Stonewater and won't be back for a long time."

The sound of footsteps clattering against the stone made Killian's voice grow urgent. "And the pilgrim? Where's he?"

"The crazed old man?" Zavros's eyebrows shot up. "He has something to do with this?" Zavros suddenly laughed. "We've been keeping him in the dungeons in Salvation, but he's dead now. The primate sent for him before he left, asking for him to be sent to the interrogation room. No one ever leaves the interrogation room alive, not once the primate's had his way with them."

As the approaching footsteps echoed through the vaulted cavern, growing louder, Killian pushed Zavros away from him. Zavros immediately dropped to the ground, fumbling until he found his oculars and placed them back on his nose.

Killian was gone.

———— ◆ ————

Killian was both furious and terrified. Evrin had been in the dungeons in Salvation, right under his nose this whole time. The lightly secured gaol for drunks and thieves was the last place Killian would have thought to look for the man who could change his appearance with a few spoken words or create objects as powerful as the destructive cubes.

The cube he'd fabricated and threatened Zavros with was so false that only Zavros, half-blind and with a templar's ignorance of runes, could have believed it was anything else. Although Zavros might have knowledge, when it came to lore, the man knew little, particularly compared with someone like Ella or Evrin.

The conversation with Zavros had filled him with confusion, but with the templar's slip he'd managed to learn something about what had actually happened.

Evrin had gone to the Pinnacle to find and destroy this book, and the chamber along with it. Something had gone wrong, and he'd been captured, but the templars thought he was just another pilgrim. Whatever the book was, it hadn't been destroyed and was now in the primate's possession.

And now the primate had tortured the old man. What had Evrin divulged? Did the primate now have the knowledge that Killian himself longed for? Could Killian have done anything to change Evrin's fate?

Killian ran toward Salvation, to the only place where Evrin might have left him a message. He would need to find Evrin's cell. Surely the old man had left him something?

When Killian arrived at the dungeons in Salvation, he stopped in shock. The gaol, where he himself was held so many times in his youth, was a smoking ruin. Charred bodies sat hunched inside the roofless remnants of cells, prisoners who would now never leave. Two of the bodies closer to the front must have been guards. One had a key ring at his belt, and the other had bits of white cloth still attached to the red flesh that had been his back.

A solitary guard in white crouched, staring at one of the corpses.

"What happened?" Killian asked.

The guard looked up with reddened eyes, perhaps from the acrid smoke. "The primate called for a prisoner, an old pilgrim, but the prisoner had escaped. The primate was angry. He ordered his men to seal the dungeon, with all guards and prisoners still inside. They tossed in prismatic orbs." He scanned the two bodies in front of him. "One of them is my brother. I'm just having a hard time figuring out which."

"I'm sorry," Killian said.

Evrin had escaped.

But where had he gone?

15

Time passed, and in the warmer lands winter gave way to spring. Daylight lasted longer, spirits grew lighter, and a new generation of young animals and wild flowers filled the air with the exuberance of youth.

In Altura's capital, Sarostar, the ferryboats again traveled the Sarsen, taking a new year of students to classes at the Academy of Enchanters. A ferryman named Fergus looked up at the azure sky and smiled, happy to be busy; his children had grown tired of old apples.

In Ralanast, capital of Halaran, the cruelest winter in a hundred years was finally over, and now it was time to count the dead. The legionnaires and regulars of the Black Army felt angry eyes on their backs as young men and scarred veterans hatched plans for liberation and for vengeance.

In rust-colored Petrya, a soldier on patrol near the capital, Tlaxor, saw a great dust storm rise in the south, in the direction of the trade town of Torlac. It wasn't the time for sandstorms, and they never traveled so far north. The soldier wiped his eyes and shrugged.

In Vezna's capital, Rosarva, spring was normally a time for growth—new plants sprouting and trees becoming saplings in a thriving living city unrivaled anywhere in the world. This spring, however, the cultivators shook their heads and cursed their young high lord, Dimitri Corizon. They remembered the days when his father, Vladimir, had ensured their neutrality in every conflict. Some began to speak of a change in leadership.

In the cooler lands, Torakon, Loua Louna, Aynar, and Tingara, the change of seasons meant little. In Torakon, families missed their fathers and sons, for the Black Army still requisitioned builders for walls and fences, turrets and fortresses, at every corner of the world. In Loua Louna the artificers waited, idle and frustrated. Essence had stopped coming long ago, and their workshops were silent and still. In Aynar, the templars watched each other; a colleague's careless word could mean instant promotion. In Tingara, the commanders and legionnaires felt proud to be ruling the world, while the common people struggled through life in the same way they always had.

There was one place where the passage of the seasons meant nearly nothing at all. The days were a little longer, but it was still cold. It was always cold.

Primate Melovar Aspen pulled the white, fur-lined robe closer around his body. He felt the chill, yet in a way, he found the climate of the icy north quite pleasant. The pain of his burned skin subsided somewhat, and he felt he was able to think more clearly. It was good to be away from the lands of the empire, even for a short time.

He'd been traveling for several weeks, time he had spent examining the book and gaining a further understanding of its contents, however incomplete. He frowned when he remembered the pilgrim. He had left explicit orders about the old man. With the pilgrim's escape, Melovar would never know if there was something locked up in his mad head that could solve his problem.

What was this powerful relic of the Evermen? What form did it take? Where was it? Why were the diagrams such strange shapes?

Melovar doubted the Akari would know either, and he would have to negotiate the coming encounter with the information he had.

The carriage bumped and jostled, and Melovar cursed when the bouncing tore at his skin, breaking it in places that would bleed anew. He hoped the Akari were worth it.

Drudges pulled the carriage over the long-abandoned road that stretched from Seranthia through Loua Louna and far into the icy north, where few men dared to go. An age ago, this road had linked Akari lands with Tingara, but since the exile it hadn't been used at all and was in poor condition, to say the least. Fortunately, once they were far enough north, snow covered the road, and as the men in front forged ahead, packing it down, it was only the occasional stone or ditch that impeded their progress.

"Halt!"

It was the voice of his detachment's captain. The primate smiled to himself; they were far enough into Akari lands now. Something told him the Akari were here.

"What is it?" Melovar called out of the open window. He could see pine trees, covered in snow, and swirling eddies of low-hanging mist. The Akari certainly lived in an inhospitable place. Melovar supposed they preferred it this way.

A templar guard came to the window. "There's a strange man standing on the side of the road ahead," the templar said, his voice betraying his anxiety.

"Strange?" Melovar asked. "In what way?"

"He doesn't come forward or say anything, or respond to our calls. He simply stands, watching. We've sent out one of the scouts."

Melovar barked a laugh. "He won't get much sense out of him. Keep us moving; the rest of them will show themselves when they're ready."

"Yes, Your Grace," the templar acknowledged.

The carriage began to roll ponderously forward again as the drudges resumed their plodding walk. Melovar leaned out the window as he saw the scout return.

"Bring the scout here," Melovar called. "Tell him to keep quiet."

The scout came to the primate's carriage, white-faced, rigidly keeping his composure.

"Well?" asked Melovar.

"He's dead," the scout murmured. "His skin glows with runes, and his eyes are white. There's the stench of corruption about him, and he stands still, as though frozen. He doesn't answer when I speak."

The primate nodded. "The rest will be close. Very close. Stay silent."

The scout nodded and moved away. The column continued to advance.

When the Akari finally showed themselves, they openly walked out of the forest, rather than materializing out of thin air. *These are just men after all,* Melovar reminded himself.

Melovar looked out of his carriage window, seeing them on both sides, edging slowly forward, encircling the carriage and the primate's contingent. The primate heard shouts as his captain formed the templars up, drawing swords as Melovar's bodyguard made a close ring around the carriage. The primate's personal guard all had the taint, and he idly wondered who would win in a fair fight between one of his templars and one of the Akari.

Melovar had never seen an Akari, and he looked at them with fascination. He quickly divided them into two groups. There were the white-eyed silent warriors, men and women both, who wore swords and armor and seemed neither angry nor scared, but simply waited. Then there were those who stood behind them, also armed, but eminently more aware of their surroundings.

The Akari were tall and pale skinned, with broad shoulders and narrow waists. They were an attractive people who almost universally had blonde hair and blue or gray eyes. The white-eyed men and women wore their hair long and loose, whereas those behind had their hair in braids, the women in a single, thick braid at their back, the men with multiple braids entwined in their hair. Many of the male warriors had forked beards, and all warriors, regardless of gender, appeared to prefer axes, maces, and hammers to swords.

One of the men at the back walked forward. Taller than the rest, with a height that must have measured close to seven feet, he had white hair, but his face was unlined. His brow was cruel, and his lips were turned down in a perpetual scowl. He wore clothing of bleached leather and a cloak of silver fur on his shoulders. At his belt he carried a two-headed war hammer, and his arms and legs were as broad as tree trunks.

The big man halted, his right hand on the war hammer, and called out, "Your standard says that the primate of the Assembly of Templars travels with this group. Show yourself, Primate; otherwise, we'll destroy this column."

Melovar opened the door of his carriage and stepped out, leaving the book of the Evermen inside. He felt the snow crunch beneath his heels and heard the wind as it howled through the trees, tossing the falling white flakes. One of the white-eyed warriors stood close by, his skin pale and the mottled flesh under his eyes showing an advanced stage of corruption. The hem of Melovar's heavy white robe trailed on the ground as he ignored the revenant and walked toward the tall warrior.

"Dain Barden Mensk you must be," Melovar said. "I heard your name spoken with fear when I was just a priest."

"That is I. You are primate of the Assembly?"

Melovar was close enough now that he could see where Barden's forked beard had been threaded with silver. The color suited the Akari. Silver-gray was prevalent in their furred clothing and the color of the older warriors' hair, in the shades of their eyes and the mood of the sky.

Melovar kept walking until he stood close enough that he knew Barden could see the countless crevices of his ruined skin, the yellow of his eyes. "I am Primate Melovar Aspen." Melovar lifted his voice. "Men," Melovar called, "this is Barden Mensk, Dain of his people. Dain is what we would call high lord, and he is the ruler of the Akari."

Dain Barden looked around him, his mouth turned down with distaste. The strange silent warriors stepped forward at some unspoken signal. Melovar could see their skin glowing softly where runes had been tattooed onto the dead flesh. With so many around him, he could see where they were in varying states of repair. Some looked fresh, if that could be said of the dead, whereas others were in an advanced state of decomposition.

At one time, the primate would have been filled with revulsion. Now he just thought of the power he would have at his disposal with the Akari by his side. Melovar looked around at his men—tough warriors, handpicked for this mission, many of them with the taint—seeing that they were both disgusted and filled with fear.

"I come to negotiate with you, Dain Barden," Melovar said, gazing up at the huge leader of the Akari, ignoring the revenants, who stared at him with their empty eyes.

Barden looked back at the primate, frowning, his brows coming together over his ice-blue eyes. "Why would the emperor send you, primate? Why not come himself?"

Melovar didn't reply immediately and instead touched the chin of one of the silent warriors, a woman with loose silver hair and a short sword on each hip. The primate turned the head, looking into the white eyes.

"Because the emperor is dead," Melovar said, "and I am the ruler of the Tingaran Empire now."

"You?" Dain Barden said. "A templar?"

Melovar turned his yellow eyes on Dain Barden, lowering his hand until he grasped the woman's neck. "Yes," he said, "a templar."

The primate began to squeeze, feeling the power of the elixir flow through his veins. The white-eyed woman flailed at her assailant with one arm while the other drew a sword, and moving with surprising speed, she plunged it into Melovar's chest.

The primate smiled as the revenant withdrew the sword; he could feel the wound resealing itself. The woman plunged the sword in again, this time pushing the point up toward Melovar's heart.

The pain was excruciating, but Melovar continued to smile, hiding the effort as he continued to squeeze the revenant's neck. If the woman had been alive, she would have choked and perished long ago, but this . . . thing . . . had no breath to yearn for. Finally, Melovar felt the vertebrae give beneath his fingers. As the woman withdrew the sword and prepared to plunge it into Melovar's flesh again, the primate felt the spine crack. He gave one last squeeze, and the revenant crumpled to the ground.

The primate turned to the ruler of the Akari, who looked at him with wary eyes. "The old ways are finished with, Dain Barden," Melovar said. "Your exile can end. We need to talk."

The tall warrior took his hand away from his war hammer, tugging on his forked beard. "Yes, Primate," Barden said. "I can see that we do."

Dain Barden entertained Primate Melovar Aspen at his frozen palace in the ice city of Ku Kara, with Melovar's men remaining outside the city. A woman bowed in front of the primate, descending to one knee to offer him strips of salted seal liver.

Melovar took one of the strips and put it in his mouth, rolling the oily texture over his tongue before biting into it. He chewed thoughtfully before swallowing. Disgusting.

Compared to the pain of withdrawal from the elixir, compared to the pain of his burned and ruined skin, it was nothing.

"I can see you admiring her beauty," Dain Barden said, gesturing to the near-naked young woman, dressed in a transparent garment of silver gauze. Her golden hair flowed to her waist, and her breasts could be seen pressing up against the material. Her narrow waist flared to hips that were round and descended to long, athletic legs.

"I am an old man," said the primate, "and a templar. Such pleasures have never driven me."

Barden gestured, and the young woman came closer to the Dain. He ran his fingers over her hair. Except for the whiteness of her eyes and the glowing symbols tattooed on her skin, she could have been alive. "My niece," he said. "She drowned in the ice a month ago. Such a shame."

Melovar nodded, shifting on the furs that cushioned his seat of ice. This was Barden's palace, and as host it was the Dain's prerogative to dictate the flow of conversation.

Dain Barden dismissed the woman with a curt gesture. "So let us be clear," he said. "You know where this relic is, along with the pool of essence?"

"That is correct," Melovar said.

Barden looked past the primate's shoulder. "Renrik?" he called.

Melovar turned in his seat to see an Akari in a silver robe approach. He had black hair, which was unusual for an Akari, and wore a necklace of what appeared to be bones around his neck.

"Primate Melovar Aspen, this is Renrik Hormundar, one of my best necromancers. Well, Renrik?"

The necromancer ignored the primate. "We have examined the book. It is authentic. We believe the relic exists, as does this pool. It must be a powerful artifact indeed to require such a large amount of essence to energize it. The structure, though, where the relic is housed . . . we cannot say where it is."

"And we can return to the Empire?" Dain Barden addressed Melovar.

"Yes," said the primate. "You can resume links with the houses, with the Assembly of Templars, and with the Empire. Your exile will be revoked."

"This relic will be ours?" Dain Barden asked.

"Yes. And the essence," Melovar said.

"And in return?"

"In return, you provide your formidable warriors to fight alongside the Imperial Legion and our templars."

Renrik spoke up. "But not in the warmer lands. Not in Altura, Halaran, or Petrya. Our warriors will decompose too quickly."

"Agreed." Melovar knew that with the Akari added to his strength in the colder lands in the east, he would be able to free up more of the Black Army to crush Altura.

"However, I know what you want most of all," Dain Barden said.

Melovar knew he was too eager and that the Akari could see it. He didn't care.

"Yes, I want the secret."

"The reason we were exiled." Dain Barden regarded him with level eyes.

"Yes, yes, I want it."

"Let us show it to you first, and then we'll see if you're still so eager."

The primate wished Zavros were with him. The sharp-eyed templar would understand much more than did Melovar himself. Nevertheless, it was beautiful to behold.

Dain Barden spoke as he showed the primate the cavernous chambers deep beneath the ice city. "The dead are animated using the necromancers' arts. Depending on the age of the body and the skills it possessed in life, it may become a warrior, or a servant, or a—how do you say it?—a creature of pleasure.

Melovar shivered. "How long do the revenants last?"

Necromancer Renrik spoke up. "We do not call them revenants. That is a word of your people." He gestured to a corpse that lay flat on a slab of ice. "To us he is a draug, the plural of which is draugar."

"Not ghouls then?" Melovar smiled thinly, his lips splitting again and blood trickling through the cracks.

"No," Renrik bristled, "not ghouls. They were once beloved, and they serve the Dain in death as they served in life. They are draugar."

"I understand," Melovar said. Not being a man of lore himself, he enjoyed pointing out their pretensions.

"The draugar are obviously better suited to colder climates such as we have here in the north. The decay is our greatest challenge, for they will remain animated long after they've started to rot, or in battle when they have lost limbs or been stabbed many times."

"Impressive," Melovar said.

With Renrik leading and the Dain and primate following close behind, the three continued past a massive vat, as high as the tallest tree and as wide around as a large house.

Renrik halted. "Here in Ku Kara, when the dead have served their purpose and can go on no longer, they are recycled. The Lord of the Night gave us something far greater than your Lexicons." The necromancer and his Dain both looked up proudly at the vat. "We Akari have no Lexicon," Renrik continued. "We have no harvesters or extraction plants, eking out droplets of essence from the plant matter and the lignite. The Lord of the Night instead gave us a method of extracting essence from those with the most life force of all. We take our essence from those with much more life than plants. We, Akari, extract our essence from the dead."

———◆———

Melovar left the lands of the Akari jubilant. He had his agreement and he still had the book of the Evermen. He would now head to Seranthia to prepare for Dain Barden's arrival. It had turned out better than he had ever imagined.

The primate would send a fast messenger to Zavros, ordering him to Ku Kara, where the templar would learn from the Akari. In particular, with the help of the Dain's necromancers, Zavros would discover how they extracted essence from the dead.

Soon the Akari would send their armies to Seranthia, and Melovar would unleash the draugar against his enemies.

When he had secured his own supply of essence, using the Akari's technique, he would once again have power at his disposal. When the primate ruled all the world, he would give the Akari the same fate he planned for all of the houses. He would destroy them and give the world peace from lore at last.

Dain Barden believed Melovar would tell him where to find the hidden relic, this powerful magic, the Evermen's greatest work. Melovar still didn't know where it was, or *what* it was, but he was determined to find it.

When he did, he had no intention of sharing it with anyone.

———◆———

Dain Barden spoke with Renrik as they watched primate Melovar Aspen's departing back. "Stick to the letter of the agreement,"

Barden said, "but don't trust them. When we have this relic of the Evermen, and when we have our avenue back into the Tingaran Empire, then we'll show them how powerful we've become since the exile."

Barden turned to his necromancer, the tall Dain looming over the man who wore a circle of finger bones around his neck. "Never forget, Renrik, never forget. They will always hate us."

16

Evrin Evenstar cursed. Limping and hobbling, he'd managed to drag himself away from Salvation until he'd taken refuge in a forest far from the road, and then his fatigue, combined with the wounds he'd received at the Pinnacle, overcame him, and he lost consciousness.

He sat up and cursed again. What time was it? Morning? More importantly, what day was it? How much time had passed since the destruction at the Pinnacle? How long had he spent in that dungeon?

He was lucky to have escaped, and lucky to be alive. A senior templar had visited the dungeon to make sure the primate's orders were being followed—that the prisoner was being fed and watered, but also being kept under lock and key.

Evrin had looked up at the templar through the bars of his cell, his eyes squinting against the glowing pathfinder the templar held in his hand. When the templar turned the device to the cell, scanning the floor and walls, Evrin could finally see.

The templar had an enchanted sword, a straight length of rune-covered steel with a bronzed grip. The sword wasn't scabbarded; the templar had it drawn and was casually leaning on it, perhaps to impress the other guards.

Evrin had quickly scanned the symbols on the sword, looking for the activation sequence, finding the upper limit of what the enchanted blade was capable of.

"*Shekular-suk. Ran-rumaya-tul-lan,*" Evrin spoke.

Evrin put his hands over his face, even as he continued to chant, and his words took effect. The templar cried out as the sword expended its energy in a blinding flare. A wave of heat came from the blade, and with the sword's length close to his legs, the templar screamed and dropped the weapon, jumping as far away from it as possible. It clattered to the ground, just in front of Evrin's cell.

Quick as a snake, Evrin's hand slipped through the bars, and ignoring the fierce heat, he gripped the hilt and pulled it through. The scratched thing was heavy, and Evrin sighed; he'd never been one for swords. At least it had been designed to project the heat forward, protecting its wielder.

He activated three more sequences, careless of how much of the sword's energy he was draining. Evrin swung at the bars, and with three mighty blows and a shower of sparks, he sliced through them like a scythe through wheat. On the other side of the new hole the old man had created, the templar stood gaping, and Evrin was relieved to see the man's eyes were clear of yellow.

Evrin felt the strength in his arms giving out, and took the sword in both hands. He swung the sword in a sweeping arc in the direction of the templar's head, a clumsy blow that missed, but nevertheless shocked the templar into fleeing.

Evrin surprised and then cut down one of the more sadistic guards before the others leapt away from the blinding light of the blade.

This old man still had some strength left.

Once outside he'd discarded the sword and then hidden among the poor of Salvation—just another dirty pilgrim—before hobbling out of town, the wounds from the explosion at the Pinnacle still causing him to wince with each step.

Evrin's thoughts returned to the present. Here he was, leaning against a tree, when he needed to get up and take action.

"Scratch you, old man," he cursed himself yet again.

Rather than destroying what he'd gone to Stonewater's summit to eradicate, he'd helped the book to fall into the worst possible hands.

There was no other course of action. Evrin needed to enhance the protection around the relic and the pool of essence that powered it. The book was gone, and only by going to the relic itself could he keep it safe.

Evrin finally stood up, ignoring the pain in his bruised body. He walked back to the road and looked along it, away from Salvation, before beginning the long walk to Seranthia.

Only much later did Evrin think of visiting the Temple of the Sky in Salvation, and by then it was too late to turn back. He could have used Killian's help, but he didn't know if the young man had waited for him, or if Killian had even made it out of Stonewater alive.

As he walked along the road toward the great city that men called the capital of the world, Evrin realized that although it was too risky for him to go back to Salvation, he might be able to send a message.

It took a few tries, and a near bite from a protective dog, but Evrin finally found a pious woman, a farmer, who felt sympathy for the old pilgrim and promised to deliver his message to the Temple of the Sky in Salvation.

"Come to Seranthia," Evrin wrote. "Meet me at the docks, at a tavern called The Floating Cork."

Evrin was going to need a scrill and essence. He needed to visit his sanctum; yet another reason to get to Seranthia.

Perhaps Killian would receive Evrin's message and find him, and Evrin would get some help.

Either way, with help or alone, Evrin was determined to see this thing through.

17

The squat trader ship rolled on the waves like an old drunk, show-ing too many years yet too little sense to head for home. The mast tilted one way, then another, as howling winds buffeted the sails and the huge waves threatened to tip the ship over again and again.

Ella balanced precariously on the poop deck, at the ship's stern above the cabin the captain called his own. She held onto a stout rail with both hands, shifting her weight from one hip to another, gazing out at the stormy sky and thinking dark thoughts.

Ella saw a figure climb the ladder up to the poop deck, and realizing who it was, she laughed. In sodden wet clothing, Jehral looked like nothing so much as a black housecat that had fallen into the bath.

Jehral glared at the young enchantress. "You are insane!" Jehral shouted at her above the wind. "This is a major storm. Don't you realize that?"

The ship crashed into the sea with a boom, and a great wave of spray crested their heads, falling down and soaking them both to the skin. Jehral cringed, but Ella laughed again; she was already wet, so what did it matter?

When they'd reached Castlemere, Jehral and the Hazaran wise woman who summoned darkness at Jehral's command had guarded Ella and Shani while the trader Hermen Tosch organized their transport. Ella had tried to engage Jehral in conversation, but he silenced her with a glare, and if she persisted, the darkness soon came over her. Jehral still hadn't explained what Prince Ilathor wanted with her.

Then Ella and Shani were again put into the covered wagon. It rumbled and bumped over the cobbled stones, and they soon heard the sounds of the sea—the crashing of waves and the shrieks of seagulls. Dressed in their simple garments, without their tools, the two captives had struggled, but it was no use. They were bundled onto the Castlemere trader ship and left in full daylight with the changing of the tide. Rescue from Miro or his men was now out of the question.

A week after departing, Jehral finally let Ella and her Petryan friend out of their locked cabin. "There's nowhere for you to go," he'd said, gesturing to the open expanse of the ocean, "and I doubt either of you know how to sail."

Even so, Ella had reveled in her newfound freedom.

Alturans weren't the greatest sailors, but Ella's people knew the river, and she was familiar with boats. As a Petryan, the only water Shani had seen was the boiling Lake Halapusa surrounding the tiered city, the Petryan capital of Tlaxor. But the worst affected by the journey was Jehral, a desert warrior born and bred. The proud leader of fierce horsemen couldn't keep his food down, and the swarthy skin of his face had turned a sickly green.

"Please come down with me," Jehral shouted into Ella's face. The sail snapped with a gust, and he looked up with fear as the mizzenmast creaked alarmingly.

"It's actually better for your seasickness up here," Ella shouted back. "Ask him." She pointed at the helmsman, a bearded Castlemere native standing at the wheel a dozen paces away, not the friendliest man Ella had met. "Keep your eyes on the horizon, and stand where the ship rolls the least, that's the key."

"Come down!" Jehral cried.

"Not until you tell me where we're going."

"We're going to see Prince Ilathor," Jehral said.

"I know that! Where are we going?"

"We're going to the Hazara Desert. We're traveling south and east, and then we'll find a river mouth hidden by the cliffs. The river will take us to Agira Lahsa, the hidden city."

Ella drew back in surprise. "Your people have a city? I thought you lived in tents and that you loved the freedom to roam the desert."

"All great civilizations have cities," Jehral said. "When our lore was lost, when the knowledge faded away, Agira Lahsa was abandoned. Prince Ilathor's father, the kalif, is rebuilding the city. We are a house now, House Hazara, and we have you to thank for it, Enchantress Ella."

"Then give me my dress back, and talk to me again as my friend, Jehral."

"We shall see," Jehral said, his voice clear against a momentary lull in the storm. "We shall see."

<hr/>

The storm passed, and the ship's motion subsided as the waves grew smaller and she made speed with a brisk wind behind her.

Ella spent much of her time on deck, sometimes on her own, other times talking with Jehral about life in the desert or with Shani about the terrible things that happened in Petrya under the rule of their high lord, Haptut Alwar.

Absent their tools, Ella and Shani initially shared their knowledge of enchantment and elementalism in hushed tones at night. Finally, they began to share their more private selves.

Petryans were fiercely competitive, and Shani had needed to completely devote herself to her calling. After initial training, the competition became stronger, even dangerous, as one budding elementalist was pitted against another. Shani didn't speak too much of this period, but her shadowed eyes said enough.

For Shani, there had been no turning back, no way to escape the training except with two red cuffs and mastery of the elements. She'd had no time for love. In fact, she had never been with a man, something Ella would never have guessed from the shapely woman's worldly wise demeanor.

Shani had transferred all of her love to her nephew, Sendak. He was a sturdy boy of fifteen years, brave and strong, skilled at contests and able to hold his own in the boys' rough fights after temple school.

Sendak and his Aunt Shani would stand on the shores of Lake Halapusa, looking away from the tiered city and skipping stones across the water. Sendak would ask Shani whether she thought he should become a warrior or an elementalist, and Shani would tell him that only he could decide. Secretly, Shani had hoped that if he really wanted to serve in Petrya's forces, he would follow in her footsteps, rather than those of his father. She had heard the rumors of war and knew only those training to become elementalists would escape the army. Nonetheless, Shani always did her best to let Sendak be the one who would decide for himself. On the day her nephew told her that he had decided, and he wanted to be just like her, Shani nearly cried.

Then came the war. One day Petrya was at peace; the next, the marshals were rallying the soldiers. The teardrop and flame *raj hada* of Petrya was raised from every tower, and rhymes mocking Altura were heard on the gleeful children's lips. Some questioned why they were fighting, but High Lord Haptut Alwar ruled his people with strength and terror, and where he led, they would follow.

Prices in Tlaxor immediately began to rise. It was difficult enough to bring goods over Lake Halapusa to the tiered city—the Halapusa Ferry could only carry so much. One silver deen bought only half of what it had days before.

The young men among the Petryans were called up to fight. Any lad over the age of sixteen would be going to war, with only those training to be elementalists excluded. Sendak, Shani's nephew, would be sixteen in a month, and both Shani and her brother knew they had to get Sendak enrolled to become an elementalist swiftly.

Shani had saved plenty of gilden. She had little to spend her money on and had been putting coins aside from her stipend for ten years. She visited the lender she had her funds with, and shaking his head, he'd told her what he was evidently telling all his customers: Shani's money had been confiscated by the high lord for the war chest.

When Shani told her brother, he'd seemed surprisingly calm, given that without gilden, Sendak's dream of becoming an elementalist would be thwarted, and the boy would soon be called up to fight Alturan bladesingers and Halrana constructs.

The truth was, Shani's brother had his own source of income: He was making money selling Alturan-made goods on the gray market. The importation of nightlamps, heatplates, pathfinders, and the like was banned by the high lord, and the man who risked the high lord's wrath could name his price.

Shani kept this part of the story short: Someone had betrayed her brother; she never found out who it was. The high lord put Shani's brother, his wife, and Shani's nephew in a cage, and they slowly lowered the cage into the boiling water of Lake Halapusa.

Along with the other residents of their neighborhood, she was forced to watch, enduring the screams and cries of her only family as the flesh was boiled from their bones.

As she looked on, Shani could take no more. With her jaw clenched tight and fists held out in front of her, the fireball appeared between her cuffs before she even knew she'd made a sound. With a flick of her wrists, Shani threw the flame at the cage, ending the cries in an instant.

The high lord's men pursued her, but Shani was skilled, and no warrior could touch her. Only another elementalist could defeat her, and none could be summoned before Shani made her escape. She forced the ferrymen guiding the Halapusa Ferry to take her across, and all alone, she made her way over the Elmas to Altura, fleeing to the very people she was supposed to hate.

"And you know what? You Alturans aren't so bad," Shani finished.

Ella's eyes were red, but her mouth was set in a grim line, her forehead creased with determination. "Don't stop, Shani," Ella said. "Don't stop until your people are free. It isn't much, but I'll do everything in my power to help you."

Shani shrugged. "There are decent Petryans and there are bad Petryans, just like anywhere else. But I've made my stand, and any who fights at the high lord's side is on the wrong side. I'm sure I'm not the only one among my people ready for change."

Ella in turn told Shani about her own childhood and about her confused relationship with Brandon, the man who'd raised her and Miro. No matter what the circumstances were, he'd loved the two children, and many times now Ella had visited his grave, laying down bunches of summerglens and starflowers. Ella spoke about the lessons she'd learned while studying at the Academy of Enchanters, for the first time able to talk about them with a steady voice and a clear mind.

"There's more," Shani said. She pushed her dark hair out of her eyes and then leaned forward to touch the pendant Ella wore at her neck.

Ella hadn't even realized she was holding it.

"Who is he?" Shani asked.

It was a long time before Ella spoke. "His name is Killian. He was a thief, from Aynar, working for the primate. He has a strange ability. It's difficult to explain, but he used his ability and the fact that I was . . . fond of him . . . to steal the Alturan Lexicon. We tracked him down. I . . . found him. Or I suppose, he found me. He had a change of heart."

"It sounds to me like you're having difficulty explaining." Shani grinned.

Ella blushed. "Nothing happened. Well, we did kiss, but that was back in Sarostar."

Shani whistled. "You really feel something for this thief, don't you?"

"He's not a thief."

"You just said he was." Shani's grin broadened.

"He had a difficult life—that's all. He grew up in an orphanage and then on the streets of Salvation, with no family and no home. Stealing was the only thing he knew. He always wanted to be something else. He even spent some time working as an acrobat."

Ella remembered Killian's sad story. The only family he ever knew was killed by the emperor's men. No wonder he'd turned to the primate.

"You love him?" Shani asked.

Ella looked down at the pendant in her fingers. "I don't know. I don't even know if I'll ever see him again."

"He stole your Lexicon, and then he had a change of heart. What made him change?"

Ella remembered Killian's initial explanation of the primate's dream. It all made sense at a basic level, but she felt that equality always needed to be balanced with opportunity. Some people needed a measure of security from poverty, disease, and the threat of violence—a kind of safety net—but people also needed freedom, and the right environment to grow and fulfill their potential. Destroying the system of houses and making everyone equal under one nation, one leader, might seem appealing, but life was never that simple.

Most of all, with each generation came new ideas, and changes to a land's culture and the way people's lives were ordered came about gradually and inevitably. Gradual change was rarely detrimental. There was only one way to bring about rapid, wholesale change in the way the primate intended.

War.

"We talked, I suppose," Ella said.

"Did you ever think it was more than words that changed his heart? That he might have been in love with you?" Shani asked.

"Me?"

"Yes, Ella, you. You're an attractive woman. Surely you've seen the way men look at you."

Ella blushed. "I don't know."

Three sharp knocks sounded on the door to their shared cabin. "Ella, Shani. Come up to the deck," Jehral's voice called out.

The ship tacked back and forth as the helmsman and captain worked in tight concert with the sailors. This was evidently a delicate maneuver: to line them up and slip the ship between two cliffs guarding a river. This river would take them into the Hazara Desert.

Ella, Shani, and Jehral stood at the rail, holding their breath as the squat ship lumbered from angle to angle, gradually growing closer to the cliffs and the rocky shores that lined their base.

This far south, the sky was clear and devoid of clouds. Ella looked down into the water and was surprised she could see all the way to the bottom. Starfish dotted the seafloor here and there, and huge fish could be seen swimming in lazy circles. Ella looked back at the wake the ship left behind, where dirty bilge water and food scraps trailed the ship night and day. The triangular fins of sharks pierced the waves.

She looked ahead again, and, high above them the tall cliffs suddenly loomed down on the ship as she passed between them. Ella could almost reach out and touch the face of the cliff, they were so close, and looking quickly to the other side of the vessel she could see that there was little more room on that side.

Ella exchanged glances with Shani and then looked at the helmsman for reassurance. There was little succor there; his usually blank face was fearful, and sweat poured from his forehead.

A sound like wood being dragged through gravel reverberated through the ship. Jehral closed his eyes, and Ella wondered what deity the desert warrior worshipped.

Then they were through.

The sound vanished as swiftly as it had started, and the helmsman broke out in a beaming grin. Jehral rubbed at the desert rose on his sash and smiled, nodding.

"Thanks for inviting us up on deck to witness that," Shani snapped.

Jehral emptied his lungs, breathing out in a slow, steady sigh. "That was even worse on the way in than it was going out."

"This isn't the first time you've done that?" Shani asked.

"Oh no," Jehral said. "My prince commands . . ."

"And you obey," Shani finished for him. "I understand, man of the desert. You have a wife, don't you?"

"Yes, in Agira Lahsa."

"Well, next time, if you're looking for a companion for the delicate enchantress here, why don't you bring her?"

Jehral was pensive for a moment, before he appeared to come to a conclusion. "I was afraid also, Petryan."

Shani glared at Jehral and stormed back below decks.

By the next day the cliffs had leveled down to rocky sands, and Ella recognized the unbroken expanse of the Hazara Desert. Waves of heat rolled off the ground, and images could be seen in the distance, shifting and changing like the illusions of House Hazara's lore.

Two days later, as the ship continued to follow the river deeper into the desert, Ella saw the light brown of the shoreline become yellow, and the rocks grow fewer in number. To either side, dunes rolled like waves, as unchanging and indomitable as the sea, but starker, for this expanse was devoid of life. The sand here must be finer, for the gentle wind Ella felt on her cheeks blew the tops off the dunes, spilling the sand into the air like the foam of a breaking wave.

She could see now why the chosen color of the Hazarans was yellow. It suited them perfectly.

Ella felt Jehral beside her and turned. "I've always found your homeland beautiful."

"My prince and I, we both knew you felt that way. Only some see the true nature of the desert, but I could always see it in your eyes."

"Have you missed it?"

"Yes, Ella, I have missed it. One more day will bring us to Agira Lahsa, and I will again see my wife. It is not just my family, though, that I miss. I miss the quiet and the way the stars shine at night. I miss the way water is valued for the precious, life-giving thing it is. I miss the different winds and the varying textures of the sand. Ah, it is good to be back."

"Jehral, when I was with your people, you were the only one I could call my friend. Thank you."

"It pleases me to hear you say so, Enchantress Ella, but that isn't true. Prince Ilathor and I, we thought you were dead. The body of Evora Guinestor was hung from the walls of Tlaxor. I even had it pointed out to me."

"I'm sorry for the deception," Ella said. "I . . . I didn't think that I would be the cause of sorrow."

"That was not why I brought it up," Jehral said. "Ella, we were both upset. I had lost one I thought of as my friend,"—he grinned—"even if she did steal my horse. But, my prince . . ."

Jehral turned away from looking out at the desert and met Ella's eyes. "Enchantress Ella, I think he grieved more than I."

Agira Lahsa, the hidden city, was not what Ella had expected. Her experience of the desert folk was that they lived in tents, yet their seemingly humble abodes didn't prevent them from displaying evident wealth. Prince Ilathor had told her of great market cities, with tents lined up as far as the eye could see. Ella had expected Agira Lahsa to be something similar.

It started as a strange shape on the horizon, jutting out of the desert in a series of stone blocks that made little sense. Then, as the ship approached, Ella saw that the stones formed once great structures that had since become victims of the elements.

Walls clustered around the city, some fallen into complete disrepair, others as tall and proud as when they were built. Ella puzzled over the largest structure, a great circular ring with blocks rising around it in tiers, finally realizing it was an amphitheater, twice as large as the Singer's Arena in Sarostar. Scaffolding formed webs around many of the buildings, and men swarmed around them. As they came to the small dock—one of the first things Jehral said they had repaired—Ella could hear the sounds of hammers hitting and saws scraping.

Facing the river, an enormous archway with a tower to each side framed the main entrance to the city. Ella could see two roads that joined and became one greater road leading to the city's entrance. One of the roads led down to the river, and the other headed into the desert.

Several oases dotted the landscape around the city, visible by their clusters of palms, and Jehral said that before he left, they'd repaired at least four freshwater wells inside the walls.

Most of the population, however, clearly still continued the nomadic life, living in black tents that sprawled in the valleys and in the shadows of the walls. Jehral had said times were changing, but Ella could detect a hint of nostalgia in the way he said it, and Ella wondered if all the desert folk were as progressive.

The ship was a flurry of activity as they docked. Hawsers were thrown, sailors called out to one another, and the ship creaked as it bumped up against the groaning wooden pier.

Ella suddenly couldn't wait to get off the ship. She caught Shani smiling at her and smiled in return, moving to follow Jehral as he tugged his loose black clothing and adjusted the silver circlet he wore at his brow.

The two young women reached the plank that led to the dock, and Jehral turned, noticing Ella for the first time. He held up his hand. "No, Ella. You'll stay on the ship until I come to get you."

Ella stared openmouthed at the desert warrior, suddenly grown serious and forbidding. "Jehral, I've spent weeks on this ship. I refuse to stay longer, and even more, I refuse to see Prince Ilathor before I've had a chance to rest and revive."

Jehral held up an admonishing finger. "Stay here. I will come for you."

Ella tried to follow him down the plank, but two warriors in black stood at its foot, yellow sashes worn proudly, ready to receive Jehral's orders. Jehral spoke to them and turned, pointing up at Ella.

With a sigh, Ella saw Shani approaching and shook her head.

———◆———

Jehral returned at sundown, more furious than Ella had ever seen him. He stormed up the plank, calling her name, pacing back and forth across the length of the deck.

"What is it?" Ella asked.

"He's gone," Jehral said. "They've all gone!"

Shani came up to join them. "What do you mean, desert man?"

"The prince grew impatient. Either that or his warriors did. He's taken the army and crossed the Hazara Desert. He plans to invade Petrya. I can't believe he left without me."

"Can we catch up with him?" Ella asked.

Jehral rubbed his forehead with three of his fingers. "They'll be across the desert by now."

"Well, I suppose we'll also have to cross the desert," Ella said.

"Ella, you don't understand. This city has remained hidden for a reason. From here to Petrya is a difficult journey, yes, but there is more to it than that. Only a large group of warriors can cross. The three of us would not make it through alive."

"Why not?"

"The Devil of Lyra. That is why not."

"What's the Devil of Lyra?" Ella asked.

"It is a creature," Jehral said. "It first appeared nearly a hundred years ago at the Oasis of Lyra, the only oasis between this city and the lands of Petrya. Sixty men stopped for water at the oasis, for the desert cannot be crossed without refueling there. Four men came out alive. I have never seen it, for it avoids large groups, but the three of us would not make it to Petrya."

"Ella," Shani said, looking intently at her. "My desire is to see a new high lord of Petrya, but I don't know how these desert men intend to treat my people. We must cross the desert."

"Then, Jehral," Ella said, "if we're going to cross the desert and potentially face this creature, I suggest you give us our possessions back."

18

Killian once more sat in the same tavern, The Light Shines Above, again glaring up at Stonewater. He took a perverse satisfaction from drinking here, with priests and templars coming and going, and scenes from the Evermen Cycles on the walls. A placard advertised, "The Evermen Shall Return!" *Not in my lifetime*, Killian thought.

He now knew why Evrin had left him and where the old man had been all this time, but he was no closer to discovering Evrin's present whereabouts. He'd returned to the Temple of the Sky day after day, but there was still no sign of the old man, no message telling him where he should go or what he should do next.

Killian again considered what he knew and what he'd learned from Zavros.

Evrin wanted to destroy a book of the Evermen. Instead, the primate now had the book. Evrin had been imprisoned, but he had escaped from the dungeons and disappeared.

Killian knew that whatever knowledge Evrin had tried to destroy, it must be important. After all the effort to cripple the primate, Killian needed to do all he could to help the old man.

Killian looked up at the mountain, home of the primate, and suddenly planted his tankard on the wooden table as an idea hit him.

Wherever he found the book, he would find Evrin.

The primate had the book.

Killian needed to find the primate.

He gulped down the dark beer in his tankard and left a coin on the table, dashing out to the street.

Killian's newfound enthusiasm waned. The primate had left on some errand, and Zavros hadn't said where he was going or when he would be back in Stonewater, if he even knew.

Who would know where next the primate would be? Zavros had said Killian would never find him, that the primate had gone on a journey. Where could the primate have gone? To Halaran in the west? Petrya in the south? Tingara in the north? When he returned from his journey, would it be back to Stonewater? Or would it be to the Imperial capital, Seranthia?

Killian turned and walked back into the tavern, sighing. When he reached the bar, he scanned the bottles of dark liquid on the top shelf.

"You look like you could use a drink," the barman said. "What'll it be?"

Killian opened his mouth to order and then had a thought. "You get a lot of people from the Assembly through here, don't you? Templars and the like?"

"Are you serious?" The barman raised an eyebrow, inclining his head at the men in white, grouped around the clean wooden tables.

"I've traveled all the way to Salvation to see the primate, even if it's just from a distance, but he's not here. Have you heard any of them say where he is?"

"Let's see. He came back from the west and spent some time in Stonewater. Something big happened there, and they're still cleaning up. Then he left for the north, but somewhere farther north than Seranthia. Now, he's on his way to Seranthia."

Killian's eyes grew round. "How do you know all that?"

The barman shrugged. "Primates need guards, servants, drudges, and carriages. Carriages and drudges need cleaning and maintenance. Guards and servants need food and drink. I know he's on his way to Seranthia because they've packed up the primate's study and sent it there, and because the rest of the primate's personal guard have left for Seranthia. People talk and it's no big secret."

Killian placed a coin on the bar. "You have that drink for me."

"Thanks," the barman said, pocketing the coin.

Killian once again left the tavern, but this time he knew his destination clearly. He would go to Seranthia, he would find this book, and he would find Evrin Evenstar.

As Killian took the road north to Seranthia, a canvas backpack on his shoulder, the setting sun cast a glow on his back, causing his red hair to shine like a flame.

Back in Salvation, a woman dressed in the rough tunic of a farmer arrived at the Temple of the Sky, a piece of paper in her hand. "I have a message I was given by an old pilgrim," the woman said to the priest. "Could you please give it to a young man with red hair and blue eyes?"

19

In the bustling merchant city of Castlemere, Bartolo Thorn sat gazing out at the ocean and fingering the threads of Ella's hair.

There was no enmity between Castlemere and Altura, and he was able to openly wear his armorsilk, his zenblade scabbarded at his side. Even so, he received some curious glances from the gruff denizens of the city—it was one thing for an ordinary Alturan to visit the city, another altogether for a bladesinger. By reputation, Bartolo could defeat their entire city guard single-handed. Bartolo grinned. Seeing the pitiful defenses of the mercantile city and the lackluster attention of the guards, it was probably true.

Still, the traders had put up a fight when he'd asked to search the wagon train, back on the road from Altura. Bartolo thought it unlikely Jehral of Tarn Teharan and Hermen Tosch of Castlemere would choose such a slow method of transportation, but he had to be thorough. The traders hadn't liked it one bit when the bladesinger had shown up, demanding to search each and every one of the forty-odd vehicles.

It took him a day to search the first twenty cargo-filled wagons from top to bottom—time Bartolo could ill afford to lose—first emptying out each cargo with the traders' reluctant help, then searching the wagon and moving on to the next.

Bartolo raged as he searched, knowing that every moment he spent with the wagons was taking Ella and Shani farther away. He owed a debt to Miro, he knew. Bartolo had been asked to take care of his friend's sister, but the woman—that scratched Petryan!—had gotten to him, and he'd left the two women unprotected.

Only for a moment, but that was all it took.

The following day, when Bartolo had demanded to search the other twenty wagons, the wagon master, a broad-shouldered trader named Ingo Bacher, flatly refused, demanding compensation from Bartolo for the lost time. Much of the cargo was perishable, he said. Bartolo had grinned, loosening his zenblade. He would give the man compensation; that was for certain.

At that moment a boy had approached, saying he'd found something. The boy led Bartolo deep into the forest that lined both sides of the road, pointing out the remnants of a fire that couldn't have been more than a day old.

Bartolo was a swordsman, not a tracker, but he recognized the white rope that the Petryan woman, Shani, had used as a belt around her red robe. Bartolo's thoughts darkened. If either of the two captors had harmed Shani, or Ella, he would face the bladesinger's wrath.

The fire proved to Bartolo that his quarry wasn't with the wagons, and anxious to make up for lost time, Bartolo walked back to where the wagon master, Ingo Bacher, stood frowning. "Sorry, trader, but you won't get anything from me. Tell your people they shouldn't consort with those barbarians from the Hazara Desert. Seek your compensation from Hermen Tosch."

Ignoring Ingo Bacher's reply, Bartolo passed the wagons that had escaped his search as he walked past.

Then something attracted his attention. Next to a wagon where an elderly woman in a black robe regarded him with cold dark eyes, he saw loose strands of golden hair, blowing gently in the breeze.

Bartolo knelt and picked up the lock of hair. "Ella," he murmured to himself.

Bartolo pocketed the lock of hair and put the white rope in his rucksack. He swiftly outdistanced the wagons, searching, zigzagging between the forest and the road, desperately looking for the women he'd been charged to find.

The road only led one way: from Sarostar to Castlemere, and now Bartolo sat alone at Castlemere's dock, breaking his vigil of the ocean and looking on disconsolately as the wagons he'd left behind so long ago arrived to unload their cargo.

Three were unloaded at one ship, four at another. Two more vehicles unloaded at a third ship, and eight at one huge cargo vessel. Bartolo squinted at one squat ship where only one wagon waited, once more seeing the distant figure of the old woman who'd watched him as he found Ella's hair.

The captors had to have come this way, he knew. Why else would they go to Castlemere, if it wasn't to take passage on a ship?

He watched the ships as they left with the changing tide, following them with his eyes until they vanished, one by one, over the horizon. The squat ship was the last to disappear, taking hours to do so, but finally even it was gone too.

Bartolo didn't know how, but he was going to get answers. He had a duty to Miro, and he knew Jehral must come this way.

Bartolo shaded his eyes as he saw a man with a round face, deep in discussion with an official, near the place where the squat ship had been docked.

Bartolo's eyes widened. The man was Hermen Tosch, the trader who'd visited the palace with Jehral.

The trader saw Bartolo even as Bartolo saw him. Hermen turned to run, but Bartolo was quick, even for a bladesinger.

Bartolo dragged Hermen through the street until he found a convenient wall. People screamed and ran from the bladesinger with the black expression, his zenblade in one hand and a local man held captive in the other. Concerned citizens called for guards, but Bartolo paid the townsfolk no heed.

Bartolo shoved Hermen high up against the wall and pressed the point of his zenblade to the trader's cheek as he squeezed his neck.

"Where are they?" Bartolo said.

Hermen's face turned red from the pressure of Bartolo's grip on his throat. Bartolo relaxed slightly to allow the man to speak.

"They've gone," Hermen gasped. "Left in a ship. You missed them."

"Scratch you," Bartolo cursed. "I don't believe you."

Bartolo spoke some words, and the runes on his zenblade lit up with the red of glowing coals. The color traveled along down the blade as each symbol lent its fire to the next. "Are you ready to die?"

"You didn't search all the wagons," Hermen said, "did you? My men left something for you in the forest. A fire. The Petryan's belt. Those you are looking for were with the wagons you never searched."

Bartolo swore. "Are they both unhurt?"

"Yes, they're unharmed. Jehral is a good man."

"Put him down, bladesinger," a voice with quavering authority instructed Bartolo.

Bartolo turned. Perhaps fifty soldiers of the city watch circled him, with swords drawn. Their officer was brave—Bartolo had to give him that. The officer's sword wasn't the only one shaking in the bunch, but he stood firm.

Bartolo spoke some more words, and the zenblade sparkled with colors of topaz and emerald. Several of the watchmen walked slowly backward. "I'm not done here," Bartolo said over his shoulder.

He once again regarded Hermen Tosch; the trader stared back at him defiantly. "Where is the ship headed?"

"The Hazara Desert. To the hidden city."

"It's a big desert. Where is this city?" Bartolo demanded.

"They don't call it the hidden city for no reason." Hermen smiled.

Bartolo moved the tip of the zenblade until it hovered in front of Hermen's eye. "Why are they being taken there?"

"To meet with Jehral's leader, the prince."

"You're going to help me find this hidden city, trader," Bartolo said.

"Bladesinger, I might as well tell you," Hermen said in his thick, guttural voice.

"Tell me what?"

"The prince . . . I've only just found out." Hermen took a strained breath. "You saw me speaking with someone just now. Jehral doesn't know, but the prince is no longer at the hidden city. I was so busy getting Jehral away that I didn't have time to get the news. Jehral is going to have to travel farther and take the women to where the prince is now. You don't need to go into the desert; you'll be able to catch up with them there."

"Where?"

"Prince Ilathor is with his men in Petrya, at the town of Torlac. The Hazarans have invaded Petrya."

Bartolo let the trader go, and Hermen crumpled, putting both hands to his neck as he recovered. The bladesinger turned and leveled his eyes at the men of the city watch, their swords still held in front of them. "You," he said to their leader, "has Petrya been invaded?"

The officer glanced at Hermen before looking back at the bladesinger. "Yes. The news is fresh, and not many know, but yes."

Bartolo turned back to Hermen. "If anything happens to them, I'm coming back for you."

Bartolo turned and walked away, ignoring the watchmen. He needed to get a message to Miro, to tell him what he knew, before he prepared for the coming journey.

Bartolo was going to Petrya.

20

Primate Melovar smiled to himself, gazing out from the tallest balcony of the Imperial Palace as the Akari paraded through the streets of Seranthia.

Dain Barden Mensk walked at the head of the vast host, his gaze stern and unyielding. Behind him were a dozen necromancers and a single company of living Akari warriors, tall and beautiful, their blue eyes contrasting with their pale skin.

Behind the living came rank after rank of the dead. Eerily silent, the revenants walked like normal men, but there was something about their stilted gait that wasn't quite right. There were so many of them that even the Grand Boulevard, the great avenue that led to the Imperial Palace, was filled from side to side, and the column of gray-clad warriors stretched to the end of the longest street in Seranthia and around the corner.

Few of Seranthia's residents turned out to welcome their new allies to their city. Melovar even saw some of his priests and templars make the sign of protection, recoiling from the white eyes of the draugar. No matter. They would be thankful enough when Melovar had pacified the lands from the Great Western Ocean to the Tingaran Sea, bringing peace to the realm. Never fear, Melovar wanted to tell them: he would cleanse the world of lore while using lore to do so.

The previous day, the primate held a Chorum, the first since the war began. He changed the format somewhat, and unlike before, he controlled events and decided who would speak. It was a strange affair, and one that left him dispirited. High Lord Dimitri Corizon of Vezna was proving difficult to handle—the elixir was taking its toll—and High Lord Koraku Rolan of Torakon could barely hold himself together. Melovar's main concern was that Dain Barden would discover something about the elixir. However, the ruler of the Akari made a surprisingly warm speech of thanks at his welcome back to the Empire.

Altura and Halaran were conspicuously absent, and Melovar knew he needed to subdue them quickly or lose credibility for his new order. All in good time; the Akari were here now.

Melovar's mission for Zavros had proven successful, and Zavros had recently returned from the icy north. Soon the primate would have his own supplies of essence, and a renewed source of elixir.

When the time came, Dain Barden would fall under the primate's power just as had Tessolar of Altura, Raoul Maul of Loua Louna, Koraku of Torakon, Dimitri of Vezna, and Xenovere of Tingara. In the end, none of them could resist the elixir.

The parade was over, and Melovar withdrew from the balcony. The Imperial Palace, huge as it was, was too small, he found, and not high enough for his liking. He missed Stonewater, but sometimes this was where he needed to be.

Melovar walked over to where Zavros sat on a plush velvet chair, thoroughly engrossed by the book of the Evermen in his hands. "I can almost see what it is," Zavros said. "Such a strange shape. It looks like the chamber is inside something, like a mountain."

"I would say it was inside Stonewater if I didn't know for myself that it isn't there," Melovar said.

"The Akari expect you to tell them where it is, Your Grace," Zavros said, placing the book to the side. "You've promised them a great deal of essence and the most powerful relic the Evermen ever created. Dain Barden Mensk isn't a man to take promises lightly."

"Which is why you've been learning their secrets, Zavros," Melovar said. "We just need to develop our own source of essence before the Akari find out how we've seized power. We must also be the first to find the relic and use its power for ourselves. So tell me—what have you learned?"

Zavros nodded. "I can do it, Primate. I can build the vats. I know how to extract essence from the dead."

"Excellent," Melovar smiled.

"But, Primate, the amount of life energy in a human is still not that great. For what you're asking for the war effort, you will need mountains of the dead. The Akari themselves cannot field the draugar in battle for long, not with the amount of essence they possess, and not in this climate, which is warm by their standards. Where do you expect to find so many of the dead?"

Melovar's smile broadened. "Why, where else do the dead come from? From the living. Zavros, I've already begun. The prison camp in Halaran was the first, but we can set up more, here in Tingara."

"Prisoners? Primate, they aren't dead," Zavros said flatly.

"Easily remedied. Oh, surely you aren't having a crisis of conscience now, Zavros? The things I've seen you do. And think, you will have free run of the camps. You can perform any experiments you want on them. Think of all you will learn."

"There is one experiment." Zavros looked up. "You wouldn't let me do it before."

"That? Zavros, you can have an entire camp to yourself, where you can do whatever you want. I will give you books, apparatus, assistants—anything gilden can buy. You can build your quarters and laboratory right next to the camp."

"The apparatus does not come cheap."

"Anything, Zavros, provided the essence takes precedence. Go and build the vats. Moragon knows nothing takes greater precedence—you can look to him for whatever you need. Bring me essence and bring me elixir. We are in a race against the Akari. Dain Barden cannot see any weakness."

Zavros stood and bowed. "It will be done."

21

Amber lived in constant fear for her life and that of her unborn child. Life in the prison camp in Halaran was hard, but since Moragon had taken over the running of the camp, it had grown much worse.

After her failed escape attempt, the guards had almost killed her, beating her remorselessly, the hilts of their swords knocking her to the ground and their heavy boots kicking at her head and back as she curled up and waited for the end.

Somehow, though, she'd found reserves of strength from deep within, and under the tending of her people Amber had survived. She had been terrified she would lose her baby, but one of the prisoners had been a midwife and assured Amber the baby was unharmed.

When the woman had finished speaking, Amber had cried, for the first time in weeks. She'd cried for Beatta, the Halrana who had died so close to freedom, and for Ness, the old woman who'd sacrificed herself just to give them their chance. Most of all, she cried for her child. Amber had tried, but she had failed. Her child deserved its chance at life.

In the time since her attempt at freedom, Amber had healed, but she now worried for the health of her child even more. She shivered at night and the pangs of hunger were like red-hot pokers in her chest.

Now the time had come, and Amber had a different plan.

It was a plan that caused her heart to quake with fear.

With her auburn hair brushed, lips ruby red, and brown eyes lowered, Amber walked toward the guard post and tried to ignore the tightness in her chest.

She was hardly showing her pregnancy, and although the rations of the prison camp meant her waist was the slimmest it had ever been, Amber still filled out the silk dress she'd pillaged from a dead woman's belongings. She had modified the dark blue dress so that the neckline was low, scandalously low, and the material was sheer, so that Amber felt almost naked.

As she picked her way through the groups of huddled prisoners, heading for the checkpoint, Amber caught the disapproving stares of both the Halrana and her Alturan countrymen. The Alturans here were mostly soldiers who had been captured at the battle at the Bridge of Sutanesta, and they'd seen their friends killed by the Black Army, by the very men that Amber was evidently giving herself to. Amber lifted her chin and ignored them. To save their children, they would do the same thing.

Amber hadn't made this decision lightly. People were disappearing from the camp. They certainly weren't being released, for the ones disappearing were the old and the infirm, the weak and the dying, but if they weren't being released, then where were they going? Then others started vanishing—those who argued with the guards or even looked at them the wrong way.

Amber's trouble started in the food line when, two days before, Hugo, a vicious Tingaran, tried to kiss her. When she'd turned her head, he'd angrily pulled her ragged dress from her shoulders, displaying her breasts for all to see. Without thinking, Amber responded by slapping him across the face.

Hugo, a big man with the typical shaved head of a Tingaran, had looked surprised for a moment, and then glared at Amber as his fellow guards hooted and jeered. "You're going next." He had prodded Amber with his finger. "I'll make sure of it," he said with venom. Amber had swiftly pulled her dress back up, before realizing what it was he meant. Wherever they were taking the vanishing prisoners, she was going too.

Amber could see only one way out, a way she could save her life and provide security for her unborn child. She had spent two days getting ready for this moment. She was beautiful, she reminded herself.

Amber reached the guard post. She saw the guard in front of her breathe in as he caught the scent of the fragrant soap she'd traded food for. The other guard looked her slowly up and then down, his gaze finally settling on her chest.

"Hello, beauty," the first guard said. "Where'd you turn up from? How come we 'aven't noticed you before?"

"I'm new," Amber said.

The second guard came forward, his mouth open and eyes still fixated on Amber's body. He leered, his reaching hand running over the soft material on Amber's waist. "Good news for us," the guard said.

Amber smiled up at him, letting his hand run over the material and up, feeling the outside of her hip, moving farther up still, to the underside of her breast. She finally stepped back and pushed his hand away. "I'm not here for you two, I'm afraid. I'm here for someone else."

"Who?" asked the first guard.

"High Lord Moragon," Amber said. "His command tent is out there, isn't it?" She smiled up at the guard sweetly.

Both men stood back and exchanged worried glances. The leering guard's expression was fearful.

"Could you let me through?" Amber asked.

The guards lived in a separate compound from the main prison camp, Moragon with them. Amber prayed to the Lord of the Sky. If they let her out unescorted, she could potentially escape, and she wouldn't have to do what she'd come here to do.

Amber remembered Hugo's words: *"You're going next."* She owed it to her unborn child to stay alive.

The first guard whistled, and a uniformed man came over. "Take her to High Lord Moragon's tent."

Amber's escort quickly looked her over but said nothing about Amber's obvious purpose. "Come with me," he said.

Amber's heart raced as her escort led her away from the fenced prison and between two pine trees. The air was sweeter out in the open, away from the stench of the prisoners. The two dozen or so tents of the guards' compound were laid out in neat rows interspersed with the occasional tree.

Some guards sat about, finishing their evening meal, sipping hot drinks from steaming metal mugs. Amber saw them nudge one another and felt their eyes on her body as she walked past. Good— the more who saw her, the better.

Six guards stood in a circle around Moragon's command tent. A tall flagpole was planted to the left of the tent, the *raj hada* of Tingara, double-circled to indicate the high lord was in residence.

Amber's escort promptly halted outside the tent. "For the high lord," he said.

One of Moragon's bodyguards came forward, a slim Tingaran who wore his sword with ease and walked with lithe grace. "I see," the slim man said. "Here," he told Amber, "stand still with your arms to your side and your legs apart. I do not do this for pleasure." He looked at Amber's escort. "You may leave, soldier."

The bodyguard's search was thorough but professional, lacking the intimacy that would make Amber feel violated. That would come.

He met Amber's eyes, made curious by her heaving chest, her breath coming fast and strong. "He's a melding, but he's still a man," the bodyguard said. "You've done this before."

Amber had only ever been with one man, Igor Samson, the husband she had lost. She almost cried, but she held it in. She wasn't just doing this for herself. She had to be strong.

"You can go in now," the bodyguard said.

Amber nodded. She stood for a moment before she could make her legs move. Her feet took her forward, and she reached the door to the tent, pushing it to the side and entering.

Swords and armor stood on racks, lining the walls at either side. The light inside the tent was dim, but a nightlamp burned at the desk where Moragon sat, a stack of papers in front of him, frowning at one in his hands. He looked up. "Who are you?" he demanded.

Amber had seen Moragon only once before, when the new high lord of Tingara had arrived in Halaran and followed his welcome in Ralanast with a tour of the prison camp. He was tall, at least as tall as Miro, with the muscled body of a warrior and the black eyes of a man accustomed to dealing out death. Amber remembered his former title: the emperor's executioner. She controlled her body, preventing the shudder trying to force its way out.

The light of the nightlamp reflected from his shaved head, and he was clad in loose garments of black with white trim, but what drew Amber's gaze was the glistening metal of his right arm. Covered with tiny runes, the metal started below his neck and moved down to his shoulder, descending to his elbow, wrist, and hand. The lore of Tingara had given him a perfect new limb, stronger than the original, if the stories were true. Amber's eyes rested on the superbly formed metal hand and fingers, matching the pink flesh of his other. It even had nails.

Amber realized he had asked her a question. "I'm Amber, High Lord. I'm a gift from the men. A welcome of sorts."

Moragon's eyebrows went up. "Come closer," he said. "I want to see if I can put a price on you. How much did they front up, I wonder? How much am I loved?" He smiled.

Amber stepped forward into the light of the nightlamp.

"Are you a virgin, girl?" Moragon asked.

"Yes, High Lord," Amber said.

All of her hopes rested on him believing her.

"And where are you from?"

"I'm from Altura, High Lord."

"Ah." Moragon grinned. "An Alturan girl. This pleases me, knowing I will be taking one of the enemy."

Amber's heart raced. She had to do this, she reminded herself. It was the only way. She had seen the promise of death in Hugo's eyes.

Moragon leaned back in his chair. "Come yet closer, Amber of Altura," he said.

Amber moved forward until the desk was barely a pace in front of her. The melding had yellowed eyes, she could see now. It made him look feverish. His teeth were sharp and jutted in different directions.

"How much are you worth, Amber of Altura?"

"High Lord?"

"How much did they pay for you?"

"They . . . they said I would be given more food and warm blankets, and that the guards wouldn't trouble me, and I wouldn't be taken to wherever the others are disappearing to."

"And you shall have all that," Moragon said.

Amber inwardly breathed a sigh of relief. She had accomplished one of the things she had come here for.

"Provided you please me, of course."

"I will, High Lord." Amber's voice trembled.

"So, a proud Alturan girl—for I can see you are proud, Amber—gives herself to the enemy for nothing more than some scraps of food and a blanket to keep her warm at night? It's good to know Alturans value themselves so little."

"Yes, High Lord," Amber said.

"Remove your shoes and your dress," said Moragon, still sitting at his desk.

Amber heard the command like a stone hitting her stomach. Lord of the Sky, she could do this. She kicked off her shoes, and then slipped the strap first from her left shoulder, followed by the one on the right. Swallowing, she reached down and pulled the bottom half of her dress up to her hips, revealing the small scrap of white underwear she wore underneath. She then gathered the dress and pulled it up and over her head, letting it fall to the ground.

Amber heard Moragon's breath catch as she hung her head, her eyes closed, resisting the urge to cross her arms over her bared breasts. It was cold in the tent, and she felt her nipples stiffen.

She opened her eyes. Moragon started intently at her, his eyes traveling up and down her form, from her calves, up to her thighs, at the white undergarment that covered the area between her wide hips at the fork of her legs. His gaze ran over her flat belly and narrow waist to her breasts. He finally looked into Amber's eyes.

"Turn around," Moragon said. "Let me get a good look at you."

Amber slowly turned.

"Stop." She heard his voice while her back was still to him. Amber halted her spin, for some reason more fearful now that she could no longer see him, her chest rising and falling.

"Take them off," Moragon said.

Amber again reminded herself why she was doing this. She had more than herself to worry about. She had to live.

She pushed the undergarment from her hips, moving her legs to allow it to fall to her ankles. Amber kicked it away.

"Good. Now turn around again."

Amber turned and felt fear course through her. Moragon was up from his desk, standing close, in front of her. He looked over her one last time, his eyes burning over the most intimate parts of her body.

He suddenly grabbed Amber's arm and twisted it behind her back. He pushed her down to the hard floor.

She cried out.

———◆———

When he was finished, he did what all men did, closing his eyes and rolling over, heedless of the hard floor.

This next part was important.

Amber thrust out her hand to where a glistening sword stood on a rack nearby. She could just touch it with the tip of her finger. Amber ran her fingertip over the edge of the blade, making no reaction as it sliced through her skin. Compared to what he had done here, the pain was nothing.

Amber thrust her hand down between her legs and let the blood drip onto her thighs.

She nudged Moragon. "See, High Lord," she said, gesturing with her head.

Moragon opened his eyes, looking to where she indicated.

"I told you I was a virgin," Amber said.

Moragon saw the blood and then grunted. "Are you still here, girl?" He sat up. "Get out of here."

Amber shakily stood, ignoring the messages of pain her body sent her. "Yes, High Lord." She looked for her dress, hurriedly pulling it on, and then slipped the heeled sandals back onto her feet.

"You'll get your food, girl."

"Thank you, High Lord."

Amber left the tent, trying to walk tall, ignoring the shared glances of the bodyguards; they'd probably heard everything.

"Here," the bodyguard who had searched her said, "I'll get you an escort to take you back to the camp."

Amber didn't reply. She was already planning.

With increased freedom, she would be able to do more to help the other prisoners.

She would wait three weeks, and then she would visit Moragon again. Amber had heard that meldings couldn't produce children. She had to hope that Moragon would think he was special, or perhaps that she was. For this next time, Amber would tell him that she was carrying his child.

22

"The gaps in a legionnaire's defenses are in the throat, the pit of the arms, and the lower legs. Go for the throat first, but don't be afraid to hold him off and await your opportunity. Your opponents will be armored and will tire faster than you will. Use this to your advantage." Rogan paused for breath, and one of the young Halrana raised his arm. "Yes?"

"What about the other men, the ones who aren't legionnaires? There are all sorts in the Black Army."

"That's a good question," Rogan said. "I spend most of my time talking about the legionnaires for two reasons. One is that they're the toughest soldiers you'll face, heavily armored and well trained with axes and swords. Another is that they're the leaders here. I don't want you to be afraid of them; I want you to go to them, and take them out first. With the Tingarans out of the picture, the other soldiers will bolt. But," he finished, "never fear. I won't go easy on you. I'll also spend some time showing you how to fight against pikemen and macemen, and how to find the weak points on an Imperial avenger."

Rogan straightened from the diagrams he'd been drawing in the sawdust he'd scattered over the expanse of the storehouse floor.

His leg pained him and he winced, leaning on the walking stick. "Use the wooden swords and fight in pairs. I want to see bruises, but no broken bones, understand?"

As the men chose sparring partners, Amelia came over and stood by Rogan, looking worriedly at the strange mixture of young and old men fighting in the makeshift arena. "I hope you know what you're doing," she said.

"He does," said Marcus Toscan, the flaxen-haired soldier Rogan had met in this very storehouse. The Halrana swordsman looked at Rogan but spoke to Amelia. "I've never met anyone like him."

Rogan harrumphed. The few months he'd known Marcus had been long enough for the young soldier to idolize him. Having young Tapel follow him around was bad enough. "Are you sure we're safe here?"

"We're safe," Marcus said. "It's a good plan."

With the population of Ralanast and its surrounding areas starving, and disease rampant throughout the conquered land, Amelia had come up with a surprisingly cunning strategy for the small army they were building.

The men of Halaran were dying.

The friends of the resistance conducted mock funerals, burying empty boxes in the earth and donning the black of mourning. Inventing causes of death was a simple matter. In fact, the women said it gave them a sense of relief to know their fathers, husbands, and sons were being kept hidden, far from the watchful gaze of the occupiers.

The deserted storehouses in Ralanast's once great cargo district provided the perfect refuge and training ground. The buildings were large enough for many men to sleep, eat, and fight, and the district was a warren of buildings and alleys that only a Halrana could find his way through. The Black Army never bothered to patrol.

That only left the question of supplies—food, water, clothing, and weapons. Once again, Amelia proved herself, finding a way to solve two problems simultaneously. The wives, daughters, mothers, and sisters wanted to visit their men, but if too many came too often or all at once, it could spell catastrophe. Amelia put out the word that with the cemeteries full, the dearly departed would have to follow a certain route out of the city via the cargo district. If the mourning parties were made up of all women, and the box on its carriage was full of potatoes, well, he was a big man wasn't he?

As the network of the resistance grew in size, and hope began to return to the citizens of Ralanast, Rogan's thoughts again turned to the prison camp, just a half-day's journey from the city. He knew thousands of Alturans and Halrana were being kept there and that the Halrana would be fearful of fighting if they had loved ones in the camp.

Rogan knew the prison camp was the first place they needed to free.

There would be men in the camp who would fight, adding to their numbers, but the effect on his men's morale would be even greater. Knowing the prisoners were free and seeing their fellows rise up against their occupiers would cause even the most jaded Halrana to join the fight.

"It's time to send word to Sarostar," Rogan said.

"Are we ready?" Marcus asked.

"We're not ready." Amelia frowned. "Even I can see that."

"No, we're not ready," Rogan said. "In three months, perhaps four, we'll be ready, but it's now time to plan. I'm going to tell the lord marshal in Altura, and you can tell your Prince Tiesto, Marcus. It's presently the middle of spring. We'll be ready at the end of summer."

"The end of summer. So long?"

"I don't know what support we can count on from Altura, but it will take them months to fight their way here, if they are even able to. The end of summer, Marcus."

Marcus hesitated but then nodded. "I'll tell Prince Tiesto."

"I need to get home," Amelia said. She paused, as if about to say something, but didn't. Instead she quickly leaned forward and kissed Rogan on the cheek. "I'll see you the day after tomorrow," she said.

Rogan watched her go, a startled expression on his face. Amelia left the storehouse, closing the wooden door behind her.

"What was that?" Rogan said to Marcus.

Marcus laughed; it was a big hearty sound that poured from his chest. "There's no better man to lead this resistance," he said. "But when it comes to women, you're as big a fool as the rest of us."

23

"I feel like I have my skin back," Shani said, grinning.

"I know exactly what you mean," Ella said, surprised at the amount of pleasure she felt to once again be wearing her green silk dress.

"Does your enchantress's dress protect you from the heat?"

"Certainly does. I'll warrant you're feeling better."

Shani looked happier than Ella had seen her in weeks. "Compared to baking under the sun, it's like being inside a shadow. Anything that can protect me from a fireball can certainly deal with this."

Ella looked at Jehral, who led the way, riding slightly ahead of them, the near-black coat of his horse shining with sweat. Unlike his two companions, Jehral had no magical protection from the intense heat, yet he appeared completely at ease in his desert garb.

Ella was pleased to see she still remembered how to ride, swiftly forming a rapport with her horse, a bay gelding named Afiri. Shani had taken to riding with surprising ease. If anything Shani saw her ability to subdue her own horse as a challenge. There was little the athletic Petryan didn't seem capable of.

Looking around her, Ella wondered how Jehral managed to navigate across the unbroken expanse of the desert. Here in the deep south, the formations of rock were a rare occurrence, and one dune appeared the same as the next.

Shani must have been thinking the same thing. "Take care, man of the desert. If anything happens to you out here, we're dead."

Once the decision had been made, their departure from Agira Lahsa had been swift. Ella saw the city only once, on their way through, but what she'd seen had amazed her. When the work of rebuilding was done, the hidden city would rival any of the other houses' capitals, with a population to match. Ella was thankful the Hazarans planned to attack Petrya and were apparently on her people's side.

They'd now been traveling for weeks, mostly by night, but also riding by day to make up time. Shani constantly urged them forward, fearful for her people and desperate to be at Torlac for the confrontation to come, and Jehral longed to be once again fighting by his prince's side. Ella had decided she could do more in Petrya than she could back in Sarostar. She'd heard Miro speak on strategy enough to know that if Altura's southern border were secured from Petrya, the allies could start to consider a re-conquest of Halaran in the east.

If Halaran were freed, maybe they could find Amber.

"We're running low on water, desert man," Shani said.

"To be expected," Jehral said. "We can only carry so much, and we're now nearing the halfway mark. Soon the Oasis of Lyra will be in sight."

"So what's the plan?" Shani asked. "Get in, grab water, and get out?"

Jehral didn't smile at her levity. "Something like that."

"Can you tell us what it looks like?" Ella asked. "This Devil of Lyra?"

Jehral shrugged, his attention on the horizon. "I have never seen it. The creature stays clear of large groups of men. I have never gone to the oasis with fewer than ten score."

"You must have heard rumors," Shani said.

"Some say it is a kind of serpent. Others, that it is a worm. I have heard it has many teeth, rows of them, and it is impervious to the stroke of a scimitar."

Shani looked down at the red cuffs she wore at her wrists. "Let's hope it doesn't like fire."

"No, Petryan," Jehral said. "Let us hope we don't see it at all."

The three riders continued in silence for a time. Ella watched the sun move inexorably to the horizon, falling as if made heavy by a hard day's work, finally glowing against the dunes, spilling radiant light on the sand, making the riders' shadows long and tapered.

Ella thought about Miro, fighting constantly to hold against the attempts of the Black Army to penetrate Alturan lands. She wondered about Layla, the Dunfolk healer, hoping the small woman was alive and safe from harm. Amber's face swam in front of her vision; she was so soft and gentle, always laughing or crying. But the chances of Ella's tender friend surviving capture by the Black Army were low.

Finally, Ella's thoughts turned to Killian. Her intuition told her he'd been successful, that something he'd done had affected the enemy's supplies of essence. It was the only reason Altura had lasted so long. She knew, though, that there was more to Killian's quest. He burned inside, desperate to know who he was and about this power he possessed.

Fingering the pendant she wore at her neck, Ella looked over at the red bracelets Shani wore at her wrists, contemplating the myriad of symbols that had been drawn with essence on the cuffs, giving Shani the ability to control the elements. Killian could wear those symbols on his skin. His skin! Like Shani, he would still need the knowledge, but the feats he was capable of, if he only had the knowledge, were staggering.

The sun dropped past the horizon, and stars began to appear in the night sky. The temperature fell away, and Ella felt a great relief; even with the protection of her dress, the heat was uncomfortable. Still, they rode on. After some hours the moon rose, casting a glow over the dunes, shimmering over the sandy ocean. Ella shivered as the night grew cold, feeling her dress adjust to compensate. Looking over at Shani, she saw that her friend wasn't coping with the chill as well as Ella was—the elementalist's robe was built to withstand heat, but not cold. The three travelers rode on.

Finally, as Ella was beginning to slump in her saddle and she could feel Afiri tiring underneath her, Jehral called a halt. He had each of them unsaddle and groom their horses with a stiff brush, before watering them a little at a time. They hobbled the horses by twisting the reins around their legs, then sank to the sand themselves, lying back against a dune while the stars looked down from overhead.

Ella tilted her water flask, surprised when she tipped it all the way and only a tiny trickle of water came out. She couldn't even remember drinking it. She felt Jehral's eyes on her and looked over at him.

"The water that is left in the bags is for the horses," he said. "We do not drink again until we reach the Oasis of Lyra." He moved his saddle behind him and sank down, using it as a pillow. "Get some rest, Ella. I will wake you in four hours."

"We will reach the Oasis of Lyra sometime today," Jehral said.

The plodding horses sweated under the morning sun. Ella's mouth was parched, her tongue dried and devoid of moisture. She was having trouble speaking, so she just nodded.

Shani appeared to be in an even worse state. Ella nudged Afiri closer to the elementalist's horse and soundlessly handed Shani her water flask. There was little more than a few drops in there, but the Petryan appeared to instantly revive. Shani smiled her thanks.

"Jehral," Ella whispered. She tried again. "Jehral, do you have a spare sword?"

The desert warrior started, evidently lost in thought. Perhaps even he was succumbing. He took some time to process Ella's words before reaching into a saddlebag. "Here," he said.

Ella reached out as Jehral handed her a large dagger, heavy and curved. "Thank you," she said hoarsely.

Ella placed the dagger in her saddlebag, leaving the strap unfastened so she could grab the dagger at a moment's notice. With no essence, the only power she possessed was in her dress. She had a couple of flashbombs in an inner pocket, but that was all; any weapon helped.

Jehral held up his hand, and the three riders pulled on their reins, halting their horses. "Ahead," Jehral said, his voice betraying the dryness of his throat. "The Oasis of Lyra. Do you see it?"

Ella squinted against the bright sunlight. At first she couldn't see anything, but she held her hand over her eyes and ran her gaze slowly across the horizon. Then she saw it, a tiny speck that could have been the spikes of desert palms jutting out from the sand. "I think so," Ella said.

"It is closer than it looks." He looked from Ella to Shani. "Are you ready?"

Shani nodded.

"Yes," Ella said. Even in her weakened state, she could feel her heart rate increase.

"The plan is to ride in fast. I do not know if the sound will attract the creature more readily, but speed is our only ally. I will stand guard while the two of you fill the water bags. Throw mine to me, and then we leave. Understood?"

"It's a good plan." Shani grinned, but her voice was weak. "Simple."

"Ready?" Jehral asked one last time. "Ride!"

He dug his heels into the flanks of his horse, and it leapt forward. Ella hardly had to kick Afiri forward; he could smell the water and wanted to follow the leader. Ella felt the wind rushing in her face as Afiri galloped over the sand, and she realized the wisdom of keeping the horses well watered. The three travelers would live or die this day based on the strength of their steeds.

Beside Ella, Shani's face was grim, her dark hair flying. Ella's feet jangled up and down in their stirrups, and she was suddenly terrified they would slip out and she would fall off her horse. She had never galloped this fast before.

The spikes became the jagged tops of palms, and as Ella crested a dune, she could see the fissure that the grove surrounded. Without breaking stride, Jehral galloped down the side of the cleft, his horse hurtling toward the tranquil pool on the gully floor.

He immediately threw his empty water bags down to the ground. Ella and Shani reached him an instant later and slipped off their horses, each grabbing their own.

"Hurry," Jehral said, turning his black horse in a single movement, drawing his scimitar, eyes scanning the area.

Ella rushed down to the water, sensing Shani beside her. She knelt down, feeling the water cool on her legs. She pulled the stopper off the first water bag and dunked the entire sack under the water, holding it down with one hand while she fumbled to open the next bag's stopper with the other.

Ella filled Jehral's two water bags and then started on her own. She turned and saw that Shani had finished filling her own two bags. "Take them to the horses." Ella indicated the four full bags. "I'm almost done." Shani nodded and ran up toward where Jehral waited with sword bared, staring out at the desert.

Ella finished filling the last two bags and reinserted the stoppers. She felt her breath coming short and fast as she put strength into her legs, running up the soft sand toward where Jehral and Shani urged her on.

Ella's fingers fumbled as she tied the water bags to her saddle.

"Come on," Shani said.

"Hurry!" Jehral called.

Ella finally put her foot in the stirrup and grabbed hold of the pommel, pulling herself up onto Afiri's back. "Go!" she cried, taking hold of the reins.

Jehral's horse shot forward, clambering up the soft sand of the hillside with great lunges. With a lighter passenger, Ella's horse had less difficulty climbing the slope, and she was the first of their group to make it out.

Ella's eyes swept back and forth as she scanned the desert. So far, luck—and speed—were with them.

"Keep going!" Jehral called from behind her.

Shani was the next to reach the top. Ella kicked her horse into a gallop, and Afiri leapt over the sand as his pace picked up.

Then the ground opened up in front of her.

Ella suddenly found herself staring into a wide hole in the desert floor, a dozen paces wide, with sand spilling into it on all sides.

Afiri reared as he halted mid-stride, and all Ella could do was hold on and pray Afiri wouldn't fall forward. Ella felt the horse tremble as his front legs slipped.

Ella stared into the hole in horror as the Devil appeared.

The first thing she saw was its head. It came out and up, mouth open and sucking as the sand poured down into its gullet. Row after row of glistening teeth lined the inside of its white lips, each the size of Ella's dagger, jagged and sharp. An eyeless head and two wide nostrils made its gaping jaw the most prominent part of its body.

The creature shot out of the hole, knocking Ella's horse backward and sending Ella flying through the air to land heavily on the sand.

Ella scrambled to her feet, then dashed over to Afiri, grabbing the dagger from her saddlebags and speaking the words that would activate the protective capabilities of her dress as Afiri attempted to get back up. She turned away from the panicked horse and faced the beast.

As the symbols that covered the silk lit up with blue and purple, the creature reared its body and plunged down at Ella, the putrid stench of its breath buffeting her as the jaws closed over her.

Ella felt the familiar feeling of the knowledge coursing through her. She was an enchantress, and this was the dress she had enchanted with the most powerful lore she knew how to create.

The Devil of Lyra's teeth bit down on a sheath of green armor stronger than steel. Closing her mind to the fear and her eyes to the creature's awful attack, Ella chanted in a sonorous rhythm, her voice neither quavering nor breaking stride.

She activated the lightning.

With a series of bright flashes, electric bolts and discharges covered Ella's form. The sandworm made a sound like breaking boulders, and the ground trembled as it reared away in pain, its head rising high into the air.

Ella opened her eyes. The sandworm had left her where she stood, and she ran toward Afiri. She tried to catch him, but the terrified horse shied away. Ella shouted to Jehral.

"My horse!" she cried.

Jehral turned his own mount with a tight sweep and galloped toward Afiri.

The giant sandworm appeared to peer sightlessly at Ella. Perhaps it had no eyes, but it could still sense her somehow.

Then Ella heard a great whoosh, and a fireball shot through the air, screaming and roiling as the sphere of flame turned over and over, flying with a well-aimed cast at the creature's head. The fireball hit the sandworm's nostrils, bursting over them in a spray of red energy.

The Devil of Lyra went mad.

It cried out in pain, and the immense head twisted in the air, finally thrusting down into the sand again as the sandworm's body formed a loop, half of its body exiting the ground at one place while the rest entered at another.

Ella turned and saw Shani behind her, still on her rearing, terrified horse. The Petryan's expression was dark as her battle instincts took over. Jehral drew to a halt beside Ella, his own horse foaming at the mouth and the reins of Ella's horse in his hand. Jehral opened his mouth to speak.

"Look out!" Ella screamed. She rushed toward Jehral as the Devil of Lyra's pointed rear came out of the sand. The sandworm's length tapered toward the end, culminating in a long, thin tail. Ella yanked the reins of Jehral's horse, pulling it away with a sharp movement.

The tail whipped out, and if Ella hadn't intervened, would have taken Jehral's head. As it was, the tail whipped across his chest. Blood spurted into the air, and the desert warrior looked down at the sudden gash.

The sandworm's body was now completely under the sand. The ground rumbled beneath them.

"It's going to come up beneath us!" Ella cried. Shani was white faced. "We need to get out of here! Here, take these reins!"

Shani grabbed Jehral's reins from Ella and dug in her heels as the desert warrior weaved in the saddle, an agonized expression on his face. They were racing away when Shani saw that the reins of Ella's horse were still twisted in Jehral's hands, and she and Jehral were taking Ella's horse with them.

Shani pulled the horses to a stop.

"Keep going!" Ella shouted.

"I won't leave you," Shani called back.

"You have to get Jehral out of here. Don't worry, I'll catch you."

"How will you get away?" Shani cried.

"Don't worry. "I'll find you," Ella said. With grim determination, she spoke a command and pulled the hood of her dress over her head.

Ella knew she would be wavering like a mirage as she chanted, activating the shadow effect.

Cloaked by her dress, she looked at the heavy dagger in her hand as Shani rode away with Jehral and Ella's riderless horse. Ella knew the sandworm didn't like heat, and she had seen that the inside of its body was softer than its tough outer shell.

It might not swallow the figure in the green dress if it could see her, and so this was the only option that Ella had. As she felt the sand begin to fall away from her feet, Ella knew the jaws would soon appear under her. Silently, she rehearsed the sequence that in an instant would change the powers she invoked in her dress from invisibility to the searing-white heat of a zenblade.

Ella felt her body fall. Looking down, she saw the mottled pink and razor-sharp rows of teeth that lined the giant sandworm's jaws. She resisted the temptation to activate the runes that would give her enchantress's dress the strength of steel.

Ella fell into the Devil of Lyra's open jaws, sliding down its throat with the sand.

———◆———

Shani laid Jehral down in the shade of a dune, then leapt back atop her horse. The poor creature had gone past the limits of endurance, yet she had one final task for her steed.

Shani galloped as fast as she was able back toward the Oasis of Lyra and the place where she had last seen Ella.

There was nothing there.

It was as if the fight had never taken place. The ground had resettled and fresh sand had even covered Jehral's blood.

Shani pulled up her horse and wondered what to do.

A hundred paces away a few grains of sand shifted, quickly followed by some more. A well appeared: an opening that grew in size as Shani looked on. Finally a deep, wide hole formed, and then the sandworm's head shot into the air before smashing back down to the earth.

Smoke poured out of its nostrils.

The Devil of Lyra opened its mouth, making a hacking, coughing sound, the segments of its wormlike form shifting and moving. It spat something out onto the sand, something that appeared to have a human form.

Shani spoke the words without thinking, and a fireball shot out of her hands. The sandworm twisted away from the new attack, the fireball barely missing its head. Shani spurred her horse into motion.

The figure on the ground picked itself up. Ella stood in her hooded dress, a blood-drenched dagger in her hand, facing the monster down.

The Devil of Lyra turned away, plunging back into the sand and vanishing into the desert, leaving Ella standing, her chest rising and falling as she gasped for breath.

24

Four weeks later, two women, one in red and the other in green, came out of the desert. With them was a wounded warrior who barely stayed upright in his saddle, leaning on the woman in green for support.

Ella recognized the rust-colored earth, stormy skies, and dark forests of Petrya, and Shani was almost overcome with emotion to be back in her homeland.

"This is the time, Ella," Shani said. "I left, and now I've returned. I promised myself that when I returned to Tlaxor, it would be to end the reign of High Lord Haptut Alwar. Pray this is that time."

"Prince Ilathor is an honorable man," Ella said. "I'll speak with him. I'm sure he also wants to liberate your people and plans to treat them well."

Ella had her own memories of Petrya. She'd traveled this land with Killian, and it was here she'd finally seen through his façade. She had slept with the warmth of his body close to hers as they camped at night, hunted by a strange creature, and for a time they'd shared a room in the trade town of Torlac.

"You're thinking about him," Shani said, indicating the pendant at Ella's neck with her eyes.

Ella looked at Jehral to see if he was listening, but the desert warrior was still, his eyes closed and his expression pained.

"It was in Petrya that I last saw him," she said.

Suddenly, Ella craved the warmth of a man with a savage intensity. She imagined Killian's strong arms and his lean body, her hands running through the fiery hair that curled down to his neck.

"And this desert prince, Ilathor. You still don't know why he wants you?"

Ella remembered another night. Another man. She remembered a night in the desert when Prince Ilathor Shanti of Tarn Teharan, now leader of the army of the desert tribes, had declared his love for her.

A love she had spurned, the very last time she and Ilathor spoke, before Ella stole Jehral's horse and left.

"Stop," Shani said. "Don't move. We're being watched."

Ella reined in her horse, and soon all three travelers drew to a halt. She looked with concern at Jehral. He couldn't survive a battle.

"How do you know?"

"There are men in those trees there. It was only for the shortest instant, but I saw them. In fact, I don't think those trees are even real. I know the trees that grow in my land."

"They aren't Petryans, then," Ella said. She called out, projecting her voice, "Warriors of House Hazara, what tarn are you?"

The copse of trees wavered, and in its place Ella now saw a band of mounted warriors, their black clothing and scimitars betraying their origin. Their leader kicked his horse forward, his men following suit.

They halted some distance away. "I am Ashnar of Tarn Bohta," the leader called. "We know what the woman in red is capable of.

Tell her to remove her robe and the red devices at her wrists and surrender herself to us."

Shani bristled. "There is no way I will . . ."

Ella hushed her before turning back to the desert men. "She is an ally of House Hazara, as am I. We have one of your warriors with us. He is wounded and needs the attention of a healer."

"How is it you ride horses?" Ashnar called.

Jehral rose in his saddle and called out. It must have taken him a great effort of will. "Salut, Ashnar. I am Prince Ilathor's man, Jehral of Tarn Teharan. These people are friends. You must take us to him." He slumped back down.

Ashnar conferred quickly with his men. "We will take you to the prince."

"That wasn't so hard, was it?" Shani muttered. Ella silenced her with a glare.

With a wary eye on the elementalist, the Hazarans formed up around the three travelers, gesturing for them to follow. "Where are you taking us?" Ella asked. "How far is it? Our friend needs help."

"Hush, woman," Ashnar said. "No one asked you to speak."

Shani opened her mouth to say something, but Ella shook her head. "Just answer me," Ella said.

"It is not a long journey," Ashnar said, "even at the pace you are able to travel. Prince Ilathor is with his men, perhaps a day's ride from here."

"Where?" Shani asked in exasperation. "We've just come from the desert."

"Why, Torlac, of course," Ashnar said. "We control almost all of Petrya. The prince has based himself in the town closest to the lake. Soon we will take Tlaxor, the tiered city, and all Petrya will be ours."

"And then?" Ella asked, paying close attention, ready to forestall any rash actions from Shani.

"And then, woman, we will continue fighting until the world is at our feet."

———◆———

They encountered more of the prince's patrols as their journey took them closer to the trade town of Torlac.

From her last time in Petrya, Ella knew that they were already on the slopes of Mount Halapusa, the mighty mountain that had erupted long ago, leaving behind a sky-blue volcanic lake with an island in the middle.

Up ahead she could now see the crater's rim, the opposite side forming a long, curving escarpment, and the near side where the ground dropped away in a steep cliff in front of them. She still wasn't close enough to see the lake at the crater's base.

Torlac had sprouted at a cleft in the rim. It was a town that wagons could pass through on their way to the Halapusa Ferry, or where the goods of far-off merchants could be purchased and taken down to the tiered city by Petryans, allowing the foreign merchants to return home.

Torlac was now in the possession of the Hazarans.

The signs of the battle fought for the town's possession were everywhere, visible long before the walls of Torlac itself. The battle had scorched and blackened the red earth, and Ella saw wooden boards covering ditches lined with spikes. They'd removed the dead, either to be burned or buried, but Ella still caught a terrible stench on the wind, the kind of smell that took an eternity to be dispelled.

Overriding the scent of corruption, the burnt odor of charred wood came through strongest. Ella looked with concern at Shani. Her friend's eyes were red, but whether from emotion or the smoke, Ella wasn't certain.

"What are you thinking?" Ella asked. "Are you all right?"

Shani turned her head. "To be honest? I don't know. I want to see my people freed, not conquered. I am no traitor."

Ashnar looked at Shani curiously.

"We'll speak to the prince," Ella said.

Casting her mind back, Ella thought about the time she witnessed Ilathor lead an attack against a rival tribe, Tarn Fasala. When Ilathor led his men to victory, and his enemy surrendered, he hadn't given them quarter. He'd butchered them to a man.

"I'm sure he wants your people to be free also," Ella said, nodding, but inwardly she wondered. How sure was she, really?

The road descended and then leveled out. Desert warriors riding past gazed at their strange party with curiosity. Jehral moaned, and Ella hoped he would get the attention of a healer soon.

The walls of Torlac loomed ahead. As they approached, Ella saw that the once formidable gate was in splinters, their escort barely giving the gate a glance as the desert men took them through.

The streets of Torlac formed a neat grid, with the central avenue leading from the main gate built wide to allow wagons to pass in both directions. The town had escaped the battle mostly unscathed, leading Ella to believe the Hazarans' plan of attack must have relied largely on stealth. Using their rediscovered lore to confuse the eyes, the Hazarans would employ deception and confusion as a key to their strategy.

With their swarthy skin, drab clothing, and flat-topped hats, Ella could easily distinguish the Petryans from the darker Hazarans. She saw a Petryan carrying a broom shy away when a rider's path took him close, the Petryan's wide eyes following the Hazaran. Ella hoped Ilathor was holding his men in check and wondered what the prince's plans were. She didn't see a single woman among the desert warriors who guarded the gates and patrolled the streets— the Hazarans certainly didn't look like they were here to stay for the long term.

Still, the Petryan common-folk who walked the streets appeared to have recovered somewhat from the battle—either that, or they were still in shock. Ella felt heartened to see some old Petryans smoking redleaf from long-stemmed pipes and veiled local women buying fruit and vegetables from one of the numerous markets. Whatever the tides of war, life went on.

Ella again glanced at Shani, but her friend's expression was blank.

Ashnar and his men led the three travelers from the market district through several wide streets to an expansive square. In the center of the square, a great marble statue of a man lay where it had fallen. Ella raised an inquiring eyebrow at Shani.

"High Lord Haptut Alwar," Shani said.

Jehral moaned and shifted in his saddle, and Ella again reached out to steady him. "He needs help," Ella said, frowning at Ashnar.

"No!" Jehral said, although his words obviously required an effort. "I need to see the prince."

A square, red-brick building opened its gates onto the square. From within the brick walls, a tall tower rose high above to dominate the square and the rest of the town. A dozen Hazarans stood guard, casually leaning on their scimitars.

"It's the old barracks—the largest building in Torlac," Ashnar said almost apologetically, looking at Jehral.

White-faced, Jehral straightened in his saddle, looking at Ashnar, but not replying.

As they pulled up outside the gates of the barracks, from the height of her horse Ella's gaze took in the guards. Her eyes widened as she recognized a Hazaran: one of Prince Ilathor's men, a thickset warrior who'd taken an instant disliking to her.

"Rashine," Ashnar said, "look who it is."

Rashine looked them over, his eyes catching on Jehral. "Jehral!" He then saw Ella and frowned, before returning to Jehral. "What are you doing here?"

Jehral smiled weakly. "Salut, Rashine. Take us to Prince Ilathor. Please."

Rashine looked at Ella and Shani, finally tilting his head at Ashnar, who nodded.

"Jehral of Tarn Teharan, I will leave you here," said Ashnar.

"Thank you, Ashnar of Tarn Bohta," Jehral said.

Ella's lips thinned with consternation as Jehral kicked his feet out of the stirrups, slipping off the side of his horse and wincing as he hit the ground.

"This is madness, Jehral," Shani said.

"Come on," Jehral said.

"You heard him," Rashine growled.

Ella and Shani both dismounted, and then Rashine prodded Ella in the back as he and three other guards formed a barrier around them. Ella glared at him.

The guards led Jehral, Ella, and Shani into the brick building. It was more functional than beautiful, with sharp angles and bare walls. Dark-skinned men walked by in small groups, heads clustered together and wicked scimitars at their sides, and the sound of crashing steel echoing through the stone signaled men practicing in the courtyard.

As she followed Jehral up a wide set of stairs, Ella's concern grew when she saw how slowly he took each step. Rashine and the other warriors ignored Jehral's plight—the proud man who was the prince's right hand would never accept assistance.

A second, narrower staircase took them higher still, and soon even Ella felt exhausted. Finally the staircase opened onto a landing, where two more guards stood outside a heavy wooden door. Ella realized they must be at the top of the tower.

"The prince cannot be disturbed," one of the guards outside the door said, holding up his hand.

Jehral sucked in his breath, and then with a bellow Ella would never have expected him to be capable of, Jehral shouted.

"It's Jehral, Prince Ilathor of Tarn Teharan. You left me with the women at Agira Lahsa, but by the Lord of Fire, you'll see me now."

"Jehral?" the voice came through the door. "Enter and be welcome, my friend."

The desert warriors exchanged crooked smiles and one of the guards opened the door.

Prince Ilathor Shanti, son of the kalif and war leader of the Hazaran desert tribes, stood looking out the open window of the chamber he'd chosen, high above the streets of Torlac, in the town's tallest structure. Ella followed his gaze, realizing Ilathor was staring into the distance at the steaming waters of Lake Halapusa and the Petryan capital of Tlaxor centered at its heart. From every turret of the tiered city below, the teardrop and flame *raj hada* of Petrya flew tall and proud. The Petryans were far from conquered.

The prince turned as they approached, his lips curved in the charismatic smile Ella remembered so well.

Ilathor had been beardless before, but he now had a thin beard, sculpted to follow the contours of his face and meeting his upper lip in two lines on either side of his chin. Ella was surprised to find she liked it. Prince Ilathor's near-black hair was very long, past his shoulders, held back with a golden clasp, and his dark skin was smooth and unblemished. He wore an earring of gold and amber in his left ear, and around his neck a golden chain supported a curved turquoise triangle.

The black clothing of the Hazarans sat snugly around the prince's broad shoulders, but it was the yellow sash around his waist that caught Ella's attention. The *raj hada* in its center was made of molded yellow gold, the desert rose of House Hazara etched into the precious metal.

Jehral entered first, the two women flanking him on either side. Jehral bowed, somewhat clumsily for the usually graceful warrior. Ella—and Shani, she was surprised to see—followed suit.

"My Prince," Jehral said. "I have been to far-off lands, but now I have returned."

"Jehral," Prince Ilathor said warmly, coming forward and clasping the man's left hand between both of his. "I never doubted you."

"Yet you left without me," Jehral said, his eyes accusing.

"I am sorry, my friend. Binding the tribes together is no easy feat. The reconstruction of Agira Lahsa is well underway, and we rediscover more of our lore every day. The men grew restless, and I could wait no longer. In my position, Jehral, would you not do the same?"

Jehral bowed his head. "I do not think to presume, my Prince."

The prince smiled. "We missed you at the fight. Rest assured of that, my friend."

Ella exchanged glances with Shani, and then, without quite realizing she'd done it, Ella cleared her throat.

"And I see you brought me my desert rose," the prince said, smiling and directing his attention to Ella.

"She . . ." Jehral said. "She . . ."

Jehral stumbled, and then, before any of them could react, fell to the floor.

Prince Ilathor looked directly at Ella for the first time. "What have you done to him?" he demanded, his eyes blazing. "He is wounded. Can you not see?"

Ella felt color rise to her cheeks. "Prince Ilathor—" she began.

"Guards!" the prince called. The door to the room opened. "Take Jehral to the infirmary. Give him the best possible care. Do you understand me?"

"Yes, at once, my Prince," the guard said.

"Then find these two some chambers. Close by. Don't let either of them out of your sight."

"Understood, my Prince."

"If he has come to harm," the prince said to Ella, "I will hold you directly responsible."

"I . . ." Ella tried again.

Guards once more surrounded Ella and Shani, and before Ella could say another word, the guards swept the two women away.

"That went well," Shani said as the door closed behind them.

25

Perhaps the mixed reception was a blessing, for Ella was travel stained and exhausted. Her next meeting with the prince was to be later in the evening, at dinner, which gave her time to rest, then bathe, and then rest again.

The chambers she'd been given were surprisingly spacious, with a deep bath in an adjoining room, where scalding hot water from the volcanic lake was piped directly. Fresh towels and linens lay stacked in a neat pile, and with joy Ella discovered the chest at the foot of the bed, filled with clean clothing.

The next time she met with the prince, she planned for things to go quite differently.

For some reason, Ella found herself spending an inordinate amount of time in front of the silver mirror. She washed her body and hair with soap that smelled like jasmine, afterward combing her pale blonde hair until it shone. She tried on the garments one after another, finally settling on a sleeveless dress of cornflower blue.

Ella suddenly stopped herself. What was she doing?

She was meeting with a powerful leader. She was representing her people, and the things she spoke about with the prince could have a great impact on the world.

Was it anything else?

No. Of course not.

With that resolved, Ella settled her silver pendant on its chain between her breasts. Was the dress cut too low? Ella felt sure it was fine.

She wondered how many people would be at the dinner. Probably at least twenty, she thought. Jehral would be there, if he was well enough, and certainly Shani and the leaders of the other tarns. She hoped she would be seated close enough to the prince to explain how Jehral had been wounded and that she'd had nothing to do with his insistence to see the prince immediately.

Ella looked into the silver mirror. Her green eyes sparkled back. When the summons came, she was ready.

———◆———

Ella once more followed the prince's guards to the room at the top of the tower. It was a small room to seat so many, she thought.

The door was open, and with a gesture the guard indicated Ella should enter. Feeling apprehensive, she stepped through the portal, noticing this time that the floor was lined with soft carpets, thick and luxurious. Maps covered the wall, and a desk rested in the corner, but even more incongruous than the carpets was the table resting in the center of the room.

Two chairs sat at the table. Only two chairs. A nightlamp formed the centerpiece of the table, activated at the lowest setting, and a wine bottle stood with two glasses. Ella's heart skipped a beat.

The prince again leaned at the window, gazing out at the starry sky. Ella walked over to stand by his side, and as she looked out, the nighttime view caused her to gasp.

A full moon shimmered over the surface of Lake Halapusa, its light broken into ethereal ripples as it was dispersed by the steam rising off the water. By night, the city of Tlaxor below was even more spectacular, with lights piled one on top of the other like the berries of a magical tree. Above the lake, the rim of the crater formed a jagged line stretching as far as the eye could see to the left and right, and above it all the stars sparkled like pinpricks in a curtain.

"You will have your own great city soon," Ella murmured.

"That is true," said the prince, still looking out. "Different, however, to this."

"All places are different," Ella said.

"Is your city, Sarostar, like this?"

"No, Your Highness. It's a beautiful city, a place I love, but nothing like this."

"So Jehral has told me." The prince nodded.

"About Jehral . . ." Ella said.

The prince cut Ella off with a chopping motion of his hand. "We have spoken at length. You saved his life, Enchantress Ella. Normally, I would grant you any wish for doing that, any wish in my power to grant. However, you lied to me. You gave me a false name, you stole my essence, and you left my people when I still needed you."

"My people needed me too!"

"Then why did you not plead your case with me? Why did you not tell me the truth?"

Ella tried to answer, but no words came out. "I . . . I don't know," she finally said. "I'm sorry."

"Thank you, Ella, for saving my friend's life. There is no debt between us," the prince said.

Ilathor turned away from the vista below, looking at Ella for the first time. A lock of Ella's hair fell in front of her eyes, and the soft light from the nightlamp shone from the strands, caressing the pale skin of her hand as she brushed it away.

The prince hadn't spoken for some time. Ella looked up at his face.

There was a fire in his eyes, a hunger she had never seen before. Ilathor reached down, and without seeking her permission, he ran his fingers through the ends of her hair, holding it up. "Like spun gold," he whispered to himself, almost inaudibly.

Ella's breath quickened, but she felt events moving too quickly and took a slight step back, though part of her screamed, telling her to move forward. The prince's hand fell down.

"Now that there is no debt between us, could you tell me why you've taken me from my home, against my will? If you'd explained your case and said you needed me, I might have come."

"Please let me explain. It was never my wish to take you from your home against your will. Those actions were taken by Jehral without my command. I merely asked him to bring you here as swiftly as he could. You are not a captive; you are free to come and go as you please."

Ella opened her mouth to speak, but the prince held up a hand.

"Yet when last I saw you, you fled without a word. I opened my heart to you, back in the desert, and your response was to steal Jehral's horse and leave. Can you blame him for being unsure of you?"

"My homeland . . ." Ella began.

Ilathor again held up a hand. "When I heard of the woman who saved her people at the Bridge of Sutanesta, I asked Jehral to discover the truth, and if you were alive, to do whatever it took to bring you here. I am sorry if your journey here was not easy, but I need you, Ella, and it is for more than my own desire that you're here, sincere as it is. Once more, lives depend on your actions."

"What is it you want me to do?"

Prince Ilathor looked out the window at the tiered city below. It was a long time before he spoke. "I need you to build the bridge," he finally said, turning to Ella.

"I don't understand," Ella said.

"I brought you here so you can build me the bridge that you built for your people after the Bridge of Sutanesta was destroyed. A bridge of light, I have heard it called. Only you can do such a thing. We have been waiting here for an eternity. The ferry has been destroyed, so we cannot cross Lake Halapusa, and the lack of supplies is having no effect on the Petryans. No conventional bridge can span such a space, and even if there were a working ferry, crossing a boiling lake by boat is no way to attack a city. I need you to build me a bridge of light across the lake."

"I see," Ella said. "I understand now." She shook her head slowly. "Prince Ilathor, you could have saved yourself some trouble, and Jehral a lot of effort. The bridge I built spanned a distance one hundred times smaller than what you need. It isn't possible."

"Please, I beg you to try," Prince Ilathor said.

Ella thought for a moment. She owed Ilathor a debt, for it was his essence that had enabled her to save the refugees and Miro's army at the Bridge of Sutanesta.

"There might be another way," Ella said, frowning.

"Anything, Ella. Anything you can do to help us take the tiered city."

Ella thought about Shani, anxious to free her people, and Miro, desperate to secure his southern border. By helping the prince, she would be helping to hasten the end of the war. "I have an idea," she said. "I'll give it some thought. Give me time."

The prince smiled. "That is all I ask. Come," he gestured, "let us drink wine together, and you can tell me who Ella is, so I may distinguish her from the woman, Evora, you said you were."

Ilathor led Ella to the table, seating her before seating himself. He poured the wine slowly, the thick, red liquid dark and fragrant, igniting Ella's senses before she'd even tasted it.

"Salut. I greet you." The prince held up his glass.

"Salut," Ella said, echoing him, not sure whether this was the correct response.

The wine tasted spicy, warm, and tart, like sweet prunes soaked in lemon and mellowed over a hundred years. Ella felt it slip down her throat, thinking that it suited this man.

"You sealed Wondhip Pass?" the prince asked.

Ella nodded.

"How did you move the stones?" He shook his head. "What does Altura's lore have to do with moving large objects?"

"It wasn't enchantment," Ella said. "I learned a few things from an old Halrana animator."

"And this bridge that saved your people . . . an incredible feat."

Ella stayed silent, remembering the soldiers and refugees who had not been saved at the Bridge of Sutanesta that day. She remembered Amber.

"Your father is high lord of House Hazara?" Ella asked, changing the subject.

"Kalif, but yes, that is what you would call it. He is an old man, Ella, and I fear he may not be much longer for this world. He tells me I am strong enough to lead the tribes when he is gone, but I have doubts. Many follow me because of who my father is."

"You have doubts?" Ella smiled. "Look at where you are. How many men do you command? Your army must be as powerful as the Imperial Legion to have taken Petrya so quickly."

"Such numbers are hard to control," the prince said. "As long as I keep them busy fighting, yes, they will do as I command. But what about when there is peace? What then?"

"I think that's the question everyone is asking," Ella said. "The Tingaran Empire is dead. Even if we can defeat the primate, what comes next? Who will lead?"

Prince Ilathor smiled. "Such intelligence. It is good to have you with me again."

Ella sipped at her wine to disguise her blush.

Yet her thoughts now turned serious. This man held the fate of Shani's people in his hands. She owed it to her friend to do her best to help her people.

"Prince Ilathor, there is a woman with me, a Petryan."

"Ah, yes. The elementalist. I have been meaning to ask you about her. To whom does she owe her allegiance?"

Ella hesitated. "It's a little more complicated than that." She took a deep breath. "Your Highness, not all Petryans were hungering for this war. Many only hate Altura and Halaran because that's what their parents have taught them to do, and most don't hate at all; they just want to raise their families in peace and prosperity. The world of leadership and the administration of the realm is a distant thing for most."

Ella thought of her brother. "Sometimes there are leaders who work to do good in the world," she said. "Brave men whose values are more important to them than doing what they think people want and expect of them. Then there are other leaders. They come to power because they inherited it or because their supporters are more vocal, more violent, and more intimidating than those who just want to live their lives. The Petryan high lord and his supporters are such men, ruling with fear, filled with hate. Hate is a disease, but it's a disease that can be cured. The greatest factor is belief that it can be cured, and this is what makes what you are doing such an opportunity. Please, Prince Ilathor, give the Petryans a chance to believe."

The prince stayed silent throughout Ella's speech, a thoughtful expression on his face.

Finally, he spoke. "May I ask you, Enchantress Ella, why you think I am here? Is it to conquer for the sake of conquering? To give my barbarian hordes some place to pillage? Perhaps to pay for all of that construction at Agira Lahsa?"

Ella opened her mouth to protest.

"No," Ilathor said forcefully. "I have eyes to see and ears to listen. I know the world is changing. This disease you speak of is an apt metaphor. I have treated the Petryans well, and I have heard their complaints. They do not know who to replace their high lord with, but that is their concern, not mine. When we take Tlaxor, there will be those who fight against us, and those who rise up against their oppressors and fight with us. We are distributing the message, and the message is clear: Petrya will be free."

Ella knew the prince was anything but a liar. As she heard the conviction in his voice, she felt closer to him than she ever had before.

"That's all I need to know, Your Highness." She smiled at him.

"Your people will also be free, Ella. The men of this Black Army attack your homeland daily, and I am told Altura may not be able to hold. With Petrya liberated, Altura may be able to break free of the encirclement. The Alturan commander's southern flank will be safe, and his strength in the east will grow." The prince looked into Ella's eyes. "I have only met one Alturan, but she taught me about her people, and I now feel I must do what I can to help them."

Ella looked down at the table. "I thank you for my people, Your Highness."

"There is more," the prince said. "I need you to understand, for it was you who first told me about these lands in a way that I could understand. I now realize it is my duty to do what I can to help the multitudes of the world. Petrya is just the beginning. With the Tingaran Empire broken, someone will need to pick up the pieces before the world falls apart. I intend to take this army to Seranthia. I will kill this primate and display his head for all to see, and put this world back on track." He paused, his eyes intent, before suddenly breaking off.

"Now," Prince Ilathor smiled, "I have done it again. I apologize if my thoughts are on the struggle ahead. Let us speak of other matters." He took a sip of wine. "Please tell me . . . who is Ella?"

"Well, the Alturan leader you spoke of . . ." Ella said, "he's my brother."

The prince's smile broadened. "And so I finally learn about Ella. Please," he topped up her glass, "tell me more about yourself. Tell me of your family and your childhood, and this incredible talent for lore you possess."

Ella spoke at length, surprised when the prince's probing questions drew more and more information out of her. She found herself telling him things she thought locked up deep inside, but there were still facets of her life she held back. She never mentioned Killian, or Brandon Goodwin, the old soldier who'd raised her. They both seemed far away now, just distant memories.

At some point food arrived, spiced lamb with roasted yellow and orange vegetables, served with a nutty substance comprised of tiny balls of grain. The flavor was intense and sweet, and left a tingling in Ella's mouth when she was done.

They finished the meal with fresh fruit and cool water, before Ella once again found herself at the window, standing side by side with the prince, gazing out at the moon's glow on the misty lake.

"It is good to have you by my side once more," Ilathor said.

"I thought you had invited me here to have dinner with your men," Ella said, looking up at him.

He laughed. "And why would I want to share you with them?"

Ella smiled. Her breath caught as the prince stepped closer to her.

"Your lodgings . . . are you comfortable?" he inquired.

Ella looked down to break the prince's gaze, uncomfortable yet excited at the way Ilathor was looking at her. "Yes, I'm fine."

Ilathor stepped closer still and lifted Ella's chin to look into her eyes. Ella felt vulnerable, even as part of her wanted to surrender.

"I . . . I'd best be going."

"That is a shame," Ilathor said, smiling. "The night is young."

She felt his hand on her hip, feeling the smooth material, running his hand up to her slim waist. Prince Ilathor leaned down, his lips parted.

Ella moved toward him, and they kissed.

His beard was surprisingly soft, and the pressure of his embrace was firm but gentle. Ella could feel him drawing her to him, and she gave in, moving in closer to him as the insistence of his lips against hers grew in intensity.

She felt his tongue hesitantly probe into her mouth, and when hers came to meet it, she felt an electric thrill run up her spine as they touched. Ella didn't care about anything else; she wanted him then, with a sensation that started below her belly and tingled through her chest, rising to the wonderful feeling of his lips on her mouth.

Ella broke the kiss, for a moment only, staring up at his dark, brooding eyes. Prince Ilathor smiled, his fingers stroking the soft hairs at the back of her neck, sending another thrill through her body. His hand moved up, outside the front of her dress, to the underside of her breast.

"It brings me joy to have you here," he said.

Ella looked down at the silver chain around her neck. Even as her body burned from the prince's touch, she felt uncertain. Things were moving far too quickly.

"I'm tired from travel," she said, stepping back but smiling to take any sting out of her words. "I should go to my bed. Good night, Your Highness."

"Good night," the prince said, bowing as he placed his hand over his heart.

Ella turned and walked away, feeling Ilathor's eyes on her back as she closed the door behind her.

Two weeks later, Ella and Shani stood on the shores of Lake Halapusa, looking down at the small pool of water they'd created off to the side of the lake itself. Ella held a book in her hand and wrote out equations while Shani crouched down beside the pool and frowned.

A contingent of fifty Hazaran warriors guarded them. Ella told Jehral she thought it excessive, but Jehral had simply shrugged and said the prince considered the two women too valuable to lose.

Ella heard the sound of hooves and looked up, now seeing Jehral approach. His color had returned in the last weeks, and she was now pleased to see him fully recovered.

"Salut, Ella," Jehral said.

"Ho, Jehral," Ella replied.

"I bring your response from the prince."

"Well? What did he say? How much essence can we have at our disposal?"

"The answer was vague. He said you can have as much as a horse can carry in its water bags, but no more. If you want a more specific answer, you will have to ask him yourself."

Ella looked at Shani. "Do you think it will be enough?" she asked.

"We will need more—perhaps twice as much. And it will only have a chance at working if we wait until after summer," Shani said. "Even then it will be close."

Ella looked up at Jehral. "Tell the prince something for me, Jehral, and this is important. Tell him we will open the way across the lake to Tlaxor, but we will have to wait until the season has changed. Tell Prince Ilathor we need more essence, as much as two horses can carry in their water bags, but that after the end of summer, we will help him take the city."

Jehral nodded, wheeling his horse, and rode away.

26

Amber stuffed three dresses, a coat, and two blankets into a sack. She picked herself up, feeling the weight of her pregnancy pull at her back, and then left the small shelter she'd been given—a canvas tent, walled on three sides—walking around to the back. She dropped the sack on the ground, before once more returning to the tent.

Summer had come and gone, and soon the weather would turn cool again. The blankets and clothing could save someone's life, and most of the things the guards gave her she didn't need for herself. Amber knew the other prisoners distrusted her, and they would never take what she gave them if she offered, but if she left the sack outside, by morning it would be gone.

Life had settled in the prison camp—for Amber, at least. With Moragon believing she carried his child, Amber now received regular meals and even had her own shelter, however basic.

The other prisoners, particularly some of the women, called her names, but Amber knew there was more to the story than they were aware of, and although she hated what she'd done, she had secured the life of her child. Her thoughts wandered. Could she ever tell Miro about giving herself to Moragon? Would he despise her too? She pushed the thought to the side.

Once Moragon found out she was pregnant, he'd made sure she was safe from harm and then left her to her own devices. Amber knew he wasn't interested in her well-being: without an heir, it was the son she might give him that was the source of his interest.

Amber felt the baby kick and sighed. She was lonely, and she knew that with her relaxed conditions, she could help her people more, if they would only let her. Although she was now safe from being taken away to where dark rumors said they were committing unspeakable deeds, more people vanished every day.

The prisoners constantly wondered where people disappeared to and speculated about who would be next. It was usually the old, the sickly, and the weak, but sometimes it was those who tried to fight back. There were rumors, horrible rumors, that the templars tortured them or experimented on them or killed them and extracted essence from their bodies.

There were constant fresh arrivals, mainly people from Ralanast. Although the spirit had left many in the prison camp, Amber felt that with the right leadership, they might be able to fight back. Some even looked to Leopold to lead them, but he had gone mad since the death of his uncle, Tessolar, the old high lord. There was no help there.

Amber stood and walked slowly around to stretch her legs, once more feeling the baby kick.

A tall Halrana woman a few years older than Amber walked in the opposite direction.

"Lina, can I speak with you a moment?" Amber asked.

"What is it?" Lina said shortly.

"You are caring for a child, a boy, aren't you?"

"Yes. What of it?"

"The guards give me oats, but I can't eat them," Amber lied, "they give me stomach problems. I could leave the bowl outside my tent in the mornings. Your boy could eat them. Do you think that would be all right?"

Lina nodded—a short, sharp gesture. "Fine. I'll . . . What's wrong?"

Amber suddenly fell, clutching Lina's shoulder for support. She waited, breathing slowly in and out, before it hit her again.

Amber looked up at Lina, knowing fear would be written across her face. "I think I'm going into labor," she said.

Lina drew herself up. "Samora," she called to another woman, "go and fetch one of the guards. Don't worry," she addressed Amber, "you'll be fine."

"I'm scared," Amber said.

"I know you are. But what is happening is natural. People have been having babies for thousands of years."

Amber felt another contraction hit her with the force of a kick in the stomach. "Lina, I have to tell you. It's my husband's child. He's dead. Moragon just thinks the child is his."

"Quiet," Lina hissed, looking around her in both directions. "Not another word, do you hear me? You stay silent about that. You're going to be fine. Let him continue to believe. You know it's the better way."

Amber nodded, grimacing against the pain. "I know."

Lina pinched Amber's arm. "The guards are here. They'll take you somewhere clean and safe." Lina leaned in close. "If you can get out of here, do it. Even if it means leaving the babe."

Amber groaned. Two men took her shoulder on either side, leading her through the camp.

Amber repeated Lina's words like a mantra. She was going to be fine.

<hr />

Just before dawn, in the dim light of the infirmary tent in the guards' quarters, Amber gave birth to a strong baby boy.

She lay back on the pallet, exhausted but happy. It was like some great weight had been taken from her and then given back to her in the form of pure joy. She held out her arms and spent the next hours in bliss, amazed by the delicacy of the baby's tiny features, in awe of the life she held at her breast.

He suckled almost immediately, feeding hungrily, gurgling and pawing, his eyes blue as the sky. Amber never wanted to let him go.

They took him from her sometime around mid-morning.

"Shh," said the Tingaran battlefield surgeon, a man more used to dealing with lost limbs than women. "He will have a wet-nurse. He won't go hungry."

"Please," Amber begged. "Please don't take him away."

Her strength gave out, and they easily pried the baby away from her arms.

"High Lord Moragon wants to see his son," said the surgeon.

"No," Amber cried. "No!"

"Shh," the surgeon said again. "No one's going to send you off to the vats; you'll still be taken care of. But the camp is no place to raise a baby. You can see that, can't you?"

Tears rolled down Amber's cheeks. She watched the surgeon's departing back as he took her baby away, then she slumped back down to her pallet, wondering how she was going to find the strength to go on.

The guards returned shortly and made her dress herself while they turned their backs. They led Amber back to her tent, where she feared she would never see her baby again.

"They took your baby," Leopold said. "I'm sorry."

Amber was taken aback when he spoke to her as she walked past. Leopold was surprisingly lucid today. She opened her mouth to respond, when suddenly she was overcome with emotion. Amber sank to the ground next to the former prince of Altura, her sobs accompanied by great wracking convulsions. Weeks had passed, but still she never knew when the grief would hit her.

"I don't blame you," Leopold said, making no move to comfort her. "There is no hope. This resistance will be crushed. Altura will soon fall."

Amber looked up. "What resistance?"

"They sent word to me," he said desultorily. "You know who Rogan Jarvish is, don't you? He's leading them, back in Ralanast."

"Blademaster Rogan?" Amber demanded. "Didn't he die at the Battle for Ralanast?"

"Apparently not." Leopold shrugged.

"Can you get word back to him?"

"I suppose so. One of the guards is a sympathizer," Leopold said. "He's in love with a Halrana woman and doesn't want to go back to Seranthia."

"Can you tell me which guard?"

Leopold nodded before returning to his contemplation of the dirt at his feet.

Amber stood up and straightened. She left Leopold behind and swiftly found Lina, Samora, and three other women, asking them to come to her tent.

She then sat inside the tent and pondered.

Amber knew who Rogan Jarvish was; every Alturan knew his name. And he was near, in Ralanast, barely half a day's walk from this prison camp!

The Halrana women arrived.

Without preamble, Amber spoke. "I've asked the five of you to come here because you know many of the Halrana here, while I know most of the Alturans."

"What's this about?" Lina asked.

"The fact that I've called this gathering, and no one can see us, should tell you something. I'm in a unique position here, and we should take advantage of that fact."

"To do what?" Samora demanded.

"To organize ourselves. I've learned that there's a resistance in Ralanast. The man leading them is one of my people, an Alturan, one of the best men we have. If we can get word to him, I think he'll help us."

"You're talking about escape? We'll get ourselves killed!" one of the other women said in a shrill voice.

"No, we won't," Amber stated. "Not if we meet here, where no one can see us, and we continue to be nice to the guards. We can all do that, can't we? There's something you need to know. The people who are vanishing . . . I don't know where they're going, but the surgeon said they're being taken 'to the vats.' I believe the rumors are true. If we don't escape from here ourselves, we'll all be dead before the year is over."

The women blanched, exchanging glances.

"This escape," Lina said, "it won't have a chance unless we have support from outside. We could take over this camp tomorrow, and they'd just send reinforcements."

"You're right," Amber said. "For now we just need to open up communication. Leopold knows about a guard here, a sympathizer. This guard can get a message to Rogan."

"Leopold?" Samora raised an eyebrow. "He's mad."

"That doesn't mean his ears don't hear. Leopold was once a prince of Altura," Amber said. "I believe him."

"So what do we do then?" Lina said.

"We think and we plan. That's enough for now. The main thing is to keep quiet. I'll get a message to Rogan Jarvish, and we'll see what he says. You'd better leave now."

The five women stood.

"We can do this," Amber said. "We must do this. There's no other choice."

The Halrana women nodded and filed out, leaving Amber alone.

Amber wondered where she would find writing materials.

27

Seranthia's huge harbor was home to scores of ships and the port of call for a great many more. People came to Seranthia from far and wide to make deals and to build alliances. The harbor was a lively, vibrant place, famed for its workshops and taverns, nearly a city in its own right.

Yet the harbor gave way to a sight more renowned still, a mighty monument second only to Stonewater in its fame.

It was called the Sentinel.

Barring the harbor, the massive statue rose from a tiny island, barely an outcrop of rock, as if thrusting out of the water. He stood tall and bold on a wide pedestal, legs outspread, with one arm raised, pointing upward as if at the stars or the sun. His features were soft, almost feminine, with hair flowing down to his shoulders, and on his head sat a strange headpiece, a crown, with a rune decorating its front. Most of the sailors navigating past the Sentinel barely gave it a second look—it had been there for an eternity, and it would be there for an eternity more. Many said it was ancient, old when Seranthia was just a fishing town. If it was old, it was barely worn, and how old would it have to be to have existed when Seranthia was small? It was yet another of the world's mysteries.

In The Floating Cork, the harbor tavern with the best view of the Sentinel, Evrin Evenstar sat nursing a tankard of black beer, glaring out at the distant statue. His wounds pained him. The journey from Salvation to Seranthia had truly worn him out.

Evrin wondered how much longer he should wait for Killian. He didn't even know if the lad had received his message to meet him here. He could use Killian's help, but he couldn't afford to wait much longer.

Seranthia was always a difficult place, and now Evrin felt for its denizens more than ever before. He still couldn't believe the Akari were here. Of all people, the Akari! Provided they kept their lore to themselves, they were no trouble, living in the north as they did, but there was danger here, Evrin knew. If their lore got into the wrong hands—the primate's hands—the world would become a dark place indeed.

The streetclans now basically ran the city, extorting the common-folk with impunity, while the increasingly corrupt templars took bribes and looked the other way.

Seranthia, a beautiful city, a grand city, with majestic cathedrals, columned arcades, arch-lined streets, and statues and fountains in every square, was becoming an ugly place.

Evrin wished he could do something to help, but he knew his own mission was more important.

He finished his tankard and sighed. He could wait no longer.

Evrin quickly scribbled onto a piece of paper, folding it up and then dripping wax from a candle to seal it.

"Another blackstorm?" the tavern keeper asked when Evrin approached the bar.

"Need to be on my way. I was wondering if I could leave a note with you," Evrin said, holding out his sealed message.

The tavern keeper hesitated, licking his lips. They were all like this, Evrin had noticed. Every honest shopkeeper and craftsman in

Seranthia was terrified. The poor fellows were only trying to make a living; they deserved better.

"Can I read the note?" the tavern keeper asked.

Evrin thought about what he had written. "I'm sorry, but no."

The tavern keeper shook his head, nervously wringing his hands. "You understand, don't you? What if someone leaves a note with me about hatching plans or saying something against our new high lord? I'm going to have to say no."

"Really?" Evrin said, feeling nothing but sympathy for the man. "Is it that bad?"

The tavern keeper looked to the left and the right, dropping his voice. "People are being rounded up, young and old, and being taken to prison camps. If you cross the templars, you . . ."

The tavern keeper's voice trailed off, and his face went as white as the piece of paper in Evrin's hand. Evrin turned, knowing what he would see.

Two templars stood behind him, their hands on their swords. Both had the yellow sheen of the taint in their eyes.

"Want to tell us what you're whispering about?" one of the templars said.

"Hand over that paper," said the other.

Evrin sighed. Two of them would be hard to handle.

"Hold on a moment," Evrin said.

Before they could react, he put the piece of paper into his mouth, chewed, and swallowed. Evrin looked from one templar to the other. He would make a dash for—

Something smashed into the back of his head with the force of a horse's kick.

Evrin's eyes slowly rolled back in his head as he sank to the floor.

The last thing he saw was the tavern keeper standing over him with a cudgel in his hand, an apologetic look on his face.

28

Killian arrived in Seranthia, weary to his core. It had been a long walk.

His journey had been slowed by the vast number of soldiers on the road. His survival instincts told him to stay out of their way, hidden behind a hedge or waiting in a copse of trees. These were strange men, a race he had never seen before, tall, with ice-blue eyes and pale blonde hair. They walked with others who were perhaps of a different race or were under the effect of some strange spell, for their eyes were entirely white, and they walked with listless movements.

Killian wasn't sure if he wanted to know more. He didn't want anything to distract him from his purpose: Find the primate, and he would find the book. Find the book, and he would find Evrin.

As he reached the hilly farmland and pasture surrounding the city, Killian saw the Wall ahead. Monstrous and indomitable, it stood impossibly tall, as only the lore of the builders could make things. Gray and forbidding, the Wall grew with each step that Killian took forward.

Killian thought about Seranthia. He wasn't from Tingara; he was from Aynar, and his earliest memories were of life on the streets of Salvation, but he still knew the city well.

In another life, Killian had been part of a troupe, a traveling show that wandered from city to city, town to town. Seranthia, with its wealthy merchants, bored administrators, and skilled craftsmen, was a frequent destination for the troupe.

Killian had always had mixed feelings about Seranthia. It was such an incredible city, but its problems were as great as its virtues. Such riches flowed through it, yet there were so many poor, sleeping on the streets, fighting each other for scraps, living in conditions akin to most dungeons.

Killian would know; he was no stranger to dungeons.

Yet the Grand Boulevard was awe inspiring—a broad avenue stretching out as straight as a rule, so wide that a stone could not be thrown across it, and so long that one end could not be seen from the other. Arguably the world's best-known street, it was lined on both sides with manicured parks, and the statues of former administrators were noble and severe as they watched the passersby.

Even more impressive, the Grand Boulevard led to the Imperial Palace, a great edifice of crenulated walls and towers, with peaked white roofs poking from behind the battlements. In the center of the Imperial Palace, a broad tower rose tallest of all, with a high balcony visible to all below, from which, over the years, Tingara's emperors made speeches to their people.

The markets of Seranthia were legendary; the eating houses, beyond compare; and the libraries, second to none. Killian wondered if one day the man would come who could take Seranthia to greatness.

As he approached the city, he again considered the Wall. It was the perfect symbol for Seranthia—tremendously huge, something that could never have been built without great wealth, yet used to impress and intimidate, to lock out and discard.

Some soldiers walked away from the city, their path taking them past Killian, but he felt safer here in the hilly land close to the city. The road was highly trafficked, and these soldiers, though Tingaran legionnaires, were commonplace compared to the strange warriors Killian had seen earlier. These men also looked busy. They were escorting several carts filled with prisoners.

Killian felt the anger rise to his cheeks as he watched the pitiful wretches go past. Untold numbers of prisoners passed in a constant stream, hundreds upon hundreds of them. They were mainly old, he noticed, but there were also some who looked starved, and even a few who might have been simpletons, unaware of what was happening around them.

And then Killian saw an old man with white hair and a beard flecked with ginger, who wasn't moving at all.

Killian's mouth opened in shock.

"Evrin," he cried. "Evrin!"

Killian ran toward the drudge-pulled wagon, desperately trying to get the old man's attention. He waved his arms and called out, running up and smacking his hand against the wood of the cart.

Evrin's eyes stayed shut, and then a legionnaire came forward. He glared at Killian, but rather than the sharp words Killian expected, the legionnaire smashed the hilt of his sword into Killian's cheek.

Killian went down, crying out with pain, but rose back up and again stood. Seeing the legionnaire's eyes still on him, Killian suppressed his anger as he watched the soldiers draw away.

All thoughts of finding the primate and his book were forgotten. He had found Evrin!

Killian waited until the last cart had passed and the soldier watching him had long gone; then he started to follow.

There was no way Evrin Evenstar was getting away from him this time.

29

Miro held his breath, barely able to watch as the warrior drew on his bow, aimed, and released.

The arrow went wide, missing the straw man altogether and sinking into a nearby tree with a *thunk*.

"I told you this wouldn't work," High Lord Rorelan said, shaking his head. "I want those bladesingers back."

"It will work," Miro said.

Prayan, the wizened Dunfolk hunter who was making the Alturans' bows, jumped up to smack the Alturan warrior on the back of the head. "No, no, no!" Prayan cried. "Your stance is all wrong. You need to hold your breath before you shoot, and then release it after. It's affecting your aim. Where do I start?"

Aglaran, Prayan's son, tilted his head as if hearing something. In one swift motion he fitted an arrow to the string of his bow, drew it to his ear, and released. Deep in the forest, Miro heard something fall to the ground.

"Woodhen," Aglaran said. "Dinner."

"Were you watching, stupid Alturan?" Prayan harassed the weary soldier. "Any child could hit the center of that target. A trained hunter like my son here can shoot a bird on the wing."

Prayan poked the soldier to emphasize his point before moving to the next, his haranguing voice coming in fits and starts as he moved down the line.

"This is hopeless," Rorelan said.

"I know it seems that way, but the men can learn, High Lord," Miro said. "You were at the Sutanesta. You saw what happened. Used in a group, these weapons are deadly."

"If the men don't have the training . . ."

"They will," Miro said with determination.

"Lord Marshal, you have—what?—three hundred of these so-called archers? That's three hundred fewer men facing the legion. Give them swords."

"How do swords beat prismatic orbs? The enemy has essence again. We won't last!"

"Give me the two bladesingers back, the ones who fight with the Dunfolk in the north."

"No. This isn't something a couple of bladesingers can solve. The enemy's strength is increasing while we grow weaker and weaker. I'm the lord marshal."

"And I'm your high lord!"

Miro lifted his chin. "I am telling you, Rorelan: This will work."

High Lord Rorelan turned and walked away, his stamping strides showing his fury.

Next to Miro, Layla shook her head. "He is correct, Miro. Your men have the strength, but becoming a hunter takes a lifetime of training."

"He's under a lot of stress," a voice said from behind Miro.

Miro turned and saw a man in a green silk robe standing nearby, watching the Alturan archers at practice. His *raj hada* proclaimed him an enchanter. Not just an enchanter, Miro realized, but a master. He was slim, with dark eyes looking down a sharp hawkish nose.

"I know you." Miro frowned. "You taught my sister."

"I am Elwin Goss," the enchanter said, "Master of the Academy. Yes, I remember your sister, Lord Marshal. How could I forget?"

"It's a pleasure to see you again, Master Goss," Miro said. He wondered what the man's purpose here was.

"You are in a difficult position, Lord Marshal," Master Goss said. "You've been charged with the leadership of our forces, yet High Lord Rorelan manages your supply of essence."

"Do you have a reserve we don't know about?" Miro said, smiling without humor.

"No, but I do have an idea."

"I'll hear it."

"Yes, I've heard you are like your sister . . . Willing to listen to new ideas."

Miro fought to control his impatience. "Please, Master Goss, I have little time."

"I want to borrow one of these bows, along with someone who knows how to use it."

Miro thought of Aglaran, Prayan's son. "Would one of the Dunfolk suit?"

"To start with, yes. Lord Marshal, my idea is based around the fact that the device already does what you want it to do, but your men are having difficulty controlling their aim. What if I and my fellow enchanters could come up with a matrix, a way to help the arrow hit its target every time?"

Miro shook his head. "I've already thought of that, Master Goss. It all comes back to essence. We've barely enough to keep five sets of armorsilk and five zenblades functioning. If every arrow were enchanted, even conservatively, it would require much more essence than we currently have."

"What if we could enchant the bows?"

Miro tilted his head to the side. "What do you mean?"

"We don't need to work on the strength of the weapons, for they already provide the force you need. Your archers simply lack the skill to aim them," Master Goss said. "What if we could find a way, with the absolute minimum amount of essence, to enchant the bows, leaving the arrows as they are?"

"That, Master Goss, would make me a very happy man."

For a time there was silence except for the twanging of bowstrings and the cursing of the soldiers.

"There is a problem, however," Master Goss said.

"Somehow I knew you were going to say that."

"I will need to convince the high enchanter that the project is worth undertaking. It will require a certain amount of essence just to test the idea."

"I see." Miro grinned. "You need to convince High Enchanter Merlon, just as I need to convince High Lord Rorelan."

"Correct."

"I'll get it done," Miro said. "You have my word."

"Don't give me your word," Master Goss said. "Just get me the approval."

Miro stood by the simulator, again redistributing his strength, moving his men, changing their equipment, assessing the potential outcomes of his actions.

Several weeks had passed since they'd received word that the desert warriors of House Hazara had taken the trade town of Torlac, from where they now controlled most of Petrya. This man, Prince Ilathor, had laid siege to Tlaxor, Petrya's capital, and rumors said he controlled even more fighting men than the Tingarans.

Miro already disliked this Ilathor Shanti. This was the man who had sent his warriors to Miro's city—to his home—and taken his sister from him under the guise of friendship. Those weren't the actions of a friend. This new power in the south didn't bode well for the broken lands of the Tingaran Empire.

It was now the end of summer. Miro had spent the season fighting grueling battles, holding Altura with nothing but hope and unflagging strength. With Petrya having her own problems, Miro had pulled his men from the south and added them to his forces in the east, but then something must have happened to resolve the Black Army's shortage of essence. The enemy once more made liberal use of mortars and prismatic orbs, and the numbers of grotesque Imperial avengers deployed against Altura increased week by week.

Rather than breaking out, Miro was bottled up with nowhere to go.

High Lord Rorelan stormed into the chamber containing the simulator, his face black with fury. "What's this?" he demanded, thrusting a piece of paper in Miro's face.

Miro read the hastily scrawled words. It was a message, addressed to Master Goss at the Academy of Enchanters. It said that Rorelan approved the use of essence for the development of a rail bow, an enchanted bow able to guide an arrow like a curtain on a rail. The signature at the bottom was Miro's.

"Oh," Miro said. "That."

"This is too much," Rorelan said. "I said nothing of the sort."

"I can explain," Miro said.

"No, Miro," Rorelan said, "I don't think you can. I've had enough."

"Let me show . . ."

"Miro Torresante, I'm promoting Marshal Beorn to your position."

Miro gaped as Rorelan spoke.

"Get out of my sight, Miro. You've gone too far. Consider yourself dismissed."

———◆———

In a city with nine bridges and a river that flowed through its center, it was inevitable that Miro would eventually be able to corner High Lord Rorelan on one of the arched pathways that spanned the waters of the Sarsen.

Rorelan reached the foot of the Lord's Bridge, the wide, wooden span constructed long ago by one of the first high lords of Altura, and stopped in his tracks when he saw the sword lying naked and shining on the bridge's bottom step. For once his guards weren't with him—just as Miro had planned.

Rorelan looked at the sword with obvious surprise and consternation, finally bending down and picking it up. Its blade was covered with symbols, and the grip fit his hand. It was Rorelan's own sword.

The high lord took a few steps forward, his boots thudding hollowly against the long, wide span rising up in front of him, but it was four more steps before he saw Miro, waiting expectantly for him on the bridge.

Tall and lean, Miro stood in the leather armor and green tabard of Altura's light infantry, having forgone the shiny suppleness of his armorsilk. Rather than a zenblade, he carried a bow in his hands, and on his back was a quiver of arrows. On his tabard was a new *raj hada*—the sword and flower of Altura decorated with a golden feather on either side.

Miro watched as Rorelan halted.

"You've picked up the sword, High Lord, which means you've accepted my challenge," Miro called across the gulf that separated them.

"Are you mad?" Rorelan demanded.

"Yours is the best single-activation sword our enchanters know how to make, would you agree?"

"I suppose so. What is the meaning of this?"

"I'm holding a bow, as you can see. Watching us are some people I've invited to observe this demonstration."

Rorelan looked out from the height of the Lord's Bridge, and saw hundreds of men in the green of Altura and brown of Halaran step forward.

"Don't worry, High Lord," Miro said. "They have orders that at the first sign of blood, they'll halt the duel. Battlefield surgeons are standing by, and Layla is a skilled Dunfolk healer."

"Duel?" Rorelan's eyes boggled. "I am no bladesinger, and I've accepted no duel."

"And I have none of the advantages of a bladesinger," Miro said. "I'm using a bow only for the second time in my life, and the first time was days ago, for minutes only. I'm lightly armored, which is an advantage, but a sword like yours can cut through stone, so it isn't much of one. The arrows I carry use no lore; they are as they appear."

"I'm telling you, I have accepted no duel," Rorelan said.

"True, High Lord," Miro said. "Let us think of it then as a contest. Your weapon"—he gestured to Rorelan's enchanted sword—"against mine. I've seen you in battle, High Lord, and I know you can fight. In fact, with your training you're more skilled than the legionnaires we battle. It's a fair contest, is it not?"

Miro withdrew an arrow from the quiver at his back and nocked it to the string.

Rorelan's eyes blazed, and without warning he spoke some activation sequences.

Miro pulled the arrow to his ear and hoped what he was doing would work. He'd intentionally provoked the high lord to fight him—nothing else would convince the stubborn noble—and now his life could very well be in danger.

Miro had been telling the truth when he'd said this was only the second time he'd used a bow. As he watched the sword light up in Rorelan's hands, he tried to ignore the distraction of the flaring blade and recall the instruction he'd been given.

"Sight along the arrow," Master Goss had said. "But remember it's the bow, not the arrow, we have enchanted, so keep your arms strong but limber. You naturally hold the bow with your left arm and the arrow with your right, so now look at this spot here, just above where your left hand holds the grip. Keep holding the string at full extension—I know it's difficult, but this bow has been made for a man of your strength. See the ringed hole in the wood of the bow, at the nock, where the point of the arrow rests against the wood? Look along the arrow and through that hole. Speak the words to activate the bow. Call the target to you."

As he remembered Master Goss's instructions, Miro's arms burned with the effort of holding the strung arrow at full extension. He sighted along the arrow. It was long and thin, made of dark polished wood, with a razor-sharp steel tip at one end and a flight of emerald-green feathers at the other. The bow itself was fashioned in layers of a lighter-colored wood, with the timeless knowledge of the Dunfolk; strong, yet flexible, creaking with pent-up power. Runes ran up and down the length of the bow, silver symbols that would light up at Miro's command. Next to the nock was a tiny hole, so small Miro could barely see through it.

Standing on the Lord's Bridge, Miro opened his mouth and spoke the words.

The symbols at the center of the bow's length lit up first, glowing with gold and silver, before the fire traveled up and down the bow, spreading away from the center. The hole was suddenly a white ring, and as Miro looked down the length of the arrow, his gaze running to the point, he looked through the hole, almost stunned by what he could see.

Somehow, the rail bow was asking him for a target. Miro's vision swam as his attention was drawn to the window of a building, far across the river, and then to a bird in a tree, farther still. Miro called his sight forward, closer, until he was looking at the wooden surface of the Lord's Bridge. High Lord Rorelan's form came to him in stark detail. Miro could see the flaring of his nostrils and the frown-lines in his forehead, even though he was fifty paces away.

"Come no closer, High Lord," Miro said.

Miro called the target to him, and he released.

The arrow sped away, launching from the bow and flying through the air faster than the eye could see, with nothing but a whistling sound to mark its passage.

The arrow buried itself deep into the Lord's Bridge, only half its length still visible. Rorelan looked down at his foot. The arrow's point had sliced a small nick from his boot, and its shaft was touching his foot.

"Lord of the Sky, you're mad," Rorelan said.

Another arrow landed next to his other foot, and the high lord cried out.

Miro grew more confident. He knew he should end this now. The demonstration was almost complete.

"Enchanted swords have been known to knock prismatic orbs out of the air, High Lord," Miro said. "Perhaps a sword can also take out an arrow?"

Rorelan looked up at him, grim-faced, the pulsing sword gripped tightly in his hands.

In one smooth motion Miro fitted another arrow and pulled on the string. He spoke the activation sequence that would allow him to call forth his target: *"Reilan-sula. Tuva-uran-surnam."*

The arrow smashed into the cross guard of Rorelan's sword, hitting it with all the velocity Miro could give it after having drawn the string as far as he possibly could.

Rorelan yelped and dropped his sword, falling backward onto his hands. He looked up to see Miro advancing toward him, another arrow fitted to the bow, his arms tensed and muscles rippling.

"You're dead, High Lord," Miro said.

Miro lowered the bow and allowed the string to slacken, replacing the arrow in the quiver at his back. He reached out his hand and grinned.

Rorelan waited a moment, his chest rising and falling.

Finally, the high lord gripped Miro's hand, and Miro pulled his friend up.

"That's an interesting way to prove a point," Rorelan said, his face still red. "You're insane, Lord Marshal, do you know that?"

"At least I'm on the right side. The enemy will fear me, High Lord. You have my word on that."

"What if I'd been killed?"

Miro shrugged. "Then I'd be tried for treason, and in a month Altura would fall. Without the rail bows, Altura will fall inside a month anyway."

"Lord Marshal, never, ever do anything like that again."

"Let's get a drink." Miro grinned. "You look like you could use one."

30

Miro gazed down at the tree-lined field, drinking in the sight. Only here, from the height of his last remaining dirigible, could his vision encompass them all: eight hundred archers armed with the new rail bows; four bladesingers, not including Miro; ten thousand Alturan infantry; four thousand Halrana pikemen; a contingent of Dunfolk, perhaps a thousand strong; and a single Halrana colossus, the animator sitting patiently inside the controller cage atop the construct's monstrous head.

Miro had gambled all of their manpower, the last of their essence, and the hopes of two nations on what would happen this day. *Three nations,* he corrected himself, for the Dunfolk had proven themselves to be staunch allies in Altura's hour of need.

The time for the simulator was past. There would never be another opportunity like this. Adding the Dunfolk to Miro's own men, he had nearly two thousand archers. Miro knew that if he hadn't helped the Dunfolk fight the Veznan nightshades in the north, they would never be here today. He also knew that the new rail bows made his own men more than their equals. It was time to show the enemy what they could do.

Miro now looked out from the height of the dirigible at the ruins of the Bridge of Sutanesta.

It had changed since the last time he had been here. The river was still turbulent, the wide, deep waters of the Sarsen surging with fury. Scattered here and there in the river, the tops of the mighty blocks of stone still poked above the water. But across the waters, on the Halrana side, much had changed. The Black Army had built walls of dark stone, interspersed with low forts. Behind the walls jutted the occasional tall lookout tower, silhouetted menacingly against the golden sky of early dawn.

It was a dangerous place to attack, but the risk was worth it. Behind the formidable defenses were the Halrana constructs they'd been forced to leave behind when they last fought the Black Army at the site of this ruined bridge. At the very rear of Miro's army were the Halrana animators, skilled masters of lore, equipped with the last essence the allies would see until the war was over. If Miro could break through the defenses and reanimate the ironmen and woodmen on the Halrana side, it could tip the scales, giving his small army the upper hand in the struggle to free Halaran.

He knew it was a desperate gamble. Miro was in a desperate position. It was a risk he had to take.

"Take me down," Miro told the dirigible pilot.

Soon the dirigible was again hovering above the floor of the field where Miro had assembled his men. He placed a hand on the rail of the dirigible's basket and leapt to the ground, spurning the ladder.

Marshal Beorn waited for him, wincing when Miro landed lightly on the ground beside him. "Well?" Beorn asked.

"It's as we feared. The walls are perhaps taller than we thought; they must have strengthened them since we last scouted. It's a bad day to cross the river, but there are no good days for these waters. How are the landing craft?"

"The boats are ready," Beorn said, scratching at his beard. "As ready as they'll ever be. We won't know if the landing craft can hold up against the river until we go across. I'm still not sure about the colossus. It's a lot to pin our hopes on."

"We've been over this," Miro said, looking across the field at the gigantic construct. The colossus made a nightshade look puny by comparison.

"Let's hope the animator is skilled indeed," Beorn said.

"We don't have another option. A runebomb is out of the question," Miro said. "Too much essence for a single explosion. A colossus will take time to burn through the same amount and is much more versatile. There's also the effect on morale."

"Let's hope you're right," Beorn said. "I still fear for the infantry. Not a man among them has enchanted armor. The enemy's orbs will tear them to shreds."

"Not if my archers do their part."

Beorn didn't reply. He simply tugged on the gray hair of his beard.

"Beorn?"

"Yes, Miro?"

"We've come a long way. Whatever happens, it's been an honor having you by my side."

Marshal Beorn grumbled something under his breath that may have been a similar sentiment.

"Lord Marshal?" One of the four bladesingers came forward. "Where do you want us?"

Miro grinned. "As a bladesinger I always chafed at the restrictions the commanders gave me. Bladesingers need freedom of movement, and sticking to a post isn't our way. You're weapons, and you should fight wherever you feel you are needed most."

"Thank you, Lord Marshal," the bladesinger said.

"A tip, though," Miro said. "The colossus is central to our strategy. See that it makes it through."

"Of course." The bladesingers left, conferring among themselves.

"Are you going to address the men?" Beorn asked.

"Yes. Please form them up."

Miro was interrupted by a slim man in the *raj hada* of an Alturan courier. The courier carried a scroll sealed with green wax and the mark of High Lord Rorelan.

"Lord Marshal," the courier panted, pulling up in front of Miro and Beorn. "The high lord said it was urgent."

Miro swiftly broke the seal and read the contents.

His eyes opened wide as he read, his heart racing in his chest, and a thrill coursed up his spine. Tears formed at the corners of his eyes, tears that Miro didn't attempt to wipe away.

Miro rolled the scroll back up and turned to Marshal Beorn, who stared at him expectantly, waiting to hear the news. "Form the men up," Miro told him. "I'll speak to them now."

It wasn't the first time Miro had addressed an army this size, but it was the first time they hadn't been fighting a rearward action, pulling away from an enemy that could not be beaten.

This time, they were fighting back.

Miro knew how to speak to such a large number of men. He mounted the wooden podium, ascending until he stood at its summit. Taking a great breath, Miro expanded his chest, projecting his voice, throwing it to the back of the field with all of his heart.

"Men! Defenders of the free world, Alturans, Halrana, and Loralayalanasa," Miro said. "You know why you fight here this day, and you know it better than I can explain it to you. You feel it deep in your hearts: It's time to end the tyranny that has taken over the world, to break Altura free from the enemy's clutching fist, and to liberate Halaran from the darkness clouded over that fair land. You know why you fight, and so I won't try to tell it to you."

Miro paused, taking a breath and then resuming. "Instead I am here to answer the question that you are asking but do not know the answer to; to put to rest any last vestiges of doubt; and to give you the courage and faith you will need to take you through this day, and the next, and to carry you forward into the shining light that we can all see awaiting us at the end of these dark times."

Miro waited, feeling his heart thudding in his chest. This wasn't a speech he had rehearsed; he simply spoke from the heart. Miro had fought alongside these men as a recruit and a soldier. They were his men, and he knew their fears, for they were his own.

"Will we prevail? That is what you ask, deep in your souls. You ask the same question now that you asked at Bald Ridge, when High Lord Rorelan and I held against a veteran army thirty thousand strong with less than three thousand. You ask the same question now that you asked when we faced an army infinitely larger than ours, here at the Bridge of Sutanesta. The answer is the same answer I gave you then. *We will prevail!*"

Amid the cheers of the men as they held their swords in the air, Miro thrust the hand holding the scroll high so that all could see.

"And in the dark times that come, if you need heart, think of this. I have in my hand a missive from Rorelan, high lord of Altura. A messenger arrived in the night. This messenger traveled through enemy-held lands, all the way from Ralanast, Halaran's capital, to bring us these words. He was captured but escaped, and when he arrived in Sarostar he was barely alive. Would you like to hear his news?"

"*Yes!*" It was a mighty roar, the sound of over fifteen thousand men shouting with one voice. Miro didn't care now if his enemies across the Sarsen could hear. Let them tremble.

"There was a man who trained me, a man who trained every bladesinger and many of our soldiers. This man was the blademaster, the leader of all the bladesingers, and he fought at the Battle for

Ralanast. You all know what happened there; it was the darkest day of the war.

"This man's name is Rogan Jarvish, and until now we thought he was dead, killed along with so many of our Alturan and Halrana countrymen. This is the news: Rogan Jarvish is alive, and he is in Ralanast. He is building an army there, leading a resistance under the very noses of the legionnaires and templars. There is no man I would trust more to see this thing through, and his message to me is thus. 'We are ready,' he says. Do you hear me, men? *We are ready!*"

Miro drew his zenblade and held it aloft. The roar of the men followed him as he dismounted the podium, reverberating through the trees of the forest.

He turned to Marshal Beorn, surprised to see the grizzled veteran wiping at his eyes. "The old rogue," Beorn said. "I fought beside him at the Battle for Ralanast. I saw him go down, surrounded by a pile of enemy dead. Somehow I knew it wasn't the right end for a man like him."

Miro clapped Beorn on the back. "It is good news, the very best. Now let's go show the Black Army some old tricks, with a few new ones thrown in for good measure."

31

The attack began two hours after dawn.

Miro deployed the landing craft first, carried upside-down on the arms of the men, who puffed and groaned as they ran toward the shore. From his command post atop a rocky knoll, Miro winced as he heard the popping thuds of the enemy's mortars, and a hail of orbs sailed over the river, through the air, and down on his men.

The flat-bottomed boats served a dual purpose here, for the majority of the orbs destined for the men landed instead on the craft. The enchanters had built them as tough as possible with minimal use of essence, and the prismatic orbs exploded against the boats with little damage to the men underneath.

Then Miro's greatest fears were realized when he saw a black cloud rise from behind the towering wall, and at least a dozen dirigibles rose into the air, heading straight for the place where the boats were slipping off the soldiers' shoulders and plunging into the raging river. Even the rail bows would be useless against the enhanced armor of the dirigibles' shells—it was the bows that were enchanted, not the arrows.

Miro's counter was weak at best, and as the enemy's dirigibles reached the middle of the river, Miro's sole remaining airship came into view, high in the sky above their counterparts. The soldiers inside cast out a massive net, weighted at the ends with balls of lead, and Miro looked on as the net plummeted to envelope four of the clustered dirigibles in its web. Tangled, the net and its prey writhed before dropping down and plunging into the river. It was the best Miro could hope for, but it left eight of the black dirigibles ready to rain terror on his unprotected men below.

There were nearly a hundred of the landing craft, each carrying up to thirty men, which meant that for Miro's army to cross, the boats would have to make return trips. If the first wave got into trouble, the boats wouldn't be able to bring reinforcements. The second wave would stay on the wrong bank, and the brave men who first reached the enemy side would be doomed.

As he scanned the sky, fearful of the enemy dirigibles, Miro suddenly noticed how low the Black Army's dirigibles flew. It would improve the accuracy of their fire, and they were still high enough that nothing could touch them. Nothing except . . .

"Send in the colossus," Miro said to Marshal Beorn.

"The plan was to wait," Beorn said.

"Unless you have a better way to take out those dirigibles, pass the order."

Beorn passed the message, frowning as he clenched and then unclenched his fists.

The thunderous shaking of the ground told Miro his orders had been followed. To his right, he saw the top half of the colossus, twice the height of the tall trees around it. Glowing colors bathed the animator in his controller cage atop its head as he moved the massive construct forward. But it was slow—too slow!

All of the landing craft were in the water now, each filled with men wearing nothing but armor of steel and leather, and many with no armor at all. Miro could see the boats being tossed around by the vicious river, but a combination of paddling and poling allowed the boats to advance. The second wave of men massed in orderly ranks on the Alturan bank.

The Black Army's dirigibles swooped low and prismatic orbs fell through the sky. Eruptions of water gushed from the river, and immediately two of the landing boats exploded in flashes of fire, the munitions throwing blood and pieces of soldiers into the air. Another craft tilted too much as a series of orbs detonated in the water around it, and the river rushed in, capsizing the craft and sending the armored men to their deaths as they spilled out.

"Come on," Miro pleaded, "hurry."

The colossus reached the riverbank. So much of their preparation had been for this moment. They had tested the idea on land, in the safety of the Dunwood, but on a wild river, in the heat of battle, was another matter altogether.

Miro knew the animator in the controller cage well. His name was Luca Angelo, and the Halrana said he was the best animator of them all. Luca appeared to be a steady man, calm under pressure, and Miro could only hope those qualities would hold now. If their plans were successful, Miro would honor Luca in whatever way he could. He knew, though, that all the animator wanted was to be reunited with his family in Ralanast.

In their preparations they had scouted and mapped the path to the river in detail. The great stone blocks of the old bridge stood impossibly far apart, too far to lay planks between, and entirely under the water in most cases.

Would they be too far apart for the colossus's great stride?

Another rain of orbs from a dirigible took out two more boats, and Miro could see the situation becoming desperate.

The colossus stepped out into the river, onto the first block they had mapped out. The gigantic form wobbled, and then the second leg came forward and the body swung, until the foot came down somewhere under the water and held.

Miro realized he wasn't breathing and tried to control the racing of his heart and get some air into his lungs.

The colossus took one more step, and then Miro saw a figure in green climbing up the construct, moving quickly from hand to hand as it reached the huge shoulder.

"That's a bladesinger," Beorn said.

The warrior's armorsilk suddenly blazed and the shining zenblade made Miro squint even from his position. The bladesinger leapt up and forward, the zenblade arcing through the air, and his fiery sword smashed into the side of a dirigible, cutting a wide gouge through the airship, before the bladesinger fell down and into the water.

The enemy dirigible spun out of control and turned into another airship close by, before both spiraled down to come crashing into the water. A moment later Miro saw a Halrana soldier help the bladesinger into one of the boats.

The great bulk of the colossus again moved forward, and then the animator struck.

A massive hand swung through the air, swatting down a dirigible like it was a tiresome insect. Another swing and one more dirigible went down. The gigantic construct's footing was precarious, and Miro saw it wobble more than once, but Luca Angelo held, and in a moment the sky was cleared of the enemy.

"It worked!" Beorn turned, grinning at Miro.

The first of the landing craft reached the opposite bank. The soldiers jumped out and lifted their boat out of the water, turning it on its side. Orbs rained down on them, deflected by the bottom of the boat, but they waited. Soon a dozen more craft had emptied their loads of soldiers. Within a few mere moments, more than twenty side-on boats formed a protective barrier at the water's edge.

More swordsmen and pikemen disembarked from the remaining boats, joining their fellows rather than turning the boats up. Their landing craft immediately began to return to the Alturan side and fetch the second wave.

The bridgehead had been formed.

The second stage of the plan now went into effect. Miro's sub-commanders deployed the archers.

They filled the gaps between the boats that made up the defensive formation. As orbs rained down on the bridgehead, arrows flew out, targeted shots to take out the mortar teams and any of the enemy foolish enough to show themselves. The frequency of the explosions began to diminish.

Another landing discharged some of the Dunfolk, who added the volleys of their fire to the targeted shots of the rail bows.

"Shine the blue light," Miro said. "It's time."

The order was passed, a signaling flag unfurled nearby, and Miro's sole dirigible shone a fiery blue light. With the bridgehead becoming crowded as more and more boats emptied, the colossus again lumbered forward.

"Please," Miro prayed, "don't slip now."

The colossus reached the bank, Miro and Beorn both breathing a sigh of relief when it finally stood tall and unharmed on the solid earth to the side of the bridgehead.

The enemy now knew where to concentrate their fire.

"What's that?" Beorn said, squinting. "It's like a blur of motion."

Miro smiled. "I think I know."

As the colossus climbed the bank, heading for the dark wall, the Black Army's fire targeted it to the exclusion of all else. But each orb hit a whirling storm of green and silver, with electric flashes of shining blue and ruby red.

Miro didn't know how many of the bladesingers rode along with the colossus, but he knew this indomitable construct would strike terror into his enemy's hearts. As an orb flew at the colossus, it hit the flash of a zenblade, which sliced it so swiftly and neatly that the device couldn't detect the contact and explode.

This was it—the moment Miro had planned and hoped for, but the one thing he could never be certain of: If the primate or one of his commanders had sent the builders of Torakon to reinforce this wall with lore, they would fail.

Miro watched as four men in green jumped down from the colossus, leaping and dodging the explosions.

Miro could almost hear Luca Angelo chanting as he activated the runes, could almost see his deft fingers touching the controller tablet at his knees. The colossus's great fists swung down, both of them with the full strength of the animators' arts behind them.

The top half of the wall smashed into pieces as the construct's huge hands collided with the stone. The arms came up, and then fell down again, as Luca kept on, oblivious to the explosions around him. The colossus kicked with one of its legs, and the wall was breached.

"Red light!" Miro cried. "Full attack!"

High above, the Alturan dirigible flashed a bright red light. With the archers providing covering fire, the soldiers at the bridgehead rushed forward in an unstoppable wave. The first through the breach were the bladesingers, followed by the colossus itself, and then there was a torrent of men pouring through.

Landing craft still crossed the river, but now the warriors who disembarked ran straight up the riverbank, shouting and cheering, swords held in the air as they joined their fellows.

Miro closed his eyes and then let out a slow, deep breath.

"Lord Marshal," Beorn asked, "are you coming?" He grinned, his hand on the hilt of his sword.

"I know a faster way," Miro said. He waved his arms, and the dirigible slowly descended. A ladder dropped down from the vessel.

"No, thank you," Beorn said. "I don't have a head for heights. I'll chance the river."

"I'll see you there," Miro said. "Bring the Halrana animators over with you."

Soon the dirigible took Miro up and over the splashing river. As he crossed he saw his men swiftly gain the advantage, and the green and brown flag of the allied army soon flew from one, then another of the squat towers. Miro was careful to display the Alturan *raj hada* on the dirigible for all to see, wary of being mistaken for an enemy.

When he was across, Miro jumped down from the dirigible and sent it back out of danger.

Officers looked to him for orders. Miro's first concern was for defenses. "Secure the towers on both sides as long as you are in view of the bridgehead, then pin the rest down with archers. Have the colossus smash up the walls and get the men to move the blocks to form a wall on four sides. Let me know the instant the Halrana animators arrive from the Alturan side. The *instant*, you understand? Tell Marshal Scola to continue the advance and encirclement. I want the river cleared in both directions. When Marshal Beorn arrives, he's in charge of the defenses."

"Yes, Lord Marshal," the officers said as he issued the orders.

"The animators are here." A soldier ran forward, six men in brown robes trailing behind him.

"Thank you, soldier," Miro said. "Please get me fifty men to form a patrol."

"Yes, Lord Marshal."

Miro regarded the approaching animators.

"You know what you're here for," Miro said.

"We do," said one of the animators, a Halrana with tapered moustaches. "I can hardly breathe. Do you think there are many still functional?"

"Calm down," Miro said. "You're in the middle of a battle."

A man in the *raj hada* of an Alturan captain came forward. "You requested a detachment, Lord Marshal?"

"Yes, Captain. We're going to find those constructs."

Amid the chaos Miro heard someone calling his name.

He turned and saw Marshal Beorn. "What is it?"

"The dirigible pilot signaled an enemy force forming in the east. They must be from the enemy's main encampment. It's a counterattack."

Miro nodded. "I understand . . . Marshal Beorn, our defenses are in your hands." Miro turned to the Alturan captain and the Halrana animators. "Come on," he said. "We don't have much time."

—————◆—————

The Halrana animators found some of the constructs almost immediately, in a field where only the ditches and gullies that were too straight for nature told that a battle had ever taken place.

Miro felt his hope fade as he looked at the huge mound of charred limbs, indicating where the enemy had gathered and burned a pile of woodmen. Of course the enemy wouldn't be foolish enough to leave them lying around.

After finding a second cluster of woodmen that had also been deliberately splintered and thrown into a pile, Miro turned to the moustached Halrana animator, expecting to see the man in tears. Instead the man in brown robes looked at the small tablet he held in his hands, where some symbols flashed and faded.

"Ironmen," the animator said. "They're close." He began to search the area.

"Stop," the Alturan captain said, waving his men back. The animator halted in his tracks. The captain walked forward, prodding the ground in front of the brown-robed Halrana with his sword.

Where the animator was about to step, the ground fell away under the captain's probing, to reveal a deep ditch lined with spikes. The animator turned, white-faced, to the Alturan captain.

"It's treacherous around here," the captain said. "Fan out!" he called to his men. "Look for ditches and traps. The animators need to search this area, and they need to do it fast. Look out for your skins, but mark out the safe ground."

The fifty men dispersed, probing at the ground with their swords and calling out when they found a trap. As Miro cursed the delay, the Halrana animators conferred among themselves, gesturing to the flashing symbols on their controller tablets.

Miro wondered how long he had before the enemy reached this area and forced them to pull back to Marshal Beorn's defenses. Miro had counted on the support of the constructs left behind last winter, and now realized how precarious the situation was.

"I'm going to see how far away the counterattack is, how much time we have," Miro told the captain.

"You can't go out there," the captain began. "Let me send . . ."

Miro spoke some words, and his armorsilk blazed as he activated its protection. "I'm the best equipped to find out," Miro said. "I'll be back."

Miro chanted as he ran, calling forth the multitude of sequences that would protect him in the event of a fall. Would the armorsilk be powerful enough to save his skin if he fell into a spiked trap? He hoped he wouldn't have to find out.

Miro opened his stride, running with long steps, barely touching the ground with his toes, expecting at any instant to plummet down into the earth. He thanked the Lord of the Sky as he reached higher ground where there would be no traps, climbing a hill where he had a vantage over the area.

The Black Army scout and Miro saw each other at the same time. Miro reached over his shoulder for the hilt of his zenblade, but seeing the green of his armorsilk, the scout turned and ran. The black-clad scout was nearly a hundred paces away, and Miro would never catch him.

Miro instead reached for the rail bow he wore over his other shoulder.

He nocked an arrow to the string and pulled it back to his ear, once again picturing Master Goss telling him how to call forth the target, bringing it into focus. Miro released the arrow, and it sped through the air, suddenly sprouting from the middle of the scout's back. Without a word, the scout keeled over, the man in black appearing close through the sight of the bow, yet incredibly distant when Miro looked on with unaided eyes.

Where there was a scout, an army would follow.

The Black Army's reinforcements were near.

Miro put his hand above his eyes, gazing at the distant hills. "Hurry," he muttered, thinking about the Halrana animators. He didn't even know if they'd found any salvageable constructs.

Concentrating on the far-off ridges, Miro almost didn't see them appear, rising up over the closest hill like a black tide.

Hordes of warriors came toward him: Imperial Legionnaires, screaming with bloodlust and waving their swords over their shaved heads; templars, their white tabards crusted with dirt and grime; and most numerous of all, a motley collection of swordsmen, axemen, and pikemen gathered from the farthest reaches of the Tingaran Empire.

Miro turned and ran, oblivious to the danger as he once again dashed over the treacherous field littered with traps and trenches from the battle once fought here. He kept his head down, his strides eating up the earth as he prayed he would be in time to warn the Halrana animators. The constructs would have to wait. Miro had brought these men here, and he was responsible for getting them out alive.

Suddenly, he stopped short.

In front of him stood a glowing man of metal, symbols flickering red over the construct's black skin. Miro looked around and saw at least forty of them in a file, all activated.

The ironmen were alive.

"They're coming," Miro gasped. "The Black Army."

The ironmen advanced, and Miro saw more rows of them behind. Miro looked around for someone—anyone—finally spotting the figure of a man in green, seen in a flash between the marching rows of constructs.

The Alturan captain unclenched his fists, looking inordinately relieved when he saw Miro. "Lord Marshal, I was worried . . ."

"They're coming," Miro said. "The enemy are right behind me. How . . . ?"

"They found a bunch in a cart that the enemy threw into a hole and buried."

"How did they get them out?" Miro asked.

"The animators had them dig themselves out. Not much stops these things."

The moustached animator hurried up to Miro as the ironmen continued their advance, passing Miro in an unbroken line.

"I'm needed to help control the ironmen, Lord Marshal, but I thought you could use a briefing. The enemy destroyed the wood-men, but the ironmen proved too difficult and were buried. Most are buried askew, in piles, but some, like these, were still filed up in their carts, and we managed to renew them."

"What about the others?" Miro asked.

"They'll take days to extract, reassemble, and renew," the ani-mator replied.

"How many do we have now?"

"We now have two hundred ironmen, fully activated and combat ready. But buried in the ground is perhaps three times that number."

Miro made a snap decision. "Captain? Send a message to Marshal Beorn. Tell him to send reinforcements, every man he can spare. Quickly!"

The captain dispatched a messenger and then glanced at Miro. "Are we holding here?"

Miro nodded. "We're certainly going to try."

———•———

One bladesinger, fifty Alturan soldiers, and two hundred ironmen held against the Black Army's counterattack of thousands for nearly an hour before Marshal Beorn arrived with reinforcements.

In the end, they held the field, and the Black Army fled to nurse its wounds. Of the fifty Alturan swordsmen, only twelve lived. The Alturan captain numbered among the dead, and as Miro looked at the brave man's body, he realized he'd never even known the captain's name.

Throughout the night, Marshal Scola harried the enemy, maintaining the initiative while Miro and Beorn consolidated their defenses. With every hour that passed, the animators unearthed more constructs, but the moment of greatest triumph came when, cheering wildly, they salvaged two massive colossi. Miro instructed the animators to keep going, rescuing as many as they could until the essence ran out.

As the next day dawned, Miro realized there had been no more counterattacks. He'd held Halrana soil for a full day. At midday the animators told him there would be no more constructs to add to their numbers.

Miro ordered the army to decamp and advance further into Halaran, and the Black Army fled in front of them.

Now Miro had the initiative.

He didn't plan to lose it.

32

Summer was over, but it was two weeks more before Ella told the prince that the time was right.

Ella and Shani had spent long hours planning while the desert warriors fought among themselves, spoiling to fight. The prince eventually took a personal hand at keeping his men in line—publicly trying eight men for insurgency and another three for their poor treatment of Petryans. All eleven men were executed by beheading. Shani told Ella she was finally beginning to believe the prince would keep his word and treat her people well.

Prince Ilathor met with the leaders of the other tarns and gave them his promise that they would be fighting when the season turned. Whenever she looked at the maps on the wall of the chamber at the top of the tower, Ella could feel the prince's eyes on her. She caught him smiling when he looked at her and couldn't help herself from smiling in return. She hadn't kissed him again, and he hadn't pushed her, but part of her wanted him to try.

The prince organized contests, something very familiar to the Petryans, who were happy to look on and supply rules and advice. The locals refrained from joining in the horse races and sword fighting, but they were glad to participate in the wrestling, running, and jumping. The games gave the desert warriors some focus, and the Petryans began to smile again. Ella's respect for Ilathor grew.

There wasn't a soul in Torlac who didn't wonder about Tlaxor. The tiered city had been under siege for months now, with no fresh food crossing the lake. The prince was obviously cognizant of the iron grip the Petryan high lord had over his people, and made his plans accordingly, but still, how could Haptut Alwar not relent?

Then, one day Shani knocked at the door to Ella's chamber. The Petryan elementalist was red-eyed and stone-faced. Ella had never seen her friend so upset. "What is it?" Ella asked, putting her notebook to the side and standing up.

Shani held out her hands, indicating she didn't want Ella to come any closer. "Bodies," Shani said. "Thousands upon thousands of them. A patrol finally found where they've all been washing up. This siege is taking its toll after all."

"I'm so sorry," Ella said.

"I made them take me to see. Most of them were starved and probably died of hunger, but not all. Some were tortured."

"It's how the high lord keeps control," Ella said. "I wish it weren't so."

"If we left, supplies would reach the city, and lives would be saved. Yet things would not change. Petrya would not be free."

"I often have the same thought," Ella said. "The best thing we can do is end it quickly. It won't be long now, I promise. They won't be expecting what we plan."

Shani nodded and left the room. That night, Ella prayed as hard as she ever had to the Lord of the Sky for the season to change. She desperately needed cooler weather.

Meanwhile, Ella worked on the most important part of her and Shani's plan. In the coolest cellars, deep beneath the barracks where the prince had made his command center, Ella had the prince's men construct huge water tanks. She kept them building night and day, and as they finished one tank, she made them start on another. Ella put some more men to work filling the tanks with water, and some others lugging sacks back and forth, adding salt to the water.

Ella kept them at it, haranguing the fearsome desert warriors and Petryan laborers until they kept their heads down and did as she said. Soon, every dark space held a tank, and every tank was filled to the brim with incredibly salty water. Ella thanked the perplexed men who had helped her and dismissed them.

Ella then retired to her chambers and spent day after day enchanting rope. Her fingers became blistered from holding a scrill, and the gloves on her hands became so familiar she often forgot to take them off. Steadily, the essence Prince Ilathor gave her was depleted, until she'd used almost half of it, and she had filled an entire grain silo with rope. Ella connected the separate ropes into one long line, and finally she split one end of the line into multiple strands.

Lastly, she enchanted staves of polished wood, long and sharpened like spears at one end. On each stave she left the sharpened half untouched, but the other end she covered in tiny runes, complex matrices she created herself, unlike anything she had ever done before. One stave was much larger than the rest, a huge pole that took six men to lift. When Ella finished the deft rune-making on its thick shaft, all of the essence Prince Ilathor had given her was gone.

She was ready.

A day later, Ella and Shani stood on the shore of Lake Halapusa, looking out at the tiered city perched precariously on its island, when the heat of summer finally broke.

A cold wind blew from the north, howling down from the mighty range of the Elmas separating Petrya from Altura and Halaran. Clouds gathered above, and the sky grew mottled with gray and black. Ella smelled moisture in the air, and looking at her friend, noted the way the gusts tore at Shani's rust-colored robe.

The two women stood fast as thunder rumbled from all directions at once. Sheets of lightning crackled across the storm clouds, and it was suddenly as dark as night.

The sky roared again, the heavens opened, and rain came down.

Moments before, Ella and Shani had been hot, sweltering in the Petryan summer. Now the chill air from the north and the cool rainwater washed over them, soaking them to the skin.

Ahead of them, the raindrops fell into the lake with little plops and splashes, sending a sound like the shaking of a crystal tree tinkling in the air. The Petryans under siege in Tlaxor would have fresh water this day, for which Ella was thankful.

It was time to return to Torlac.

"Wait? Please, Ella, I cannot wait further. You said you needed the weather to change. It has changed," Prince Ilathor said.

"We must wait for the rain to stop," Ella said.

"How long?"

"I can't say," Ella said. "When the rain stops, the city will be yours. That's the best I can give you."

The prince sighed, rubbing at his forehead. Controlling the men under his command was taking its toll.

"You'd better go," Jehral said.

Ella touched the prince's shoulder and turned, leaving Ilathor staring out the window at the Petryan capital below.

As she reached the bottom of the stairs, Ella cocked her head.

Silence.

She left the barracks completely—the guards were accustomed to her presence by now—and looked up at the sky.

The clouds had parted, and the weather was still cool.
The rain had stopped.

———◆———

With Shani's help—Ella would never have understood the thermal
equations without the elementalist—Ella built her great magic at a
hundred points around Lake Halapusa.

Their loose clothing fluttering under a brisk breeze, a detachment of twelve horsemen kept a wary eye out for the enemy as Ella
reached the first point. Shani was working in the opposite direction,
and the two women would meet at the opposite side of the lake, a
place they had chosen to be the section of lake closest to the trade
town of Torlac.

Taking a deep breath, Ella halted her horse and dismounted at
the place she and Shani had previously marked. She walked down
to the lakeside until she stood beside the shallows, wary of touching
even the smallest amount of the scalding water. Careful not to splash
herself, Ella lifted her arms and plunged the first of her fifty sharpened staves into the water. A warrior tried to come forward to help
as Ella then lifted a heavy hammer, but she waved him back. Ella
smashed down on top of the stave until she was sure it was secure.

Ella spoke the activation sequence. *"Simela-atun. Sunala-arun.
Mulan-turapela."*

The runes she had inscribed on the top half of the stave lit up
with power, each shining bright and blue. Satisfied, Ella hefted her
hammer and remounted her horse. Forty-nine to go.

When she was sinking the forty-fifth stave, Ella looked back
along the shore the way she had come. Her breath caught. She
could see a plume of gray steam rising into the air, tapering down
to a point where the previous stave must be. Looking further still,
along the shoreline, Ella could see more plumes, many of them.

It was working.

Deciding it was worth the risk, Ella crouched down beside the lake and dipped her finger into the water of Lake Halapusa.

"Lord of Fire, what are you doing?" one of the desert warriors called out, leaping down from his horse and running toward her.

Ella smiled and stood. Her finger smarted from where it had been scalded by the water. Yet it was just a minor burn.

"I'm fine," Ella said.

Ella continued her task, sinking the last five staves, and then Shani was in front of her, watching as Ella sank the fiftieth stave into the lake. As Ella finished activating the complex lore she had imbued the stave with, she looked up and saw Shani grinning.

"You need to work on the muscles in your arms," Shani said, pointing at the bicep of her own right arm. "You're struggling there."

"Perhaps you can do the big one then," Ella said with a wry grin.

Ella's escort merged with Shani's, and they rode along the lake until they came to the place at the lakeside where Torlac was at its closest, a small speck in the cleft of the crater high above.

Jehral and the prince stood holding the reins of their horses, with perhaps sixty desert warriors ranged behind them.

Shani looked up at Prince Ilathor. "Why so few?" she demanded.

Ella grabbed Shani's upper arm. "Look." She pointed.

"What?"

"The fissure in the crater's edge, in front of where Torlac is— see? It's much smaller than usual."

"I don't understand."

"The Hazarans have built an illusion around the cleft. Lord of the Sky, it's massive. I can't believe how many men must be hidden there."

"Every man I could spare," the prince said. "We will take the city quickly, so that the high lord's men have little chance to react.

My men have instructions to be swift and to concentrate on those who lead the defenses. The common people will be as safe from harm as I can make them without endangering my own men."

Ella looked up at Prince Ilathor. "Thank you," she said. "Good luck today. Fight well."

He nodded, his dark eyes sending a familiar thrill through her. "Good luck to you also, Enchantress Ella. All of our hopes are with you."

"It's time," Ella said. "Bring it down!"

Ella turned back to the volcanic lake. In all directions she could see plumes rising from the hundred staves. She wondered what High Lord Haptut Alwar would make of them. She doubted he would expect what was to come.

Six men carried the huge, rune-covered stave down to the lake's edge. They hesitated as they reached the water—the pole was unwieldy, and none of them had any desire to see the flesh boiled from their ankles.

"It's fine," Ella said. They still looked fearful, so she stepped forward. "Watch."

Ella walked down to the water's edge, and, without dwelling too long on what she was about to do, she stepped into the water. Ella took two steps more, until the water of Lake Halapusa was up to her calves.

She turned around to face the stunned men carrying the stave. "It won't harm you," she said. "I need you to drive it in hard, out there, where the water is deep."

Ella felt a thrill to see the lore was working. Steam no longer rose from the lake itself. The water was actually cold, and felt like it was growing colder all the time.

The six men waded into the water until it came up to their waists. With a heave and a splash, they lifted the metal-bound shaft and drove it deep into the bed of the lake until only half of its length poked above the water. Two men each hefted a sledgehammer, pounding at the top of the stave until Ella was satisfied.

Ella returned to Prince Ilathor. "Are you ready?" she asked.

"We're ready," he said.

On the path down from Torlac stretched the length of cord that she herself had made. Shani handed Ella the end, and Ella's eyes followed it up the path until she could no longer see it.

Ella pictured the other end of the cord. The end she carried was like the rest, a single woven piece; but high above, in Torlac, the line split into several strands. Each strand rested in a tank of cold, salted water.

Ella hoped the prince had remembered to evacuate the barracks.

With all eyes on her, Ella waded into the lake until she was beside the thick stave. She ran her eyes over the wood, decorated with as many tiny symbols as her enchantress's dress. Ella threaded the cord through a hoop on the side of the pole and tied the end.

"We should get back now," Ella said, returning to the shore. "Everyone, stand back!" she cried. She hardly needed to; the desert warriors stood nervously beside their horses, far from the lake's edge. Even Shani took a few steps back, leaving only Ella next to the lake.

Ella lifted her arms, taking in a deep breath. Her voice came strong and certain as she chanted with a steady rhythm, activating the capabilities of the cord and then calling forth the powerful conductive magic she had imbued the stave with.

The top of the shaft lit up, white and pure as the snow. The light traveled from the shaft to the cord and then continued along its length, moving along the line with the speed of a bird in flight.

All eyes followed the light as it traveled up the slope, heading directly for the town of Torlac. In an instant the whole line glowed piercingly white, and Ella closed her eyes, praying the lore would work.

She again caught the eyes of Prince Ilathor. He regarded her with hope in his eyes.

Please let it work, she prayed silently.

———◆———

In the tower where Prince Ilathor Shanti had made his headquarters, high above the streets of Torlac, a Petryan named Leptar stole into the prince's chamber.

He knew about the warning to stay clear of the barracks. It made his task that much easier. Leptar had received a message from High Lord Haptut Alwar. His ruler wanted to know what this lore was that the Hazarans were preparing.

Leptar hardly needed to be quiet; the barracks were completely deserted. Discarding all caution, he began to rummage through the papers on the prince's desk, searching for some clue to what the man was planning. Giving up, he moved to the maps on the wall, but the squiggles meant nothing to him. He could see the borders and rivers, the great lake and the mountains to the north, but what were those other lines? Were they plans of attack? There were many lines plotting a course leading from Petrya to Tingara, through the Gap of Garl, but what would the high lord care about that?

Then Leptar heard a great thudding boom followed by a strange hiss. He wondered what it was, and then it came to him.

The great magic—it was here. It was the reason the prince didn't want anyone going near the barracks. He'd warned everyone else away, and now he was secreted away with his loremasters, building some powerful weapon.

Leptar knew it was risky, but he was brave, and loyal to the high lord, who had promised him riches and a harem of young concubines. He decided to follow the sounds and see if he could get a look.

Leptar descended the steps from the tower, being a little more cautious now that he realized the creators of lore were somewhere in the barracks. Another hiss came from deep below, guiding his footsteps, and soon Leptar was on the ground level.

They must be in the cellars.

The air grew warm as Leptar descended. He turned a corner and saw a strange glowing cord enter a room at one end and plummet down some stairs at the other. Congratulating himself on his intuition, which had never served him wrong, he followed the cord down the stairs and into the cellars.

Leptar reached the foot of the stairs and saw that the pulsing cord vanished under a heavy wooden door. He suddenly felt he should leave. There were those with powers he didn't understand on the other side of this door. Yet what could he say to the high lord if he didn't open the door?

Leptar drew the heavy bone-handled knife he wore at his side. There were no guards, and the men inside wouldn't be expecting him.

With a mighty pull, Leptar hauled the door open.

A loud bubbling and hissing assaulted his senses, and clouds of hot steam rolled at him, so that for a moment he couldn't see.

The glowing line broke into strands, each strand running into a tank. As Leptar looked on, his mouth agape, the sides of the tank closest to him began to glow.

About the same time Leptar realized it wasn't the glow of runes, but the glow of heat, the tank melted from the intense temperature as the salted water vaporized to steam, and the superheated steam reached higher and higher pressures in the sealed tank.

Leptar opened his mouth to scream, but there was a series of explosions, and flying slag splattered into his face and chest.

He didn't make a sound.

33

Ella chanted constantly as she stood just beside Lake Halapusa and transferred the lake's heat into the tanks under the barracks in Torlac.

This lore was far too powerful for a single activation sequence, and her lips moved continually as she called the names of the runes, reading the colors of the symbols on the thick shaft sunk into the lake, noting which were brightest and which grew dim.

Cracks appeared under the surface of the lake, and Ella heard murmurs behind her—cries of wonder.

Deciding it was time, Ella called forth the final activation. *"Luktar-loklur!"*

With a mighty crack like thunder, Lake Halapusa froze as the water turned solid.

Ella's arms flopped back to her sides, and she turned back to where Jehral and Prince Ilathor sat astride their horses watching her. Shani stood nearby. Ella smiled—a weary smile of triumph.

"I should never have doubted you," the prince breathed, awe-struck. "Both of you," he said, turning to Shani.

"How long will it last?" Jehral asked.

"The heat has been sunk into salted tanks of water underneath the barracks in Torlac," Ella said. "The salt allows the water to hold much more heat. If our calculations are correct, they should hold enough heat for the lake to stay frozen for at least a day."

"And if they are not?" Jehral said. "Sorry, Ella, but I have to ask."

"Then, man of the desert," Shani said, "you'll be swimming in boiling water before the day is out."

"My Prince," Jehral said, suddenly urgent, "the Petryans will know what we have done. It is time."

The tall leader of the Hazarans shook himself as if out of a trance. His horse turned as he wheeled it around. The prince signaled to his men, and they galloped up the slope toward where the Hazaran warriors lay in hiding, calling out to initiate the attack.

Ella turned to Shani. "Where should we watch from?" she asked.

"Watch?" Shani said. "I don't plan to watch."

Ella then noticed the Petryan held reins in her hands. Beside Shani's horse was Ella's own horse, Afiri.

"It will be dangerous," Ella said.

"Life is dangerous."

The two women mounted up. Ella felt her heart race as she looked back over her shoulder toward the cleft in the crater's rim. A great dust storm rose out of the red earth, rushing forward in a way Ella knew wasn't natural, a cloud of sand and wind where the flashes of steel and horses could be seen among swirls of air given form.

In an instant, the two women, one in green and one in red, were swept away with the horde of riders.

Thousands of Hazarans leapt from the lakeshore onto the ice. Ella held her breath, but it held, and Afiri also ran onto the blue ice. The first wave of horses slipped and scrabbled, but the going was made easier as their hooves chewed up the ice, finally digging into the slippery surface.

The riders raced across the surface of the frozen lake. The dust storm covered their approach, yet from inside the illusion Ella could perfectly see the tiered city grow in size as the horde of riders approached.

Ella reached down to the hilt she'd attached to her saddle. Her fingers closed around the curved dagger Jehral had given her. She had since enchanted it, and as she withdrew the blade and activated it, the heavy knife instantly felt as light as one of Ella's scrills.

Ella looked behind her, back at the shore of the lake where the sunken pillar stood bright and tall, surprised at how far they'd already come.

Was that a figure in green, a man, running down the slope toward the lakeshore? Before Ella could look more closely, her attention again returned to her horse as Afiri slipped on the ice before regaining his footing.

She held the knife in one hand, and with her other hand Ella held her reins against the pommel of the saddle. She gave Afiri his head. She couldn't have stopped him if she'd wanted to, and then suddenly there were balls of fire flying through the air around her.

They were mostly untargeted, wild shots thrown from the terraces and walls of Tlaxor. Ella was thankful for the illusionary storm surrounding them—the Hazarans had no method of striking from a distance. Yet the illusion gave them no actual protection, and blasts caught many of the Hazarans, warriors screaming and falling off their horses as red energy smashed into their faces and torsos in clouds of sparks. Ella cried out when a flaming ball struck the horse of a warrior riding next to her. She smelled burning hair and heard the sound of sizzling flesh as both horse and rider erupted in a gush of fire.

They reached the main gate, set into sloping walls with no protection for the struggling Hazarans. The storm was of little value here, for the high lord's elementalists could hurl fire at the foot of the gate and were bound to strike someone. Some valiant warriors left their horses and, with knives between their teeth, began to scale the slanted walls. Most exploded in screaming flame, but a few made it to the top, giving the men below a few moments' respite from the relentless fire.

Ella saw Shani holding a great fireball between her wrists, the biggest Ella had ever seen. Sweat dripped down the elementalist's forehead, and if she hadn't been wearing her protective robe, Ella knew her friend would have been scorched.

With a shout Shani launched the ball at the gate. Twisting and turning through the air, it made a sound like tearing paper as it flew at the center of the dark wood.

Ella could see builders' runes on the gate and knew what would happen next. The huge ball of flame fell apart in a flurry of sparks. The gate was scorched, but it held.

The Hazarans crowded up against the gate, and soon it would be a massacre as the packed warriors proved themselves easy targets for the high lord's elementalists. Realizing the danger, the horsemen peeled to either side, some heading to the left and others to the right as they encircled the tiered city.

Ella saw Prince Ilathor ride forward and dismount from his horse as he drew the huge scimitar he wore at his side. Ella watched openmouthed as he called a series of runes, the scimitar blazing with blue fire. Reading the colors, Ella knew only Alturan enchanters could have made such a sword, but it was a scimitar, a style of blade that was definitely not Alturan. She wondered how old it was and how long it had been in Ilathor's family. She wondered if the prince even knew.

Ella could predict what was coming. The prince took the scimitar in two hands and swung at the gate. The sword that could cut through stone smashed against the gate that had been reinforced with the lore of House Torakon's builders.

Prince Ilathor's sword bounced off the gate with a fountain of sparks as the enchanted blade met the strength of builders' runes, and the gate won.

With no siege weapons—no battering rams or mortars, scaling ladders or catapults—Ella realized the Hazarans still had much to learn about warfare. The prince needed her help.

"Prince Ilathor," Ella called.

He looked back at Ella as she leapt off her horse's back.

"When the gate opens, hit it with everything," Ella said as she reached him.

The prince dodged a fireball. "What are you going to do?"

"Whatever I can," Ella said.

Ella pulled the hood of her dress over her head and started to chant. In an instant she could see from the prince's stunned expression that she'd activated the shadow effect and in the chaos of battle could no longer be seen.

Before fear could take hold, Ella ran to a place where the sloped wall was free of climbing desert warriors and plunged her glowing dagger into the stone. Sparks and pieces of stone flew out, bouncing off the material of her dress.

Ella cut a wide gouge in the stone of the wall and placed her foot into the cut, hoisting her body up. She cut another hole in the stone, resting her other foot in the second hole. Two more holes gave her hands something to hook onto, and Ella hoisted herself up, one limb at a time.

It was painstaking work and would never have been possible without the slope of the wall, but gradually Ella climbed, never looking down, cutting hole after hole in the stone until soon she was halfway up the wall.

Ella looked up, just in time to see a fireball screaming at her head. She tucked herself into her dress and prayed that the enchanter's arts would beat the lore of another house.

The heat washed over her, and Ella knew that she would be illuminated as the fire covered her shadowed form, outlining it like a tree hit by lightning.

Looking up, Ella saw an elementalist prepare another fireball, but the man was forced to duck when a huge ball of flame came from below, bathing the wall in its glow, giving her the time she needed.

Ella knew how hard it must have been for Shani to send that fireball at her countryman. She knew she couldn't afford to miss the chance.

Ella climbed the wall at a furious speed, cutting the holes just in time to enter her foot or hand, and then already gouging the next as she moved up.

Then she was at the top. Looking down, Ella saw the prince's men under heavy fire; they wouldn't hold much longer. In front of her a parapet lined the top of the wall, and below, inside the gate, Ella could see ranks of Petryan soldiers awaiting any breach by the Hazarans.

Climbing onto the parapet, Ella saw the gate's opening mechanism, a little to the side of the gate. She breathed a sigh of relief—she'd been hoping it wasn't manually operated. The runes would be coded, but Ella was confident she could break the obfuscation and find the activation sequence.

"Your path made it easy to climb," a voice said behind her, "but how do you plan to get down?"

Ella turned, and the prince was standing beside her on the parapet, the glowing scimitar in his hands and the wind in his hair.

Fireballs flew at them from several directions. Petryan soldiers on the parapet ran toward them, swords bared and cries of battle rage on their lips.

Prince Ilathor blocked a fireball with his sword, speaking words that caused a white shimmer to solidify the air around his scimitar and shield them both. Ella put her body between another fireball and the prince, once again feeling the heat wash over her. They needed to get down from the wall.

"Stairs," Prince Ilathor pointed.

"I need to get to the gate's mechanism," Ella said. "Protect my back."

Ella and the prince dashed down the steps from the parapet. Ella chanted under her breath to enhance the protection of her dress, but was fearful for the prince in nothing but ordinary clothing. She threw a handful of flashbombs into the ranks of the soldiers, pandemonium following in their wake as flashes of light blinded the Petryans. Ella and Ilathor rushed to the gate, and Ella started to decipher the runes on the mechanism while Ilathor stood at her back, sword extended, ready to face thousands of Petryan soldiers on his own when they restored order.

"Quickly," the prince said.

"I'm going as fast as I can!" Ella cried. "Aren't you a bit busy to be harassing me?"

The Petryan soldiers at the back pushed past those disabled by the flashbombs, and the swordsmen in red rushed forward to take down this foolish solitary man.

Prince Ilathor's scimitar whirled, flashing through the Petryan soldiers as he cut first one way and then another. In a moment he would be overrun, and Ella would be cut down from behind. There were simply too many of them.

"I've got it!" Ella shouted.

She spoke the words, and the gate's mechanism lit up as Ella decoded the symbols, seeing through those that had been placed there simply to hide the activation sequence.

The gate opened quickly, and Jehral, Shani, and thousands of yelling horsemen rode past Ella to support the prince against the Petryan soldiers.

The Petryans weren't used to fighting men on horseback, and one by one they began to bolt. The heavy sabers of the Hazarans bit down into the soldiers, blood spurting up into the air in their wake.

The whirling storm of illusion now twisted around the forms of the horses, making the warriors appear otherworldly, some terrible vengeance sent down from heaven.

Shani halted, her horse rearing up into the air. "Ella! Will you come with me?"

"Where?"

Shani pointed up into the air. "The Poltoi Palace. We need to find the high lord before he tries to escape. It's at the summit of the city."

Ella took Shani's arm and was lifted up to the horse, sitting behind her friend. The horse whinnied as Shani kicked it forward, and Ella nearly fell.

"Hold on!" Shani called.

Ella knew the Hazarans would be opening the other gates, and saw the retreating Petryan soldiers now fully in rout. A soldier in red cringed as Shani's horse surged forward, and Ella looked around her, knowing the scene in front of her would always be remembered.

Now that she looked, Ella could see how starved, weak, and dispirited the Petryan soldiers were. Many dropped their swords at their feet and fell to their knees in supplication. For a moment it seemed that the Hazarans would run riot through the city, burning and pillaging, but Prince Ilathor and the other tarn leaders soon called their men to order, and the ruthless discipline of the commanders began to take effect. Petryan soldiers still ran ahead of them, but the prince first formed up his men—there would be no mad dashing through the terraces and cobbled streets of the tiered city. They would instead methodically search out pockets of resistance.

"This way," Shani said, turning the horse down a side street, leaving the scene behind. "I know a shortcut."

They took one street, and then another, each leading them higher above the city. Ella couldn't escape the feeling that she didn't belong here in Tlaxor, the capital of Petrya. The horse heaved and puffed out of its nostrils as it leapt up the long sloping path that lay in front of them, occasionally taking a series of steps as they gained height.

"We need to go up that path," Shani said, pointing to a narrow set of stairs rising through an area of rocky gardens. "The horse won't make it."

"Shouldn't we wait for the prince?" Ella asked.

"We can't risk the high lord going into hiding," Shani said. "He's crafty. If he weren't, he wouldn't have lasted so long."

The pair dismounted from the horse, where it stood blowing, flecks of foam at its lips.

Shani led the way as the two young women climbed the steep steps, taking them two at a time. By the time they reached the summit, Ella was fatigued, but they still weren't at the Poltoi Palace.

"Where is it?" Ella asked. They were once again on a sloping road, wide enough for two carts to pass each other.

"At the top of this road. Can you see the iron fence?" Shani asked. "The grounds are on the other side of that fence."

"More climbing," Ella said.

Shani ran up the road, Ella close behind her. When they came to the fence, Shani didn't halt. She simply gathered a fireball, and in an instant there was a hole in the fence, the iron bars melting around the hole.

Shani dashed across the grounds at Tlaxor's very summit toward the palace of red stone and dark wood that gazed out at the sky-blue expanse of Lake Halapusa below.

Shani reached the palace, pausing at an ornate set of double doors only long enough to grab a handle.

"Shani," Ella called. "Wait!"

Shani heaved open the door.

A man in red robes waited on the other side.

Ella screamed her friend's name as Shani was instantly bathed in fire, the flames pouring out of the doorway in a gushing cloud.

After the red dissipated, Shani crumpled.

Rushing forward, Ella felt something hit her from behind. She experienced the familiar surge of heat as a fireball scored a direct hit on her body, knocking her face forward onto the ground.

Ella looked up at Shani's motionless form, smoking on the doorstep. An elementalist stood over Ella's friend, a fireball dancing in the palm of each hand. The elementalist looked down at Ella and smiled.

Ella tried to get up, but she felt the pressure of a boot on her back. She could see two more men in red robes, moving to stand between her and Shani, yet the pressure on Ella's back didn't let up.

Four elementalists—maybe more.

Ella looked at her green sleeve, noticing how the runes on her enchantress's dress had dimmed. She knew she couldn't withstand another onslaught of fire. *Burned alive,* she thought. She hoped it would be quick.

As Ella waited for the end, she heard chanting, an eerie, sonorous sound, completely incongruous in the setting. The voice was surprisingly rich, a male baritone, clear and growing steadily in volume.

Impossible as it was, the realization came to her.

Ella heard a sudden squelching sound, like a knife slicing through a piece of fruit. Lying on her stomach, she couldn't see behind her, but she saw a spray of red, and the pressure of the boot on her back fell away, followed by the thump of a body hitting the ground.

A shadow moved through the air, flickering and dancing, and this time Ella saw the flash of white-hot metal as it took one of the elementalists in front of her from neck to waist in a fountain of blood.

The next elementalist spoke some words in quick, harsh syllables. Three balls of fire left his hands in rapid succession to strike the shadow, smashing against it again and again, coating it in flame.

The singing grew louder to compensate, and even as the shadow blackened, it wavered, finally displaying a man in green, a fiery sword held in his hands. As he sang, he leapt forward, and a single blow tore through his red-robed assailant, sending a wave of gore splattering onto the ground.

The elementalist standing over Shani's smoking form launched the two balls of fire he carried in the palms of his hands, and then gestured wildly as he screamed a stream of words, powerful activations that turned the cuffs at his wrists purple.

A wall of fire rose up between the elementalist and the swordsman in green. The flames crackled, sending forth a furious wave of heat that drove the swordsman back. The elementalist then put his wrists together and pulled them slowly apart. In between his wrists, connecting the cuffs, there was now a single line of purple fire, too bright to look at.

The elementalist looked down at Shani. He started to crouch down, ready to drive the line of fire across her neck.

A cry came from the swordsman. He leapt through the wall of flame, his song forgotten, completely disregarding the danger. Once on the other side, he spoke a sequence and flung out his arm, pointing his blade at the elementalist. A bolt of pure energy left the point of the sword and struck the Petryan in the throat.

The elementalist toppled over, his eyes already sightless as he hit the ground.

"You women are a lot of trouble," Bartolo said before he too fell to his knees, his blackened armorsilk flickering as the magic left it.

34

After a short time that felt like an eternity, Ella finally rushed back to the Poltoi Palace with healers. Fortunately, no more surprises awaited the prince's men, and they quickly secured the palace. While Shani and Bartolo were treated by two Hazaran elders and Ella paced outside, Prince Ilathor came to her to confirm that the battle was over.

Tlaxor was taken, yet High Lord Haptut Alwar had somehow escaped.

The prince tried to talk to her, but Ella left him and walked back down to the city's gate, looking down at the splashes of blood on the ground. *It's over now,* she thought, still dazed, realizing she was lucky to be alive.

She looked out the gate and over the frozen lake at the shore. She had enabled this city to be taken. It was a strange feeling.

A Petryan suddenly rushed up to the gate, staring out at the lake, soon joined by another. The prince's men stirred and kicked their horses into motion, coming over to where a growing crowd of Petryans stood looking out the gate.

"What is it?" Ella asked.

"It's Haptut Alwar," the Petryan said, pointing. "I would stake my life on it."

All thoughts of confrontation forgotten, the Hazarans and the Petryans stood side by side, looking at the man walking on the expanse of frozen water.

The solitary figure moved across the ice, richly dressed, a chest in his arms.

"We'll catch him," one of the Hazarans said.

"Will you put him on trial?" said one of the Petryans.

"If that's what you want," a voice to Ella's side spoke, and turning, she saw Prince Ilathor beside her.

"No," the Petryan said, his words tinged with venom. "Trial would be too good for the man whose favorite method of execution was to boil a man in the lake."

"Or a child," said another Petryan.

"Or a woman," said another.

"You might have your wish granted," Prince Ilathor said.

Ella looked at the lake and realized what she had been staring at but was too dazed to realize.

Steam rose from the ice.

"I thought you said a full day, Ella," said the prince.

Ella looked out in the direction of Torlac. A thin trail of smoke curled up from the area of the town. She hoped no one had been hurt. The cellars under the barracks were far from the homes of the locals.

"It's good to know that sometimes even you can be wrong." Ilathor smiled.

When Haptut Alwar, the tyrant high lord of Petrya, was halfway across the ice, he suddenly stopped.

"How long will it take to change?" Prince Ilathor asked.

"At a guess? The sheet on top is the last of it. Underneath, it's already boiling hot."

The richly robed figure took one more hesitant step. By now, a large crowd of Petryans had gathered, all watching the drama unfold, everything else forgotten.

On the shore, close to where the crowd stood, Ella could see the water bubbling and boiling as Lake Halapusa returned to its natural state.

High Lord Haptut Alwar took three more steps.

Then, with a blood-curdling scream, the Petryan high lord fell through the ice.

———◆———

Ella left when the Petryans and Hazarans started to take bets on how long he would take to die. Haptut Alwar thrashed and cried, moans of anguish coming from his throat as he tried to swim through water that grew hotter with every passing second.

It was even better than it would have been before, the Petryans said, with the water slowly heating up. The longer he lasted, the better.

Ella returned to the Poltoi Palace as singing and dancing started in the streets. The high lord's most fervent supporters were rounded up, and she tried to ignore their screams as they too were thrown in the lake. Ella was glad the Petryans saw it as liberation rather than conquest. She hoped the future would now be brighter for these passionate people.

"Salut, Enchantress," the Hazaran guard said when Ella approached the chamber at the palace where the healers had taken Shani and Bartolo. The guard shook his head, a strangely bashful expression on his face. "I am sorry, but you cannot go in there."

"Why not?" Ella demanded. "Are they all right? I want to see my friends."

"They are fine," the guard soothed. "Please come back another time."

"What's wrong?" Ella said. "Are they badly hurt?"

Ella pushed forward, and the guard tried to stop her, grabbing onto her wrist, but she spoke a word, and he snatched his hand away with a yelp.

She turned the handle of the door and opened it. "Shani? Bartolo?" she called. "Oh . . ."

Ella stepped back and immediately closed the door. She knew her face must be bright red.

"I tried to warn you," the guard said.

"I see," Ella said. "Well . . . I'm glad to see they're well and recovering, both of them."

"It seems that way to me." The guard grinned.

"Good night," Ella said.

Ella walked back out of the Poltoi Palace and onto the terrace where Bartolo had saved Shani's life and hers. A bladesinger and an elementalist—who would have thought? She knew they would be good for each other, and most of all she was happy for Shani. Love came from the strangest of places.

She could hear singing and warbling music wafting up from below, carried on the warm, moist breeze. Looking out, Ella saw that the sun was about to set, and she was again taken by the view from the top of the tiered city. It had been a long, eventful day.

"Always I come to you, and always you leave me," a male voice, smooth as silk, came from behind her.

Ella turned and caught Prince Ilathor's smile, even as the sun fell behind the crater's edge and the first stars came out. "Does it seem that way?" she said.

Barely visible in the rapidly fading light, she saw the prince shrug. "It does. The first time was in the desert, when I thought you were Evora Guinestor, high enchantress of Altura. The second time was high in the tower above Torlac, when I again felt the connection between us. The third time was just now, by the gate of this city. Here I am. Please don't leave me a fourth time, Ella."

"Everyone is celebrating," Ella said.

"But not you?"

"I'm tired. I don't even know where I'm sleeping tonight."

"It has all been taken care of. Just down the hill from the Poltoi Palace is the house of a merchant, a man kind enough to put his rooms and servants at our disposal. I do not know if 'house' is the appropriate term; his manse is nearly as big as this palace."

"Thank you, Your Highness."

"No, Enchantress Ella. Thank you." He paused. "For today, I mean. You were . . . amazing."

"I think I'm going to lie down," Ella said. She reached out and squeezed the prince's hand. "Good night, Your Highness."

Prince Ilathor didn't let go of her hand. Ella could feel his cool, dry touch, her hand enveloped in his larger one. His thumb ran over the skin on the back of her hand, sending a tingle traveling up Ella's arm and down her spine.

"At least let me walk you down," Prince Ilathor said.

Before they left, Ella took one last look at the view from the terrace. Once again the moon was out, but this time the shimmer on Lake Halapusa was closer, and even the sparkling stars were reflected on the water. Ella's hand was still held in the prince's, but she didn't let go. She'd seen so much horror and death this day that his touch held a strong affirmation of life.

The prince spoke as they walked. "I received a message today," he said. "Something I have been saving for you."

Ella turned her head sharply. "What message?"

"The allied army of Alturans and Halrana has crossed the Sarsen into occupied Halaran. Your brother, the lord marshal, led his men to a great victory. They have salvaged many Halrana constructs, and they have a thousand of the small hunters with them."

"Dunfolk," Ella whispered.

"Yes, Dunfolk," the prince said, squeezing her hand. "Not only do they have Dunfolk archers with them, but they have Alturan archers of their own, carrying a new weapon they call a rail bow. These weapons have proven to be decisive, and the Lord Marshal is penetrating deeper into Halaran. Some say he is heading directly for Ralanast."

"Truthfully?" Ella said. "Do I have your word?"

"Ella, do you need to ask?"

Ella felt tears come to her eyes at hearing her brother was not only alive and safe, but actually pushing the enemy back. "That's . . . that's wonderful news," Ella said.

Perhaps there was some end to this war in sight after all. Ella thought about Bartolo and Shani, desperately locked together in embrace. There was still love in the world, even amid the horror. She thought about herself and the little experience she'd had with love. After the day of bloodshed, the terror stronger than any she'd felt before, didn't she deserve to feel someone warm beside her?

Prince Ilathor led her to the wrought-iron gates of a three-storied stone building. Some Hazaran guards nodded and placed their hands on their hearts when the prince and Ella walked through the gates. The pair followed a paved path through a garden to the door of the manse.

Without knocking, Prince Ilathor pushed open the door, holding it open so Ella could walk in and then allowing it to shut behind them.

"*Tish-tassine,*" the prince said, and instantly nightlamps set into the walls and ceiling lit up from one end of the manse to the other.

"I suppose I should get to bed," Ella said. "Where is everyone?"

"The master of the manse and his family have vacated at my request," Prince Ilathor said. "There is no one here but you and I."

Ella and the prince stood in an expansive entertaining room. The floor was marble, and framed canvases dotted the walls: Petryan landscapes and even a haunting image of the Hazara Desert at night. At the back of the room were thick carpets, low benches, and piles of embroidered cushions with patterns of crimson and gold. A squared column stood in the middle of the room, rising to the high stone ceiling, and each facet of the support carried a tall rectangular mirror, so that Ella could see the prince's broad shoulders; tall back; and long, dark hair as he stood facing her, with his back to the mirror.

Ella could also see herself reflected in the silver. Her straight, blonde hair fell past her shoulders. It had grown long, she realized, nearly to her waist. Ella's green enchantress's dress, long-sleeved and hooded, clung to her body, the silk soft and supple. The lore in her dress meant it looked new and fresh, as if she hadn't just fought in a great battle—hadn't nearly been killed. It followed the contours of her body in a way she had never been fully conscious of before.

Had her body filled out more in the last year? Her calves were lean, and her legs tapered only slightly from her hips. But her hips seemed a little wider and her waist a little narrower. Her breasts were never large, but the silk of the dress pressed up against them, and if the dress had been lower cut, Ella was sure she would have been displaying cleavage. The skin at her wrists and throat was pale, infinitely lighter than Ilathor's, and Ella's green eyes looked seriously back at her from her heart-shaped face.

"Is it really just us?" Ella said in a small voice.

"Yes." The prince said the word like a whisper or like the hiss of a snake, soft and sibilant.

He took a step forward and gazed down at her. Ella looked up at him, suddenly afraid. They were from such different worlds. Was this really going to happen?

"You are my desert rose," Ilathor said. "It was in memory of you that I chose the symbol for my house." His voice dropped to a whisper. "Lord of Fire, how I wept when I thought you were gone."

Prince Ilathor lowered his head, closing his eyes as his lips found hers. This time when the shock hit her, it was powerful, so strong that she almost made a sound. Ella's mouth sought his as tingling waves ran up and down her spine, and as their tongues met, she felt a melting warmth welling up from inside her.

The prince's arm came round behind Ella's back, and she felt his hand caressing the small of her back.

Then, as they continued to kiss, with a smooth sensation of pleasure flowing through every fiber of Ella's body, the prince's fingers found the buttons at the back of Ella's dress.

Ella tensed, suddenly as taut as a drum, before she again relaxed as the prince undid the topmost button and moved to the next. His other hand caressed the hair on the back of her head, stroking the soft silken strands, then following down the contours of her back, feeling where her hips curved in at her waist.

He had now undone four of the buttons, and there was no sign of him stopping. Ella wasn't sure if she wanted him to stop. Part of her was frightened, but the prince was gentle. As he moved on to the fifth button, his other hand moved around to her front, traveling up the smooth silk and cupping her breast through the material.

Ella's tongue and his sought each other, his lips strong and insistent, their mouths wet and hungry.

The prince undid the last of the buttons and broke off their kiss, pushing her away from him. As Ella's lips left his, a tiny moan escaped her lips. She could feel the back of her dress open to her waist, her skin bared to the warm air. The prince's expression was intent as he reached forward and pulled the material away from Ella's left shoulder.

Without being fully aware of what she was doing, Ella slid her arms out of the sleeves. Ilathor reached forward to assist, but she held his hands away, and in the end she did it herself. She pulled the dress down to the tops of her breasts, and with each motion, revealed more of her skin to the prince's hungry gaze. Her left breast came free, and then her right, the nipples round and pink. Ella blushed; she had never willingly revealed herself to a man in this way. She pulled the dress down still further, to her narrow waist, the material growing tight when she reached the top of her hips.

Ella looked past the prince, at the mirror, where she could see herself exposed, her golden hair falling over the tops of her breasts. It somehow drove home what she was doing so that she knew it deep in her core. She was undressing herself for a man.

She pushed the dress down past her hips, past her black undergarment, and let the dress fall down to the floor, stepping out of it. She blushed again when she looked up at the prince and could see herself in the mirror behind him. Ella's flat belly led to the small triangle of material she wore over her womanhood, and the black against her white thighs drew attention to her hips and legs. Embarrassed, Ella hung her head.

She felt her head tilted back up, and the prince kissed her. She felt his hand on her left breast, teasing the nipple between his fingertips, each touch sending a shiver through her body. The warmth beneath her belly was growing so intense that she knew she could never stop . . . didn't want to stop. She felt his left hand now move to her right breast, the nipple there also becoming hard, so sensitive that her breath caught. His right hand traveled down over her belly, tickling the little dimple there for an instant before he reached the sheer black undergarment.

He ran his hand down to her thighs, and without meaning to, as their tongues caressed and his touch on her breast gave her feelings she'd never felt before, Ella moved her legs slightly apart.

His fingers ran over her thighs, feeling the smooth texture of her skin, and then, even through his kiss, Ella gasped.

The prince ran his fingers over the top of the black material, feeling both over and then underneath, and he pressed in gently. Waves of incredible pleasure flowed through Ella's body.

His other hand left her breast, but the kiss continued. He took hold of each side of the black fabric and pulled it down. Ella broke the kiss and moved away slightly, looking up at the prince and feeling the undergarment fall down her legs, finally kicking it to the side.

He looked down at her, not hiding the intensity of his gaze. A small triangle of hair, sparse and light-colored, covered the cleft between her legs. Under his gaze Ella felt wicked to be revealing herself, which strangely sent more pleasure running through her.

He resumed their kiss, and she whimpered into his mouth.

Ella made him stop, holding him at arm's length while she removed his clothes. Ilathor's chest was muscled, with dark hairs curling in a line from his navel. Ella gasped when she saw three faint lines, the scars of past battles, and she reached forward to run her fingertip along one of the marks.

Soon they both stood naked.

Prince Ilathor pulled Ella down to a place where carpets and cushions lined the floor.

Her legs opened as he found her, and Ella cried out into the night.

35

Miro knew that all people suffered from doubts, but he also knew that not everyone's decisions affected as many people as his did. He didn't know if that made his doubts greater or more important. Were a father's doubts when worrying about a sick child, wondering whether to sell his tools to pay for a healer, any less important? Miro didn't know.

He knew he was rash and intemperate, and sometimes too informal both with his men and his superiors. He was often ruled by his heart, a trait he tried to temper with sleepless nights at the simulator and long discussions with Marshal Beorn or High Lord Rorelan. He didn't always know that what he was doing was right, but he believed that doing something was always better than doing nothing.

This time, Miro knew without a doubt that what he was doing was right.

"Beautiful, isn't it?" Marshal Beorn said.

"Undoubtedly," Miro said, feeling the wind sting his eyes as he gazed out at the great city, far away, but unmistakably in view.

"Can you see the spires of the Terra Cathedral?" Beorn asked.

"The four tall towers, near the dome in the north?"

Beorn laughed. "Your eyes are better than mine. But yes, that's it. Ralanast lies before us."

"Lord of the Sky, we've come a long way."

"That we have, Lord Marshal." Beorn peered intently at the horizon.

There were three factors without which they would never have made it.

The ironmen had proven to be invaluable, tough enough to push through places where the explosions of prismatic orbs made the use of men in light armor suicidal. At Carnathion, the glowing constructs smashed through the enemy, preventing a near disaster when eight Imperial avengers tore through Miro's pikemen, and at Goldhaven the walls that the Black Army boasted were unbreakable fell.

More decisive still were the archers, one group comprising of Dunfolk with hunting bows, the other made up of Alturans with rail bows. Along with his archers, Miro used all his divisions like pieces in a war game, the lines and strategies of the simulator constant in his mind. He destroyed the enemy's mortar teams at Norcia and routed the legion—the Imperial Legion!—at Cortona Gap. He quickly realized his bowmen's weakness was close combat, and invented new tactics as he went along: the running line, the forked envelopment, and the rearguard folly.

The third factor was the most influential of all, and without it the liberation of Halaran would have come to naught, no matter Miro's skill or that of those under his command.

The people of Halaran were rising up.

For many in Miro's army, this wasn't a journey—it was a homecoming. The Halrana who'd fled their homeland after the battle at the Bridge of Sutanesta were now making good on their vows to return. Many were from Ralanast, but many were also from the towns the allied army liberated: Carnathion, Norcia, Goldhaven, Lonessa, Sallat . . .

As the Black Army fled before them, Miro's men entered each town to a hero's welcome. People threw flowers in the streets and openly wept tears of joy. Singing and dancing carried on into the dawn, and as the Halrana under Miro's command were reunited with their families, even Miro felt tears come to his eyes.

Miro always gave these Halrana the day and night to spend with their families, and to Miro's pleasant surprise the soldiers always returned to his command. Before departing, Miro also gave a speech to the townsfolk, in particular directed to those men who'd survived the depredations of occupation.

When they left each town, every man who could hold a sword came with them.

Miro's ranks swelled to such an extent that he sent word back to High Lord Rorelan in Altura for more weapons and armor. Soon Miro's new recruits were armed with sharp swords and leather armor, unenchanted but durable. Rorelan even sent two hundred more rail bows; it seemed he'd found a little more essence tucked away.

The most emotional time for Miro was when they reached the small town of Sallat.

Once, not long ago, but far back in the events of the war, Miro had been a bladesinger recruit billeted in Sallat while Prince Leopold awaited orders. Miro had met a woman there—in fact, she was still the last woman he'd been with—but when the orders came, the Alturan army had left Sallat behind. Less than a day later, the Black Army hit the town. The Alturans had done nothing to stop the slaughter that came.

Now, after nearly a year, Miro walked alone through the streets, remembering Varana, the Halrana woman who had taken him to her bed. Half of the town had been destroyed, and Miro was sad to realize he didn't recognize any of it. He took a bearing at the remains of the town hall, confirming in his mind only that Varana's house was one of those blackened hulks. The survivors told him she was almost certainly dead, killed when the legion came through. Miro felt a small sadness; he'd always known she was gone. He had been another person back then.

"What orders, Lord Marshal?" Beorn asked, bringing Miro back to the present.

Miro turned away from his examination of Ralanast to speak to Beorn. "Marshal Scola will need to take his three divisions toward Mornhaven, to head off any attack at our rear from the Ring Forts. He won't have enough men to attack; we just need him to secure our rear from the enemy."

"What about us?"

"Have the scouts returned?" Miro asked.

"Yes. There's a good place between here and Ralanast. It's high and well protected. The enemy know we're here, so there's little risk in being so visible."

"Good," Miro said.

"Lord Marshal?" a courier called, coming up the hill with a piece of paper in his hand. "A message from Ralanast."

Miro swiftly broke the seal and read the note. "It's from Rogan," he said. "The signal is a plume of green smoke."

Miro looked at Beorn, who nodded his understanding. Miro then turned his attention back to the distant spires of the Terra Cathedral and the one hope he had never dared to mention, not even to himself.

Thoughts that couldn't be dispelled came to him, however, now that he was so close. He tried to quell the stirring in his breast, but her face was there in his mind. He'd known her since she was a girl, and deep inside he'd always known she loved him, but she was his sister's friend, and he'd thought it the puppy love of a child.

When he'd finally seen her as a woman, it was too late, and then it wasn't just her marriage to Igor Samson that drove them apart but also the war, and finally she was taken from him, perhaps a prisoner somewhere, but most likely dead.

Amber.

"Miro, are you all right?" Marshal Beorn asked.

Miro realized he held his fists clenched at his sides. He forced himself to relax. "Yes, I'm fine," he said. "Pass the word. We advance."

36

"Woman, you're staying here," Rogan said, putting all of the force that could command an army behind his voice.

"May the Lord of the Earth scratch me if I am," Amelia said, her brown eyes blazing.

"The fight is going to be dangerous, and if I'm worried about you, I'll be distracted," Rogan said, changing tactic.

"Then I'll have to stay right by your side, won't I?"

"You'll stay put here with Tapel," Rogan said. "I command it."

"You command it, do you? Listen to me, Rogan Jarvish: You don't command me. I'm coming with you."

"Please, Amelia," Rogan said. "The coming fight will be no place for a woman. I intend to be at the heart of it."

"No," Amelia said. "That armorsilk doesn't fit you anymore."

"What do you mean? Of course it does!"

"No, it doesn't." Amelia's voice softened. "You aren't a young man, Rogan. Yes, the armorsilk fits, but it's no longer right for you. You were badly wounded in that battle—you're a warrior, and you know it as well as I do. Bladesingers always go where the battle is thickest, isn't that what they say? Well, not you. Your men need you to stay alive."

Rogan spluttered for a moment. "I'm mostly recovered, and you know it."

"You're no longer a young man," she said.

"Don't change the subject, Amelia. We're talking about you, here, not me."

"We're talking about *us*," Amelia whispered.

Rogan suddenly couldn't speak. He was as speechless as he'd been while recovering from his wounds. He simply gaped, staring at Amelia, looking into her eyes. Lord of the Sky, she was a beautiful woman. He stood silent and mesmerized by her. He realized he loved her smile, and her golden hair, the color of wheat. What was she doing here, arguing with him?

"I'm not staying home either," Tapel said, his piping voice rising up over the silence.

Rogan and Amelia both rounded on the boy. "Yes, you are," they said in unison.

"You can't make me," Tapel said.

Rogan loomed over the boy, who cowered under him. He spoke slowly in the voice that had handled countless boys a lot tougher than this one. "Yes," Rogan said, "I can."

"Will you come for me after?" Tapel asked in a small voice.

"Boy," Rogan said, "I'll come for you after. I'll come for you after the battle, and I'll come for you the next day. Now, get gone with you." He cuffed the air, and Tapel ran away.

"Do you mean that?" Amelia asked.

"I do," Rogan said. He hesitantly reached forward and took her hand.

Amelia closed her eyes and breathed deeply, a sigh of mixed pain and pleasure, and when she opened her eyes, Rogan was surprised to see a tear glistening there. "I'm coming with you," she said, "and I won't hear another word about it. You can wear your armorsilk and carry your zenblade, but I don't want you doing anything foolish, do you hear me?"

"I hear you," Rogan said. "Nothing foolish."

He leaned forward and kissed her gently on the lips. He knew she was a good woman, and Tapel would be the son he had never had. "I'm going to say this now before I lose my nerve. I want to stay with you," Rogan said.

"I want you to stay alive," Amelia said, and then she was crying.

"And I'm not saying this for your benefit. I'll be a father to the boy too, if he'll have me."

"He doesn't like it when you call him that," Amelia said, laughing through her tears.

"When he learns some respect, then I'll call him a man."

———

Prince Tiesto Telmarran, the man who would be high lord of House Halaran, was obviously nervous. Dressed in full ceremonial gear, he wore a brown robe, the *raj hada* of Halaran—a hand with an eye in the center—displayed on a torc around his neck. His hair was shaped tall and erect in the formal style, and his aides stood clustered around him. Seeing Tiesto in this light, for the first time Rogan believed that this man could become high lord.

Closest to Prince Tiesto were Marcus Toscan, the soldier who had been by his side since the beginning, and Salvatore Domingo, a stiffly abrupt loremaster Prince Tiesto had named high animator.

They were in the manse of a Halrana merchant, a man playing the dangerous game of sycophant to the occupiers while giving every aid to the resistance. The merchant's house was close by the storehouses of Ralanast's cargo district, which made it the perfect place from which to organize.

"Blademaster Rogan, how go the preparations?" Prince Tiesto asked.

"Just Rogan," he said, "and the preparations go as well as can be expected. The men are ready. We are in communication with Lord Marshal Miro. In three days we put the plan into effect."

There was a soft knock at the door, and everyone in the room exchanged glances. Marcus opened the door, speaking quickly to someone outside before shutting it again.

"News," Marcus said. "The allied army is just outside the city. From a high vantage our men in the city say they can see the green and brown banner."

The men in the room erupted in cheers, and Prince Tiesto smiled. The high animator looked as dour as ever.

"This is the best opportunity we will have, Prince Tiesto," Rogan said. "The morale of the men is high, and with news of the army just outside, the people of Ralanast will need only a little push for it to turn into a full-scale revolt."

"What about the Halrana Lexicon?" High Animator Salvatore Domingo asked.

Rogan sighed, and even Prince Tiesto looked exasperated.

"It's in Altura with High Lord Rorelan," Rogan said. "You saw the lord marshal's message." How many times had the man asked?

"When will we get it back?"

"When Halaran is safe enough to send it through to you, High Animator," Rogan said. "Or you could depart Ralanast and go to Sarostar to get it yourself."

The high animator harrumphed and walked away. Marcus stifled a grin.

"He is a skilled man," Prince Tiesto said, "one of the best. He simply cares for his craft."

"I know," Rogan said. "When this is over, I'll apologize."

"Have you heard from the Alturan woman again?" Prince Tiesto asked.

"Amber says she's ready, but I'm still concerned. The prison camp is on the opposite side of the city to the allied army, in a region well defended by the Black Army. To reach the camp, we first have to get past the fortified city walls and then through a series of smaller checkpoints until we reach the farmlands. The camp itself is also fortified with a steel fence and a nearby encampment of guards."

"Must we stake everything on freeing the camp?" Prince Tiesto questioned. "Between the allied army and the men under your command . . ."

"We must," Rogan said with finality. "At least half of my men won't fight unless we free their friends and family being held in the camp. Then there's the rest of the city folk. We're counting on their help, and they'll be as hesitant as the fighters—probably more so."

"Go on," Tiesto said.

"We'll divide into two groups. The first, larger group, led by you, Prince Tiesto, will lead the revolt here inside the walls of Ralanast. Your objective is to wait for the right moment and then to let the people know you're here. Shout the message loud and clear, and take out every man in black you can get your hands on. Then head for Ralanast's eastern gate, where the second group, led by me, will need to get back into the city with the prisoners."

"Understood," Marcus nodded. "Gather men and open the eastern gate. You'll return with prisoners."

"That's right," Rogan said. "A simple plan is a good plan. You know timing's critical, so keep your eyes on your timepieces."

"What about you?" Tiesto asked.

"Obviously, I'll need to get my men out of the city to free the prison camp. That's going to be difficult. We'll leave in small groups throughout the day. We'll be disguised as farmers and workers, and there'll only be a hundred of us."

"Is that enough?" said Marcus.

"It'll have to be. Each man has been handpicked—sorry, Your Highness, but I've got the best of 'em—and we're actually replacing a hundred real farmers and workers, who will give us their clothing and wait here in the city while we exit in their stead."

Marcus frowned. "It's risky."

"Nothing comes without risk," Rogan said. "These workers we're replacing also have loved ones in the camp. If questioned on their way out of Ralanast, my men will each have a new name, new clothing, a new family, and a new home. Let's just hope our enemies don't notice the deception."

"Which is why we've planned it for the day of the new guard rotation," Marcus said.

"That's right." Rogan smiled grimly at the young soldier. "We'll leave during the day; then after sunset I'll assemble my men in the forest outside the prison camp. When we get the signal from inside, we'll strike."

"What signal?" Tiesto asked. "What if you don't see it?"

"Amber is an Alturan enchantress, Your Highness," Rogan said. "She said she would raise a green light—green for Altura. She'll make sure we see it. And when we see the light, that's when we strike."

"The timing's tight," Tiesto muttered.

"It is," Rogan said. "We only have the night to free the prisoners and march with those who are able back to Ralanast's eastern gate, keeping the enemy at bay the entire time. Your Highness, you must start the revolt at dawn."

"And finally . . ." Marcus said.

"Finally we all march through the city for the main southern gate, where the lord marshal and an army of Alturans and Halrana will be itching to get in."

"It's a good plan," Tiesto said, nodding. "But it all comes down to the prison camp."

"It comes down to a lot more than that, Your Highness," Rogan said.

"Marcus, please leave us alone for a moment," Prince Tiesto said.

Marcus placed his hand over his heart and looked briefly at the ground before glancing at Rogan and then departing.

"Look, if this is about the high animator's request, I'm afraid this is one battle that won't be won by lore. In three days' time, it's the hearts of men that will be the deciding factor between victory and defeat. Without essence and a lot of time . . ."

Prince Tiesto smiled. "No, Marshal Rogan . . ."

"Marshal . . . ?"

"This isn't about the Halrana Lexicon, Rogan; this is about you."

Rogan scowled. "What about me?"

"It isn't right to call the man who trains bladesingers 'just Rogan.' Like it or not, you are a leader, and you need to have a leader's title."

"Who says so?" Rogan asked.

"I say so," Prince Tiesto's voice firmed, and Rogan's eyebrows went up. "Here," the prince said.

The Halrana noble handed Rogan a device to be worn on his breast. It was a *raj hada* with the hand of Halaran on one side and the sword and flower of Altura on the other. The colors green and brown were interwoven. The insignia was that of a marshal.

"What is it?"

Prince Tiesto snorted. "Don't be a fool, Rogan. You know what it is. I'm making you a marshal, and don't think High Lord Rorelan or Lord Marshal Miro won't back me up."

"Don't expect me not to wear armorsilk," Rogan said.

"Marshal, underneath that, you can wear whatever you like. Lord Marshal Miro is a bladesinger; why should you be any different?"

Rogan thought about what Amelia had said about leading rather than fighting. Perhaps this was his destiny?

"Fine, Your Highness." Rogan frowned, taking the badge. "Marshal it is."

As the newly promoted marshal turned to leave, Prince Tiesto spoke again. "And Marshal Rogan?"

"What is it?"

"Thank you. From the bottom of my heart. Thank you for helping my people."

"Prince Tiesto?"

"Yes?"

"You've got a busy few days ahead of you. You'd better get to work."

37

"I swear that's what the guard said," Samora declared. "Moragon's away in the east, and the babe went with him. I'm sorry, Amber— don't be upset."

"I just hate not knowing where he is and whether he's safe." Amber wiped at her eyes.

"It's better that the babe isn't here. He might get caught up in the fighting."

"I know," Amber said. "Scratch it, I know. But how will I ever get him back to me?"

"You'll find a way," Samora said.

"Thanks for getting me the information. I know it wasn't easy." Samora shrugged. "He just wanted a grope. I've had worse."

"You'd better go," Amber said. "In fact, we'd better not speak again until tomorrow night."

"I understand." Samora nodded. The Halrana woman squeezed Amber's shoulder and then left the tent.

When she was alone, Amber waited for the space of twenty breaths and then lifted up her sleeping pallet to reveal a place where the dirt had been recently stirred. With her wooden plate she scooped at the loose dirt, digging deep and forming a pile at the side of the hollow. Finally she hit something hard, and with ears pricked for the sound of anyone approaching, she dropped the plate and felt in the hole with her hands. She withdrew the big glass bowl, and then a moment later Amber withdrew the tiny flask of essence and the scrill that just a few days ago Lina had brought her.

In the time since Amber's son had been taken from her, the unlikely friendship between the two women had grown. Lina was a tall, stern Halrana with an unforgiving manner and the lines of a hard life written across her face. In contrast, Amber was young and pretty, with dimples when she smiled and gentle eyes. Yet here in the prison camp, both women were determined, more than any of the rest, and both shared the loss of a child. Lina had seen her babe trampled to death at the battle at the Bridge of Sutanesta, but still the woman hadn't given up. Amber knew she too would never just fall down and die like so many others in this terrible place.

Lina had taken care of Amber after the baby's delivery. They began to take walks around the camp together, ostensibly to help Amber regain her strength, but in reality so the two could talk together and deliver instructions to the other prisoners. With the lean diet and regular exercise, Amber's clothes fit her again, and her belt was as tight as it had ever been.

The guards also knew Moragon had laid claim to her, and she could earn small indulgences without having to compromise her safety.

One day Lina showed up with the essence and scrill. Lina knew Amber was an enchantress and that they needed a way to signal their liberators. She didn't tell Amber how she'd managed to get the essence, and Amber never found out more.

Amber sent a message to Rogan Jarvish to say that she would signal the way with a green light. She'd then set about enchanting some flashbombs and a few other tricks. But she knew the light would have to be bright, and with one night remaining, Amber still hadn't finished.

With a sigh Amber set to work. She knew it was dangerous beyond belief to use essence without metal gloves—a single spilled drop and she was dead—but gloves were the one thing she'd been unable to procure. Amber sat the glass bowl, as large as her head, on her knees, and dipped the scrill into the mouth of the vial of essence, holding it there for the barest instant before withdrawing it and setting to work on the glass.

Smoke rose from the glass, and Amber turned her head to prevent it from going into her nostrils. Her hand moved with slow, careful movements as she struggled to remember her classes at the Academy of Enchanters. She was only trying to enchant a nightlamp, she reminded herself. Well, perhaps a very powerful nightlamp, but a nightlamp nonetheless.

It would serve a double purpose. As bright as she knew how to make it, the light would shock the guards, and hopefully some would be blinded. It would also be a rally call to the Alturans and Halrana, both inside the camp and out. The many thousands of prisoners would be certain to know what was happening, and hopefully they would fight.

Amber knew she was taking a terrible risk. If a guard came to her tent, she would need to move quickly to hide what she was doing. With no gloves, fast movements were more than just risky. Amber could only pray to the Lord of the Sky and continue what she was doing.

Suddenly, she heard movement outside.

Amber's eyes grew wide with fear as she panicked. Fingers fumbled at the knots at the tent—she'd tied them intentionally tight, but they would only hold a man for so long—and Amber heard breathing.

Amber's allies in the prison camp knew better than to disturb her. She had made it very clear that any disturbance would compromise their whole plan.

Which meant it could only be a guard.

Amber's hands shook as she looked for somewhere to put the scrill. A single drop flew out, and her eyes watched it as with terrifying slowness the droplet fell through the air, landing on the sandal of Amber's left foot. She held back a scream and kicked the sandal off with her other foot, waiting for the pain to hit her. When the tent opened and a head poked in, Amber still had the vial on the floor in front of her, the scrill in her hand, the glass bowl on her lap, and tears of terror trickling from the corners of her eyes.

The pain didn't come, and the head was Lina's.

"I'm sorry," Lina said. "I know . . ."

"Scratch you," Amber whispered. "I almost died just now. Do you realize that? You almost killed me."

Lina came in and closed the tent flap behind her. "Is it that bad?"

"That bad?" Amber said. "It's *essence*, Lina. You might not realize how deadly it is, but I know. I'm an enchantress. I've seen what this does to people. Lord of the Sky, you nearly killed me."

"I said I'm sorry," Lina said, "and I wouldn't have come if it wasn't important. Rayna is about to break."

"What do you mean?"

"Rayna's scared about tomorrow night. The woman is crazed. She's going to tell the guards. I mean it. Samora has her, and for the moment she's keeping her calm, but in moments Rayna will be screaming our plans to the world."

"Can't you take care of it?"

"No, Amber, I can't. Rayna's a friend of Samora. I need you."

"All right. Help me put all this back under the pallet. Then let's go and see them."

Rayna was just as Lina had described. The woman rocked back and forth, mumbling words no one could understand, repeating them over and over. Samora spoke to her friend with low, soothing tones, but how long Rayna would stay quiet was a mystery.

Amber and Lina sat down next to the two women, looking at Rayna with consternation. Amber looked around. The sight of four women huddled together was a common one. Amber met Lina's gaze, and the tall Halrana woman shook her head.

"What does she know?" Amber asked Samora under her breath.

"Everything," Samora whispered back.

"Can't do it. Can't do it," Rayna's words suddenly became clear, and her volume increased.

"Shhhh," Samora soothed, but to no effect.

"Dead outside. Dead inside. We're all dead anyway. Should I die tomorrow? Why wait? Why not die right now? Get it over with. End it in an instant. Dead already. Dead-dead-dead-dead-dead-dead . . ."

"We have to do something about this," Amber said.

"I know," Samora said. "She was fine, but then she just . . . snapped."

"I'm sorry," Lina said, "but you know what has to be done."

"Wait," Amber said. "Do we have rope and something we can make a gag out of?"

Lina looked at Amber scornfully. "You know that won't work. We tie her and gag her, and then what? And no, we don't have rope."

Samora looked from one woman to the other. "No," she said. Tears began to slide down her face.

"I'm sorry," Amber said. "I know she was your friend."

"*Was?* What do you mean? She's right here!" Samora cried.

"And in a few minutes, she's going to start screaming," Lina said.

"Samora, you know what we have to do," Amber said.

Amber exchanged glances with Lina and then shuffled along the ground until she was close to Samora. She put her arms around the Halrana woman while Lina went over to Rayna.

Samora began to sob in Amber's arms.

"Shhhh," Lina said to Rayna, whose mumbling rose in intensity and then quieted before rising again.

As Amber looked on, holding Samora to her breast, Lina reached her arm around Rayna's neck until the woman's chin was in the crook of her elbow. With both arms, Lina began to squeeze, and Rayna's ranting was suddenly cut off.

Lina must have been stronger than she looked, or Rayna must have been ready to go. With barely a gasp, a red-faced Rayna kicked once, then suddenly went limp. Samora's sobbing intensified. Finally, Lina laid Rayna gently down, closing her eyes and placing the woman's hands together on her breast.

"It's over now," Amber said to Samora. "I'm so sorry."

Amber stood and walked away. There was little light left in the day, and she would need to finish the nightlamp before nightfall.

Amber struggled to maintain her composure.

She wondered what had happened to the little girl from Sarostar she had once been.

38

On the third Gathering of autumn, a day usually reserved for the harvest, when child, parent, and grandparent would head out into the fields to reap the rewards of their sunny land, long-laid plans were finally spurred into action at Ralanast.

The officers of the Black Army were the first to play a part, although for them it was nothing far from the ordinary. An hour after dawn, the guards stationed at Ralanast's eastern gate were relieved. Those finishing their tour would immediately return to Tingara, but the new soldiers settled in for a long spell and wondered if the rumors they'd heard about Halrana women were true.

The sun climbed the sky, with nothing special to note as farmers brought drudge-pulled wagons carrying loads of grains, fruits, and vegetables into the city. The new guards examined several carts for weapons, but couldn't see much reason to be meticulous, and eventually waved the lot through.

To the south of Ralanast, an army of grim-faced men in green and brown looked down from a distant hill, maintaining a rigid formation as they gazed at the indomitable southern gate. They had been waiting for days, and with little in the way of siege weapons, the Black Army's officers were starting to believe they wouldn't attack after all—they hadn't even encircled the city in an attempt at siege! If this was out of sentiment for the Halrana, who would be the first to starve, then perhaps the Alturan commander didn't have the stomach for what it took to win in a war like this. The allied army would be crushed, the same way they had been crushed at the last Battle for Ralanast.

The heat started to leave the day as the sun crossed the center of the sky and began to fall toward the horizon. In the cool autumn evening, the farmers who'd dropped off the products of the harvest for the city's workshops and mills left Ralanast's eastern gate to return home to their fields. The soldiers at the gate remarked that they seemed a reticent, sober-faced bunch, but then their speculation dried up as they too felt the import of the day, without quite realizing why.

At the prison camp, the soldiers in black sensed that their prisoners were stirring. Their captain warned his men to be especially vigilant, although there was nothing specific he could point to—no rebellious behavior that could be punished with whipping, hanging, or a brief and educational visit to the vats.

In Ralanast itself, a man in the attire of a Halrana high lord stood at the vortex of a constant stream of activity, issuing orders and receiving messages from his command center in one of the four great storehouses in Ralanast's cargo district. There was a whisper, a hum that was impossible to suppress, as the number of men under Prince Tiesto swelled at the last minute, with every young Halrana wanting to play a part and join his fellows in this moment. The newly created officers—recruits whose only credentials lay in the fact they'd been with the resistance since the beginning—tried to keep the murmurs of anticipation quiet, but the Halrana could not be silenced. By nightfall the storehouses were filled to bursting, and still they came. Prince Tiesto would not turn any away.

Expectancy hung in the air.

———◆———

Amber looked around her, nodding in satisfaction. To all outward appearances, the density of the clustered groups of prisoners was the same as it always was, but she and Lina had coordinated a shifting so that the most able-bodied prisoners now clustered near the gate.

Their task was made increasingly difficult by the various personalities of the prisoners. Some were willing and ready to fight—desperate to, even—whereas others were terrified, their spirit crushed by the constant fear and merciless beatings. Amber often felt that more of their efforts had gone into handling the other prisoners than anything else.

There were many more prisoners than guards, but the guards had sharp swords and long pikes, steel armor and prismatic orbs. The tough warriors of the Black Army would cut through the weak and unarmed prisoners with ease.

Amber sat with Lina and Samora, wondering if she looked as nervous as the other two women. "What if they noticed the food was tainted?" Amber asked Samora.

"Then it's over before it starts," Samora said.

Amber looked at the guards, men who were on duty and wouldn't be eating with the others, knowing that no matter what, they would need to take these men out. At best, the poisoning would only reduce the numbers of their reinforcements. "Are you sure she used enough?"

"How would I know?" Samora said. "I'd never even heard of celemar three days ago. It's not like I was there to watch her."

The off-duty guards always took an evening meal at their own encampment. There were three shifts in a day, which meant that, at any time, two-thirds of the total complement of soldiers would be resting, ready to come to the prison camp at a moment's notice in the event of trouble, while those on guard duty, who would take their meal later, cursed their luck.

During mealtimes, an officer had drafted one of the prisoners, a fifteen-year-old girl named Merri, to serve the guards. He evidently considered the stick-thin waif of a girl harmless enough to serve out bowls of meat stew, scrub the dishes after, and clean out the latrines.

Lina had procured the celemar from one of her secret sources, but when they first spoke to Merri, she refused outright to have anything to do with slipping it into the guards' food. A brown knob of root the size and color of a large mushroom, the celemar looked far from appetizing, and Merri said she had no involvement with the preparation of the food anyway.

After the conspirators gave it some thought, Amber was tasked with obtaining a canister of salt. This time she used a man's typical reluctance to think too hard about anything womanly. Amber told the guard that she needed salt to mix with water to prevent infection. What infection? The guard asked. Amber had simply looked down. Embarrassed, the guard had lived up to expectations and provided her with a canister of salt from his meal table, fear of Moragon written across his face.

The three women then spent hours with stones, grinding up the celemar until it was a fine, light-brown powder. Amber and Lina remembered to wash their hands afterward, but Samora forgot, and even now she was still sick in her bowels.

They poured the celemar powder into the salt canister, mixing it with actual salt, and appraised their handiwork. The color was definitely off; would the guards notice?

Merri finally agreed to the plan. She would smuggle the canister in with her, placing it on the bench next to the steaming pot of stew she served the soldiers. Many would automatically season their monotonous fare, and if the chance presented itself, Merri herself would try to sneak some of the powder into the pot.

"How long until sunset?" Samora asked.

"Less than an hour, I make it," Lina said, the tall Halrana woman frowning and looking up at the sun. "It gets dark late this time of year."

"The guards are going to wonder why some prisoners aren't returning with their bowls," Amber said worriedly.

"No they won't," Lina said. "We've spoken about this, and the bowls are the one thing they'll never think of us using as weapons. The guards will just count their blessings that mealtime finished early today."

"Look." Samora nudged Amber.

Merri was returning to the camp. In her hands the thin girl held a tray, and from where they sat the three women could see steam rising.

With a shaky smile on her lips, Merri took the tray to a pair of guards, who greedily took a plate each. Merri then moved on to some more guards, a soldier pinching her on the rear as she departed, causing her to squeal.

"Lord of the Earth, bless that girl," Lina said. "She's done more than we ever asked of her. I don't know how she convinced them to let her serve the men on duty, but I'm naming my next child after her."

Amber smiled, suddenly feeling a surge of hope to hear Lina, a woman who had been given her fair share of life's painful moments, talk about again having a child.

"It's nearly time," Samora said.

"Give it a bit longer," Lina said. "Everyone knows to wait for nightfall."

Amber looked down at the sack at her feet, where the glass globe of the nightlamp was covered from prying eyes, trying to slow the racing of her heart as the sun steadily dropped toward the horizon.

"The man who commands the allied army," Amber said suddenly.

"What about him?" Lina asked.

"He's the man I love."

"You're in love with the lord marshal?" Samora said quizzically.

"Yes," Amber said.

"I pray you'll soon be reunited," Lina said, squeezing Amber's knee. "Come on. It's time. They're here." Lina looked up.

Against the afterglow that remained after sunset, six men carrying a makeshift litter were silhouetted against the sky as they wended their way through the camp, carrying a seventh man, immobile and groaning in pain, to where the three women sat waiting.

This part of the plan was a calculated risk. Moving anything large through the camp always attracted attention, but the guards generally left the prisoners to their own devices, particularly when it came to injuries. When a prisoner was hurt or sick, there were no visits from healers; it was left to the prisoners to tend to their own kind. The litter had been made from Amber's wooden sleeping pallet, modified by some of the men who were good with their hands, to form a platform of planks. The six men who bore the litter were the strongest of the prisoners, and the prone figure they carried was neither injured nor unwell. All seven men had been soldiers in the allied army, and all had a debt to repay to their enemy.

"Put him down here," Amber said. From now on, they would give up any pretense; the most casual glance would reveal the revolt. "Now, quick, before the guards notice, everyone stand back and get ready."

The man on the litter rolled off to join his fellows while Amber heaved and, with help, turned the door-sized piece of wood over.

Spidery symbols covered it, drawn with as much skill as Amber possessed. *"Sahl-an-tour,"* she said.

The runes blazed to life, and immediately a wave of warmth washed over her from the makeshift heatplate. The growing temperature forced Amber to step back, beads of sweat breaking out on her forehead.

Shouts and cries were heard from the guards. In their section of the camp, near the gate, the most able-bodied prisoners all stood in accord, wooden food bowls in their hands.

"Now!" Amber cried.

Some of the men had fashioned sacks, which they carried over their shoulders, and the women hefted the pouches they'd brought with them. They'd been scrabbling at the dirt for days, gathering up the small pebbles and specks of gravel. They now poured their sacks out on top of the heatplate.

Amber spoke some more words, invoking the power she'd built into her device. She was forced to step back farther, and the gravel began to glow a fearsome red.

As she knew would happen, Amber's plan now dissolved into chaos, and all she could do was pray and do her part.

Prisoners ran forward with their wooden food bowls and dug at the gravel on top of the heatplate, heedless of the burns on their hands as they made a weapon from the most mundane of substances. Guards moved against the rising prisoners and began to shove them out of the way to see what was happening.

Amber saw a prisoner run forward and fling out his arm, tossing the contents of his bowl at a soldier in a spray of red-hot stones. The soldier screamed in agony as the fiery substance hit the metal of his armor, burning his eyes and getting into his hair. The prisoner ran forward and, after a brief tussle, stood holding the guard's steel sword. The prisoner then ran the guard through, blood gushing from the black-clad soldier's mouth.

Men and women everywhere emptied the contents of their bowls at the guards, and Amber realized the power of a weapon any fool could use. She knew, though, that the heatplate wouldn't last long. What they were doing was a distraction, but without Rogan's men, the revolt would be ruthlessly crushed. The prisoners were simply too weak for a sustained fight.

Amber hurriedly took the glass bowl she'd enchanted. She looked out at the closest of the sentry towers. Rogan didn't know Amber and was unwilling to risk his men in an attack without timing it to her signal. Amber needed to raise the green light now.

"Fight!" Lina cried. "It's now or never!"

All around them prisoners grappled with guards, the soldiers shocked at the ferocity of their captives.

Darting among them, Amber ran toward the guard tower, the glass bowl clutched to her chest. A ladder ran up the side of the tower to a small platform, where two guards stood throwing orbs down at the prisoners.

An explosion tore the earth apart just ten paces in front of her, knocking Amber to the ground. When she gathered herself, she realized the glass bowl was no longer in her hands. Where was it? There! She dashed toward it but a man in black stepped in front of her and a mailed fist smashed into her stomach. Amber crumpled to the ground.

Hugo, the particularly cruel Tingaran who had once threatened Amber with the vats, loomed over her, a blood-drenched sword in his hand. "I always thought you were too clever for your own good," he said.

Lying on her back, Amber grabbed the glass bowl and clutched it to her chest, eyes transfixed by the droplets of blood that fell from the end of Hugo's blade.

Out of the corner of her eye, Amber saw Samora running toward her, a wooden bowl in her hand.

"You piece of filth!" Samora cried as she flung out her arm.

Nothing happened. Samora's bowl was empty. The woman looked at it dumbly and then threw the bowl itself at Hugo. The warrior laughed and took a step forward, swinging his sword like a woodcutter attacking a tree. As Amber watched in horror, Hugo sliced through Samora's skull, sending bone and brain matter flying through the air. The Halrana woman's body crumpled to the ground.

Hugo turned back to Amber, raising his sword over his head with two hands. In desperation, Amber held the glass bowl out to block the blow. She knew that this makeshift nightlamp, the signal for Rogan, was the thing that must be protected above all, but she couldn't control her limbs; her body simply wanted her to survive.

A sword came out, blocking Hugo's stroke a hair's breadth from the glass. Amber's eyes were closed, and as she realized she was alive, she heard yet another clash of swords and opened them.

Leopold stood grimly facing Hugo as both men circled each other, swords extended in front of them. Amber saw the former prince of Altura wobble and place a hand at his chest, grimacing. Flecks of red appeared at Leopold's lips, and he coughed. Amber didn't know if he'd been hurt earlier, or if Hugo was responsible, but she knew Leopold was mortally wounded.

"Go," Leopold choked. "Get out of here."

Amber stood, the glass bowl in her arms, looking at Leopold one last time before running toward the tower.

She couldn't tell if the revolt was being crushed or if the prisoners were holding their own against their tormenters. Explosions came from all directions, and screams of agony echoed along with cheers of victory. There were simply too many figures running about. She could see guards fighting, but prisoners also ran in all directions as they finally expressed their frustrated desire for vengeance.

The two guards on the platform at the top of the tower continued to throw prismatic orbs, adding to the chaos. Amber awkwardly held the glass bowl at her side, climbing the ladder one-handed, leaning into it to steady herself, wondering how she was going to defeat two healthy, trained, and armed warriors.

Her only advantage lay in the fact she hadn't been seen. Amber's chest heaved and her breath came in gasps as she put all her strength into climbing. She ignored the precariousness of her position and pulled herself up one rung at a time, panting with exertion.

The two guards drew back in shock and surprise when they saw Amber pull herself up to the platform, and then, realizing it was a woman—and a young and pretty one at that—they laughed.

Amber hefted the glass bowl, covered in symbols drawn by her own hand. She planted it down on the platform and looked away.

Amber said the words that were said the world over every time a nightlamp was activated. *"Tish-tassine."*

This nightlamp was different.

The device lit up with a green of such intense brightness that, looking out over the camp, her gaze directed away from the glare, Amber could see the entire scene laid out before her in detail, revealed in the light of an artificial sun.

The prisoners were creating havoc throughout the camp, but a core of soldiers had formed up near the main gate. Any who came toward them died in a flurry of flashing swords and blood. Amber knew the heatplate would have exhausted itself long ago. The black-clad soldiers moved forward as they restored order to their ranks.

Behind her on the platform of the tower, Amber heard the two guards scream as the makeshift nightlamp blinded them. As the light began to ebb, Amber turned back to the platform, one of her hands held in front of her eyes, the other holding onto the low rail.

Against the brightness she could see the two guards, struggling to stand, clutching the rail for support. These two men had thrown murderous orbs into the middle of Amber's fellow prisoners. She couldn't begin to estimate how many they'd killed.

Amber moved forward, her eyes mere slits against the glare, and heaved. She pushed first one guard and then the other from the top of the tower, hearing satisfying screams and crunching thuds when they hit the ground.

Leaving the nightlamp where it was, Amber again took stock of the revolt as she descended the tower. The flash of light hadn't been as much of a distraction to the soldiers below as she'd hoped it would be, and she realized that in moments the prisoners would give up hope as they saw they couldn't escape through the gates.

Amber still had some flashbombs. She ran back to where the guards stood blocking the gate, and rejoined the prisoners.

As she rallied the prisoners in a final surge at the guards, and sparks of light burst in the soldier's ranks, breaking them apart, Amber saw movement on the other side.

39

"That's the signal," Rogan said.

"Are you sure?" Amelia whispered.

"Lord of the Sky, woman, what else is it?"

Rogan and his hundred men crouched in a clearing, hidden from the road by a screen of trees. He had taken his men as close as he was able, but the frequent patrols meant he couldn't be as close as he would have liked.

Rogan stood, all efforts at silence forgotten. "Men," he cried. "Do you see that light? That's the light of a brave woman and her fellow prisoners who are rising up to give us this one chance. Are you with me?"

"Yes!" shouted Rogan's handpicked Halrana.

Rogan drew his zenblade and pointed it ahead. He started to sing in his gravelly voice, and first his zenblade and then his armorsilk lit up with fiery colors of emerald and gold and starbursts of purple. He began to run, heedless of how much noise he made, throwing off the shackles of the hushed resistance, finally able to take the battle to his enemy's heart.

Rogan's men rushed past him like a wave of the ocean splitting around a tall rock. He ignored the pain in his leg's bruised tendons and the stitch in his side, the occasional faltering of his voice, and the way he could only keep up with the slowest of his men. He was running, and once again his weapon was in his hands.

Rogan settled into a wincing, lumbering gait, but eventually he was pleased to see he could stay with his men. He allowed his blade-singer's song to fade; it was simply too difficult. Soon all Rogan could hear was the puffing and panting of the men as they ran. He concentrated on putting one leg in front of the other, listening intently. Finally he could hear it.

"Do you hear?" Rogan asked Amelia, who was handling the mad dash surprisingly well. "Sounds of fighting."

"It mustn't be far now," she panted.

Ahead the dirt road passed a guard station. The black-clad warrior who manned it stared in the direction from which the sounds were coming, scratching his shaved head as if wondering what to do.

Rogan's lead man cut him down with a single slice at his legs, the next brown-clad warrior then opening up the guard's throat, barely pausing as they ran past.

Rogan felt proud then. He knew these men, all of them, and a few months ago most of them had never held a sword. They would remember this moment until the end of their days.

The shouting and clashes of metal grew louder, and Rogan could now distinguish screams of agony from roars of triumph, the shrill cries of women from the calls of people holding on to their courage with every bit of strength they possessed.

A steel gate suddenly barred their way. They had arrived. Rogan prayed it wasn't too late. Through the bars Rogan could see people fighting, falling, fleeing, and dying.

Rogan's men threw themselves at the gate, but it held fast. Through the narrowly spaced lines of steel, Rogan saw some of the Black Army's soldiers turning to take stock and prepare themselves for this new threat.

"Make way!" Rogan roared, brandishing the zenblade over his head.

In that moment the difficulty of his song, the searing pain in his chest, and the aching of his leg were nothing. Rogan was the blademaster. The activations poured from his throat, strong and clear, and Rogan planted his legs on the ground, tightened his grip on his zenblade with both hands, and swung once, twice, and a third time. It was a move Rogan had devised to fight Veznan nightshades and Tingaran avengers.

With a sound like a tree being struck by lightning, the zenblade cut through the steel. Sparks flew in a fountain, raining down on the black-clad soldiers on the other side of the gate, and Rogan completed his arc, kicking fragments of molten steel out of the way, before leaping through to the other side.

Against the blademaster, the stunned prison guards didn't stand a chance.

Rogan's men poured through the opening he'd created, taking the enemy warriors down, one by one. The superior numbers of the Halrana, and Rogan's training, instantly began to tell, and with renewed vigor the prisoners who held swords continued the fight. Rogan dispatched one man with a thrust to the upper chest, and then turned on his heel, making a complicated twist of his wrist and taking a second Black Army soldier's head clean off. A Tingaran with a blood-drenched sword and the sun and star tattooed across his shaved head came at him with his sword raised; Rogan opened him up with a sweeping blow.

They kept coming at him, and Rogan kept taking them down. The corpses piled up at his feet, and as Rogan thought about what he'd heard went on in this camp, he snarled and launched himself at another soldier, taking the battle to his enemy.

Rogan's song came strong and fierce, the blood sliding away from his armorsilk as the lore prevented it from sticking, so that he looked new and green as a blade of grass, lit up by the morning sun.

"Marshal, there are a bunch of them in their own camp nearby," a male voice called, cutting through Rogan's battle haze. "They're fleeing into the forest."

"We have to let them go," Rogan said, panting. He lowered his zenblade, realizing there weren't any more of the enemy to kill. The pain came to him then, and he grimaced as he felt the soreness in his leg come back a hundredfold, his throat hoarse and his chest wheezing.

"Rogan?" a soft voice said behind him.

Whirling on his feet, Rogan saw a young woman gazing at him intently, a stout piece of wood in her hands, which she'd evidently been using as a club. She was a pretty thing, and he instantly felt his heart go out to her when he saw the bruises on her arms and the splashes of blood on her dress.

"What?" he panted.

"I'm Amber."

"You're too young," Rogan blurted. When she'd said she was an enchantress, he'd pictured a matronly woman with steel-gray hair and a parade-ground voice. He looked then at the young woman's eyes, and with the wisdom of his years he could see that she had seen much, too much perhaps. "Sorry," he said.

"Thank you for coming," she said. "I know it can't have been easy for you. We couldn't have held much longer."

He still couldn't believe this was the woman who had organized the revolt. Rogan, a man uncomfortable with women at the best of times, suddenly knew then what he needed to do.

"Can't have been easy for me?" he asked, shaking his head.

Amber's eyes began to well.

Rogan took Amber by the shoulders, looking down at her from his height. "I am so sorry for what you've been through here. It's over now." He repeated the words twice more before she seemed to realize. "It's over," he whispered, opening his arms.

Amber fell forward as she let go of the iron restraint she'd held over herself, and realizing her ordeal was over, she fell into the fold of the tall warrior's arms.

"They took him from me," Amber said as she sobbed.

"Shhh," Rogan said as he hugged her. "I know they did."

Rogan felt a squeeze on his shoulder, and opening his eyes, saw Amelia give him that special look she gave him alone. He let Amber cry herself out, and rather than feeling proud of what he'd done here, he cursed himself that he had taken so long, that any of the prisoners had spent one second longer here than they needed to.

Finally Amber let go of him, and he saw the strength once again go into her brown eyes, her lips setting with determination.

As Rogan felt the rage build within him, he let it feed him, giving him energy. He gathered himself for the long night ahead, and looking around him, he saw his men do the same.

"Men and women," he said, "people of Altura and Halaran, I'm afraid the night is far from over. This area crawls with the enemy, and your friends and families are anxious to have you safely home. At the speed we will travel, Ralanast is a half-day's journey from here, which means walking through the night. I know it will be difficult, and I'm sorry to ask more of you when you have already been through so much, but there will be light at the end, for with the dawn, the people of Ralanast will show those who would believe otherwise that they are free. Your people will welcome you with open arms, and even the Alturans among you will soon be among more of your countrymen, just as I will, for a great army lies outside the walls of Ralanast, an army of Alturans and Halrana, and we intend to welcome this army with the new day. Now, please gather yourselves. We have water and we have some food. It will be a long night."

As Rogan's men gathered the prisoners, Amelia came forward. "Rogan?" she asked.

"What is it?"

"We always knew this might be the case: Many of the prisoners are unfit for travel. I need twenty of your men."

Rogan closed his eyes. He could hear the steel in Amelia's voice and knew it wasn't worth the attempt to argue. He sighed, opening his eyes again. "You'll have twenty-five men," he said, "but it's all I can spare. Lord of the Sky, I wish I could give you more."

"It'll be fine," she soothed. "They just need to help us hold here until tomorrow. I'll do what I can for these people's injuries and illnesses. Some of them have been very poorly treated."

"If anything happens to you . . ."

"It won't," Amelia said.

"I'll come back for you," Rogan said. "As soon as I can, I promise."

"And I would say that I will fear for you,"—Amelia shook her head—"but after seeing you fight tonight . . ."

Rogan saw Amber come forward, a tall Halrana woman at her side. "This is Lina. She'd also like to stay to take care of the others."

Amelia nodded.

"And you, Amber, will you make the journey?" Rogan asked.

Amber looked up at him with a disturbing amount of steel in her eyes. "You remind me of someone," she said. "He always thought I was just a little girl. Don't make the same mistake."

"I won't." Rogan grinned.

He looked around him at the burning mounds of rubble and the pits in the earth where orbs had exploded. Corpses were scattered at all ends of the camp, most wearing black, he was pleased to see. His men gathered the freed prisoners in a column. They were ready.

"Move out!" Rogan called.

40

The uprising of Ralanast commenced at dawn.

Prince Tiesto had scattered his men throughout the city so that a multitude of armed companies, each at least fifty strong, ran through the eighteen avenues and twenty-six streets that made up the city's central zone. The uprising began in earnest when the rising sun touched the easternmost spire of the Terra Cathedral, and the Halrana patriots began to shout the mantra that would signal the start of the battle for liberation and call their people to arms.

"Brown for the earth! Green for life! The birth of a new day!"

Some of the patriots were met by curious citizens, woken by the commotion. All questions were answered: "Meet at the Terra Cathedral! Freedom for Ralanast! Freedom for Halaran!"

Others met the swords of the Black Army's soldiers. The clash of steel broke the morning stillness. Blood pooled in the dusty streets, and as the call to arms rang through the Black Army's barracks and the sound of marching boots echoed in the streets, some of the Halrana chose to stay at home.

Prince Tiesto, with Marcus at his side, led his men toward the eastern gate and his rendezvous with Marshal Rogan.

Tiesto had never fought in a battle before, and even though part of him was terrified, he also felt the thrill of the uprising course through his veins. With five hundred men at his back—most either boys or old men—Tiesto waved his shining sword over his head and shouted encouragement. The boys' faces flushed with excitement, and even Marcus grinned like a fool.

They passed unchallenged through the cargo district, heading for the eastern gate in a direct line, and Tiesto felt hope rise when he saw the twin towers of the gate only a few blocks ahead.

The Tingaran legionnaires met them in the broad avenue leading to the gate.

Rogan had tried, but nothing could have prepared Tiesto for the chaos of his first engagement. Both Tiesto and Marcus were trained in swordsmanship, but Marcus had been a palace guard, his experience confined to only border patrols before that. Tiesto had never before had a man try to kill him.

It was worse than he'd imagined.

For some reason, when Tiesto saw that his numbers were greater, he'd expected the legionnaires to surrender or, at the least, for some kind of discussion to take place.

Instead, the men of the Imperial Legion tore into his ranks like a storm, blood spraying through the air as their swords slashed and thrust into Tiesto's men. Ranks of enemy pikemen marched forward in disciplined formation, the front of their column bristling with lowered weapons.

Tiesto remembered Rogan's advice for dealing with pikemen. He turned to Marcus. "Hit them from the side!"

Marcus vanished, taking a squad with him, and Tiesto found himself battling both the column of relentless pikemen and the flashing blades of the legionnaires.

"To me!" Prince Tiesto called, launching himself at the legionnaires. He hoped that the pikemen would have difficulty continuing their advance if his men were tangled with the legionnaires.

Immediately his hunch was proven correct, but it didn't escape his notice that the Tingarans were the superior soldiers, better armed, stronger of muscle, and more disciplined.

Tiesto thrust his sword at a Tingaran's round face, the point penetrating into the man's mouth as he died with a scream. The prince pulled out his sword with an effort and then raised it to block an attack. He countered with a classic riposte, taking down another of the enemy.

"To me!" he called again, drawing both the enemy and his own men to him.

Over a legionnaire's shoulder he saw Marcus lead his squad smashing into the side of the pikemen. The enemy pikemen were soon tangled in their gear as they tried to turn their long weapons, and Marcus penetrated deep into their ranks.

Prince Tiesto continued to hack and slash his way through his enemy, narrowly escaping being skewered by the bloody sword of a snarling Tingaran. Then a space opened up in front of him, initially filling him with relief.

Until he saw it.

A monster stood in front of him, an apparition of man and molded flesh, with a black sword in place of one arm and a flail held in the grip of the other. The creature's face was a horror of metal and cloth, with red slits where eyes should be. It lurched and twisted as it moved forward, directly into Prince Tiesto's path.

Tiesto was unable to tear his eyes from the long twists of braided steel that jangled at the end of the flail, each length ending in a spiked ball the size of a man's hand.

Behind the creature was another, and a third lumbered forward behind that. These were Imperial avengers, three of them, and Prince Tiesto's ragtag army didn't stand a chance.

Tiesto thought about Rogan Jarvish, charging toward the city's eastern gate with only a hundred men and a mass of half-starved prisoners, desperate for the gate to be opened—something that would never happen. He pictured the Alturan lord marshal, waiting vainly for the main southern gate to open, and Prince Tiesto realized that all their planning had been in vain.

Tiesto had tried. Perhaps he had never been cut out to be high lord. He'd never even wanted the position—only to help his people.

The prince raised his steel sword, wishing he had the enchanted blade he'd lost long ago, and with a muttered prayer he prepared to defend himself from the avenger.

The flail whipped forward and Tiesto ducked, hearing the whistle as it flew over his head. He ran forward, weaving as he went, rolling to the side as the black sword skewered the ground where he had been a moment before, and then thrust his sword at the avenger's body.

The glowing runes on the metal torso flared and hummed, and the jarring turned Tiesto's fingers numb as his blow was easily deflected.

Without an enchanted sword, Tiesto couldn't penetrate the protective power of Tingara's lore.

Tiesto rolled again as the spiked steel balls smashed into the cobbled street, bits of stone flying in all directions. He coughed as he realized he was on his back, willing his body to rise up from the ground. A pointed length of black metal whistled through the air, and barely in time, Tiesto raised his sword in front of his face to block.

The avenger's black sword broke Tiesto's blade in two, the top half clattering to the street. Suddenly the prince was helpless, prone on his back, holding the hilt of a broken blade. The avenger lurched forward, ready to finish the fallen man in brown. The sword arm hovered over Tiesto's chest, where he wore the Halrana *raj hada* proudly over his heart.

Something moved to Tiesto's right, and a colossal foot planted itself down next to the prince.

Tiesto looked up at the enormous foot. His gaze continued upward, higher, until, at a height taller than the avenger's body, the lower leg developed a knee joint.

Higher still, taller than the tops of the two-storied buildings, the leg forked where it met the other leg. A hand came down from above, plucking the avenger from the ground as easily as a child picking a flower.

Tiesto stared openmouthed at the colossus, at the huge limbs made of wood and steel, and the matrices of runes, glowing golden and bright, covering its skin. It was a strange design, almost . . . old-fashioned.

But it was big.

High above, the hand holding the avenger squeezed, and bright-red blood gushed from the red slit of the avenger's eyes. The colossus dropped the avenger, and then, as the remaining two Imperial avengers turned to face this new threat, the colossus lunged forward, and for an instant Tiesto saw the controller cage atop the construct's gigantic head.

The prince picked himself up off the ground as the colossus grabbed the next avenger and then threw it hard to the ground before crushing it with a massive foot. The last creature leapt up, the length of the flail lashing in the direction of the controller cage, but the animator easily moved the colossus's head back out of the way. As the animator again moved the colossus's hand forward, the avenger swung its enhanced sword, taking off one of the fingers. The animator curled the remaining fingers into a fist, swinging at the avenger's head. Two blows at the avenger's head knocked it to its knees. The colossus's second hand came down, pinning the avenger to the ground on its back. The animator pushed down on top of its head with the heavy fist, and with a terrible squelching sound flattened its skull. The avenger's legs kicked, and then it was still.

Tiesto finally remembered where he'd seen the colossus. He saw Marcus approaching, his sword dripping red. "It's from the museum," Marcus cried, laughing. "It must be a hundred years old!"

Looking up, Tiesto saw High Animator Salvatore Domingo sitting in the controller cage. As dour as ever, the high animator pulled the colossus back to allow Tiesto's men to regroup. The high animator had mentioned nothing of his plan to recover the colossus from the museum.

"What about them?" Marcus said, pointing.

Tiesto saw the remaining legionnaires and pikemen fleeing, scattering to the streets. He then looked at the twin towers of the eastern gate. His objective was just ahead, and with no prearranged signal there was no way to tell if he was early or late. Marshal Rogan could be just outside, his small force being slaughtered by the enemy.

"Leave them," Tiesto said. "We need to get the gate open."

He waved his arms to get the high animator's attention. The colossus tilted its head forward until Prince Tiesto was nearly eye to eye with the animator. He wanted to shake the stern high animator's hand or pound him on the back. Instead, Prince Tiesto pointed at the gate.

"We need that opened!"

High Animator Salvatore nodded, turning the colossus toward the gate.

Marcus and the prince regrouped their forces, neither commenting on the fact that barely half of their five hundred men remained.

"Men!" Prince Tiesto cried. "Your countrymen are on the other side of that gate!"

With a resurgence in strength, they ran forward, those alive realizing that they had survived their first engagement and their goal lay ahead.

The high animator led the way, the colossus eating up the distance with ground-eating strides. Orbs flew at the colossus from the two towers, but the animator, from his high perch on a level with the soldiers manning the towers, looked straight into their eyes before smashing the construct's fists into first one, then the other.

Then Tiesto saw the colossus's left arm suddenly drop as the runes went dark. The right arm followed. The symbols on the construct's back, feet, and legs began to fade.

As the ancient colossus reached the gate to stand towering over it, the animator brought back the construct's right leg, but before the high animator could bring the leg smashing into the gate, the limb went limp.

Black-clad soldiers started to pour out of the doors at the base of the towers.

"Lord of the Earth, please," Prince Tiesto prayed.

Prince Tiesto had been told the new high animator was skilled, more skilled even than his predecessor. He didn't know how Salvatore Domingo did it, but in one final burst the symbols on the colossus flared red. The colossus began to rock, and then tilt, and finally Tiesto realized what the high animator was doing.

The colossus leaned forward, tipped over, and crashed its great mass through Ralanast's eastern gate. Stone flew in all directions as the gate was flattened, the colossus leaning at an awkward angle, the controller cage torn open.

Prince Tiesto waved his men forward. High Animator Salvatore was still in the controller cage, dazed and unarmed, with the soldiers in black swarming forward to man the breach in the gate.

Tiesto ran as hard as he could, but the enemy reached the high animator first, two legionnaires climbing up to the torn cage. One raised his sword above his head, preparing to deliver the death stroke that would end the high animator's life.

Then a blazing shadow shot through the breach, moving so fast, it was like trying to focus on a ray of light. The legionnaire standing over the high animator exploded in a wave of blood and gore. The second followed straight after. Tiesto caught a flash of green as the newcomer leapt down from a block of stone to launch himself into the place where the enemy numbers were thickest.

It must be a bladesinger. Tiesto had never seen one in combat, but watching this one fight, he knew the stories were true: They were the world's finest swordsmen, each worth a thousand men in battle. The blade-singer pirouetted and thrust at a legionnaire, taking out the warrior's throat, before ducking an attack and cutting another swordsman in two. The bladesinger's armorsilk deflected a blow, and now Tiesto and his men were close enough that the prince could hear the deep growl of the man's singing, an eerie sound that sent a chill up his spine.

Tiesto's men cheered. "Blademaster!"

Prince Tiesto blinked. His men were telling the truth—it was Rogan!

More men in brown joined the bladesinger, coming in from the other side of the gate, and soon the black-clad soldiers were under heavy attack. When Prince Tiesto's men joined the fray, it was too much for the enemy, and they were swiftly overwhelmed.

More people poured through the gate to enter the city: soldiers in brown; thin, but determined, former prisoners holding swords; and even a few women with clubs. They kept coming, and Tiesto gasped when he saw how many prisoners had been freed.

"Well met, Your Highness," a hoarse voice said, panting and wheezing.

Tiesto turned to Rogan as the symbols on the man's armorsilk dimmed with the halting of his song. He saw the hollowed pits under Rogan's eyes, the drawn skin, and heaving chest.

"You came at an opportune time," Rogan said.

"As did you." Tiesto gripped Rogan's shoulder.

"You must be Prince Tiesto," a woman's voice said.

A young woman, battered and bruised, with auburn hair that curled at the ends, addressed Tiesto before shifting her gaze to look at Rogan with concern.

"I am," Tiesto nodded.

"There is an army outside that needs us," she said.

Tiesto glanced up at the sky. Morning was well underway.

"Marcus?" Tiesto looked around. "Marcus?"

A Halrana soldier came forward. "I'm sorry, Prince Tiesto," the soldier said, shaking his head. "A sword took him in the thigh. Unlucky hit; he bled out. He didn't say a word—just kept fighting until he fell."

Tiesto looked into the distance, and the grief came to him all at once. Surely the soldier must be wrong. He looked at his men, expecting to see Marcus's face among theirs.

Tiesto hadn't even known the young palace guard when Marcus had spirited the Halrana heir out of Ralanast's Rialan Palace. For a long time it had just been the two of them, and then a small network of defiant townsfolk, before Rogan came. Marcus had been the rock by Tiesto's side. The prince realized he hadn't even given the man a title. What did you call the soldier who was simply there when you needed him to be? Captain? Marshal? Lord? Friend?

Tiesto felt a hand grip his shoulder. "We need to move on," Rogan said. "He was a good man, and we will mourn him later. Your men in the city need you. Until a plume of green smoke rises from Terra Cathedral, Miro won't attack."

Tiesto nodded.

Rogan called out to the men. "Spread the word: The prisoners have been freed. I want every Halrana to know it. You hear me?"

"Yes, Marshal." Men leapt in response to Rogan's orders.

"I want these two groups combined and formed up into order. We're the only sizeable force inside the city, and the army outside is relying on us to open the main gate. When we encounter the Black Army—which we will—and when you take on Imperial avengers, hold fast. Do you hear me, men? Hold fast."

"Yes, Blademaster."

Tiesto felt a hand clap his shoulder as Rogan met his eyes. Tiesto knew they were red. He expected Rogan to say something about how he must fight on, or Marcus's sacrifice would have been in vain.

Instead, Rogan squeezed his arm. "You did well, High Lord. You did well."

41

Miro paced back and forth, doing his best to ignore Marshal Beorn. From below their vantage, the city of Ralanast appeared tranquil and calm in the morning light. The allied army waited on the broad hillside in rigid formation, any protest or wavering met with instant discipline, as Miro waited for the signal that would herald the start of the battle to liberate Ralanast.

"We should attack now," Marshal Beorn said again.

"No," Miro said shortly. He had rarely had such a contest of wills with the veteran commander before.

"Something has gone wrong. Look at the city—does it look like a city in revolt to you?"

"We can't see the whole city from here," Miro replied.

"You know they'll be sending reinforcements from the east. We can't afford to wait here like this, so close to the city, with our flanks and rear vulnerable to attack."

"I've told you my reasons," Miro said. "How many lives do you think will be lost if we attack with the gate closed instead of open?"

"How many lives will be lost if we're attacked here? We're like a hunter who has moved so close to his prey that he can no longer guard his back."

"We wait for the signal," Miro said.

"For how long?"

"As long as it takes."

Beorn took Miro roughly by the arm. "You trust your old teacher; I respect that. But Rogan Jarvish is just a man like any of us—he's no miracle worker. If the uprising was crushed, then the best thing we can do is attack now, while the enemy is distracted. If the Halrana come through and open the gate while our attack is underway, even better."

"Beorn, you've seen how well defended that gate is. Even our colossi can't touch it. Without siege weapons, we'd be dashed against the gate like a wave on the rocks. The wave breaks, but at the end of it all, the rocks are still there. I won't be responsible for losing that many of our men. This war doesn't stop in Ralanast. You know as well as I do that it won't be over until our army marches into Seranthia."

Marshal Beorn opened his mouth to reply, when a soldier spoke.

"Lord Marshal, look!"

From the four spires of the Terra Cathedral, four plumes of green smoke rose into the air. The city may have appeared peaceful, but inside those walls, Miro knew, people were dying.

"Fly the countersignal!" Miro called.

The command passed down the line, and a light flashed where it could be seen high above. The dirigible far above the city released its massive banners, and both the sword and flower on green and the open hand on brown flew high above the city of Ralanast.

Miro heard it then, a sound, carried on the air, rolling up from the occupied city below.

The sound of hundreds of thousands of voices all raised in unison.

"It's not so quiet now," Miro said to Beorn. He grinned. "You can buy me a drink in Ralanast tonight."

"With pleasure." Beorn smiled back.

"Lord Marshal!" an Alturan soldier called. "The dirigible has raised a new signal flag. Red and gold on a blue field."

Miro could never remember the signaling system. "Don't tell me what it looks like. What does it mean?"

"Some of the enemy are fleeing the city through the northern gate!"

Miro and Beorn exchanged glances.

Another soldier called out. "The southern gate is open, Lord Marshal!"

Miro drew his zenblade and raised it high for all to see. He spoke the words that made his armorsilk blaze like the sun, the zenblade red with deadly intent.

The time for speeches was past. Miro opened his mouth and shouted one word with all of the strength he could muster.

"Ralanast!"

The army of Halrana, Alturans, Dunfolk, colossi, and ironmen flew down the hillside, gathering momentum as they ran. A contingent of Tingaran legionnaires awaited them, vainly attempting to close the southern gate.

On one flank, hundreds of massed ironmen strode forward, lacking in grace but more than making up for it in indomitable strength. The other flank was led by the three colossi, with Luca Angelo, the animator who'd broken the enemy's defenses at the Sarsen, at the head.

Never one to hang back, Miro led the charge, the foremost of a wedge of bladesingers, with two of them running on his left and two on his right. The lightness of their armorsilk, their peak fitness, and their agility meant the bladesingers swiftly outdistanced the heavily armored infantry and the columns of pikemen.

Miro and the four other bladesingers crashed into the massed defenders, penetrating deep into their ranks as Miro's archers followed close behind. Ahead and above him, Miro saw arrows flying through the air to come raining down on the legionnaires' unprotected heads, wiping out hundreds of men at a time.

Miro slowed due to the sheer number of his opponents, but he was desperate to be first through the gate. He had to know what waited for him on the other side. As his sword rose and fell, blood spraying and splattering over his armorsilk, Miro knew he was fighting the same men who had launched constant sorties against his homeland. These soldiers in black had attacked the massed Halrana refugees at the Sarsen, intentionally cutting down men, women, and children. They had imprisoned the survivors and occupied their lands, raping and pillaging at will. The Black Army had taken Amber away from him.

Even the other bladesingers couldn't keep up with their lord marshal. He spun and in a mighty arc he cut through two men with one blow. A pike thrust at his unprotected face, but he cut the pole in half and slashed the throat of the warrior who held it. Miro sang in a clear, crisp voice, the words part of who he was. The song came unthinking from his lips as he caused his armorsilk to become transparent and his zenblade to grow blue and ethereal. He caused waves of heat to pour from the runes, burning through his enemy's clothing and searing their limbs, causing them to drop their weapons from the pain.

Then Miro was at the gate, a tall tower of stone to either side of him. Orbs rained down, the Black Army insanely killing their own men. Miro's armorsilk shielded him from the explosions, but he still felt the bite of shrapnel on his cheeks.

He dispatched a Tingaran with two blows, the warrior falling to one knee, and then Miro saw an Imperial avenger make its way toward him, twisting and turning with its strange gait. Miro used the Tingaran's back as a springboard to launch himself high in the air, his zenblade held over his head, the song from his lips never ceasing. The barbs of the avenger's flail clutched in vain at his armorsilk, but still Miro continued his trajectory. He took the avenger's head from its shoulders, landing with both feet on the ground as the body crumpled to the earth.

Miro next took down two surprised legionnaires; then he saw Halrana soldiers in brown, to the rear of his opponents, and sensed the press of his own army behind him. Crushed between the two forces, the warriors in black started to throw down their swords. Those of the enemy who didn't surrender turned and fled. The two forces met and Miro's army surged into the city. The gate was won.

Marshal Beorn swiftly gave assignments to the green- and brown-clad soldiers. Panting, Miro lowered his zenblade, allowing the runes to fade. He knew Beorn would take control, sending the men throughout the city—although it seemed the rising Halrana had done most of the hard work already. Calm began to descend as the allied soldiers crushed the final pockets of resistance, one by one.

Another bladesinger stood in front of Miro, with his back to him. He was a tall man—as tall as Miro himself—and lean, with gray in his dark hair, yet he wore his armorsilk like it truly belonged on him.

Soldiers in brown ran up to the bladesinger, the man responding with curt orders. Then the bladesinger turned, and as Miro saw the man's face in profile, the ugly scars and weathered features, and noticed the *raj hada* across his breast, he began to smile.

"So they made you a marshal?" he called above the explosions and shouts of a battle still in its last throes. The bladesinger turned in surprise when Miro called out. The two tall men in green faced each other. Miro knew this was the man who'd made him who he was.

"I always knew you couldn't follow orders," Rogan Jarvish said in the same voice he'd once used to berate Miro at the Pens in Sarostar. "Lord marshal, eh?"

"Something like that," Miro said, grinning. "We all thought you were dead. Lord of the Sky, I could have used your help." He looked around at the blood-splattered Halrana. "But it looks like you found some people who could use it more."

Rogan stepped forward, and he and Miro embraced, Miro's old teacher evidently embarrassed when a cheer sounded from the soldiers around them.

"Ah, there he is. High Lord Tiesto Telmarran," Rogan said when they separated, "this is Lord Marshal Miro Torresante, my best student."

"I had a good teacher." Miro smiled. "It's an honor, High Lord."

"Thank you, Lord Marshal," Tiesto said. "I still have not been named high lord . . ."

"But you've earned it," Rogan growled. "Don't be a fool. After today, there isn't a man here who won't follow you to the ends of the empire."

"Which is where we'll likely end up," Miro said. He shook his head. "Please don't thank me, High Lord. Half of my men didn't even participate. The uprising has been well planned and bravely fought."

"There's still more to be done," Tiesto said. "I must go." He turned to Rogan. "Marshal Rogan, I've sent five hundred men to the prison camp. Amelia will be fine."

Tiesto departed, and with his final words Miro was aware of a terrible squeezing feeling in his chest. "I've heard about the camp. Where is it? I'm leaving to—"

"Miro," Rogan said, "we've freed the camp. It's done. A woman there helped us."

Miro opened his mouth, and suddenly the act of asking about *her* was the hardest thing he'd ever done.

"The prisoners . . . ?"

"It was a dark time for them. Many were taken away, murdered to feed some evil magic of the primate's. We were able to free thousands of them. That's all I can say."

"There was a young woman," Miro said. "I don't know if she was with them or even whether she was taken prisoner. I lost her at the Bridge of Sutanesta."

"I'm sorry, Miro," Rogan said. "If she's living, I promise you, I'll help get her back to you."

Miro nodded, unable to ask more. He took a deep breath and opened his mouth to ask Rogan where the rescued prisoners had been taken.

"Ah," Rogan said, looking past Miro's shoulder, "here's someone I'd like you to meet."

Miro turned.

"Enchantress Amber Samson, meet Lord Marshal Miro Torresante."

42

"I suppose my last name is Rosalie now," Amber said. "My husband was killed."

Amber had thought about this meeting for so long that she couldn't believe it was happening. He had changed—Lord of the Sky, he had changed—but if anything, the resolve in the lines of his mouth and the thin scar that ran from below his left eye to his jawline added strength to his face.

The last time she'd seen him was at her graduation from the Academy of Enchanters in Sarostar—what felt like a lifetime ago. He'd told her then that he was being sent to the front—and now he was the lord marshal.

Amber remembered the day so clearly because it was the day she'd realized that he'd finally come to terms with the way he felt about her. It was nothing he'd said; it was in the way he'd sat close to her, their legs touching, and the surreptitious glances he'd given her when he'd thought she wasn't looking.

Amber had been married then, but now Igor Samson was gone. There was so much she knew she should tell Miro but was too terrified to say. How could she ever tell him about how she'd given herself to Moragon? How could she mention her baby, when Miro hadn't even known she was pregnant?

She had forgotten how tall he was, as tall as Rogan. His dark eyes looked down at her past his sharp nose. Stubble lined his angular jaw, and his black hair was tied back with a cord. He was finally saving her, just as she had always imagined him doing.

All of a sudden Amber felt frightened and dropped her eyes. Of course he would be pleased to see her, but what if it was just as his sister's long lost friend, as the girl he had grown up with? She knew she looked terrible. Why did he have to see her like this?

Amber felt fingers on her chin. She once more looked up into Miro's dark eyes and saw them welling with water.

Miro spoke for the first time since he'd seen her. "Never again let me forget how beautiful you are," he said.

He lowered his head, and his arms went around her. The last thing Amber saw from the corner of her vision was Rogan as he wiped some speck from his eye.

Then she forgot everything else, as finally Amber had what she had wanted ever since she first saw him in Sarostar, so many years ago.

Amber had the kiss of the man she loved.

By the end of the day, Ralanast was secure, and with every hand turned against them, the soldiers of the Black Army fled the city's environs in droves.

After a quick ceremony, Tiesto Telmarran, the new Halrana high lord, took charge of Rialan Palace, dedicating his first words as high lord to a fallen soldier named Marcus Toscan.

Marshal Beorn took command of the army, seizing the former positions of the Black Army as far as halfway to the Louan border.

Marshal Rogan set men to work repairing the demolished eastern gate, and in the afternoon Amelia returned to Ralanast with the last of the liberated prisoners.

With the city finally safe, sympathizers, and even those who had simply preferred to stay clear of the fighting, were rounded up by those who'd suffered at the hands of their occupiers. Stones were thrown and names called, but the Halrana had seen enough of bloodshed, and little more was done.

An hour before sunset High Lord Tiesto ordered the streets to be cleaned up. Soldiers and volunteers from the citizenry set to willingly. The streets were cleared of rubble. The bodies of the enemy were taken outside the walls to be burned, and those of the brave Alturans and Halrana who gave themselves for the city were taken to the cargo district to later be buried with full ceremony.

As the sun sank below the horizon, the high lord ordered the bells of the Terra Cathedral to be rung for an hour. The buildings emptied of people as Alturan soldiers and Halrana of all stations massed in the streets, in the square outside the palace, and in front of the Terra Cathedral.

Music floated up from several places in the crowd, and the people's voices rose as they sang simple Halrana songs about the harvest and the beauty of their country. There was little in the way of food and drink, but every man with food in his shop or beer in his cellar sent it into the crowd. They thanked the Evermen they were alive, and they mourned the dead. Every Alturan soldier was kissed at least once, and those with no place to sleep soon had one, many by the side of a dark-haired Halrana woman. Husbands kissed their wives, and children were clutched to their fathers' chests. It was a night when no one was alone.

At a small house in one of Ralanast's poorer districts, an exhausted man opened his front door and slumped against the frame, looking at the sight that greeted him. Tapel squealed and ran to Rogan's side, hugging him around his waist, while a smiling Amelia came forward and rubbed the soot from Rogan's cheeks.

"You stayed home, son," Rogan said. "Good for you."

Far away, in a cool chamber in Rialan Palace, where the songs of the crowd could be heard wafting in through the open window, High Lord Tiesto Telmarran stood by the body of Marcus Toscan, gently pulling away some blood-crusted flaxen hair from the young soldier's face.

"Be at peace, soldier of Halaran," Tiesto said. "No one should be alone tonight, least of all you."

At the Terra Cathedral, a young man and a young woman, both clean and fresh, mounted the steps hand in hand, climbing up to the tall wooden door that barred the entrance to the spectacular building the Halrana had dedicated to the Lord of the Earth.

Two red-faced guards, evidently jovial from the empty wine bladder at their feet, rose to bar the entrance, but then one of them grabbed his fellow's arm when he saw who it was.

"Lord Marshal," the guard said, "it's all as you asked."

Amber thought about the prison camp and placed her hand on Miro's arm. "Miro, I . . . I don't like enclosed spaces. Or even dark ones."

Miro turned to Amber and smiled. "Amber, I'm a soldier. I've spent the last year or more sleeping outdoors, in pavilions or under the stars. I like the Crystal Palace—it's light and airy; you'll like it too, but anywhere else is too confining for me."

Amber smiled in return, following Miro into the cathedral as he pushed open the door.

The domed room was massive, spacious and light, with nightlamps in sconces and scenes of growing life decorated on the inside of the dome.

With Amber's hand still clasped in his, Miro led her up the stairs that wound along the inside of the dome. At the top, they went through a tiny doorway, and Amber once more smelled the freshness of the air outside. The night was cool, but there was no chance of rain. From below, they heard the sounds of the people singing.

A wide platform rested against the outside of the curved dome, and Miro now led Amber along the walkway to a flat area, open to the air and fenced by a low stone rail.

Thick cushioned carpets covered the expansive floor, with piles of pillows, plates of food, shining nightlamps, and flasks of water and wine. Coverlets lay folded near the pillows.

"Only the priests come here," Miro said. "Do you see where we are? We're on top of the Terra Cathedral, close to the spires."

Amber looked up and gasped. The stars shone down from an amazingly clear sky, and at the top of each of the four spires, a glowing prism cycled through a series of warm colors.

"I asked the high lord for somewhere special," Miro said, "and this is what he gave me. There's a bedchamber just through that door there, if you'd prefer to go inside, and there's a washbasin in a second chamber."

"Miro," Amber said, "it's beautiful. I've never seen anything like it."

"I know you've had a tough . . ."

"Shh," Amber hushed. "Yes, it's war, and it's been difficult for everyone. But thinking of you is what got me through. I love you. I always have."

"I'm a fool," Miro said.

"No you're not," Amber said. "You're a man." She pulled him down to the soft covers. "Please show me that you're my man."

That night in Ralanast was a night when no one was alone. Some slept in a lover's arms while others danced the night away.

And at least one couple made up for lost time.

43

Primate Melovar Aspen brooded in his lush chambers at the Imperial Palace in Seranthia, when two separate messages came, telling him he was losing the war.

When Melovar had first heard about the desert men and their siege of Tlaxor, he'd diverted the legionnaires he was sending to Halaran and instead sent them toward Petrya. While the reinforcements were still traveling and couldn't do anyone any good, the first message arrived to tell him that this desert prince had conquered the unconquerable city. Prince Ilathor had somehow crossed the boiling waters of Lake Halapusa to the Petryan capital, storming the gates and taking the city.

The Petryans were now out of the war.

Haptut Alwar was dead—caught trying to flee, they said—and the warriors of House Hazara would soon be pouring through the Gap of Garl and heading for Tingara and their evident goal, Seranthia.

Then the second message arrived. Moragon, the fool, had been touring Loua Louna when the Alturans crossed over into Halaran, and by the time he'd turned back to seize command of the situation, the Alturan commander retook several towns and then liberated Ralanast itself.

Moragon's men in the Ring Forts tried to drive through to the city but encountered a second army left in waiting for that very eventuality. After a great battle near Mornhaven, the Alturans left the field victors, and soon the Ring Forts would once again be in the possession of the Alturans and their allies.

Moragon had been forced to pull back to the Azure Plains in Torakon. His position in Loua Louna was untenable, he said.

He then told Melovar the latest piece of bad news with his customary directness. After a coup in Vezna, High Lord Dimitri Corizon had been removed from power.

Now the Veznans were also out of the war.

The primate looked at the ancient book of the Evermen, holding its secrets fast as it sat innocuously nearby. He picked it up and hurled it at the ground.

A guard poked his head in.

"Get me Zavros," Melovar thundered. "Now!"

As he waited for Zavros, the primate gathered his thoughts. The Akari had rejoined the Tingaran Empire, and Dain Barden was at Melovar's disposal. The primate would continue to dangle the relic in front of them, but first it was time for the Akari to show their worth.

They'd said they wouldn't fight in the warmer lands. Perfect— Moragon was now in Torakon, and the desert men were heading for the Gap of Garl. It was time for Melovar to find out if the revenants' reputation was deserved.

"You summoned me, Your Grace?" Zavros asked, bowing as he entered the room.

"You told me the new plants were functioning well, Zavros. Obviously, not well enough. They've taken back Ralanast. Moragon is giving up Loua Louna and pulling back to Torakon."

"It isn't my plants that are to blame. The facility near Ralanast was the first, so problems there were inevitable, but the two other facilities in Tingara are functioning well. Each body has a certain cost to transport to the facilities and dispose of, as I'm sure you can imagine, but we are easily recouping this cost in essence using the Akari's technique." Zavros paused. "However, Primate, essence isn't everything. You know that better than anyone. There is no substitute for enchanted weapons from Altura, constructs from Halaran, and Louan orbs and mortars. Half the world's industry is gone, Primate. We've been set back a hundred years."

"It won't matter when I send in the Akari," Melovar said. "Perhaps it's time to convert our friend Dain Barden."

"Are you sure that's wise, Your Grace?" Zavros said. "The Akari are a tight-knit people, and the revenants can just as easily be turned on us as our enemies. It might be better to save that card to be played later, when the revenants are far away."

"Fine," Melovar snapped, the pain of his ruined flesh returning. "I can control the Dain with or without the elixir." He looked around for the one thing that seemed to ease the pain. He finally found his crystal goblet resting on a nearby table and drank the foul black liquid greedily. "We'll send the Akari to combat the Alturans in the west and the desert tribes in the Gap of Garl," the primate said, setting the goblet down. "Moragon's legionnaires will fight with them, and we can control Tingara with the templars."

"A wise decision." Zavros nodded. "Sending the Tingarans away is a good idea."

Melovar caught something in Zavros's tone. "Why?"

"Primate," Zavros licked his lips, "word is starting to get out. Think about what the first emperor did to the Akari. He cast them out and banished them to the north because people find the idea of animating the dead repulsive, and the concept of recycling the used-up bodies even more so." Zavros let his words sink in. "Then think about what we're doing. We're not the Akari—we don't ask our people to serve in death as they did in life. We're taking prisoners of war and killing them for the life energy in their bodies. Even our own people with the taint won't stand for it, Primate, the Tingarans especially."

"You're one to lecture," Melovar growled. "What about the things I hear you're doing at your laboratory? Playing with the stuff inside people's skulls, testing how much pain a person can endure before he is rendered insane? Trying to breed women with other creatures?"

"What I do," Zavros said stiffly, "I do for knowledge."

"And what I do, I do for the masses of the world, to show them all that there's another way to rule, with unity above all else," the primate said.

"I know," Zavros said. "I am with you, Your Grace. I am merely showing you what other eyes see. The masses still respect the Assembly, as they still worship the Evermen. But be careful, Primate. I merely ask that you be careful."

After Zavros left, Melovar picked up the book of the Evermen. Now, above all else, he longed to find this powerful relic. It was a weapon. He knew it would be a weapon. He lusted after it, thought about it night and day.

Where was it?

44

Amber was stunned by the wonderful normalcy of what she was doing: she was at the market, shopping for the ingredients she would use to cook Miro's supper.

She knew she was welcome at the conference, but Amber had no desire to be with all the lords and officers as they discussed supplies and casualties. She knew Miro would come up with a good plan, and she would have an opportunity to talk to him afterward.

But even as Amber picked up and examined withered yellow peppers, squeezed old potatoes, and weighed onions, she still felt apprehensive. It was only days after the liberation of Ralanast. What if some of the Black Army's soldiers were still in the city, desperate men who had taken to hiding and hadn't yet been found by Miro's men? Amber tried to force down her fears. Surely she had nothing to worry about.

Miro had tried to reassure her. "Remember," he'd said, "to the guards you were just another prisoner."

Amber had thought about Moragon and the son the Tingaran high lord thought was his. "I know," she had said, knowing it was a lie.

More afraid of telling Miro her secret than facing the streets, Amber had refused Miro's offer of an armed escort, eager to turn the conversation to another topic.

Part of Amber thought the journey to the market would do her good. Amber loved to cook, and the act of doing something she was familiar with, on her own and completely independent, away from talk of death and destruction, felt like just what she needed.

As she looked at her basket and the items she'd procured, Amber realized she was starting to enjoy herself. She would finely slice the mushrooms and olives and crush the walnuts, combining the trio over a hot pan. After she scooped out the seeds from the peppers, she would stuff the mixture into the cavity of each and roast them in a hot oven.

Having finished up at the vegetable market, Amber turned down a side street. She wanted to purchase a whole chicken, flattening it and seasoning it with herbs and lemon zest. She thought she'd seen the butcher's stall down this alley . . .

When she didn't find it, Amber halted and turned around, then took a left turn, still looking for the butcher's stall.

Amber suddenly stopped in her tracks, realizing she was lost. She began to tremble but held herself stiff and strong, promising herself she wouldn't be afraid. If she simply followed this street to its end, she would soon be back to where there were more people.

Her face set with determination and her elbow looped through her basket, Amber walked forward, trying to ignore the cloaked figure huddled in a doorway as she passed.

Amber wrung her hands as she walked, so nervous that when a hand thrust out and grabbed her shoulder, she didn't even scream, only whimpered. She looked up into the round face and tattooed cheek of a Tingaran.

Surely this was a nightmare. It wasn't happening.

He pulled her roughly to him, so close Amber could smell the stench of his breath. The basket fell out of her arms, clattering on the cobblestones. A few mushrooms rolled down the street, down, down, down . . .

"You're the whore what gave Moragon that brat," the Tingaran said, holding Amber's arm in a grip of iron.

Amber opened her mouth to scream, but his hand clapped over her mouth.

"None of that, love," he said. "You talk nice and quiet, else I gut you here." The Tingaran slowly lifted his hand away from Amber's mouth.

"I . . . I don't know what you're talking about," Amber said.

"Yes, it's you. Luck, she's with me. They can't call me deserter if I bring you in."

"Please let me go," Amber said.

She felt herself turned around and pushed against the wall. The Tingaran tied her hands behind her back at her wrists and then thrust a balled up piece of dirty cloth into her mouth.

"There's a few of us," the Tingaran said when he was done, "all wondering how we can get home without the officers hanging us as deserters."

Amber cried out, but the sound was muffled. Lord of the Sky, was this really happening?

"Don't worry, girl. We'll get you back to your one-armed lover safe and sound. I expect the high lord will reward us for bringing you in. You're coming with me."

Miro was glad Amber hadn't come to the conference.

As the area of land under the allies' control grew, the truth about the prison camp became impossible to hide. It sickened them all to their core, and if there was one thing they agreed on, it was that they needed to push all the way through to Seranthia, removing Primate Melovar Aspen from power and ridding the world of his evil.

Much was clear now that had previously been rumor and speculation. Amber shouldn't hear this.

Miro knew the whole picture now.

Some valiant men, perhaps templars rising up against the primate, had destroyed the Assembly's relics in Stonewater. With their destruction, the primate's source of essence vanished. This courageous act leveled the playing field, as both the Black Army and Altura's supplies of essence dried up, and the primate could no longer produce the elixir he used to control his minions.

Yet in the last few months the Black Army's devastating use of orbs, dirigibles, and avengers had increased. The primate had some new source of essence.

And now they knew what it was.

"We've destroyed the facility completely," Marshal Beorn said, "and the vats with it. I don't think it would do the common people any good to know what went on there."

"Agreed," High Lord Tiesto said. "However, I think we can safely assume this wasn't the only site."

"Rumors are there are two more, both in Tingara. I think Tingara makes sense," Miro said. "Simpler logistics and faster transportation of the essence to where it's needed."

"Lord of the Earth, what a mess," High Lord Tiesto said.

"We should make the location and destruction of these facilities a priority," said High Animator Salvatore.

"There just happens to be an army in the way," a moustached Halrana lord whose name Miro couldn't remember said wryly.

"There are some items of good news," Miro said. "First: the situation in Vezna. Marshal Rogan?"

Rogan spoke, "The Veznan high lord, Dimitri Corizon, had the taint." Rogan inclined his head to acknowledge Miro. "The lord marshal here was on a fact-finding mission in Rosarva when Dimitri was first given the elixir." Rogan paused. "However, just over a week ago, a minor lord and the captain of the high lord's personal guard swept Vezna's leadership clean."

"It couldn't have been easy," Miro said.

"That's incredible news," High Lord Tiesto said. "How did they succeed?"

"Well," Miro said, "as you know, Vezna is administered from the Borlag, in the heart of Rosarva. Around the Borlag is a moat, and the only way to cross the moat is via the Juno Bridge, a living system of vines and plants. An activation sequence must be spoken to cross the Juno Bridge. Otherwise, the bridge . . . reacts."

"The two conspirators changed the sequence at a very opportune moment," Rogan said, "and let the Juno Bridge do the work for them. They took out Dimitri Corizon and his coterie in a single sweep."

There were murmurs around the chamber at the news.

High Lord Tiesto turned to Miro. "Yet you've been there your-self, Lord Marshal, and survived to tell the tale. One day you'll have to tell me that story."

"At your convenience." Miro smiled. "So, High Lord, we can safely assume the Veznans are out of the war."

"Can we expect any assistance?"

"It's highly doubtful," Rogan said. "The Veznans, true to form, are already withdrawing and closing their borders. I'm sure they wish they'd never entered the war."

"Leaving us to pick up the pieces," Tiesto said.

Miro looked at his second in command. "Marshal Beorn, you're the most up to date with the Petryan situation."

Beorn scratched at his beard before speaking. "The second item of good news is that the desert men of House Hazara have taken Tlaxor, the Petryan capital."

There were gasps around the room as those who hadn't heard the news reacted.

"They say a great magic was performed at Lake Halapusa"— Beorn looked sidelong at Miro—"and the unconquerable city was taken in a day."

Miro had the news secondhand but had been relieved beyond belief to hear about the incredible freezing of the lake and the golden-haired woman who'd saved innumerable lives both in Petrya and here in Halaran. It could only be Ella.

Miro's thoughts darkened, however, when he thought about an eventual meeting with this desert prince. No one, not anyone, came to Miro's home under the pretence of friendship and took his sister away from him.

"The Petryans are also out of the war," Beorn said, "but these horsemen are heading for Tingara as we speak. They move faster than we do, and they haven't made clear their intentions. Rumor says the Hazarans are building a city, deep in the desert, and I hear they are a violent people."

"This is a matter for concern," High Lord Tiesto said. "We have to place this at the top of our agenda, even higher than the destruction of these horrific essence plants, I'm afraid. The Hazarans cannot be the first to reach Seranthia. The empire is in ruins, and what happens to Seranthia will determine the future of the world."

"I agree wholeheartedly," Miro said. "We must be first to Seranthia. This Prince Ilathor is not to be trusted, and his motives are unclear. Which brings me to the next item on the agenda." He paused, licking his lips. "The Akari."

One of Tiesto's lords, a man Miro didn't know, raised his eyebrows so high it looked like they would jump off his head. "The Akari? Tales to frighten children. Any rumors about them should not be credited."

"Let the lord marshal speak," Rogan growled.

"We've sent some scouting patrols into the Azure Plains—risky ventures behind enemy lines. We expected losses, but nothing of this scale. Hardly any of our patrols have returned, but those who've made it back alive speak of white-eyed warriors who cannot be defeated."

"Revenants?" the Halrana lord snorted. "I thought we were here to discuss strategy."

"I've questioned them all myself," Miro said, his patience growing thin, "and my men are not prone to delusions."

"Think about it," Rogan said. "It makes a horrible sense. The Akari are said to have been exiled to the north by the first emperor, Xenovere the Great, when the Tingaran Empire was newly formed. The story is they used their dead in unholy ways. What if this has something to do with Primate Melovar Aspen's new source of essence? What if the Akari have allied themselves to the primate? Or are perhaps under the thrall of his elixir?"

"Preposterous," the lord said haughtily.

"We'll soon find out," Miro said, grim faced, "for our objective of reaching Seranthia ahead of the Hazarans means we will need to move quickly. I would have preferred to move into Torakon via Loua Louna, leaving a small force behind us to lay siege to the Ring Forts, but for expediency we will now need to assault the Ring Forts directly. Marshal Scola has a large force with him, which, added to ours, will give us the manpower we need to take back Manrith, Penton, Ramrar, Charing, and finally the great fortress Sark. We will, however, suffer heavy losses."

"When we once more have control of the Ring Forts," Rogan continued, "we'll have a strong base from which to launch a direct assault on the Azure Plains in Torakon. Our objective is to push through quickly and decisively, using every weapon at our disposal, until we are standing in the streets of Seranthia."

There was a hesitant knock on the door, causing every man in the room to frown, a situation that would have been comical if their words weren't so grave. "What is it?" High Lord Tiesto called. "I left orders that we weren't to be disturbed."

A steward popped his head in. Miro recognized the man who had been planning the evening meal with Amber.

Suddenly, Miro felt a shiver of fear run through him. Why was the steward here?

"What is it?" Miro demanded.

"I'm sorry, terribly sorry, but I need to speak with the lord marshal."

"Tell me now," Miro said, unable to wait until he was outside the chamber.

"Lord Marshal, it's about Miss Amber . . . She was due back from the market hours ago. I went looking for her, but it appears she's gone."

As lord marshal, Miro had the prerogative of telling his men what to do. He felt no guilt at ordering the city of Ralanast to be searched from one end to the other.

He had never felt so furious, but the anger was directed completely at himself. His men leapt at every snapped command, fearful of their commander's rage, and soon there wasn't a soul in Ralanast who didn't know the lord marshal was looking for a young Alturan woman with brown eyes and auburn hair.

Miro put all battle plans on hold, forcing down any objections with an iron will. Yet, when two days had passed and Miro still hadn't found her, he finally stood on the steps of the Terra Cathedral, his fists clenched at his sides, impotent and uncertain, when Rogan Jarvish placed his hand on his shoulder.

"I lost her before," Miro whispered. "Why do I keep losing her? And it's always my fault. I lost her when I let her marry someone else. I lost her when I left her behind at the Bridge of Sutanesta. I lost her when I left her on her own in a city that I told her was safe, a city that I thought, in my arrogance, I had made safe."

"You can't control everything," Rogan said. "You're right— you're being arrogant, but not because you thought the city was safe. You're being arrogant because you think that the destiny of other people can be controlled by your actions. You aren't all powerful, Miro."

"It's my fault," Miro said.

"You're probably going to believe that you made a mistake, no matter what I say," Rogan said. "So I'll just say what I've always said: You learn from your mistakes and you move on."

Miro looked up at Rogan. "I never knew I took those words from you."

Rogan squeezed Miro's shoulder. "What are you going to do?" he asked.

"I keep losing the people I love. First it was Ella, when that desert man Jehral took her from me, and now it's Amber, the woman I want to be my wife. Rogan, I have to find her." Miro looked down at the floor. "Something happened in the prison camp, something she didn't tell me. I could see it in her eyes. Her disappearance must have something to do with it. If Tiesto discovers her here in Ralanast, he can keep her safe for me, but there are many who can search this city. If the enemy have her, they will have taken her to Torakon."

"If that's the case, your chances of finding her are slim," Rogan said.

"I have to try," Miro said. "Rogan, you will be commander for the next few days until I return. I know I'll be leaving the men in the best of hands. I give you my word that I'll be back as soon as I can."

45

"Stop," Prince Ilathor said quietly. "Do not move a muscle."

Ella froze, halfway through crouching at the little pool, cupping water in her hands to splash on her face. She looked sidelong at where the prince slowly reached forward to the flat rock beside her, and then with horror recognized the dark shape basking in the sun.

Ella's eyes grew wide, and she held her entire body rigid. The prince reached forward, and with incredible speed he snatched at the long shape. A moment later Ilathor held the snake by its neck as the lower half of its body writhed and swayed.

Ella drew back, looking frantically around for more snakes, but this was the only one. She stepped away from the prince as he grinned at her.

"What kind of snake is it?" she asked.

"It is called a death adder," he said.

"Lord of the Sky," she breathed. "I could have been killed."

"Not a chance." Prince Ilathor's smiled broadened. "This poor fellow is suffering from a misnomer."

"What do you mean?"

"He is very slow and rarely moves away when approached. So he was named a deaf adder. Over the years the name has become distorted, and now he is a death adder. Yet he harms no one."

"Why do you think the name changed?"

Ilathor shrugged. "Perhaps so that a man like me can impress a woman like you."

"You can let him go now," Ella said, looking askance at the prince.

He flung out his arm, the snake flying through the air to land in a nearby bush.

Ella quickly washed her face and then was silent as she walked by the prince's side, returning to where the Hazarans gave their horses some respite from the journey, on the sandy banks of a small river.

As they remounted and Ella kicked Afiri forward, she looked back the way they had come. The long column stretched as far as the eye could see, thousands of horsemen and many more on foot. Camp followers trailed in their wake: cooks, tinkers, grooms, and whores. Ella was glad she rode with the prince and Jehral at the head of the column; otherwise, she would have been as covered with dust as those behind. Bartolo and Shani also rode at the head, along with ten Petryan elementalists, friends of Shani's from Tlaxor.

Ella was surrounded by friends, and Prince Ilathor was always nearby, yet she felt alone. Since their night together she'd told the prince she needed time to think, and he'd respectfully honored her request. Ella felt guilty when she thought about Killian. Did that mean she didn't love the prince?

As Prince Ilathor took the column through the Gap of Garl, away from Petrya and toward Tingara, Ella realized she had never been this far from home. She wondered where Miro was and whether he was safe. She fingered the pendant on its chain at her neck, wondering what Prince Ilathor planned to do when they reached Tingara. How far did his ambition extend?

The temperature turned cool as they left the warm Petryan lands, and the mountain ranges no longer blocked the cold weather from the north. On one side, to the west, Ella could see the jagged tops of the Elmas, the range that separated Petrya from the lands of Altura and Halaran. On the other side of the Gap of Garl, the mighty Emdas rose in the east, looming over the column of riders, the mountain tops white and covered with clouds, the summits so high they could hardly be seen.

A speck grew on the red horizon, a returning scout from the flat land in the north. Their journey through the Gap of Garl took them first north and then east. It was a long way around, but it was the only way.

A cloud of dust rose behind the single rider. He was clad in Hazaran costume, and soon his yellow sash could be seen against the black. The scout pulled up in front of Prince Ilathor.

"A small army," the scout said, his breath coming between gasps, "up ahead. Just past that rise."

"What banner?" Jehral asked.

"A withered tree on gray," the scout said.

The prince looked first at Jehral, who raised his eyebrows, and then at Ella, who shook her head. Bartolo shrugged, and even Shani's face said she didn't know the markings.

"How many?" Prince Ilathor asked.

"Perhaps two thousand. It is hard to say."

"Go and speak with them. See if you can find out who they serve."

"Yes, my Prince," the scout said, wheeling his horse and riding away.

"If he doesn't come back by the time the sun hits that tree," the prince said, "he isn't coming back."

"You have a cold heart, desert prince," Shani said, low enough that the prince wouldn't hear, but close enough that Ella could.

"This is a poor place for a battle," Bartolo said. "There are hills to either side. We should move to the higher ground and fortify our position."

"He speaks sense, my Prince," Jehral said.

"Thank you, Bladesinger," Prince Ilathor said, "but that is not our way. Two thousand is nothing to an army this size."

———————

As they waited, more and more of the Hazaran riders arrived, to be deployed in fighting formation as a long line of riders, but the scout did not return.

Prince Ilathor prepared for battle.

The elders—those women who had been chosen to receive the lore of House Hazara—summoned illusionary warriors, storms, and whirlwinds. The sky overhead flashed, and lightning stabbed down at the earth. Dust rushed one way and then another as the elders struggled to keep control of their lore.

The open field was where the desert warriors fought best, and as Prince Ilathor's deadline for the scout's return approached and then passed, he signaled his tarn leaders and launched his army into action. The infantry and Petryan elementalists were to stay behind. They couldn't keep up with the horsemen, and of the Petryans only Shani was comfortable on a horse.

"Stay back, Ella," the prince commanded, as he spurred his black stallion into action, determined to be at the forefront of the attack.

Seeing her friends in the line, Ella ignored the prince and joined Shani, Bartolo, and Jehral, keeping her horse close by her red-robed friend.

Ella had to admit she was impressed, even exhilarated, to be traveling with such an army, imagining the fear that the lightning, storms, and the horses themselves must strike into the enemy's hearts.

Yet as the air filled with the thunder of hooves on the hard earth, the temperature suddenly dropped, giving Ella a premonition that something terrible was about to happen. She gripped her reins tightly in her hands, her knees pressed hard into the horse's flanks.

Ella saw Afiri's breath steaming in the chill air; surely such a rapid decrease in temperature wasn't natural?

The ground before her rose in a steep incline. Ahead, the thundering mass of riders crested the rise in front of her and then vanished under the hill as the warriors went down the other side. As the steepness increased, Ella leaned forward in the saddle and spurred Afiri on, realizing she had lost sight of Jehral, and only Shani and Bartolo were with her now.

Ella reached the crest, and the vista opened up before her. An army such as the world had never seen raced down the hill: horses' hooves thundered, desert warriors raised scimitars above their heads, and lightning crashed around them. A single cloud became a multitude in an instant, so the Hazarans appeared to be flying out of a storm that a moment ago had simply not been there.

Ella could now see the gray banner flying over the tightly formed ranks of their enemy, with the opposing soldiers arranged into three columns. In the centermost column, pikes rose up into the air, the first dozen ranks holding theirs bristled in front. The column to the left consisted of heavily-armored men and women in gray tabards, each holding a sword or an axe. On the right was a smaller column of warriors with maces, and half a dozen men in silver robes clustered at the rear.

Ella knew something was terribly, desperately wrong. They were too disciplined, too still. Surely no one faced an attack like this without some men breaking?

The gray-clad axemen and swordsmen all held their weapons in the air, moving in perfect unison. The pikemen braced themselves, grim and unwavering. One of the silver-robed men raised his arms in the air, as if summoning powerful magic.

The column of axemen and swordsmen on the left moved forward at an angle, the macemen on the right following suit, and the pikemen in the center began an orderly retreat backward, with the pikes in front still facing the screaming riders.

Unwittingly, Prince Ilathor's men became funneled into the space opening up ahead of the retreating pikemen. Some of the long line of riders smashed into the swordsmen and macemen on the left and right, but the majority fell in behind those ahead, forming a spearhead that thrust into the space opening up in front of them.

Ella was no strategist, yet even she could see the disaster about to unfold. Placed as she was somewhere in the middle, she could see that the gray warriors now flanked the riders on the left and on the right, like the horns of a bull. Ella wondered at the incredible discipline of the enemy. They still hadn't made a sound, and their ranks were in such tight formation, they reminded Ella of Halrana constructs.

Then the riders in front hit the bristling wall of pikes, and the gray warriors to the sides closed in.

The sound of hundreds of horses being impaled was something Ella never wanted to hear again. The prince's army, however, was by far the larger, and the momentum of the horsemen took them deep into the ranks of the pikemen. Desert warriors slashed down from horseback, their heavy sabers designed specifically for this type of combat, and Prince Ilathor turned them in an arc, evidently intending to drive into the swordsman on his left flank and burst through to regroup outside the enemy's attempted encirclement.

It might have worked, but the majority of the riders faced forward, and the enemy swordsmen were on their left. With unbelievable ferocity, the flanks closed in, attempting to envelop the Hazarans in front, on the sides, and—most dangerous of all—the rear.

Ella's eyes widened with fear as she saw enemy swordsmen and axemen closing in on her left, the gray warriors wielding huge two-handed swords, battle-axes, and some even with two smaller axes held in both hands. She saw every rider around her becoming embroiled, preventing any movement. The whinnies of horses, jangles of armor, and clashes of weapons split the air.

Nearby, a Hazaran warrior slashed down with his scimitar at a huge man wielding a two-handed broadsword. The desert warrior's saber bounced off the gray warrior's armor, and the Hazaran quickly raised his sword to block his enemy's two-handed counterstroke. The clang of steel rang like a bell, and the Hazaran grimaced at the numbing strength of the gray warrior's blow. Then the broadsword came swinging down again, not at the rider, but instead at his horse. With a single blow the horse's head came off at the neck, blood spurting in a fountain as the animal collapsed and rolled, trapping its rider underneath. Ella turned her horse in the stricken man's direction to help, but the swordsman in gray thrust down at the Hazaran, opening up his throat.

"Ella, look out!" she heard Shani scream.

A warrior held Ella's leg by the stirrup as he copied the swordsman's maneuver, swinging his axe at Afiri's neck. Ella couldn't believe how utterly fearless these men were. The Petryans had found confronting skilled warriors on horseback terrifying, yet these soldiers simply attacked horses and men alike.

Ella kicked out with her leg and reared Afiri out of the way, one hand clinging to the reins, the other reaching for her pocket. She spoke a rapid series of activations, calling forth the blinding light and protective power of her enchantress's dress.

The warrior holding Ella's stirrup looked up and snarled silently, his lips curled to bare his teeth. His skin was the color of snow, his long hair loose and as gray as the withered-tree tabard he wore on his chest. A chill ran up Ella's spine as she realized his eyes were entirely white. She saw rotten flesh at the edges of his eyes, his nostrils, and his mouth.

He was dead.

Ella had heard of revenants, sometimes referred to in the stories as draugar. Now she was confronting one in the flesh, on the field of battle. Terror struck Ella at the knowledge that they weren't just the creations of stories. Revenants existed.

One was trying to kill her.

Ella now realized what she was seeing. A Hazaran sliced at the neck of a warrior, creating a deep gash, yet no blood came out, and the warrior kept fighting. One revenant crawled on the ground, an arm and a leg hacked away, yet he continued. Underneath their armor Ella could see the eerie blue glow of runes seeping through the cracks.

House Hazara's lore relied on illusions to strike terror into their enemies. Ella now wondered whether the tough desert men would be able to keep their own fear at bay as they battled an enemy that wouldn't be killed, didn't bleed, felt no remorse, and fought with incredible savagery and discipline.

Ella's fingers found what she was looking for. She took the wand out of her pocket, hoping it would work against the revenants.

After the liberation of Tlaxor, Ella had decided she needed a weapon to take into battle. She didn't want to ever again be in another situation like she had when Bartolo had rescued her and Shani at the Poltoi Palace.

It had been a long time since enchanters had themselves fought in battle. Unlike animators and elementalists, who were both the rune-makers and the users of their magic, enchanters created a much wider range of items, but typically preferred to stay clear of any fighting.

Yet there had been a time when enchanters fought, before bladesingers, zenblades, and armorsilk. In the time of Maya Pallandor, the woman who had invented armorsilk, there were objects that were common in those days but had since fallen out of use.

Wands.

The prince wouldn't give Ella any more essence, even after her success at Tlaxor, so she had simply lied, telling Jehral that rather than saying no to her request for more essence, Prince Ilathor had agreed wholeheartedly.

Jehral hadn't been too pleased with Ella when he'd discovered the deception, and the prince had been furious. Ella ignored them both and finished her work.

The wand Ella now held in her hand was as long as her forearm and tipped with a prism of gold-flecked quartz. It was made of dark hazel wood, with three facets rising to the tip, and was strangely warm to the touch. Tiny symbols covered its length, so small that Ella had needed a lens to draw the runes with the finest of scrills.

Ella fought to control the quaver in her voice as she began to chant. The revenant thrust its sword up at her head, but she turned and it instead hit her dress with a blow that would have skewered her through. Ella chanted the runes without pausing, still muttering under her breath as she pointed the wand at the soldier's rotting face.

A bolt of energy left the wand, tearing a coin-sized hole in the revenant's neck. Ella chanted some more, and a second circle of white fire left the wand to strike its forehead. The warrior fell down, twitching once before lying still and unmoving.

Ella looked around her at the battle. A ball of fire flew through the air, sizzling with red energy before it struck a revenant warrior. The warrior burst into flames, and Ella's eyes traced the fireball back to its origin to see Shani on horseback nearby, the palms of her hands centered over a growing bud of fire as she prepared to launch another.

Ella continued to chant, keeping the magic of the wand alive, even as she knew it would drain rapidly. Two revenants ran at Shani, one bursting into flames, the other crumpling to the ground as Ella's bolt of light created a fist-sized hole in its temple.

Ella realized all the Hazarans around her and Shani were dead. The two women brought their horses close together as the swordsmen and axemen closed in. Ella and Shani faced in opposite directions, balls of fire and bolts of light flying again and again from their hands.

"This way!" a man's voice called.

Ella saw a fiery sword tear through three draugar. She heard the song of a bladesinger join her own chanting as Bartolo slashed toward them. Seeing he was on foot, Ella incongruously wondered if he preferred it to horseback.

"Come on!" Bartolo cried.

Ella whirled Afiri, and she and Shani spurred into action. Fireballs tore through the air, and bolts from Ella's wand took the revenants down one after the other. Yet they kept coming, their inevitable destruction from the two women meaning nothing to those already dead.

Shani took Bartolo's wrist, and with the incredible agility of a bladesinger, he swung up behind her on the horse.

Ahead, Ella could see the Hazarans finally break free of the enfolding formation of revenants and slash their way through the axemen and swordsmen, moving in the direction from which they'd come. Ella and Shani joined them, and as the desert warriors galloped as fast as they could for safety, the revenants continued to chase on foot until they gave up pursuit.

◆━━◆

"It is as the rumors stated," Jehral said, shaking his head.

"Wait," Ella said, rounding on the prince. "Are you telling me you knew something like that was out there?"

"They were rumors," Prince Ilathor said. "Nothing more."

They were in the prince's command tent, raised high on a hill with a complete view of the land below. The Hazarans had spent a day recovering and building fortifications—even now they were checking their positions, digging pits, and erecting barricades—and on the second day Prince Ilathor had called this hasty gathering.

"Yet you still attacked without first scouting the land, assessing their strength, forming a battle plan . . ." Ella said, her eyes blazing.

"Women," Prince Ilathor snapped, "are not normally allowed at these discussions. Hold your tongue, Ella, or speak with civility."

Ella opened her mouth to retort, but caught Shani shaking her head.

"Revenants," Bartolo murmured. "Who could have known?"

Ella was still angry, part of her wondering if it was a reaction to the fear. She'd almost died. Prince Ilathor had lost a third of his army. *A third!*

"And you know what the scouts say now," Jehral said. "There is another army also flying the gray banner, behind this one. This second force is at least five thousand strong."

Everyone in the tent silently digested the information.

Jehral looked at Prince Ilathor. "Tell her," he said.

"What?" Ella demanded.

"A messenger came last night," the prince said. "Ella, Halaran has been liberated. Ralanast is once again a free city, and the allied army of Alturans and Halrana have occupied the Ring Forts."

"That's wonderful news," Ella said. "Did you hear about my brother?"

"There's a new commander. That's all I know."

Ella put her hand to her mouth.

"Ella," Jehral said. "There could be many reasons for someone else to lead them."

"There is more," the prince said. "This news is not good, I am afraid." He sighed. "The army of green and brown recently suffered a great defeat. I wish we had received this message just one day earlier, for our own disaster could have been averted. On the Azure Plains, the Alturans and Halrana, like us, faced those who carry the gray banner. They are called the Akari—perhaps that name has meaning for you. The allied army fell back after suffering heavy losses."

Ella felt Shani squeeze her shoulder. Anger and frustration coursed through her in equal parts. Overriding it all, she worried for her people, and for her brother.

"Ella," the prince said, "this is lore I cannot comprehend. What can you tell us?"

Ella forced herself to concentrate, to use her mind and ability to reason. Nothing was impossible. Everyone had a weakness.

"Supposedly the first Tingaran emperor banished the Akari to the north. It's cold there, so the dead would decompose more slowly. Bringing them to life must use a large amount of essence, I can guarantee that," Ella said. "Shani's flame worked well against them, and I would guess they don't much like heat."

"Good, good," the prince said. "Go on."

"The men in silver robes could be similar to Halrana animators. Try taking them out." Ella paused. "The fact is, I need to learn more about them."

"What do you need?" the prince asked. "Essence? You shall have it. Anything else?"

Ella suddenly knew what it was she needed to do. Her people needed her just as much as the Hazarans. Even if she found a weakness and told it to the prince, the Alturans would still be in the same position they were in now. Ella needed to help not just the Hazarans against the Akari, but also Miro and Altura, in any way she could.

"I need to leave," Ella said, "to travel ahead of this army, into Tingara, where I can learn about these revenants. I promise you I will find a way to defeat them. I know it will be risky, and so I'll go alone."

"Ella, no," Shani said.

"No," Prince Ilathor said, "I forbid it."

"Your brother asked me to keep you alive," Bartolo said.

Ella knew this was what she had to do, but she also knew it wouldn't be right to risk her friends' lives as well as her own.

She reached back and pulled the hood of her green silk dress over her head.

"I command that you stay!" Prince Ilathor said.

"You can't command me," Ella said. "You never could."

Ella spoke the words and vanished.

46

Moragon was too busy to see Amber, and for that she was grateful. Not knowing what to do with her, some legionnaires manacled her legs and gave her a small tent, their treatment somewhere between solicitous and hostile. After weeks of hard travel, Amber was once again under lock and key, with warriors in black surrounding her. This was no prison, however; this was the main enemy host, deep within the Black Army's encampment, where escape was impossible.

The soldiers who had abducted Amber from Ralanast went on to rejoin their comrades, and she was once more alone. Their plan was a success, and rather than being named deserters, an officer sent them back to their commander with a grunt. Any reward for bringing her in was laughed at, but the warrior who had first found Amber tried anyway, persistently harassing the officer who said he was the closest he'd get to High Lord Moragon. A dagger in the chest silenced the soldier's demands, and his companions decided not to argue the case further.

Amber tried not to think about where she was and what it was they would do with her, but her mind wouldn't let go. She wondered what death would feel like when it came. Most likely it would be the swift and painful death of a sharp sword thrust. Perhaps they would slice her throat or put a blade into her chest. She doubted it would be the rope, for these men weren't squeamish when it came to shedding blood, even the blood of a woman.

From what she'd seen on the journey and heard from the soldiers, Amber knew she was in Torakon, somewhere in the Azure Plains. The blue haze on the horizon extended in all directions, never obscured by hills or forests. The land was flat and covered with wiry grass, and the men of the Black Army spread across it like flies, so numerous that Amber wondered how Miro's army could ever hope to defeat them.

After several days in the tent, Amber's legs hurt, and she shifted them, wincing at the hard iron digging into the tender flesh of her ankles. She knew Miro wouldn't have any idea why she had disappeared or where she had been taken.

There was one night, though, when there was a great commotion she thought might have been him. It sounded like an animal ran wild, causing cries of confusion and shouts of anger. Amber waited that night, hoping it would be Miro, but she waited in vain.

Amber heard the sound of approaching footsteps, and her heart started to race. She looked around desperately for a weapon, but the only furniture in the space was a sleeping pallet and the post Amber was chained to, hammered into the ground.

Fingers untied the knots on the flap of the canvas tent, and Amber was surprised to see the face of a woman. She was young— younger even than Amber—and wore the simple tunic of a farmer's daughter. Her curly dark hair made Amber think she might be Halrana.

Then Amber noticed the small bundle held in the girl's arms, and realization hit her like a hand squeezing her heart. Amber would know that beautiful baby from among a thousand others.

"Ohhh," Amber breathed and held out her arms. "Please. Please! May I hold him?"

"Here, miss," the girl said, squatting down on the earth next to Amber and passing her the bundle. "He's yours, in't he?"

Amber clutched him to her breast and felt a feeling of such intense joy to be reunited with her son that for a long time she couldn't speak. She marveled at how much he'd grown in the several weeks she'd been separated from him, and couldn't stop herself from playing with his tiny fingers and cooing at his constantly changing expressions. Amber lost track of time, holding and rocking him, never saying a word, simply smiling and kissing him gently on the forehead time and time again.

"I'd best go," the girl said, as the babe made an urgent, distressed sound. "He's hungry and wantin' a feed. Anyone catches me here, I'll be whipped."

Amber realized she hadn't spoken at all to the woman who was taking care of her son. This must be the wet nurse, she realized, a girl who had probably lost her own child shortly after giving birth. It must have taken a lot of courage for her to come here.

"Can you come again?" Amber said. "Please . . . I just want to see him."

"I'll try, miss," she promised.

"I'm Amber."

"Casey," the girl said.

"Thank you, Casey," Amber said. "I know coming here is a big risk."

"I know I'd want to see my boy, weren't he dead," Casey said plainly. "Better go. I'll try come back."

———◆———

Another week passed, and Amber counted herself lucky that in that time Moragon was still away or too busy to deal with her. Then she overheard some soldiers talking outside her tent and discovered what it was Moragon was busy with.

A battle was about to be fought against the allied army of Alturans and Halrana. It was time for Moragon to bring out his "secret weapon," something called the Akari. Or perhaps someone? The name was familiar.

Amber heard the sound of marching footsteps all throughout the day and night as the Black Army's soldiers departed for the coming battle. It was going to be a pitched effort, an all-out struggle between the two armies. Amber worried endlessly about her child, and she feared for Miro. Between the two, she was so worried that she couldn't eat the thin stew the soldiers gave her.

With the encampment nearly deserted, Amber began to think about escape. Casey was a simple girl, but she seemed to be free to wander about the camp. When Casey came a second time, Amber asked the girl to visit one of the blacksmiths and try to procure an iron file.

Casey's face screwed up as she thought about it, but in the end she promised to do what she could, and Amber spent yet another day worrying and fruitlessly running one escape plan after another through her mind. If she could get out before the Black Army's soldiers returned, she could flee with both Casey and her son. There was a chance, a small one, but a chance nonetheless, that Amber could escape, this time with her child.

Amber desperately hoped that Casey would bring her the file soon. She would use it to escape the manacles, and while the soldiers were distracted by the battle, she and Casey would get away. Amber didn't know how much interest Moragon was taking in the babe he thought was his son, but with other things on his mind, he might just let her go.

It was raining on the day the soldiers returned. The Black Army had won a great victory against a larger number of Alturans and Halrana, holding against the allied army and eventually pushing them back to the Ring Forts in Halaran.

For some reason, though, the soldiers were far from jubilant. It appeared they owed their success to the Akari. With a jolt Amber suddenly remembered the stories from when she was a child, and as the accounts of the overheard soldiers sent shivers down her spine, she realized what the Akari were.

Revenants were fighting with the Black Army.

Amber jumped when she heard gruff voices outside and fingers fumbling at the knots in the tent flap. Realizing it must be Casey, she calmed herself, feeling the familiar warmth of excitement to see her child and wondering if the girl had been successful in her quest to get the iron file.

But instead of the girl, a man thrust his head through the opening. Amber put her hand to her mouth with shock, and a horrible sinking feeling settled through her stomach as he pushed into the tent and settled down, crouching on the floor, grinning at Amber.

"We won today, Alturan woman," Moragon said. "I couldn't tell you how many of your countrymen we killed."

"Who are the Akari?" Amber asked. "Would you have still won without them?"

Moragon frowned. "The Akari are our allies. Their lore allows them to animate the dead. I'm sure you can imagine a dead warrior is hard to kill."

"So they are your superiors, then?"

"No, woman, not even our equals." He pointed to his metal arm and the runes covering it. "I would like to see the Akari replace a limb with one twice as strong. They have weaknesses, many of them, but for now they are proving useful."

"What weaknesses?" Amber asked. "Your men seem to think they're anything but weak."

Moragon scowled. "The bodies don't last long in this climate," he said. "But most of all, they require a fearful amount of essence. Their leader, Dain Barden, is fielding an army of draugar so large he can hardly control it, and we're providing the essence from our new supplies, but even that isn't enough. With the Akari dependent on us for essence, we can curb their power at any time."

Moragon reached behind him. "Much as I enjoy speaking with you, the reason I'm here is that I brought you a gift," he said, handing her a covered basket.

"Open it," Moragon said.

Amber cautiously lifted the lid on the basket. She saw brown curls, a simple face, an expression of pain, and the horrible flaps of skin and gashes of red that remained when a head was taken off. Amber recoiled in horror and pushed the basket away from her.

"No," Amber moaned. Who could do such a thing to a woman?

"You're very crafty," Moragon said. "I gather you must have been jealous of her taking care of your child, so you gave the simple girl a task you knew would see her killed."

"That's not true!"

"Now that she's dead, who's going to feed the boy? You've killed your son's wet nurse, and now he's going to starve."

"Please, no. Give him to me."

"Bring the boy!" Moragon called.

A moment later the baby was in Amber's arms.

"Let's hope you can feed him," Moragon said. "Else I'll need to find a new wet nurse, and it'll be your head we deliver to the next girl as a warning."

Moragon left the basket with Casey's head in the corner of the room. Amber continued to tremble, but she realized the position she was in. If her milk had run its course, Moragon would do the same thing to her that he had done to Casey.

Amber hated him. She hated him with all her heart.

As the babe made sucking motions and little urgent noises, Amber gave him her nipple and prayed.

Her prayers were answered when she felt him taking from her greedily.

The next morning when Amber woke with the babe in her arms, the basket with the head was gone.

47

"Three men," Layla said, "and one woman who struggled. Her arms were tied behind her back, but her legs were free." She pointed out the tracks, but all Miro saw were slight scratch marks in the dirt.

"How long ago?" Miro asked. His blood ran cold at the thought of Amber being under the power of these men.

"Three days. They were moving quickly."

Miro didn't know how the Dunfolk healer had found out about Amber's abduction, but as he'd left Ralanast, she was suddenly there beside him. He'd tried thanking her and releasing her to go home— it would be dangerous, heading into enemy lands, he told her—but Layla had said she owed him a debt for helping her people against the nightshades.

The soldiers who had taken Amber had found a way down to the Azure Plains from the tall cliffs above. It was tough going, and Miro's heart reached out to Amber. The journey would have been a nightmare, and she would have been filled with constant dread about what would happen at the end.

Why were they so interested in her? Miro was thankful that they hadn't just killed her and left her by the side of the road, but he realized there must be some reason for the special interest these soldiers had taken. What would happen to her once they reached the Black Army's encampment?

"There it is." Layla pointed.

From their rocky trail still high above the plains, Layla indicated a cluster of black spots against the blue haze on the horizon. Shading his eyes, Miro peered at the enemy encampment. The soldiers had taken Amber somewhere Miro would never be able to free her from.

"Stop," Layla said, holding Miro's arm when he tried to continue forward. "There is nothing for you here."

"She's in there somewhere!"

"There is no way for you to get in, and you have no way of knowing if her journey ended here. You do not keep your prisoners with your soldiers, do you? They would have sent her away, wouldn't they?"

Miro knew he couldn't answer Layla's questions, because he didn't know why they had taken Amber in the first place. Layla was right though. It stood to reason that she would have been taken to another prison camp rather than being kept with the men. Miro had a duty to his command back with the army. Every part of Miro's reason told him to turn back with Layla.

But his heart told him he had to try.

"I need you to go back," Miro said. "Go and see Marshal Beorn, and tell him I'll be behind you."

"There is a big battle coming," Layla said. "You might be too long."

"I know," Miro said, "but I can't leave her."

"I understand," Layla said, "but if the battle is fought and lost without you there, you will never forgive yourself."

"You're right," Miro said, "but if I don't try to find her, I'll never forgive myself either."

Moragon sat in a thronelike wooden chair, broad and high-backed, discussing the coming battle with Dain Barden.

The melding high lord of House Tingara and the leader of the Akari were as different as two men could be. Moragon was tall, tanned, and broad, with a shaved head and an arm of metal covered in silver runes. He wore a leather jerkin on his otherwise bare chest and tight-fitting black trousers with heavy brown boots. The yellow tint of his eyes gave him a feverish look, and the servant who topped up his mug with the oily black elixir looked fearful.

Dain Barden was taller even than Moragon, the top of his head nearly touching the roof of the command tent as he paced. His muscled legs stamped heavily on the ground, and he occasionally looked at the war hammer at his belt as if wanting to use it on someone. Silver fur covered his shoulders, and his leather armor was bleached to a deathly near white. His lips turned down in a scowl, and his brow furrowed in cruel lines.

"We want to crush them, completely and overwhelmingly," Moragon said.

"And I keep telling you, we don't have the essence for such a long engagement. We're losing draugar daily due to rot and depletion," Dain Barden said. "You can't do it without us, no matter what you think. Their army is too large."

"Then, Dain Barden, what do you suggest?"

"We have to make this first engagement decisive, yet at the same time conserve our strength until the next carts of essence arrive from Tingara. We're fielding so many draugar—and spread so thinly—that if it weren't for the supplies coming from the primate, we would have headed back to the north long ago."

"Why don't you?" Moragon asked.

"The man you serve gave us a promise. We intend to make sure he fulfills that promise, and as long as he keeps the essence coming, we'll be able to make sure he does. As he strengthens our numbers to fight these rebels, he also gives us more draugar to make sure he fulfills his end of the bargain. We want this relic of the Evermen."

Moragon shrugged. "You can have it, for all I care. My task is to defeat our enemies."

"And bring the world under one rule. Yes, I've heard the speeches."

"You don't think it's possible?" Moragon asked.

"I think it's possible. But is the primate the man to do it? Are you?"

"We have the essence," Moragon said.

"You do. Using the techniques we gave you. I find myself wondering how you manage to glean so much, where we ourselves struggle to accumulate just a small percentage of what the primate sends us. I've heard rumors, Moragon. They say you aren't just extracting the essence from your dead. They say that when you need more bodies, you just go and kill yourselves some more."

"Rumors," Moragon said. "It's war. There's never a shortage of bodies."

"We'll see," Dain Barden said.

"Wait," Moragon said, holding up his hand.

"What is it?"

"I sense something," Moragon said, standing. "A presence."

Miro had been lucky to have escaped notice this long. Several times he'd noticed Moragon tilt his head or pause mid-sentence. Once the melding even shifted in his chair, glancing around the shadowed command tent.

Miro had been whispering under his breath, a trick he'd used before to keep the shadow ability of his armorsilk activated while hiding. But shadow drained his armorsilk at a phenomenal rate, and in his desire to learn more, he had waited, hidden in the dark corner of the command tent, too long.

Worst of all, he still didn't know where Amber was.

Miro made a decision. He let the shadow effect go, changing his song to give the protective power of his armorsilk priority. He drew his zenblade from behind his back, cursing that he hadn't brought his rail bow.

"A bladesinger!" Moragon shouted. "Guards!"

Dain Barden pulled his war hammer from his belt, eyes roving with menace, but Moragon didn't bother to grab a weapon; his grafted arm was weapon enough.

Miro spun and tore a huge hole in the side of the tent. He hadn't learned as much as he might have liked, but he knew the knowledge he had would still be vital to the struggle. He ducked as he heard a sizzling sound and Moragon's arm tore through the air where a moment ago his head had been.

Every instinct told Miro to turn around and face his enemies. He didn't know if he could defeat both Moragon and the leader of the Akari, but he could try.

But if he failed, the men he was responsible for would never know how sparse their enemy's supplies of essence were. If he failed, who would care about Amber in his stead?

Miro turned on his heel to delay his opponents, thrusting his zenblade at Moragon's head before leaping outside, into the open air. Faster than Miro would have thought possible, the melding ducked and ran forward with the speed only those with the taint of the elixir possessed. The metal arm smashed into Miro's side, knocking the wind out of him. Miro fell to the ground, choking and coughing.

Miro tried to regain his breath, rolling to the side as his second opponent exited the tent and Dain Barden's hammer smashed the ground where he'd been a moment before. Miro jumped back to his feet but the Akari leader changed tactic and thrust the head of his weapon into Miro's face. Miro managed to pull back, but the hammer still hit his temple with the force of mountains, nearly causing him to black out.

Miro gulped a breath of air and forced out the words that would strengthen his armorsilk. He faced his two opponents with the zenblade held out in front of him.

Even if he could take them both, in moments Miro would be overwhelmed by sheer numbers.

"I recognize you," Moragon said. He grinned. "You've got a nerve, Lord Marshal, I'll give you that. Just so you know, when I'm done, every Alturan woman will be shared among my men. They'll thank me for the opportunity to serve."

Miro heard shouts and cries. He scanned to both sides. "I'll see you on the battlefield," he said.

"You'll never get back to your men in time," Dain Barden said. "In fact, you'll never get out of here alive."

"We'll see," Miro said.

There was one last sequence Ella had built into Miro's armorsilk. He used it now, hoping it would be enough.

Miro chanted the runes quickly, one after the other.

A second bladesinger stood beside him, every movement a copy of Miro's own. As his lips moved, a third appeared, then five more, and then ten more.

The illusions appeared all around him. As Miro used the confusion to escape from the very heart of the enemy camp, he again thanked his sister for saving his life.

In the end, though, Dain Barden was right, and Miro missed the battle. He saw it unfold from a distance as he returned to the west, watching in horror as the revenants of the Akari tore through the ranks of the soldiers in green and brown, eventually causing the allied army to break, fleeing back to the protection of the Ring Forts.

Miro hated himself for missing the battle, and now that he hadn't managed to find Amber, he hated himself for trying. He knew he was being foolish, that if he'd managed to find Amber, he would feel differently.

But when he made it back to Sark and saw the expression on Rogan's face, it didn't make him feel any better.

48

Ella had never been so filled with rage. She thought about all she had seen and all she now knew, and she wanted to hurt the ones who had done this. She wanted to hurt them badly.

She ate a cold meal of dried fruit and biscuit and tried to formulate a strategy, to use a clear head and intelligence when what she really wanted was to feel emotion. Through the trees ahead of her, she could see three sets of twinkling lights. One set was the prison camp, the second was the camp of the soldiers, and the third was the terrible place where they took the bodies.

It was located near the road from Seranthia to Sakurai, capital of Torakon, which meant Ella was in Tingara somewhere. Once she made the decision to leave the Hazarans, she had swiftly outdistanced the army, able to make her way through smaller paths and back routes, traveling night and day, burning with her desire to find a way to defeat these Akari and their revenants.

When she'd come across this place and seen the vats, her intuition told her there was something here that wasn't right. She had explored the facility, using the shadow effect of her enchantress's dress, and had spoken to some of the prisoners. She had deciphered the runes on the bubbling vats as well as she was able to, given the strange lore she had never encountered before.

And Ella heard the screams.

She told the prisoners to have heart, for she would be back, and soon Ella knew everything there was to know about what went on at the facility. She knew there were two of these places: the one close to her, and another not far away, also in Tingara. There had been a third, in Halaran, but it had been liberated at the same time as Ralanast.

Ella wondered whether Miro knew about the facility in Ralanast and what he made of what the primate was doing. She hoped the allied commanders realized this war wouldn't be over until the primate was dead, and allied soldiers walked the streets of Seranthia.

A constant flow of essence departed from the facility, stored in conspicuous glass canisters and piled atop drudge-pulled carts. Ella knew the essence was going to the Akari and that without the constant supply they wouldn't be able to field so many revenants.

She had found her enemy's weakness, although even if she hadn't, Ella still wouldn't have been able to pass this place by. Filled with rage, Ella knew she had to free the prisoners and destroy this place.

Ella was glad she had her wand. Without it, her difficult task would have been made impossible.

She would wait until the middle of the night.

Then she would strike.

49

Killian spent his last hours thinking.

His thoughts twisted and turned as he dwelled on what he could have done differently. He pondered the secrets the old man had promised to reveal but never did. He wondered if he was ready to die.

He thought about Ella.

She would never know what had happened to him. Did she even care? A girl like her, she would probably have found herself a strong lover by now, someone to see her through the war. Killian wished he could see her one last time.

This was his last night, the guards said. Killian had been deemed a troublesome prisoner. The guards hadn't bothered to hide what would be done with him—why hide it from those who would soon die anyway? With the morning light they were going to take him out and slice his throat. His blood would sluice into a special well, and when it was all drained out of him, they would toss his corpse into one of the huge vats. Killian's body would provide the fuel that powered the enemy's war machine.

Perhaps he'd been too arrogant, too confident of himself. When Killian saw Evrin on the cart with all those other prisoners, back near Seranthia, he'd followed them to this camp. He had been looking for Evrin, and after finding him, Killian could hardly restrain himself. It was all about to be revealed. He would find Evrin, they would escape the camp, and Killian would help Evrin with his quest after Evrin told Killian who he really was.

His mind so fixed on his objective that he could think of little else, Killian had scouted the terrain before deciding he was ready to break into the camp and free Evrin.

The defenses had been stronger than he'd expected, or perhaps he was simply unprepared. He didn't even have a sword; just himself and his stealth, his strength, and his agility.

He had clung to the bottom of a goods cart to get in, then let go when the guards became distracted by a commotion in the yard. He'd hidden behind the base of a guard tower, getting his bearings and deciding on a course of action after the camp went to sleep. and then he realized what the commotion was.

At the same time that Killian saw the cause of the tumult and recognized that the fleeing man in a scraggly white robe was Evrin, he'd felt a sword prick under his armpit.

So close, but not close enough.

Evrin had made it out, but his rescuer had not.

Now, after living in the camp on starvation rations, after a recent failed escape attempt, with three guards killed and two gravely wounded, it was Killian's time to die.

He almost wished they hadn't told him. The knowledge made Killian's last night torture. Somehow the night both dragged interminably and passed much too fast for his liking.

Killian wished he could have a chance to fight, but his legs were manacled, tied by a chain to a sunken stake, and his bound hands afforded little movement. He was to spend his last night in the small hut where they put those who were destined to die.

With nothing better to do, Killian decided to work on the stake. He knew that even if he made it outside, the guards would simply beat him until he couldn't think and then tie him even more tightly, and he wouldn't get far with his legs manacled and wrists bound.

Yet Killian decided to try anyway. It was better to die fighting than to give up all hope.

***

It was nearly the middle of the night, and Killian's ankles were bleeding freely as he pushed the stake away from him and then pulled it toward him, again and again. Killian's wrists became bruised and the skin red and torn, but he kept at it, pushing and pulling, pushing and pulling . . .

He stopped, breathing heavily, and decided it was time to try to get the stake free again. He squatted down with his hands clasped around the pole and slowly tried to stand, feeling the veins throbbing in his forehead as he pulled on the stake.

He could feel it coming! Killian groaned with effort, stifling the sound, until he finally felt the stake slide out of the earth, before rising to his full height.

His legs were still manacled, but he could now hold the chain in his hands. Positioned at the end of the chain, the stake now made a handy weapon. His wrists were still bound, but Killian had been a thief and an acrobat. He could still move—enough to take some of the enemy with him, at any rate.

Killian retreated to the hut's far wall, as far as he could get from the door. He tucked his head into his shoulder, and with the clumsy gait his manacled ankles gave him, he ran at the door.

Killian knew how to move so that all of his power was directed to one part of his body, and this time he put all of his energy into his shoulder.

The poorly built frame splintered instantly. Killian's momentum took him forward, and he tumbled onto the ground, rolling and then picking himself up as best he could.

He looked around him. Killian knew what he was doing was suicide, but if he could take one or two of the sadistic guards with him, it would be worth it.

Strangely, the guards hadn't come at the noise of Killian bursting through the doorway. Where were they?

Killian ducked his head as the sound of a thunderous boom came from everywhere at once. Thousands of huddled prisoners came to their feet uncertainly, wondering what was going on.

He saw a guard looking around with sword bared. The guard's back was turned, so it was a simple matter for Killian to come forward and wrap his chain around the guard's neck. He pulled and counted. The guard kicked once, twice. Killian let the guard's body slide to the ground.

There was another explosion, and this time Killian saw an accompanying flash of light. Guards fought prisoners, and with each blast an armored man went down.

The prisoners rallied and called out to one another, the number of combatants growing and adding to the commotion. Killian looked down and found the strangled guard's sword. He didn't know much about sword fighting, but its presence felt comforting in his hand.

Nearby some prisoners had formed a group and battled a guard, swarming him with sheer numbers. Killian saw the guard go down, and a tall man in rags grabbed the sword, waving it in the air.

Killian wanted to help them, but he couldn't seem to run fast enough. He hobbled forward in the direction of the gates, and it seemed everyone else had the same idea.

"This way!" Killian called to those who still stood by uncertainly. "It's either now or never. Come on!"

Guards formed a line between the screaming prisoners and the closed gates. Killian looked on in awe as a wavering figure appeared, and a beam of light tore a hole in a guard's side, sending a gush of blood spurting out before the guard crumpled to the ground. The shimmering form appeared at another place, and still another guard went down as a bolt of energy opened a wound in his throat.

A guard swung his sword at Killian. Ducking, Killian felt it whistle over his head, before swinging his own sword in a clumsy arc at the guard's chest. The guard blocked and the vibration that went through Killian's wrist was so strong, he dropped his blade. Killian swung the stake on the end of its chain, catching the guard under his left eye and tearing open his cheek. When the guard screamed in pain and placed his hand on the left side of his face, Killian swung again, smashing the heavy piece of wood into his opponent's temple. The guard went down.

The shadow appeared again. This time a bolt of light came out of its middle, tearing a fist-sized hole in a guard's stomach. Another guard swung at the figure with his sword, but the figure became illuminated with an electrical discharge that sparked across the blade, turning the soldier's sword hand into a blackened mess. As the guard screamed in pain and dropped his weapon, the ragged prisoner with the sword ran forward and slashed twice at the guard's neck and chest.

The hairs rose on Killian's neck as he heard the sound of chanting, and a blinding light suddenly flashed a dozen paces from where the guards stood. Another bolt came from the shining figure to take another soldier through the forehead.

The guards broke. One of them hurried to the gates to activate the release mechanism while his fellows urged him on. As the gates started to part, the guards poured through the widening gap. The prisoners stormed forward, screaming and shouting and pummelling their captors with anything they could lay their hands on.

Killian tried to run with them, but he took two steps and then fell down as he tripped on his chains. He raised himself onto his hands and knees and looked up.

The shining figure stood in front of him. It reminded Killian of nothing so much as Saryah, the evil creature he had faced in Stonewater. Whatever it was, it filled him with terror.

The shape's hand held a wand that sparked and flickered as waves of energy sizzled from its base to its tip.

Killian heard some words of magic spoken by a surprisingly female voice, and out of the shimmer a person slowly materialized, a young woman in a green dress.

"It's you," Ella said with surprise.

Killian gaped, for a moment unable to speak. How could she be here?

"I'm back in the hut, aren't I?" Killian said. "I'm dreaming. You're the last person I ever expected to see here. But please, don't wake me up."

Ella looked just as shocked as he was. She stood staring at him until Killian wondered if she was going to speak at all.

"Well?" Killian said.

"Well what?"

"Are you going to get me out of these chains?"

"Soon." Ella smiled. "It's nice to finally have you as my prisoner rather than the other way around."

50

Ella tended Killian's wounds as they rested within the trees under the flickering glow of firelight. She could have activated a nightlamp, but it was a cool night, and the warmth would be good for him. Perhaps it would be good for her too.

The freed prisoners had fled into the forest, knowing better than to stay anywhere near Seranthia. Now there was just one more facility Ella needed to destroy with the help of the vengeful prisoners.

"You look like you're thinking," Killian said as Ella touched a damp cloth to the sores on his wrists.

"I was thinking about that place," Ella said. "How long were you there?"

"Not that long. Most people were there a lot longer than me."

Ella moved on to Killian's ankles, making a sound when she saw the bloodied mess he'd made of them. "How could you do this to yourself?"

"Fear of dying does that to a man," Killian said. "For some reason you become a little desperate. Aren't there others out there who might need your help more?"

"To be honest, I don't know what I'm doing," Ella said. "But I've been in a few fights now, and I'm pretty sure you're supposed to clean wounds. At least with you, if I get something wrong, it isn't much of a loss to the world."

"I'm glad to know you feel like that," Killian said wryly. "I've thought about you. Thought about you a lot. Yet the girl I've been thinking about doesn't care about me."

Ella's smile faded at Killian's words. She'd slotted back so easily into their companionship that she hadn't taken note of the way he was looking at her.

She pressed the bandage down a little too hard on one of the wounds on Killian's ankles, making him gasp. "Let me see. We were in Petrya, if I recall correctly. We spoke about the Halrana Lexicon, and I could see you considering something. You told me you were going out for a short while. I never saw you again."

"Might that be because if I stayed with you, High Enchantress Evora Guinestor would have carved me into little pieces?"

"You could have told me."

"What would I have said? Ella, I'm going to Stonewater to recover the Halrana Lexicon I stole. You can have your own Lexicon back. Don't let your boss catch me."

"Something like that."

"I did what I had to do," Killian said. "I had to go back. Something told me I could find the answers I was looking for in Salvation. You have a brother, Ella, and a people. You have a last name and a home. Maybe I have family out there somewhere. Or maybe I'm just some orphan thief. I have to know."

"You're more than that," Ella said softly, "and blood doesn't make anyone who they are."

"Even so, Ella, I was right. When I got to Salvation, I met someone who knew about me. He knew about how some lore doesn't harm me and how essence doesn't kill me. He helped me destroy the primate's relics, and in return he said he would tell me who I am. *What* I am."

"Did he tell you?" Ella asked. Maybe he was right. Maybe she didn't know what it felt like to have no home, no relatives, and to be different.

She looked at Killian again. The red hair, the piercing blue eyes; Ella had never seen anyone with his features. His strong jaw and athletic build made him handsome, but there was some other quality to him as well. There was something almost fey about the way Killian looked.

"I destroyed the relics," Killian said. "I did my part to end the primate's evil. In return Evrin Evenstar promised to tell me what I wanted to know. But he never made it to our meeting. I waited, but he never came."

"Evrin Evenstar?" Ella started. She took a breath. "At the beginning of the Alturan Lexicon there's that writing. It's also in the Hazaran Lexicon."

"I've seen it." Killian nodded. " '*To the common people of Merralya, one and all, I give you this, the third volume in my Tomes of Lore. Evrin Evenstar.*' I read that in the Halrana Lexicon."

"I once met someone who said his name was Evrin Alistair," Ella said. "He taught me animator's runes. He was clever and strange and funny, all at once."

"Did he have a white beard flecked with ginger?" Killian asked.

Ella's eyes widened. "And blue eyes," she said. "Blue, like yours."

"It was him." Killian nodded.

"How?" Ella asked. "How could Evrin Evenstar have created the Lexicons yet be alive today?"

"I don't know," Killian said. "It's somehow tied in with who I am. What I am."

"Please go on," Ella said. "Evrin—what happened to him?"

"I've only learned this since, but while I tried to destroy the relics the primate used to create essence, Evrin went to a different part of Stonewater, the Pinnacle, to destroy something he considered at least as important."

"I knew something had happened to disrupt the primate's supply of essence. You saved countless lives. What could be more important?"

"I don't know exactly," Killian said. "There's a templar named Zavros. He's the templar who perfected the primate's elixir, and he's probably the one who built these vats. He's an evil man. I questioned him back in Stonewater, and he let slip something about a book. Evrin tried to destroy it, but he wasn't successful, and now the primate has it."

"What happened to Evrin?"

"The primate had him locked up in Salvation for a time, but he escaped. Since I couldn't find Evrin, I decided to look for the primate and try to find the book, so I headed to Seranthia. On the way, I saw Evrin with some prisoners. I tried to free him, but I was captured, although Evrin escaped. And here we are."

Ella was silent for a moment while she digested Killian's words.

She realized she was still holding a damp cloth, now stained red with Killian's blood, and she threw it into the fire.

Obviously, the book that was in the primate's hands was of the utmost importance.

"You said Evrin escaped the primate in Salvation?" Ella asked.

"Yes," Killian nodded. "The primate wasn't happy. He had all the guards killed."

"Yet you found him with some prisoners near Seranthia. What was he doing in Seranthia?"

"I don't know," Killian said. "All I know is that Evrin needs my help, and he's the only one who can tell me who I am."

"Whatever it is Evrin's worried about, it has something to do with Seranthia," Ella said, "and it sounds dangerous."

"Will you help me?" Killian asked.

"I have my own task," Ella said. "There's one more facility like the one you were in. The essence is being used to fight my people, and the prisoners deserve to be freed."

"I could help you," Killian said. "They say it's a bigger facility than this one, which means it will be more heavily defended."

Ella nodded. "If you help me destroy this last facility, I'll help you find Evrin."

"Agreed," Killian said.

She and Killian clasped hands, the act strangely formal. His strong hand easily held her delicate fingers within it.

"You never told me what happened to you?" Killian said, releasing Ella's palm.

Ella told Killian about High Enchantress Evora's sacrifice to save her and the Alturan Lexicon. She skimmed over her capture by Prince Ilathor and his men, telling Killian simply that she'd helped the Hazarans rediscover their forgotten lore, and in the process she herself had learned about the power of illusion.

Ella explained how she'd blocked the Wondhip Pass, using the animator's runes Evrin had taught her, and built the ethereal runebridge when the Bridge of Sutanesta was destroyed, saving the refugees and enabling the Alturans to fight another day.

Finally, Ella told him about the battle against the Akari in the lands between Petrya and Tingara, and how she had come here to see what she could learn and, hopefully, do.

"You've learned a lot," Killian said. "You've changed."

"Not too much, I hope?" Ella said, smiling up at him.

"You're more beautiful than ever," Killian said, and Ella blushed. "But that's not what I meant. You've grown."

"War will do that."

"You've learned illusionist's runes, elementalist's runes, and animator's runes, as well as being a trained enchantress. I don't know if anyone has done that before."

"There's still so much I don't know," Ella said.

"You should see what Evrin can do," Killian said, shaking his head. "I know nothing about lore, but when he drew the runes on my skin . . . I can't describe it."

"Where did he draw them?" Ella asked.

Killian touched his chest with both hands, gesturing then to his arms and his neck, his legs and his face. "Everywhere."

Ella moved a little closer to him.

"I have essence," she said. "When we take this second facility, we'll need to hit them with everything we can."

Killian stretched and moved closer to the fire, inadvertently shifting closer to Ella so that their legs were touching. Neither of them moved apart.

"I agree," he said.

The firelight danced and played across Killian's face. Ella's leg was pressed only slightly against his, yet she felt incredibly conscious of the contact.

"I've always wanted to see what we could do together," Ella said. "I have some runes in mind."

Ella's chest heaved, her breasts rising and falling with her breathing. She realized she was wearing the same dress she'd worn when she was with Ilathor, and she suddenly felt heat come to her face.

"You're blushing," Killian said.

Ella wondered if she should tell Killian about Ilathor, but she pushed the thought away. After all the horror and bloodshed, the time with Ilathor had been a rush of emotion, as Ella craved the warmth she'd seen Shani and Bartolo share. Prince Ilathor had pushed Ella, and she'd succumbed. With Ilathor, however, she'd felt none of the kinship she now felt with Killian.

"The night's a bit cool," Ella said.

Killian looked over at the fire, which glowed with red embers, and raised an eyebrow.

"It's a little warmer over here," he said, opening the crook of his arm.

Ella shuffled over until she was sitting beside him, leaning back into his arms. Killian moved to sit with his back to a tree, and Ella snuggled in to his body, feeling safe in a way she never had with another man.

Comfortable tiredness washed over her. "You still have me at a disadvantage," Ella murmured. "You've seen me naked."

She felt a hand stroking the side of her cheek, and then Killian's soft touch was on her neck. As Ella drifted off she realized it was the necklace at her throat that he'd found.

"You do care for me," Killian said.

Ella didn't hear him. She had already closed her eyes, sleep coming to her instantly.

51

"This enemy can be beaten," Jehral said.

Prince Ilathor nodded. "Their numbers are fewer, and even in battle some of the revenants are falling down without being struck at all. Whatever she has done, it is working. Yet still no word."

"I am sure she is safe, my Prince," Jehral said.

"Salut!" a voice called from outside. "Your Highness, the Petryan and the Alturan are here."

"Send them in," Jehral called.

Shani and Bartolo entered the prince's command tent. Without preamble, Prince Ilathor spoke. "The new tactics are working. Elementalist Shani, Bladesinger Bartolo, I have you to thank."

"We need to move more slowly," Bartolo said. "I know your men value speed and surprise, Prince Ilathor, but we can't keep this pace up. Today's battle was lucky. Tomorrow's battle might not turn out as well."

"I hear you, Bladesinger," Prince Ilathor said, "and I do not wish you to think your arguments fall on deaf ears, but the Tingaran winter is coming, and if we want to reach Seranthia before the advance of the cold, we must press on. My men are not equipped for winter."

Bartolo shrugged. "Then many more of your men will die than is necessary. The speed you want will mean sacrifice."

"It cannot be avoided."

Shani spoke. "The essence we captured today . . . If our elementalists can have some, we can create more walls of fire."

"You shall have it," Prince Ilathor said, "as much as you like. Nothing is as successful as fire when it comes to destroying these creatures."

"We can see if our elders can create some illusionary fire as well," Jehral said. "The enemy won't know where the fire is real and where it is not."

"Good, good." Ilathor smiled. "These are all excellent ideas. You've done well, all of you."

"What do you intend to do with the necromancers we captured?" Bartolo asked.

Prince Ilathor exchanged glances with Jehral. "They have been killed. Jehral and I have seen to it."

"That's not customary . . ." Bartolo began.

The prince looked up at Bartolo. "Not customary in these lands? Not customary practice in war? You have heard the same things I have, Alturan. Do not let your honor get in the way of ridding the world of this evil."

"We don't know if it's true," Shani said.

"But if it *is* true about how the enemy is obtaining their essence, then it isn't just my duty, but all of our duty, to see this thing through. It won't be over until my men are in Seranthia."

"Have you heard anything from Ella?" Shani asked.

"Nothing," the prince said.

"Her brother is my friend," Bartolo said, "and he will want to know that she is no longer under your protection."

"I don't know if she ever was under our protection," Jehral said, smiling thinly.

"That doesn't change the fact that the Alturan lord marshal needs to know," Bartolo said. He turned to the prince. "Either you send word, or I will."

52

The land of Torakon was the last to be freed from the Black Army before the allies advanced into Tingara itself.

Moragon and Dain Barden fled before the allied army, the Black Army inflicting heavy losses before falling back to the next strong position. Nevertheless, the men in green and brown were advancing. As winter drew near, and they pushed relentlessly eastward, the Torak capital of Sakurai was declared an open city, and the Black Army fell back to the Tingaran border without a fight.

Miro was surprised, although he soon realized he shouldn't have been, when the allied army was hailed in Sakurai as liberators. House Torakon had been one of the first houses to ally themselves with Tingara, yet here they were cheering wildly and celebrating in the streets when the army marched through the city. Then Miro heard about the dark days of High Lord Koraku Rolan's rule while under the primate's control, and began to understand. Koraku's body was discovered in his chambers, swinging from a rope. The Toraks raged that it was too clean a death. Miro knew it was better for it to be over; they would move on all the more quickly.

"Something's changed," Miro said to Rogan.

They were in Miro's tent at the allied army's encampment outside the walls of Sakurai. Both men preferred the austerity of the tents to the strange structures and giddy heights of the builders' capital.

"They're running out of essence," Rogan said. "I've seen it before, back in the Rebellion."

"That's not the only thing, though. You know what I'm talking about."

"The Hazarans," Rogan said.

Miro nodded. "The Hazarans. We're in communication with this Prince Ilathor, but his replies are guarded and ambiguous. He doesn't sound like a man accustomed to the bargaining table."

"You know their reputation," Rogan said. "Kill first, ask questions later."

"We need an alliance," Miro said. "Our information says they're ahead of us in the race to Seranthia."

"Your sister would be the natural go-between," Rogan said. "She travels with them."

"I don't know how I can get a message to her," Miro said. "Anything I send to her will be intercepted by the prince. I don't trust him, Rogan."

"If the Hazarans are the first in Seranthia, she'll be the only Alturan there," Rogan said.

"Miro," a new voice said. Marshal Beorn entered the tent. "There you are. A Hazaran messenger arrived." He held out a piece of paper. "It's from Prince Ilathor."

Miro exchanged glances with Rogan and then took the scroll, quickly breaking the seal: a desert rose in yellow wax. Miro scanned the paper while the other two commanders looked on.

"Prince Ilathor says fire is the best weapon to use against the draugar. He also says to cut off the revenants' heads, something we've already learned. The Akari are short on essence, but their warriors drain faster in warmer weather, so once winter settles in, we'll find it harder to wear them out. He mentions nothing about an alliance." Miro looked up. "And finally he says my sister is no longer with him. She's out there somewhere on her own, in the enemy-held lands near Seranthia."

Miro handed the note to Rogan, who scanned it swiftly.

"What does this mean?" Marshal Beorn asked.

"He's sending us a message," Rogan said. "He's telling us he intends to be in Seranthia before winter sets in properly. We need to press on. Some of the Toraks might join our cause, but they'll need to be trained as we march. We can't be the last to reach Seranthia. The future of the world depends on it."

"I've come to a decision," Miro said, standing.

Rogan and Beorn regarded him. "Tell us," Rogan said.

"Freeport is to the north. I'm going there, alone."

"Freeport?" Rogan frowned. "There's nothing there but fish and trader ships."

"It's a frequent port of call for the Buchalanti," Miro said, "and I can be in Seranthia in days on one of their storm riders."

"Alone? You're mad," Rogan said. "Let me send some men with you."

"The Buchalanti are neutral," Miro said. "If I have a company of soldiers with me, they'll never give me passage."

"What will you do when you reach Seranthia?" Beorn asked.

"If the city is still in the primate's hands, I'll keep my head down and do what I can until either the Hazarans or you two arrive. I'm counting on it being you two, but I'll be prepared if it's not. If my sister isn't there, there'll be at least one Alturan in Seranthia when the primate is taken from power. I can make sure the Tingarans aren't butchered out of hand and can negotiate our position, knowing you'll soon be arriving with strength."

"It's a brave move," Rogan said. "I promise you, we'll do what we can to get there first."

"I also plan to look for Amber," Miro said, "and for Ella."

Miro walked to the corner of the room where his zenblade hung on a rack. Next to it was his rail bow and a quiver of arrows, fletched with green feathers. He started to pack.

"You've leaving right now?" Beorn asked.

"Why wait?" Miro said. "I trust both of you. Let's see this thing through."

"Take care," Rogan said, "and don't do anything rash. I'll see you in Seranthia."

53

Seranthia, capital of the broken Tingaran Empire, was the largest city in the world. The numerous districts stretched to cover land that was once hills and valleys, from the wide-open mouth of its massive harbor to the unbroken gray line of the Wall.

Seranthia was a city with a unique mix of lawlessness, vice, and brutal punishment. Newcomers and strangers thought there were no laws at all, but the truth was the laws that existed were few, but rigidly enforced.

The old emperor, Xenovere V, like all of the Tingaran emperors before him, took great offense at anyone making light of his position, and so anyone overheard disparaging his name was thrown over the Wall.

Recognizing the importance of respect for the Assembly of Templars, those caught denigrating the Evermen, the primate, or the Assembly itself were thrown over the Wall.

The laws were all simple, and those remaining no less so. Essence was the most valuable substance in the realm, and even small amounts on the gray market could cause the destruction of the powerful merchant families and result in chaos. Anyone caught possessing essence without a license had his or her lands and possessions confiscated before the person was thrown out of the city. Distributing essence resulted in torture and the execution of one's family.

The final law was the simplest of all but was the one broken the most. Vagrants were not tolerated, so anyone without the price of a loaf of bread on his person was forced to leave the city. If the vagrant struggled or protested, the legionnaires were authorized to throw him over the Wall.

Those vagrants that didn't end up as mangled corpses at the bottom of the Wall generally headed to Aynar, where they became burdens on the Assembly of Templars.

Now there was a new place where the legionnaires could send the poor of Seranthia: a facility managed and run by Templar Zavros.

True to his word, the primate gave Zavros whatever he needed to conduct his experiments, provided the essence kept flowing. With the price of a loaf of bread in Seranthia now a silver deen, there was no shortage of prisoners for the facility Zavros had named Angelmar.

Zavros didn't care about the primate's constant demand for essence, or even about the elixir. For Zavros, Angelmar was the opportunity of a lifetime. He'd already learned more about the mind and the way it controlled the body than he'd read in any books—and Zavros had read everything written on the subject. He had as many subjects for his experiments as he could wish for, and as isolated as Angelmar was, there was no one to bother him with details, ask him for reports, or question his methods.

Today he was excited. Ahead of him as he walked, two templar guards dragged his next subject along the corridor. The youth was a troublemaker, a wild one from Seranthia, who had fought like a demon when they took his mother and sister from him. Zavros intended to find out if such aggressive tendencies could be curbed.

Could he turn this useless creature into something of worth to the world? Perhaps the boy's muscles could haul stone, or build fences, or dig holes. The things Zavros learned here had the potential to change the world for the better.

The chamber where Zavros did most of his work was built of brick, double-thick and painted white. Zavros didn't want any noise to escape the chamber, but more importantly, he didn't want to be distracted while he worked. If the prisoners rioted over their rations or tried to escape, Zavros didn't want to know about it. He was no soldier; he preferred to let the guards sort such matters out.

"Sit him down in that chair," Zavros said, looking down his nose through his oculars and gesturing to the guards.

The youth writhed and struggled as they set him down, but his efforts were useless against the burly templar guards. Even if they hadn't been given the elixir, the guards could easily control one such as this. Zavros thought it interesting that the boy likely knew his struggles were useless, yet the aggressive streak in his mind caused him to fight nonetheless. He couldn't wait to see if he could restrain such instincts with the judicious use of his scalpel, and then test the results of his efforts to see what it took to once again bring out the boy's aggression afterward.

"Strap his arms into the chair," Zavros said. "Good. Thank you, gentlemen. You may go now."

A faint, hollow boom answered him. Zavros frowned when he heard the sound. This was the second time he'd heard it, so slight he wondered if he imagined it. He considered whether he should investigate, but he was eager to test his theories on the boy. The officers outside would sort it out, whatever it was.

The templar guards exchanged glances and then left. Zavros smiled without humor at the quick pace of their footsteps. Men like these would never have the courage to make discoveries such as those Zavros had made, and would continue to make. Too much of the world was controlled by men who understood the language of physical aggression, yet shied away from knowledge. When the primate's vision for the world became a reality, Zavros planned to change that proportion.

Zavros heard the metal door to his special chamber clang heavily against its frame. He frowned; his guards should know better than to make such a racket.

Still frowning, he took out his small scissors and began to cut away the hair on the boy's scalp, quickly forgetting the guards and anything beyond the room. He then took a razor in his hand and bit his lip with concentration as he prepared to shave the top of his subject's head. He didn't want to slip here, for though blood was inevitable, too much made things messy.

Zavros felt a sudden pressure on his wrist.

Whatever it was, it squeezed, harder and harder, until the razor fell out of his hand, tinkling as it landed on the hard floor. Zavros scanned wildly but there was no one to be seen. The force on his wrist increased until with a sickening crunch Zavros felt the bones break. The splintering fragments mashed together, and Zavros screamed with the excruciating pain of it. With one last squeeze, the force crushed Zavros's right wrist, bones poking through the skin.

The pressure ceased, and Zavros looked at his wrist in disbelief, the shock so strong he didn't even scream. He tried to see where his assailant was, whatever it was, but there was nothing; even with the oculars Zavros's vision wasn't the best.

As Zavros's breath returned, he screamed, waving his arm around. Blood splattered, dripping onto the wide-eyed boy in the chair. Every sound Zavros made echoed throughout the chamber. He was used to the screams of others, but this was the first time he had heard his own voice bouncing off the walls. The pain was so great that he gasped for breath, and in the silence he heard a male voice speak arcane words.

A form materialized out of the air where before there had been nothing. A bare-chested man, his face as grim as death, now faced Zavros, peering into his eyes. Through the haze of pain, Zavros suddenly recognized his assailant's red hair and blue eyes. "Killian," Zavros whispered.

Zavros saw the symbols that covered Killian's face, neck, arms, and chest. Zavros knew they were runes, and even as he fought the pain, he wondered again what power enabled runes to be drawn on a living man.

Killian looked at his hand. *"Lok-tur,"* he said.

The runes on the palm of Killian's hand blazed red, and Zavros felt heat pour from it in waves. Killian lifted Zavros's wounded arm and looked at the crushed wrist.

"I can't make this too easy for you," Killian said. "The last time we met, you told me to do my worst. I remember I said I would destroy your library. Unfortunately, I can't threaten you with that now. It's already been done."

"No," Zavros said. "You wouldn't. You couldn't."

"Do you really want to test what I'm capable of? The building we're standing in is the last one left in this place, Angelmar, or whatever you call it. I thought this last structure might be some kind of prison. Look what I've found instead. Those things in the other chambers . . . they were once people. I didn't realize an evil such as yours could exist."

Killian held his burning palm in front of Zavros's face. "Unfortunately, I can't destroy your library because it's already gone. The good news, however, is that this time there's no one coming to help you. So there's nothing holding me back from doing my worst, as you boldly requested."

Killian held his palm against Zavros's forehead, ignoring Zavros's screams, searing the flesh with the intense heat. When the oculars fell from Zavros's face, Killian stooped and retrieved them, picking up the razor as he did so.

Sweat poured from Zavros's forehead as Killian held the razor out, but Killian simply bent down and cut the bindings holding the boy to his chair.

"Go, lad," Killian said. "You don't want to see this."

The wide-eyed youth shakily got up from his chair and stumbled away.

Killian placed the oculars back onto Zavros's eyes.

"It's time for me to do my worst."

<hr />

Ella saw Killian come out of the white building with the thick walls and called out to him. When she saw his face, she almost recoiled—his eyes were murderous—but then she realized she probably looked little better. The things she had seen at Angelmar would haunt her nightmares for years to come.

"Anything still standing?" Killian asked when he saw her.

"All gone," Ella said. "The prisoners did most of it." She looked out at the smoking ruins and torn fences, at the scene of terrible destruction left behind. "Zavros?"

"I found him," Killian said. "The primate is definitely in Seranthia. We don't know where Evrin is, so finding the primate is our next best bet."

"I thought you said he'd never talk."

"He talked."

54

A single flake of snow floated through the sky, twisting first one way and then another in the unpredictable gusts of wind that blew in from the ocean nearby.

High in the clouds, the snowflake hovered over the immense city below, ignorant of the fear pouring from the city's residents. A puff of wind from the harbor pushed the snowflake away from the city, past the imposing walls and further inland, where the object of the residents' fear straddled the hills around the city.

The snowflake was the first of its fellows to fall down toward the earth. As it passed the endless ranks of horsemen encircling the city, an undercurrent tossed it back up again, but its reprieve was short lived, for it came back down again and settled on the nose of a dark-skinned warrior.

The warrior brushed the snowflake away from his nose irritably. He rubbed at the thin, perfectly groomed beard on his chin and frowned. His skin was as smooth as a young man's, yet his bearing was regal and his eyes were dark. The man's hair was very long, past his shoulders, and tied back with a golden clasp. He wore a gold earring set with amber in his left ear, and around his neck was a chain with a curved turquoise triangle.

"Tell the tarn leaders we attack with the dawn," the dark-skinned man said. His eyes blazed as he regarded the huge city below, but anyone who knew him very well would have said he was fearful.

There was only one man present who knew him to that degree, yet he was a man who would never challenge his leader.

"Yes, my Prince," Jehral said.

There were two others present: a warrior in loose clothing of green silk, decorated with arcane symbols, and a woman in a rust-red robe with a white cord tied around her waist. The woman in red stood close to the warrior in green, and when he stepped forward, she tried to hold him back, but he pushed her away angrily.

"This is madness," Bartolo said. "This isn't Torlac. It isn't even Tlaxor. This is Seranthia. You remember what happened the last time you attacked a fortified city with no siege weapons, don't you? You'll be sending your men to their deaths."

Prince Ilathor turned to the bladesinger. "Watch your tongue, Bladesinger, else I'll have it removed." He waved to the hills around him. There were so many horsemen that they stretched in an unbroken line in either direction as far as the eye could see. "There are plenty of men here who would be honored to do the task for me."

"I'd like to see you try," Bartolo growled. He placed his hand on his zenblade.

Shani and Jehral both opened their mouths, but it was a new-comer's voice that rang out.

"Your Highness, a message," the approaching courier said.

"Give it to me," Prince Ilathor said. He swiftly broke the seal and scanned the contents of the scroll. He leveled his gaze on Bartolo triumphantly. "Your people are encountering fierce resistance in the west. You may go to them, if you wish, Bladesinger."

"No!" Bartolo cried angrily. "Do you think I would be anywhere but here? I want to see this finished as much as you do."

"Yet it will be I who ends it," Prince Ilathor said. "I will hang this primate from the Wall, and I will not stop until his evil is scourged from the land."

"Many of Seranthia's citizens are victims as much as my people were," Shani said. "Please, Prince Ilathor, extend these people the same mercy you gave Petrya."

"No," the prince said. Even Jehral's eyebrows rose. "I must not show weakness to this enemy who uses the dead to kill the living, and kills the living to bring the dead to life. I have been weak, and now I must be strong. Jehral!"

"Yes, my Prince?"

"I gave you an order. Tell the tarn leaders. We attack with the dawn."

Storm clouds gathered over Seranthia before the sun had fully set, plunging the city into darkness. Yet these storm clouds produced no rain, and as sheets of light flashed from one cloud and then another, no thunder could be heard. Forks of lightning plunged down to strike the earth, yet caused no destruction. The sky grew ever darker, and the ordinary citizens of Seranthia locked their doors, held their children close, and prayed to the Evermen for deliverance.

Some brave ones climbed up to the top of the Wall and returned pale and anxious, reporting what they had seen with voices that shook. Clouds were moving against the direction of the wind. Ghostly figures could be seen riding about the hills, and dust storms billowed up and then vanished again just as quickly as they had appeared.

The Akari were bad enough; what could the denizens of Seranthia expect from the ruthless warriors of House Hazara? What were these creatures they rode? The drunks and children told tales of the barbarians who hated the idea of walls, or any kind of structure at all for that matter, and traveled the world tearing down any sign of civilization they found, slaying all they came across. The learned men knew in their hearts the darkness that lived within the core of Tingara and the deeds done in the Tingaran Empire's name. Any conqueror of Seranthia would have a score to settle.

The fear was the great leveler. It could be felt throughout the market houses in the financial center, in the docks and taverns, and in the Imperial Palace itself. The rough men of the streetclans armed themselves, and the ships of the Imperial fleet took stations outside the harbor, ready to face any attack from the sea. The city's landward gates had closed long ago.

Seeking solace, many of Seranthia's residents headed for the Imperial Palace. The Grand Boulevard became choked with their numbers. They knew the primate was in residence. Why didn't he speak?

By the middle of the night, they gave up waiting for the primate to show himself and went home.

At dawn, the desert warriors attacked.

55

From his vantage high in the Imperial Palace, Primate Melovar Aspen could see everything.

He liked being at a height. There was something about looking down on the people below, scurrying like insects, that lifted his spirits. He imagined a bird of prey must feel the same way, wheeling and spying out the land before seeing a victim and then hurtling down, flying through the air with claws extended to suddenly strike, before flying up into the air again to devour its prey.

Melovar often visited the Imperial Palace's highest chamber when he was feeling troubled. It reminded him of his workroom in Stonewater. The view from here wasn't quite so impressive, but it was high enough for Melovar to watch his doom unfold.

From his vantage he could see over the Wall, and his gaze was on the west as he watched the commencing battle outside the gates of Seranthia. The primate almost laughed. He had been deceived, or perhaps he had deceived himself. While he had been busy worrying about the Alturans and the Halrana, a greater enemy was rising in the south, closer to his borders, with only Petrya between them. He was going to be defeated by an enemy he knew almost nothing about. Zavros would smile and say something about the power of knowledge.

Melovar heard footsteps behind him, but he didn't turn. He knew Moragon was out there, fighting to the last, and so was Dain Barden.

The primate held the Evermen's book in his hand. He carried it with him always, although he now wondered why he bothered. Did Dain Barden still think the primate knew where the scratched relic was? The primate knew he had been caught out in his lie, for if he knew where the powerful weapon of the Evermen was, surely he would have used it by now.

Behind him, a throat cleared, and Melovar turned irritably. "I left orders I was not to be disturbed."

"Your Grace," the templar said, "the harbor is still clear. The Imperial fleet is at sea. We do not doubt High Lord Moragon's leadership, but it is safer if you take a boat now, while it's still easy to do so."

"Why?" the primate said. "If they win, they'll just follow me to Aynar. I prefer to stay here where I can watch it all unfold. Our enemy has proven resourceful. How do I know there isn't a surprise waiting in the harbor?"

"Your Grace, please, look for yourself," the templar said, pointing. "You can see the harbor from here. Those are our ships keeping guard outside the Sentinel."

Melovar sighed, and then without warning spun and smashed the book in his hand into the man's face. He began to use his fists, punching again and again, pouring his rage on the templar until he was spent. Finally when the templar was on the ground, perhaps dead, the primate threw the book onto the templar's bloody face.

The pages of the book fell open to the oddly formed diagram, and Melovar was once again looking at the image of the pool of essence, and the obscured relic above it. A chamber enclosed it all. Such a strange shape.

Melovar glanced up.

He looked at the diagram again.

"All this time," he muttered, but he felt excitement course through his body as realization dawned. "All this time it was here, right in front of me."

The dimensions. The strange shape of the chamber.

The most powerful relic the world had ever seen.

They said it was old, older even than Seranthia itself. They said it had been here when the city was just a small fishing town.

The features that made no sense. The angles and turns.

Melovar picked up the book and looked at the diagram, and then gazed again at the harbor. If he completed the shape . . .

The Sentinel. Of course. *The relic was inside the Sentinel!* Perhaps the relic *was* the Sentinel.

The statue wasn't solid.

It was hollow.

56

Dain Barden Mensk of the Akari rested the bloody head of his war hammer on the ground, panting as he watched the riders once again break away to regroup on the hills surrounding the city.

"Tough fighters," he said to no one in particular.

He looked down at his bleached leather armor, now splotched red with blood. He'd killed more of the desert men than he could count, but the scratched Hazarans kept pulling away, harrying his flanks, protecting the fire-wielders before regrouping again out of range.

Barden felt a surge of pride when his gaze swept the ranks of his draugar, still holding formation, pikemen bristling and swordsmen holding firm. He was using the draugar sparingly, and they were holding out well. It would be close, but at the end of the day the fight would be his.

The Dain of the Akari was surprised at how tired he felt. What was he doing here anyway? He felt a fool now for being tempted by the primate's hidden relic, the prize that had been dangled in front of him. Yet Dain Barden was an honorable man, and he would live up to his end of the bargain. He'd promised the primate he would defend Tingara against her enemies, and he'd given that strange templar, Zavros, the secrets of the necromancers. In return the primate had let him rejoin the Tingaran Empire. Even so, Barden felt he had let his people down the day he made that deal.

When the battle was over, Dain Barden decided he would take his people home to Ku Kara, the ice city. He'd known not to trust the primate, but he'd been eager to rejoin the other houses and open up discourse and trade. How could he have known the mighty Tingaran Empire built by Xenovere the Great would have been in such a state? The relic, whatever it was, and the pool of essence he'd been promised—they were only ever a possibility, and the primate was evasive when pressed about the relic's location—but what was the use of rejoining an empire at war, led by one such as the primate?

Dain Barden had promised to defend Seranthia, and as a man of his word he would, but then he would leave.

"Dain," a young Akari said, his blonde hair wild and wispy and his chest heaving.

"What is it, lad?" Barden said.

"The primate's left the Imperial Palace."

Dain Barden grunted. "What's he doing? Fleeing?"

The Dain knew that if the primate really had access to this relic, something he appeared to believe was a weapon, he wouldn't be brooding in the Imperial Palace, nor would he be fleeing.

"He's asked to be taken to the Sentinel."

The Dain's eyes widened. "What did you just say?" Barden fixed his full attention on the man. "Did you just say 'the Sentinel'?"

It made sense all of a sudden. Fearing the loss of the Imperial capital, the primate was finally desperate enough to use the relic for himself.

The relic had been hidden in plain view the entire time.

"The weapon," the Dain muttered to himself, "it's something to do with the Sentinel." He thought for a moment. The primate had promised it to him! He turned back to the young Akari. "I must get there before the primate uses it. It's ours, in the name of the Nightlord. Get me two draugar as guards."

As Dain Barden departed the battlefield, he heard someone call his name. Turning, he saw Moragon waving at him.

"Your master's trying to take the relic for himself," Dain Barden said. "I haven't fought your battles for nothing. Don't try to stop me, melding."

"Give me command of your men," Moragon said.

"What?"

"We need to combine our strength, and your necromancers won't listen to me unless you tell them to. Please,"—the word sounded strange coming from Moragon's mouth—"you made a bargain. You can have the relic, and when we win today, your help won't be forgotten."

Barden knew that every moment he waited, the primate was getting closer to his goal. "Can I trust you to lead them?"

"I've no wish to see these barbarians in the streets of Seranthia," Moragon said. "I would say my motives are stronger than yours."

"You'll lead them well and wisely? On your honor?"

"On my honor," Moragon said.

Dain Barden made a quick decision. "I'll put out the word. Take care of my men, melding. I will be back."

<hr />

Moragon watched the Dain's departing back. The leader of the Akari took only two revenant bodyguards.

Moragon summoned four of his meldings.

Like himself, each had an arm of metal, and they carried enchanted swords by their sides. Fearless fighters and skilled swordsmen, they were loyal to their high lord.

"Follow him until he's out of his people's sight," Moragon said. "Kill him before he finds the primate."

"Yes, High Lord," they acknowledged.

Moragon now took command of the whole battlefield. With the Black Army and the draugar all under his control, he could finally fight the battle the way he wanted it to be fought.

"Sound the clarion. I want to pull back behind the Wall. They will dash themselves against the gate, and that's when we'll come out and strike with everything we've got. I want every revenant, every avenger, and every legionnaire lined up behind the gate, with nothing held in reserve. They will think we've gone behind the Wall to lick our wounds. We'll crush them with one final blow."

57

"There's fighting outside the gates of Seranthia," Ella cried. "I need to help my friends!"

"Ella, you know this is more important," Killian said. "If Evrin was trying to keep the primate from a powerful weapon, now is the time he'll try to use it."

"I know," Ella said, tearing her eyes from the scene below the hill they'd just crested. The prince's men fought in open battle outside Seranthia's gates, a swarming force of legionnaires and revenants pouring out of the city, rivaling even the numbers of the Hazarans. "We need to get into the city. How will we get in?"

"Not this way," Killian said. He was pensive for a moment. "The harbor. We'll take a small boat and enter from the harbor."

"Where will we find a boat?"

Killian looked at her. "Do you have a better idea?"

He took her by the hand, and they started to run.

Ella and Killian kept their distance from the city as they ran up hills, along gullies, through forests, and over farmland. Finally they reached a river, flowing out toward the sea.

Ella saw a blue horizon ahead, an expanse of sea that grew in her vision as they ran headlong down the slope of a hill that terminated at the water's edge. Ahead she could see a few shacks and a small jetty. They were well outside the walls of Seranthia, in a region likely occupied by fishermen.

When they reached the water, Killian headed for the jetty. He ran along its length, following it for as long as he could before reaching the end. He stopped, gasping for breath and holding his hand to his eyes as he shielded his gaze from the sun.

A moment later, Ella stood beside him. "Can you even see the harbor from here?" she panted.

"We're too far to see," Killian said.

"What's that?" Ella said, pointing.

"That's the Sentinel," Killian said. "Surely you've heard of it?"

"Not the Sentinel," Ella said, "that boat heading out. Farther over there, see? It's flying a black sun with a gold rim."

Ella and Killian squinted, looking out over the harbor.

"It's the primate," Killian said. "That cruiser is flying his flag. Do you see? It's landing at the Sentinel. Of course," he suddenly cried, "the Sentinel! There's something there. Why else would the primate be going there now?"

Ella gazed at the statue, distant and yet so huge she could see the fingers on the man's pointing hand. "Lord of the Sky," she breathed, "you're right."

"We might already be too late," Killian said.

He turned to Ella and grabbed her arm. "I need you to draw the runes on my skin. Can you do it quickly? Just do whatever you can."

"What are you planning?"

"I'm going to swim," Killian said.

"Killian, no." Ella looked at the distance in horror. "You'll never make it."

Ella still hadn't told him how she felt. She wasn't even sure herself, but she knew she cared for him, with a sensation that tore at her heart when she thought of him coming to harm. She opened her mouth to tell him, realizing this might be her last chance, when he spoke.

"Ella, what if there is a truly powerful weapon there? The primate has nothing to lose. He's backed into a corner, and he's mad, completely mad."

Killian started to tear at his clothing, ripping off his shirt and kicking off his sandals until he stood in just a faded pair of trousers.

In a daze, Ella reached into a pocket of her dress, taking out her vial of essence and scrill. "Killian, I . . ."

"Quickly," he said. "Please, Ella, hurry!"

Ella fumbled with her gloves, her hands shaking so much Killian had to help her put them on. Finally she dipped the metal rod into the small bottle, waiting the count of a single breath before withdrawing the scrill and starting to draw on Killian's skin.

Smoke rose from the end of the scrill as Ella worked, and soon blue lines appeared where she drew. Ella worked quickly, yet at the same time she knew Killian's life would depend on what she was doing. Who knew what he would find when he reached the Sentinel?

"I'm going to go for help," Ella said when she was nearly finished. "I've given you strength and shadow, but it's not perfect invisibility, and you have very little protection. Be careful, Killian, please."

"Who will you go to for help?" Killian asked.

"The desert men. I know their leader, Prince Ilathor. He'll believe me, and he'll come."

"Good luck," Killian said.

Ella opened her mouth and then closed it again. She felt a burning sensation behind her eyes. Suddenly, she had a terrible premonition, a deep dread telling her she would never see him again. "Good luck," she finally said.

Without another word Killian turned, ran, and dove into the freezing water of Seranthia's harbor.

58

Bartolo spotted Jehral nearby and nudged his horse forward, Shani close behind him. "Where is the prince?" Bartolo asked the weary-looking desert warrior.

Jehral pointed to a hill close to the rise they'd fallen back to, where the prince's personal banner flew high. "He's with the tarn leaders."

Around them hundreds of riders waited impatiently while many thousands more waited on the other hills for the order to attack once more.

"This isn't a victory," Bartolo said. "I hope he realizes that. They've retreated behind the walls to regroup. Who knows how many of them there are behind there?"

"The prince is conferring with his commanders," Jehral said. "They will make the right decision."

"And why aren't you with them?" Shani asked.

"Because I have been asked to lead the vanguard," Jehral said, somewhat stiffly. "It is a great honor. The prince must make decisions, but I have been entrusted to lead us into the city."

"Or die trying," Bartolo muttered.

"Don't feel like you need to stay with me, Bladesinger," Jehral said. "Your skills are impressive, but we will take this city, with or without you."

"Jehral, we aren't going anywhere," Shani said. She turned to Bartolo. "What do you think they're saying?"

"The ladders are coming forward," Bartolo said. "I don't need to tell you what that means."

"The prince plans to attack again today?" Shani asked. "But we've lost so many men."

"The enemy have lost as many," Jehral said.

"You're right," Bartolo said, "but attrition isn't how you win wars. Lord of the Sky, I miss Miro."

"That's the signal," Jehral said. "We're to advance. The ladders will follow."

Bartolo and Shani exchanged glances as Jehral kicked his horse forward.

"Bartolo," Shani said. "I . . . I want to thank you."

"For what?"

"For helping me find hope again. Even if it ends here, I didn't realize how dead I was inside until I met you."

"Don't worry, Shani, we'll make it."

"How can you be so sure?"

Bartolo thought for a moment. "Because I have to be. I'm not going to let anyone or anything take you from me, and that's all there is to it."

Shani grinned. "That's what I like about you. So sure. Lord of Fire, where were you in Petrya when I needed you?"

"Practicing," Bartolo said.

"For what? How to love a woman?" Shani's smile broadened and then faded when Bartolo looked into her eyes.

"For this battle. It's not going to be easy. Come on. Jehral needs us, whether he knows it or not."

◆

The Hazarans wheeled, galloping in a circle around the field, gathering numbers and momentum before turning and rushing forward in a mighty column. The fastest riders outdistanced the others to form a wedge like the point of a spear, and at the very tip rode Jehral, flanked by Shani and Bartolo. The elementalist in her red robe and the bladesinger in green stood out against the uniform yellow-on-black colors of the Hazarans, and the sound of the hooves on the earth formed a roar that provided a thunderous counterpoint to the jagged lightning that danced in the clouds above.

The gates stayed shut when they pulled up in front, halting their wild momentum, and Bartolo looked up fearfully, but when no orbs rained down, and no enemy came to meet them, he immediately knew something was wrong.

The Hazarans kept coming, forming a great mass of riders that milled in front of the gates, with Jehral, Shani, and Bartolo the foremost of all. Desert warriors lifted ladders, each ponderously moving through the air, incredibly long to reach the top of the Wall. The riders kept coming, but with no enemy to fight they were forced to wait as the ladders rose. The horses stamped, and the men astride them stirred impatiently.

"We need to get out of here," Bartolo said.

"The prince has ordered that we stay here to guard those who carry the ladders," Jehral said. "We cannot leave."

A chill went through Bartolo's spine as the gates started to open. "Form your men up. Do it now."

"Lord of Fire," Jehral breathed as the gates drew wide.

The enemy commander must have stripped the Wall bare of defenders; there was no other way to account for the force that now challenged the Hazarans.

Sixty Imperial avengers led them. Behind the rank of avengers was a column of legionnaires—the elite Imperial guard, with Alturan-made enchanted armor and swords. Thousands of revenant swordsmen and axemen stood side by side with pikemen. Bartolo could see three columns of templar warriors in white, and then more men in black—legionnaires and Black Army regulars as far as the eye could see. Bartolo had never seen so many men formed up in disciplined ranks. He knew a superior force when he saw it.

"Sound the retreat," Bartolo said harshly. "Do it!"

Bartolo heard the sound of trumpets, but it was the enemy's call to attack. The sixty avengers led the charge.

"I cannot retreat," Jehral said.

"Scratch your honor!" Bartolo said. He turned to Shani. "Stand by me. I'll carve a way out."

Shani smiled sadly. "You know that's impossible."

"Then I'll take as many of them with me as I can."

Bartolo drew his zenblade and called forth its power. His armorsilk flared as he pointed his weapon at the avengers leading the charge.

Jehral lifted his scimitar above his head. *"Charge!"* he cried.

The Hazarans cried out as one, spurring their horses into action.

Just outside the gates of Seranthia, the two forces met in one final cataclysmic crash of blood and death.

59

Evrin Evenstar sighed as he regarded his handiwork. He'd done what he could, built what wards and traps he was able to, but he was too weak, his injuries too great, and now he could do no more.

He lay on his back, his breath wheezing as he looked at the still, reflective surface of the pool. The stone was hard behind his back, but if he moved, the pain would overwhelm him. Better to stay like this.

He glanced at the bloodstained bandage on his right leg and chuckled. Even with the cloth wrapped crudely around the gaping wound, he could still see down to the bone. The skin around the lesion was mottled with colors of blue and black, puffy and inflamed. The bones in his other leg rubbed against each other whenever he moved. It took all of Evrin's effort to suppress the pain and stay conscious.

The source of Evrin's humor wasn't his injuries; it was the fact that here he was with all the essence in the world in front of him, and yet he lacked the strength to do anything with it. There was a time when he could have repaired his flesh without a second thought. Those powers were forever lost to him now.

"Evrin Evenstar. Killed by gangrene," he muttered. "What an epitaph. Could at least have been a sword."

Evrin had done what he could. Now he could only wait.

Two days ago, passing time in the chamber with only himself for company, Evrin had run out of food. Perhaps an hour ago he'd drunk his last bit of water. The pool was tantalizing, but it wasn't filled with water. Unlike the primate's foul elixir, this oily black liquid was tasteless, but quenching Evrin's thirst was impossible. The *raj ichor* wouldn't kill him, but drinking the essence would give him no benefit besides making him quite ill.

Evrin looked around the vaulted chamber, wanting to fix his eyes anywhere but on the reflective surface of the pool. It was hard not to, however, for there was only a crescent-shaped gallery of stepped stone; everywhere else was taken up by the walled pool.

At one end of the crescent, a hole indicated where the spiral stairway led down to the base of the statue. Evrin lay in wait, propped up against the stone tiers at the opposite end, where he would see any who made it this far.

The pool was perhaps fifty paces across, lined with a stone wall where it met the crescent, its opposite walls formed by the shell of the statue. It had been filled to the depth of a man's knees.

In the very center of the pool, a stepped island of stone emerged from the liquid. On this platform, the relic of the Evermen dominated the room, graceful and beautiful, ethereal and otherworldly.

It was an oval mirror, twice the height of a man and unbelievably thin, hovering in the air without apparent support, with no part of it touching the stepped island in the pool. The oval mirror initially appeared reflective, but on examination it was not. Its shimmering silver surface was difficult to focus on.

On the mirror were three seals: one at the bottom, on the outside of the mirror's rim; a second on the left; and a third on the right. The seals were made of a glossy, metallic fabric, akin to the material of the Lexicons' pages, and runes covered each seal.

The pool was simply the power source for the lore. Creating the relic had required breakthroughs of knowledge even for the Evermen, yet gathering such a large amount of essence hadn't required skill, simply dedication and ruthlessness. Evrin glared at the essence now. Every drop was obtained by blood. The gods had betrayed their worshippers.

Long ago, when Evrin had last been here, he had put the three seals in place. He didn't have the power to destroy the portal—it was indestructible, and even his cubes couldn't harm the relic or the Sentinel itself—but he could turn his brothers' lore against them. All of the energy provided by the pool of essence was now being drained by the seals. The pool now powered the seals that kept the portal closed.

Evrin cast his mind back to the events that had brought him here. It had seemed so simple, back when he'd charged Killian with the task of destroying the primate's refinery and set himself the task of destroying the knowledge hidden at the Pinnacle.

But he had failed at his task, and whether the primate discovered the location of this place or not, Evrin knew he would die here.

For he hadn't been able to build the traps with a mechanism to allow his passage back out. Evrin's harmful wards might prevent anyone from entering, but they would also prevent him from leaving.

Guarding this place was the whole reason for Evrin's existence. He might have liked to share this burden with Killian, but perhaps the lad was better off not knowing about the portal, just as the rest of them were better off in their ignorance.

The devout of Merralya prayed for a day when the Evermen would return and take them to a land of golden skies, far from the pain of this world they lived in.

Evrin knew the truth. The return of the Evermen was the last thing they should pray for.

Evrin would stand guard at the portal for as long as he was able.

When thirst overcame him, he would join his maker.

60

Bartolo fought two avengers at once while at the corner of his eye he saw Shani battling a third from atop her horse. He vaguely remembered leaping from his horse when he'd seen blood gushing from its neck after a legionnaire's sword blow.

He ducked under the whistling blur of a flail and then thrust at the red slit in the foremost avenger's face, his bladesinger's chant coming full and strong, the sizzling zenblade penetrating the defenses of the avenger's mask. As the avenger fell, Bartolo barely moved fast enough to block the sword blow of yet another. Bartolo's song faltered for an instant, allowing a legionnaire's sword to bite through the armorsilk on his side. Bartolo gasped with pain, turning on his heel and taking the warrior's throat. Two spiked balls of metal smashed into Bartolo's legs, knocking him from his feet.

He rolled and leapt back up, his sword arcing through the air to take an avenger's head clean off at the shoulders. Swiftly scanning, Bartolo saw Shani, still astride her horse, throwing ball after ball of flame at avengers and legionnaires alike. The smell of burning hair and cooking flesh combined with the cries of men, clashes of weapons, and whinnies of horses to fill the senses. Bartolo tasted blood on his tongue. He didn't know if it was his own or someone else's.

Bartolo beheaded a revenant and searched again for Shani. He finally found her screaming as two pikemen thrust forward with their weapons, withdrawing the dripping points of their pikes and plunging them a second time into her horse's chest. Shani cried out and fell, tangled in her stirrups.

"Shani!" Bartolo roared.

There were too many avengers and snarling legionnaires between Bartolo and Shani, but he still pushed forward. Rushing toward her, with two successive blows he took down a yellow-eyed templar in white and a round-faced Tingaran legionnaire. He leapt up, springing from the legionnaire's back and sailing over a group of the enemy. Where were the rest of the Hazarans? Was it just Shani and he against this horde?

A legionnaire butted his forehead against Bartolo's unprotected face, breaking the bladesinger's nose and sending waves of pain through his consciousness. Stars sparkled at the edge of his vision, but he ignored them, crashing his shoulder into the Tingaran and eviscerating him with the zenblade.

Bartolo finally reached where Shani lay half-buried beneath her horse. "My legs," Shani gasped. "I don't think I can get up."

"Nonsense," Bartolo said, gasping the word between his bladesingers' chant as he cut down two more of the enemy.

He crouched down again and with a heave lifted the dead horse so Shani could roll away. He saw one of her feet twisted at an angle, the ankle already swollen.

"I'm not leaving this spot," Bartolo said.

"Look out!" Shani cried, as she launched a fireball past Bartolo's shoulder. It scattered harmlessly on the rune-covered chest of an Imperial avenger but gave Bartolo time to face off against his enemy.

He blanched when he realized he faced three avengers. No, there were four. Two moved to his right while the others shifted to Bartolo's left. He would never be able to take them all.

Then Jehral came surging through the battle, his horse charging into the avengers on Bartolo's left side, knocking them back. One of the avengers stumbled, and Jehral's scimitar rang as it struck its neck, but the avenger's armored body deflected the blow. Jehral wheeled his horse to strike again.

A second fireball flew past, striking one of the avengers directly in the creature's face. Shani launched them in a volley, a rapid succession of discharges that leapt from her fingers, one after the other, and the metal on the avenger's face began to melt. It screamed then, a nightmare sound.

Bartolo ducked under the flail of the next avenger and then blocked the black sword with his zenblade, breaking the avenger's sword into two pieces.

Jehral fought from his horse by Bartolo's side as Shani staggered on one leg, an expression of agony on her face as she attempted to hold the enemy back with ball after ball of flame.

Then a revenant cut Jehral's horse from under him. The desert warrior fell heavily to the ground, then leapt back up in time to block an axe blow from a tall warrior in gray with half his face rotted away.

Jehral, Shani, and Bartolo fought side by side. The man from the desert saved the Petryan's life, and the bladesinger then saved the desert warrior. Clustered around the bodies of the horses, the corpses of their enemies piled up around them.

But it was three against a horde, and they all knew it was hopeless.

Even as Bartolo fought legionnaires, avengers, templars, and revenants, his mind took note of the carnage around him. Fallen Hazarans fought beside their dead horses, their honor forcing them to stay against all odds. Bartolo realized he stood directly between the great gates to the city of Seranthia. How close they had come.

Bartolo missed blocking a revenant's sword and felt fire in his arm as the blade tore into his fading armorsilk. Beside him he heard Shani's scream, a sound he never wanted to hear from the woman he loved. Turning, he saw her high in the air in an avenger's grip. "No," he cried weakly. Tears ran down his cheeks as he saw the avenger's black sword rising.

Bartolo prepared to leap forward. He knew he wouldn't be quick enough, but he would destroy the creature that ended Shani's life.

Suddenly, Bartolo heard a rumbling sound from all directions and felt the ground heaving beneath his feet. Were the walls falling down? What else could make such a sound?

Clarions sounded behind the enemy's lines. The avenger dropped Shani; she fell heavily to the earth, injured but alive.

"They're regrouping," Jehral gasped. "I don't know why."

As the enemy drew back into the gate and once more formed up ranks, the rumbling grew louder, and Bartolo turned back and looked at the hills surrounding the city.

It was the most beautiful sight he had ever seen.

61

Rogan Jarvish and tens of thousands of men from Altura, Halaran, Loua Louna, and Torakon had marched for two days and two nights. They were exhausted, but they were determined, and they were ready to fight.

"Are you sure?" Marshal Beorn asked.

"I'm sure," Rogan said. "There's a time to lay plans, and there's a time to roll the dice and join the battle. The gates are open but the Hazarans are nearly done for. Proper battle order will have to take second priority. Marshal Scola has the left flank, Beorn you have the right. I'll take the center. Call the men to arms immediately."

Heralds ran along the lines, and messengers dashed to and fro. Rogan had hardly finished speaking when he heard the clarions, and then the thumping of the colossi drowned all other noise as they took positions up front.

Down below, the enemy began to realize their grave danger. Some astute commanders pulled the warriors back and reformed ranks, but Rogan intended for them to be too late.

Rogan drew his zenblade as he gazed down at the city of Seranthia. "Let it end here today," he murmured.

To the left the Alturan heavy infantry stood formed up with Torak spearmen and Halrana pikemen, and the thousand Dunfolk archers stood side by side with their taller allies. There wasn't time to separate the men into their divisions, and in a way Rogan found the idea of them all fighting together somehow fitting.

To the right the Halrana animators and ironmen they controlled were mixed up with Alturan archers and the youngest, newest of the recruits, most of them farmers who had never held a sword.

In the center Rogan would command the men he'd trained in Ralanast, along with the multitude of Halrana who had fought by his side since the liberation of Halaran. With them were the three Halrana colossi, the largest under the control of the animator Luca Angelo.

The last four bladesingers fought at Rogan's side. These were men he had trained and led in a brotherhood that once consisted of more than seventy, yet whose numbers could now, at the war's end, be counted on one hand.

The call to arms had barely sounded when Rogan ordered the troops to advance. Even mixed up as they were, the men ran forward together, tight and controlled. Soldiers in green and brown, and blue and tan poured down the hillside, the ground trembling under the strides of the colossi. As the enemy drew back to reform, the Hazarans rode away to regroup before joining the great mass of marching men, scimitars waving above their heads as they cheered wildly.

"The revenants are pulling back, leaving just the templars and the Tingarans," one of the bladesingers shouted above the din.

"Some of the legionnaires are trying to close the gate," another called.

"We need speed!" Rogan cried. *"Attack!"*

The men around him took up the cry, passing it along to those farther away, until the multitude of soldiers shouted with one voice.

"Attack!"

The three colossi hit the gates first. All three pushed against the closing gate on the left while the ironmen under Beorn's control hit the right-hand gate. The gates' halting motion ceased, and then with a crash they opened wide.

Rogan was the first man through the portals of Seranthia, but once he was through he stopped, remembering Amelia's words, knowing he was no longer a young man. Soldiers passed him on both sides, pouring through the gates like a rushing river, unstoppable and inexorable. *This is their moment,* Rogan thought. *Let them go first.*

Then Rogan saw he hadn't been the first man through after all. A warrior in the green of a bladesinger slumped against a wall, just inside the gate. A woman in a red robe leaned against him, and beside them both was a dark-skinned warrior in loose black clothing with a yellow sash.

Rogan walked over and grinned at Bartolo. "Looks like you beat me inside the city."

Bartolo opened an eye, the other so encrusted with blood it stayed shut. "Looks like we did, Blademaster."

The Hazaran warrior coughed, blood trickling down the corner of his mouth. "I would say we all came in together. Thank you, Marshal. You saved the lives of many of my people."

"You got the gates open," Rogan said. "I would think that makes us equal."

"I thought you were dead, you know," Bartolo said.

"I keep hearing that," said Rogan. "Have you heard from Miro?"

"No," Bartolo said. "He's not with you? Wait, I'm coming with you."

"You'll do nothing of the sort," Rogan said. "Take care of your friends, and we'll speak later. I'm sure Miro's fine."

Rogan knew the city was far from won.

He headed for the Imperial Palace.

62

Moragon cursed the Akari as he stormed into the Imperial Palace. Cowards! He had ordered them to stand their ground, but when the time came, the necromancers had run like the skulking curs they were.

Guards and servants got out of his way as Moragon searched the palace for his son.

He climbed the wide marble stairs and then ran up a second stairwell. The living chambers inside the palace were all clustered on the fourth and fifth levels, and still clouded by battle lust, Moragon momentarily couldn't remember which chamber he'd left the Alturan woman in. Finally it came to him, and he climbed yet another set of stairs and turned down a corridor, his boots leaving bloody footprints on the white floor. Moragon hit the wall with his metal arm as he walked, so filled with rage he could hardly think.

He had held victory in his grasp! The Hazarans should have been crushed beneath his boot heel, and Moragon could have closed the gates before the reinforcements arrived.

Scratch it all! The scouts had said the Alturans were far away. How could such a thing have happened? Even so, if those craven Akari hadn't fled, he could still have held. He hoped the four meldings he'd sent after Dain Barden made a bloody mess of the Akari leader.

Moragon came to the door and kicked it open. The heavy wood fell back on its hinges, bouncing off the wall behind it.

The Alturan woman, Amber, stood by the window, looking out at the commotion below. Even she must realize the city was lost. All Moragon wanted was his son. He drew the long sword from the scabbard at his side. He planned to disappear into the wild lands of northern Tingara or perhaps head for one of the free cities. The woman wouldn't be coming with him.

Amber turned and fixed a sad smile on Moragon. In her arms she held a bundle, and Moragon had a sudden premonition that she was going to do something rash.

"I'm not letting you take my son," she said.

"He's my son, woman, and you'll give him to me or I'll run you through."

Amber inched closer to the open window.

"What are you doing?" Moragon demanded. He could see through the window how far below the streets of Seranthia were.

"I said I'm not going to let you have my son," Amber repeated. She held the bundle out through the window and turned back to Moragon, her eyes threatening. "Do you understand me?"

Moragon continued moving toward Amber, the light from the window glinting from the steel of his sword. "I don't believe you. You wouldn't do it."

"Don't come a single step closer," Amber said. Her eyes were wild, and there was a hysterical note to her voice.

"Give him to me," Moragon said. He laid down the sword on the floor and held out his hands in supplication.

Moragon wanted his son more than anything. With the end of the primate's vision for the world, the child was now the only thing he had left. The Tingaran loremasters who gave Moragon his arm of metal, making him into a melding, had told Moragon he would never father a child as a result of the lore. They had been proven wrong. The child was a miracle.

As Moragon took one step closer, Amber leaned out the window as far as she could and let the babe in swaddling go.

With a cry, Moragon shoved her to the side and leaned out the window. The babe had slid a short way down the sloping wall and then stopped when it hit a gutter. Below the gutter there was nothing more to stop it from tumbling down to the ground far below, where Moragon's son would certainly be killed.

Moragon leaned out as far as he could, but his son was too far out of his reach. He pushed himself through the window, heedless of the danger, with only one foot now on the floor and his body precariously positioned out the window.

He heard a voice behind him. Where Amber's voice had been meek, it was now strong and confident.

"Let's see you regenerate your way out of this," Amber said.

Moragon felt a brutal shove, upsetting his precarious balance. He made one last attempt at smashing Amber with his metal arm but she ducked out of the way, and Moragon's blow instead took a bite out of the stone of the window frame.

He scrabbled and slid on the sloping wall, his eyes still on the bundle that perched against the lip of the gutter. Moragon reached the bundle and grabbed at it even as he tried to arrest his motion, his hands closing on nothing but cloth.

"You witch!" he screamed up at Amber.

Moragon slipped down and over the gutter, catching onto the lip of stone with his fingertips. He looked up at Amber, who watched him from the window with cold eyes.

Moragon saw she held the babe in her arms.

"The child isn't yours," Amber said. "It never was. I was already with child before we met."

They were the last words Moragon heard before he fell through the air, screaming as he tumbled, until he hit the hard stone of a garden wall.

Moragon's back broke instantly, and his skull caved in as the back of his head struck stone. His arm of flesh and both legs shattered, splinters of bone ripping through the skin.

The pain was beyond belief.

Moragon was conscious throughout; he knew exactly what had happened to him. The elixir coursing through his veins tried to rebuild his body even as his organs ruptured and he bled internally, even as bits of matter from his head dripped on the stone, and his blood welled in a pool around him.

Then his body gave up.

"Thank you, my sweet," Amber cooed to the babe. Tears ran down her cheeks as she rocked him in her arms. Even the slightest thought of harm coming to him was too much to bear. "Thank you for staying quiet. You knew, didn't you?"

Amber heard shouts and the sound of running boots outside the chamber. She frowned and with the baby in the crook of her arm, she bent down to pick up Moragon's sword. Nothing would stop her now.

A man appeared in the doorway. When Amber saw his scarred face and dark hair lined with gray, she breathed a sigh of relief.

"I've found her," Rogan Jarvish called over his shoulder. "Lord of the Sky, Amber, am I pleased to see you."

He walked past her and leaned out the window, looking down. "Was that Moragon?"

Amber nodded.

"Is he dead?" Rogan asked.

"He's dead," she replied. Rogan turned his eyes on the baby.

"He's my son," Amber said.

"He's beautiful." Rogan smiled at her.

"Where's Miro?" Amber asked.

"He left to take a ship so he could enter Seranthia by way of the harbor."

"Please, Rogan, can you help me find him?"

"Nothing would give me greater pleasure."

63

Dain Barden was angry, and when he was angry, men jumped when he told them to jump. With satisfaction he saw that the skiff he'd commandeered was gaining on the primate's slower vessel.

He wasn't sure if it was the bloodstained war hammer he held in his hands or the two draugar by his side, but the six men who rowed the boat pulled on their oars as if their lives depended on it, which, he supposed, they did.

Barden was in a foul mood. Not only had the primate proven himself to be a man without honor, but the melding, Moragon, had betrayed his trust.

Even so, sending only four meldings after the Dain had been foolish. He was the ruler of the Akari. His race was the strongest of all the peoples of the world, and Barden was the strongest of his race.

After he'd killed Moragon's would-be assassins, the Dain sent a message to his captains. He ordered his necromancers to withdraw the draugar immediately, leaving the Tingarans to their fate. All of the Akari would return to the north.

Now Dain Barden was angry and wanted revenge.

"Hurry," he muttered to the rowers. "Hurry!"

The rower in front of him whimpered. There was a slight increase in speed.

Both the Sentinel and the primate's cruiser grew larger as Barden's skiff approached. In the distance, Barden could see ships of the Imperial fleet, but they were far away on the Sentinel's other side, looking for enemies coming in from the ocean. Barden saw with satisfaction that the primate had no soldiers with him. He was accompanied by his ship's crew, but no one else.

Barden knew, though, that he needed to be careful. He remembered seeing the primate take a revenant's sword thrusts in the chest without a hint of pain. Additionally, he might need to keep Melovar Aspen alive for a time, for the primate had knowledge that Barden himself lacked.

Dain Barden thought about the primate's description of the relic, words verified by his own necromancers when they examined the primate's damaged book of the Evermen.

The most powerful relic the world had ever seen was somewhere inside the ancient statue. A pool of essence was there for the taking.

No matter what, Dain Barden Mensk wasn't going to let the primate have it all to himself.

64

Ella breathed a sigh of relief when she found the prince.

She had Jehral to thank, who she'd found, covered in blood, with some Hazarans just inside the city. In the maze of Seranthia's streets, she never would have located the prince on her own.

Prince Ilathor was the center of a flurry of activity, with messengers and warriors rushing up to him and then leaving as he gave them orders.

"The Alturans have captured the Imperial Palace, Your Highness," a Hazaran rider called above the din, pulling up his horse beside the prince's, "and the Tingaran high lord, Moragon, is dead, but there is no sign of the primate."

"They are welcome to the palace," Prince Ilathor said. "It's the primate I'm after. He cannot be allowed to flee. This will not be over until I have his head. If he isn't at the palace, where will he be?"

"How about the harbor?" one of the tarn leaders said. "Between the two armies, we have the city surrounded on all landward sides. They say the Imperial fleet is keeping the harbor in the hands of the enemy. It's the only route of escape left."

"My Prince!"

Prince Ilathor turned when he heard the cry, and then drew back in shock when he saw Jehral. "Jehral, Lord of Fire, man, you need to see a healer."

Ella rode just behind Jehral, her arms around his waist as he weaved in the saddle. A shallow wound on his neck seeped red, and he held his left arm awkwardly. Ella had felt terrible asking him for help, but she'd had no one else to turn to.

"You need to hear what she has to say," Jehral said.

Prince Ilathor scowled. "There's a battle going on, Jehral, and I have to find . . ."

"Ilathor," Jehral said, and the prince's eyes widened at the use of his first name. "I know there's a battle going on. I've been at the front of it. Listen to her."

"Prince Ilathor," Ella said. "There's a statue on an island, just outside the harbor. It's called the Sentinel."

"I know what it is. What of it?" the prince demanded.

"I believe there's a great magic there, something very powerful, and our enemy is prepared to use it. I need your help. Please."

"Explain to me. I don't understand."

"I don't have time to explain. I need you to help me."

The prince tilted his head for a moment. "No," he finally said. "Jehral, you may help her, but there is too much here to do."

Ella's heart sunk.

"My Prince . . ." Jehral began.

"Ilathor, if the primate reaches his goal, nothing you're doing here will matter!" Ella cried.

"The primate?" the prince asked. "You know where he is?"

"Yes," Ella said. "That's what I'm trying to explain! He's on his way to the Sentinel. He may be there by now."

Prince Ilathor issued swift orders.

Ella breathed a sigh of relief. She just hoped they would be in time.

65

"The cruiser ahead, heading for the Sentinel—it is flying the primate's flag." Sailmaster Scherlic pointed.

"Can you get closer?" Miro asked.

As if in answer, a boom sounded as one of the Imperial warships fired a warning shot across the bow of the *Infinity*, a splash of water erupting from the sea as the orb exploded. Miro could see a catapult mounted on a swivel on the warship's deck.

"This is as close as I will take you," said Sailmaster Scherlic.

Miro fumed as he saw how close he was. The wide mouth of Seranthia's harbor lay in front of him, and he could see the primate about to pass the Sentinel and make his escape under the protection of the Imperial fleet.

Miro saw smoke rising from the city in several places. He didn't know if the Hazarans had taken the city or if Rogan had led his men to victory, but he knew momentous events were occurring there. Yet Miro also knew it wouldn't end until the primate himself was taken. He couldn't miss this chance.

Miro turned to the stocky loremaster of House Buchalantas.

"Every house has fought in this war," Miro said. "The terror, the bloodshed—it has touched all of us. I have lost those I loved, and

I have fought this enemy with all my strength. I have sent men to their deaths, knowing their sacrifice would save a larger number, yet knowing it was my decision that ended their lives."

Stone-faced, Sailmaster Scherlic looked at Miro, his expression unreadable.

"Every house has fought in this war," Miro said, "except yours. House Buchalantas is neutral. That's what you say, isn't it?"

"It is not our fight," Scherlic said in his deep, accented voice.

"When does it become your fight? How do you think the Buchalanti would fare under the single rule the primate desires? Do you think you'll keep your much-vaunted independence?" Miro thrust his finger at Scherlic's chest. "We've given a lot to get to this point. More than you'll ever understand. Now it's time to make a choice, Sailmaster."

Scherlic looked out at the warships and then back to Miro.

"The time for neutrality is past," Miro said. "This ship is a Buchalanti storm rider. Those Tingaran-made ships over there? They're just ships." Miro gestured at the glowing runes that covered the sails and coated the decks of the *Infinity*. "Why have this power if you aren't prepared to use it?"

"One ship, against—what?—twenty ships of the fleet?" Scherlic finally spoke.

"One Buchalanti storm rider, fighting for freedom."

Six of the Tingaran ships approached, sails unfurled as they gathered speed and attempted to head the *Infinity* off.

Sailmaster Scherlic made a choice.

"Battle stations!" he called. "Prepare to increase to ramming speed."

"Thank you," Miro said.

"Now get out of my way," Scherlic said.

The Buchalanti Sailmaster raised his voice and began to chant.

Miro was blinded by the flash of runes, and the deck trembled beneath his feet as the *Infinity* came to life.

66

Primate Melovar Aspen stood on the wide circular base of the statue, looking up at its leg and wondering how to get in. He tilted his head back until, high above, he could make out where the leg bent at the knee, then even higher until he could see where the two legs met. Melovar turned back to the book of the Evermen, swiftly turning the pages in his hand.

"Try looking down rather than up," Melovar heard a voice behind him say. Turning, the primate saw the last person he expected to see.

Dain Barden stood watching him, the muscles in his arms tense, the head of his war hammer on the ground. Behind the leader of the Akari, two revenants looked on with their white-eyed gaze, silent and impassive.

Melovar looked down at the smooth stone of the Sentinel's pedestal, a single piece of marble so expansive a thousand standing men would not have been crowded.

At the primate's feet, directly under the statue's center point, was a circle of runes.

"Well?" Dain Barden said. "Is it what you're looking for?"

Melovar allowed the arm that held the book to drop to his side. "I don't know," he said. "I've only been able to glean fragments of knowledge from the book."

"I gathered as much. Is it a weapon?" Barden asked.

"I don't know."

"Can you open it?"

"I can try," Melovar said. He examined the circle of runes for a moment and then flipped through the book, turning the pages one after the other.

The primate felt his heart race when he recognized the circle of symbols on the page in front of him.

He called out in a clear voice. *"Mulara-latahn. Sunara-latahn. Sumayara-sulamara-latanara."*

The runes carved into the stone, still looking as fresh as if newly inscribed, lit up with a slow fire of green light that traveled from one symbol to the next.

A seam appeared on the inside of the circle of runes, and Melovar heard Dain Barden draw in his breath. There was a grinding sound, as if one stone moved against another, and the seam flared with golden light.

The stone disk moved downward, falling into a rapidly opening hole. A moment later the grinding ceased, and Dain Barden stepped forward to stand with the primate so that the two men stared down into the glowing opening in the ground. As he squinted against the bright light, Melovar saw stairs inside the hole, and he took a step forward.

"Wait," the Dain said, holding Melovar back with his arm. "Let me send in one of them."

Barden motioned, and one of the revenants took clumsy steps down into the opening before disappearing down the stairway. The primate waited for the count of ten breaths and then once more moved forward.

"Stop!" Dain Barden shouted.

With a sound like the roar of a forge, the golden light turned to red, and both Melovar and Barden looked away, shielding their eyes. When they peered back into the opening, eyes following the steps, only a pile of ash indicated where the draug had been.

"I don't think we're welcome here," Dain Barden said. "It's warded."

"Send in the other one," Melovar said.

The light had shifted hue back to soft yellow. The second revenant stepped forward, taking the steps one at a time, walking for the count of twenty steps without coming to harm, and with a shrug Dain Barden followed, the primate close on his heels.

The light appeared to emanate from the walls themselves, with no obvious source. The two men and the revenant descended for a short way before the passage leveled out. Melovar felt both trepidation and anticipation. The battle for Seranthia was inconsequential now. It was what happened here that would determine the fate of Merralya.

The short corridor at the base of the stairway was tall enough that even Dain Barden didn't have to stoop and wide enough for the two men to walk side by side behind the revenant. Made of the same white marble as the Sentinel, the corridor was smooth to touch and unblemished by runes or artwork.

"I don't know how they built this," Barden said. "Look at the walls. Those aren't blocks of marble; it's all of one piece. It doesn't even look like the floor is made of a separate piece from the walls."

"There are chambers within Stonewater like this," Melovar said, "but nothing on this scale."

Ahead, the corridor ended in another set of stairs, spiraling upward this time. Once more, Barden sent the revenant ahead, but these twisting stairs didn't appear to be warded.

"One of the legs," the Dain explained as they climbed the interminable steps, eyes carefully watching the draug ahead of them. "We'll soon be in the body. I suppose it might open up then. Why build inside a statue?"

"The Evermen work in mysterious ways," the primate said.

"Save me your cant," Barden said. "We're in a place where ordinary men may have never set foot. The last who came this way could have been the Evermen themselves. You must be burning to know what it is."

"And wondering whether what we'll find is something that can be shared?" the primate asked, glancing sideways at the Dain.

"You need me, Primate," Dain Barden said. "If there's another of those traps, only my draug will find it."

"Just as you need me," the primate said. "I have the knowledge, and I am the representative of the Evermen in this world. The Evermen will not allow harm to come to me."

Melovar heard Dain Barden grunt as he put one foot in front of the other, the spiral stone staircase going on and on. The primate knew that without the elixir coursing through his veins, he himself would never be able to ascend as quickly as he was. The burning fire in his blood gave him strength. The pain told him he was alive.

At the top of the stairway, a steady blue light revealed a chamber beyond. The revenant emerged without pausing, while the two men followed more cautiously.

A cavernous hall opened up in front of them, so large that it must occupy the statue's entire torso. A stone gallery, tiered with steps on the left and a low wall on the right, spread in a crescent shape ahead, a curve that followed the wall. Each tier was perhaps wide enough for five men to walk abreast, and the winding stairway they'd just crested opened onto the bottom tier. Even from their low position, the two men could easily see over the wall.

In unison, Primate Melovar Aspen and Dain Barden Mensk turned their heads and gasped.

67

Evrin's eyes opened weakly as he heard the sound of footsteps break the silence. Dread hit him in his chest as he realized someone had made it past the first of his wards.

Three men stood on the lowest tier of the gallery, facing the pool. No, Evrin realized: two men and a revenant. So that was how they had passed his ward.

The primate in his white robe stood beside a huge man, a commanding figure in blood-splattered armor of bleached leather. The pair walked forward slowly, gazing at the shimmering pool with both lust and fear. A single drop of the essence would kill them, yet they were looking at more wealth and power in one place than any man had seen before.

As they grew closer, Evrin saw that the huge man wore the *raj hada* of a Dain of the Akari. Of all peoples to get mixed up in this war, the last Evrin had wished to see join the fight were the Akari.

"What is the oval mirror?" the Dain whispered to the primate.

"It's a portal," Evrin spoke up, answering for him.

Both men jumped when they heard him, but the revenant showed no reaction. Evrin watched them turn to face him, knowing what they saw: a broken old man, unable to stand, unable to move, lying prone across the tiers in the far corner.

"You," Melovar said. "The old pilgrim. What are you doing here?"

"Protecting the portal from men like you," Evrin said, his voice weak, but clear. "Stop, please. While you can." He tried to move, but the pain was nearly too much for him, and Evrin closed his eyes momentarily.

"Primate, who is this man?"

"I thought I knew, Dain Barden, but it seems he is more than I once thought he was. Tell me, old man, why so much essence?"

"My name is Evrin Evenstar, and the essence powers the portal, but my seals absorb the power so the portal cannot be used."

"Portal? A portal to where?" the Dain asked. "How did you cross the pool to place them there? What happens if the seals are removed?"

"I placed the seals there to block the portal long ago," Evrin said. "If the seals are removed, the portal will open. But you must understand—"

"You haven't answered the most important question," the primate interrupted, his eyes calculating. "Where does the portal go?"

"Where the Evermen went, of course," Evrin said. "But, Primate, you should know the truth. The Evermen were no gods. They were evil."

"What makes you say such a thing?" Primate Melovar asked.

"Because once I was one of them."

Dain Barden didn't appear to have heard the exchange. He stared at the silver surface of the portal in awe. "The Lord of the Night? He is through there? He can return?"

When the primate's gaze followed the Dain's, Evrin opened his mouth and spoke the words to activate his final ward. The two men and the revenant were all standing on the gallery's bottom level. There would be no better time.

At Evrin's command, symbols appeared on the white surface of the stone, flashing with angry crimson on the lowest tier. A purple haze welled up to the height of a man's knees, transparent like water, fading nearly as quickly as it appeared, but with a power Evrin knew was deadly beyond belief.

Melovar Aspen screamed, a cry of pure agony that reverberated through the chamber, as first his feet, then his ankles, and finally his lower legs melted away, until the purple subsided and he fell down, staring down at the bloody stumps of his knees in horror.

As soon as Evrin started to speak, the revenant reacted, somehow aware of the nature of what was to come, its memories of life in the Dain's service telling it the Dain must be protected at all costs. The revenant grabbed Dain Barden, and with a surge of lore-enhanced strength, threw him up to the higher tiers of the gallery, before it too succumbed. In moments the purple haze ate through the draug's legs also, the revenant still and uncannily silent as it fell down face-first and looked up at Dain Barden with its blank-faced stare.

The Dain looked in horror, first at the draug, and then at the primate's legs, now nothing more than stumps.

The chamber was silent.

Evrin slumped back against the stone in his corner of the room while the Dain panted, sprawled on the stone steps, turning his wide-eyed gaze on the old man.

The silence was broken by an ear-splitting wail. "My legs!" the primate screamed.

Evrin sighed. He'd activated the last of his wards, yet the Akari was unharmed. "Leave this place, I beg you," he said. "Do not remove the essence, and do not remove the seals. Those on the other side will know the moment the portal is open."

"How will they know?" asked the Dain. "If you tell me how it works, I can help you."

"A beacon on the other side will alert them that the way is open."

"Good," said Barden. "If the beacon's on the other side, then you won't be able to stop it."

"Listen to me!" Evrin tried to shout, as loudly as he could. "You don't know what you are dealing with. You would visit on the world a horror greater than you can imagine."

"The Lord of the Night is our god," the leader of the Akari said. "We are his chosen people. Perhaps you are afraid, old man, but for me there is nothing to fear."

68

Dain Barden looked at the pool of essence, the thoughts spinning in his mind. There was no way across. To touch the essence would be to die the most painful death imaginable. Yet what if he only had this one chance? The old man was powerful, whoever he was. If Barden left this place, he doubted he would be able to return.

"I do not wish to die here," the Dain said. Then it came to him. "You," he pointed at the revenant, "remove the seals."

Moving laboriously, the revenant began to crawl forward, using its hands and elbows to pull itself forward. It hauled itself over the wall, and with a splash it landed in the pool of essence.

The Dain released his breath when he saw his guess proven correct. The substance couldn't harm a creature that was already dead. Dragging itself along, worming and wriggling through the oily black liquid that trickled over its body as it moved, the draug clambered toward the oval mirror and the three seals that kept the portal closed.

Barden focused his gaze on the old man. "If you had any more tricks you would have used them, but"—he walked over until he stood in front of the old man, looming over him—"not a word, even so."

Evrin looked up at the Dain.

"Not a word!" Barden said.

The revenant reached the platform of stone steps that jutted from the pool and clambered up to the oval mirror. With a swipe of its arm it knocked away the seal on the left. A second swipe took the seal on the right. Only the third seal on the bottom remained. The silver surface of the portal shifted color, now tinged with gold.

"Soluara-sonur!" Evrin called out.

The final seal lit up with a flare of heat, bathing the room in red. The revenant began to smoke and burn, finally falling back into the pool, its body destroyed while it was still short of its goal. Evrin closed his eyes.

The last seal was still intact.

Enraged, Dain Barden reached down and grabbed Evrin by the throat, lifting him up high. Evrin barely struggled as the Akari began to squeeze.

A shadow moved. Water dripped to the floor.

Something smashed into the Dain's armored body with the strength of iron, hitting so hard that it punched through the leather, and he felt the snap as three of his ribs broke from the single blow.

Dain Barden dropped Evrin and turned just as a second blow hit his jaw with the force of a mountain. When the Dain stumbled, a third punch closed his left eye; then a fourth hit his lower chest, knocking the wind out of him before he fell to the ground.

"Where are you?" the Dain said, coughing and spluttering as he rose once more to his feet.

He took his war hammer in his hands and swung it in the air, first striking left and then right. Barden's third blow jarred his arms to the bone as he hit something hard.

In front of him a shadow flickered as drops of water fell down from the shape of a man. "Now I have you," the Dain snarled.

Dain Barden swung his hammer in quick, successive blows, trading strength for speed. There was some figure that weaved and dodged but wasn't fast enough to escape all his strokes. Each time the Dain struck, the figure's skin sizzled and Barden could see runes outlined, allowing the Akari to see more of his opponent. He felt his hammer starting to have an effect, and finally he heard a cry of pain when he swung with all his strength at his opponent's chest.

As the air shimmered and the form of a man materialized, Dain Barden saw that whatever his opponent's abilities were, the man was young, with red hair dripping wet to his shoulders and a bare chest covered with fading runes. The young man punched at him again, but the Dain was a skilled warrior, and he blocked easily. He raised his hammer to strike at the young man's face.

"The portal!" Evrin suddenly cried in anguish.

Barden and his opponent both turned to the relic. The Dain couldn't believe what he was seeing.

Primate Melovar Aspen had dragged his broken body into the pool. There was something in the strange power the primate possessed that allowed him to survive the touch of the essence for the time it took for him to cross the pool and pull himself onto the raised platform.

When the primate reached the last seal and struck it away, Barden heard a ragged chuckle come from the primate's lips.

Even as the primate's face contorted from the terrible agony of the essence, there was an expression of triumph on his face.

69

Surely no one could stand such pain. Then Killian thought of the primate's elixir. Would it keep Melovar Aspen alive?

Killian shifted his gaze and saw that the Dain's mouth was open, their struggle forgotten.

What would happen now that the last seal had been removed?

The primate's eyes opened wide as he looked at something past Killian, and then the screams of Melovar Aspen were forever silenced. An arrow fletched with green feathers suddenly sprouted from the primate's throat. It was swiftly followed by another that plunged into the primate's eye, and a third appeared in the center of Melovar Aspen's mouth.

The primate fell back down into the pool of essence. His screams were terrible as his insides liquefied, even as the elixir tried to heal him. The primate's skin hissed and bubbled as if acid fought to escape the confines of his veins, and then his skin began to fall off his body in pieces swiftly devoured by the essence. The primate tried to push with his arms, to keep his head above the surface, but then his left arm fell from his body. He opened his mouth, and a stream of red and yellow fluid gushed forth as the pressure inside his body forced his insides out. The screams became gurgling moans.

The primate's death was horrific, yet Killian couldn't help but think this was a fitting end for the ruler of the Assembly of Templars, to be killed by essence.

The primate's body sank under the surface of the pool, hissing and steaming, bubbling as it broke into little pieces, until it was as if Melovar Aspen had never been.

Killian turned. A dark-haired man in the green silk of a bladesinger stood by the edge of the pool. He carried a bent piece of wood in his hands, shining with activated runes, the string still thrumming from the release of the last arrow. He had angular features and the white line of a scar rose from his jaw line to his left eye. A cord tied his long hair back from his face. He was perhaps the same age as Killian.

Instantly, Killian knew this was Ella's brother. Their hair was different, but the features were the same. Ella's description hadn't done her brother justice. The man's character was written in the lines of his face: this was a warrior who would fight to his last breath in the pursuit of his ends. Killian doubted even the Dain of the Akari would be a match for Miro.

Miro fitted another arrow and then turned, holding both Killian and the Dain in sight. "No one is to move," the bladesinger said, his voice firm, and Killian knew he meant it. "I don't miss."

"The seals!" Evrin's cry brought Killian's attention back to what the primate had done. "The beacon!"

The last seal was gone. The primate had struck it away, and now the three seals lay on the stone just below the tall oval mirror. The way was open. The beacon would call.

The sound came all at once.

Dain Barden dropped his hammer and put his hands to his ears, his face twisted at the deafening note resounding through the chamber.

Killian, the runes on his body now faded, put his own hands against his head.

The sound grew until Killian thought his head would explode, and then it fell away again until it nearly stopped altogether. It rose once again to the volume where Killian could hardly think, the pain like a prismatic orb bursting inside his skull.

The next time the sound fell, Killian looked at Evrin.

"It must be stopped or the Evermen will return," Evrin gasped. "Now that it has activated, it can only be stopped from the other side. The seals must be replaced, but they won't work if the beacon isn't stopped."

Killian turned back to Miro. With a shock he saw two more people enter the chamber, but he had eyes only for one of them.

Ella stood next to a man from the Hazaran desert, his bearing regal and gold thread in his clothing. The desert man tried to hold Ella protectively behind him, and instantly Killian knew that this man loved her.

Ella and Killian's eyes met. He had never spoken about his life with anyone in the way he had with Ella. No one had ever cared to ask.

Killian wanted Ella to live in a world free from men such as the primate. If great danger was on the other side of the portal, Killian wanted Ella to be safe from it. He knew there was no other option.

The beacon could only be stopped from the other side.

Calmly, Killian walked forward. For some reason the intensity of the beacon's call no longer hurt him. He reached the wall around the pool and stepped over it, plunging first one leg, and then the other into the oily black liquid.

Where the essence touched his skin, Killian felt a strange tingling sensation, but nothing else. He walked forward, wading through the essence toward the oval mirror of shimmering gold that stood twice the height of a man.

Toward the portal.

"No. No!"

Killian heard her even above the deafening wail of the beacon. He turned and looked at her. Ella gazed back at him, pushing the desert man away as she came forward, crying out as the Hazaran held her back.

Killian reached the center of the pool. At the foot of the shimmering portal, he could see the seals resting where they had fallen to the stone of the platform.

Killian climbed the stone steps, retrieving the seals and hanging each on the portal where it had been before, where Evrin would be able to activate them once he had crossed through to the other side.

Killian glanced at Evrin.

"You'll know what to do," Evrin said.

Killian turned to Ella again. He looked into her eyes as he mouthed three final words, directing them at her.

He was making a journey that would have no return. Without another glance behind him, Killian stepped forward, through the burnt gold of the portal's curtain.

Into the unknown.

70

Killian's last words were to tell Ella he loved her.

The surface of the mirror rippled like molten gold. Killian's expression was set with determination as he took a breath and then walked through. Ella looked for his body to emerge on the other side of the shimmering curtain.

But he was gone.

Moments later, the sound of the beacon ceased as abruptly as it had started. Ella heard Evrin's voice as he reactivated the seals, and the reddened shade of the portal shifted steadily back to silver. Evrin sighed and hung his head.

For a long time there was silence.

The Akari was the first to speak. "You can lower your weapon, Bladesinger. I won't fight."

Miro slowly relaxed the arrow he had nocked to his ear.

Ella wanted to go to her brother, but there was still too much she needed to know. Instead, she bounded up the tiers to reach Evrin. The old man was badly wounded: one of his legs was clearly broken, and the other bore a gaping wound that might be infected. His lips were parched and cracked. "Water!" she cried.

Miro threw her a sloshing flask. Ella snatched it out of the air and pressed it to Evrin's lips, waiting until the old man took a large gulp, before she spoke.

"Where did he go? When will he come back?"

"I'm sorry," Evrin said, appearing to revive in front of her. "He cannot come back."

"No," Ella said. "I don't believe you. How could you let him go if you knew he could never come back? Bring him back." She shook the old man, heedless of Evrin's moans. "I know about your secrets. I know you have powers. Bring him back!"

"Ella," Miro and Prince Ilathor both said in unison. They then looked at each other as if each man was noticing the other for the first time.

"Who are you?" Miro said.

Ella looked at her brother and Prince Ilathor. It was like a meeting of two black-maned lions, circling as they took each other's measure. Both were tall, but Miro was slightly taller. Both men were lean and broad-shouldered, but Ilathor's shoulders were a little wider. Each wore the right of command like a mantle.

"My name is Prince Ilathor Shanti of Tarn Teharan. I take it you are the brother of Ella?"

"Miro Torresante, lord marshal of the allied armies of Altura and Halaran."

Dain Barden picked up his war hammer and leaned on the head. "I remember you, Lord Marshal. We met on the Azure Plains."

"We should get out of here," Ella said, breaking the tension in the room. "Miro, Ilathor, help me with Evrin."

The two warriors lifted the groaning old man between them and carried him out of the chamber.

"Don't even think about it," Ella said, glaring at the Akari and looking pointedly at his war hammer. The Dain surprised her by spreading his hands in a gesture of peaceful intent.

Ella followed the Dain down the spiral stairs, but before she left, she saw a book on the ground. Its pages were seared at the edges, and part of it was missing completely, but it was made of the same metallic fabric as the Lexicons. She bent down and picked it up.

Soon Ella, Miro, Prince Ilathor, and Dain Barden all stood on the pedestal below the Sentinel.

"Please, put me down here," Evrin said. "Lean me up against the foot. Yes, that's it. Before I speak, there is something I must do."

The old man called out a series of activations, names Ella didn't recognize at all. The circle of runes around the opening in the pedestal flared blue, and there was the sound of stone moving against stone. In an instant the opening closed, sealed as if it had never been. Only the circle of runes remained.

Now that they were safely out of the chamber, and Miro and Ilathor held the Akari in check, Ella rounded on Evrin.

"Where did Killian go?" Ella demanded.

"He went to another place, removed in both time and space from this world. I am sorry, but where he has gone you cannot follow," Evrin said sadly.

Ella's mouth set with determination. Killian had given himself so they could be safe from the danger on the other side of the portal. He couldn't be gone forever. He simply couldn't.

"I promise you, I will find a way," Ella said in a voice of steel.

"Ella," Miro's voice spoke behind her.

Ella saw his open arms and fell into her brother's embrace, closing her eyes for a moment. She looked over Miro's shoulder and saw Prince Ilathor, looking at her as if seeing her for the first time. Ella remembered Killian's last words as she looked farther still.

"Look," Ella said, pushing her brother away and pointing, laughing despite herself. "It's Jehral. He has Bartolo with him. And Shani. And . . ."

71

Miro released his sister and turned. Five figures were walking across the tiny island toward where their group clustered at the base of the Sentinel.

Miro saw the Hazaran first, recognizing Jehral from long ago in Sarostar, though he was now covered in blood and walked with a limp.

Supporting Jehral on each side were Shani, the Petryan woman, and a bladesinger. Miro grinned when he recognized Bartolo, smiling broadly despite his wounds.

Then Miro saw Rogan Jarvish, whose tall body obscured the woman beside him. Rogan smiled wearily.

And then Miro was running. He didn't remember telling his feet to move; they were simply propelling his body forward. "Amber," he whispered.

Amber held something in her arms, and Miro suddenly drew up short, staring at her in shock.

Amber looked up at Miro, and he could see trepidation in her eyes. She pulled the soft wool from the bundle in her arms so that he could see the tiny babe she carried.

"Miro," she said, "this is my son."

Miro gazed down at the baby, looking at clear blue eyes and a dimpled chin. The baby held his hand in front of his face and then reached out, as if trying to touch the chin of the warrior who loomed over him.

Miro stared at Amber, and then his eyes returned once more to the baby. The babe's hands were tiny, each little finger grasping at the air. Miro reached down with his own hand, and the boy grabbed hold of his finger with surprising strength.

"What's . . . what's his name?" Miro asked.

He looked up at Amber when she didn't reply, and then he saw the tears rolling down her cheeks. Miro reached out and pulled her close to him, with the baby held between them.

"He doesn't have a name," Amber said through her tears. "I never gave him one."

"He's beautiful," Miro said, and he meant it. Here, with her baby held so naturally to her breast, Amber looked lovelier than ever. "You're beautiful."

Amber's eyes shone through her tears. "He's Igor's," she said. "I never told Igor I was with child."

"Amber . . ." Miro was suddenly unsure of himself. He shook his head. "Actually, I don't . . ."

"What is it?"

"Do you think . . . ?" Miro hesitated. "Do you think we could name him together?"

Amber laughed. "Of course we can. I'd like that very much."

Miro beamed. "I would too."

"Amber." Ella's arms went around her friend. "I've missed you so much." Then the baby started crying, and Ella laughed. "He's beautiful."

"The city is secured," Rogan said to Miro. "The desert men, like Jehral here"—he nodded to indicate Jehral—"and our soldiers are working well together as we restore order."

Miro locked eyes with Prince Ilathor.

"There's one score I need to settle first," Miro said, frowning at the prince. "No one comes to my city under the guise of a treaty and captures my sister. No one."

Prince Ilathor scowled. Accustomed to deference, he dropped his hand to rest on the scimitar at his side.

Miro reached around to the hilt of the zenblade on his back.

"Miro, stop," Ella said. "He needed our help to take the Petryan capital. By knocking Petrya out of the war, he enabled you to take back Halaran."

"My Prince, listen to me," Jehral said. "It was not our people who took this city; it was those from all over the world. They come from Altura and Halaran and from Torakon and Loua Louna. It is for no one house to claim victory. We are in their debt."

Prince Ilathor took his hand away from his sword, and after a moment, Miro followed suit. The prince held out his hand, and Miro hesitated, but a moment later, he reached out, and the two men shook.

"There is one more," Rogan said. "All others have either surrendered or come to our side." He looked pointedly at Dain Barden.

The ruler of the Akari shook his head. "We won't go against the wishes of the houses. It's too hot here. I've already sent the orders. I'm taking my people back north, if you'll let me."

Rogan growled, "You can help us rebuild, and then you can go back north."

"What did you really want?" Miro asked.

Dain Barden shrugged. "We wanted to join the empire. People find our lore repulsive, but it is who we are. No one is harmed except for the dead and those we send them to fight."

"Provided you keep your lore to yourselves," Rogan said.

"Yes, I'll give you that. Provided we keep our lore to ourselves. The first emperor—Xenovere the Great they call him—exiled us because of who we are. All we ever wanted was to have our own place in the world."

"Then go back to the north," Miro said, "but this time not to exile. The Tingaran Empire is gone, and the brief rule of the primate is over. It is up to men like us to decide what comes next. Whatever happens, we must never again let any one man control the world's essence, just as we need to keep a wary eye on the relics the Evermen left behind."

"A worthy sentiment," Evrin spoke from his seat, leaning against the Sentinel's big toe. "As soon as I'm well enough, I'll help you rebuild the machines that once resided in Stonewater. Extracting essence from the dead may work for the Akari, but essence taken from lignite works just as well."

"Wait," Ella said, causing all eyes to be on her. "Before we say anything more, I think it's time."

"Time for what?" Miro said.

Ella turned to Evrin. "It's time to know the truth. Killian left us," her voice caught, "so that he could prevent the return of the Evermen. Twice now you've asked everything of him, and twice he's given you everything. All he ever wanted was to know the truth. Yet he left without ever knowing. It's time we knew, Evrin Evenstar."

"I'm wounded," Evrin protested.

"Then the sooner you start telling us, the sooner you'll see a healer," Ella said. "None of us are leaving this island until we know the truth. It's time," she repeated.

Evrin bowed his head. "I suppose it is. I used to think the best protection lay in ignorance, but the primate has proven me wrong. Listen to me well, for I will not repeat myself."

Ella and Miro exchanged glances. Soon they all clustered around the old man.

72

"My name is Evrin Evenstar," he began. "I'm not sure how old I am, but I have walked Merralya for at least a thousand years. Please put aside everything you have learned from the Evermen Cycles, for what you have learned is a lie, and what I am now telling you is the truth."

Ella and her brother exchanged glances. Ella looked at Evrin and now saw the passage of centuries behind his eyes, and as he spoke power came to his voice. Ella could believe that this was the man who created the Lexicons.

"Long ago, the Evermen ruled the world. Not just these lands here that you call the Tingaran Empire. No, I speak of long before the empire even existed. We Evermen ruled all of Merralya, and everyone in it."

The sounds of waves crashing against the island combined with Evrin's words. Evrin closed his eyes for a moment and then resumed.

"Humans were our workers. You could use the term 'slaves.' Like all slaves, you were given work."

Evrin looked into the distance, and Ella wondered what he saw.

"Some of you processed essence for our use," Evrin said. "You were taught to use the machines, but you didn't need lore of your own and were never taught any."

"Templars," Amber murmured.

"Some of you, however, were taught to utilize lore. You built our cities, and you manufactured tools and machines to do the labor that you were not capable of doing yourselves. Some of you created illusions to entertain us."

Evrin moved his leg and winced before he continued.

"Ours was a beautiful world, filled with wonder. Yet when I say 'ours,' I do not include you humans, I refer to my brothers and myself. You were our playthings, our toys, and our slaves. You did what we commanded, and we did with you what we willed. Your lives were in our hands, and you lived, loved, and gave birth at our command. You were no threat to us, for we were all powerful. We lived forever and we knew everything."

Evrin licked his lips. "Or so we thought."

Ella looked up at the Sentinel and thought about Stonewater and the Pinnacle and the incredible power the Evermen had possessed.

"My brothers and I each took a god-name to impress our subjects. There was Varian Vitrix, who you might know as the Lord of the Earth. Pyrax Pohlen was the Lord of the Sun. I am Evrin Evenstar, but you would know me as the Lord of the Sky."

Ella couldn't believe what she was hearing. It turned upside down everything she had ever been taught about the Evermen. She could understand now why Evrin had kept them all in ignorance. Who would cast down their own gods?

"There was one of us, Sentar Scythran, the Lord of the Night . . ."

Dain Barden looked up, his gaze intent.

"You," Evrin said. "Dain of the Akari. You need to hear this most of all."

Barden's knuckles were white as he gripped the hammer at his belt.

"Sentar Scythran found his slaves' free will to be offensive. He didn't want humans having emotions or singing songs. He didn't want his subjects speaking to him out of turn or breeding without his permission. To avoid what he saw as these inefficiencies and insults, Sentar Scythran preferred to be served by the dead."

Ella wondered how the Dain would react to Evrin's words.

"None of us took much notice. We were powerful and knowledgeable, and we could do almost anything we set our minds to. Drawing runes on a corpse and teaching it to pour wine was nothing to us."

Evrin coughed for a moment, and Ella looked over at Seranthia, wondering if the world would ever be the same again.

"However, something happened that made us take notice. For, being constantly around the dead as he was, the Lord of the Night discovered a new source of power. Sentar discovered that essence's power comes from life. We all knew that, of course, but we always thought the essence itself had to come from lignite, from below the ground, where the life energy of a thousand trees or a million blades of grass condenses over eons.

"Yet Sentar Scythran, the Lord of the Night, made a new discovery. He found a way to harness the life energy of humans."

Evrin looked down at the ground as if filled with shame.

"My brothers, the Evermen, began to adopt this process. At first we were pleased. We had found a use for the dead humans, and our power was never greater. We could do anything. We pooled our knowledge, and we discussed ways of exploring worlds beyond this one."

Ella thought about the hidden relic, a portal to another world. She wondered if Killian was lost to her forever.

Evrin looked up again. "But then I fell in love with a human."

He took a deep breath. "You have to understand, this was something unheard of among my people. Unimaginable—perhaps that might be a better word. We Evermen did with our slaves whatever we willed. We bedded those whom we ruled whenever the mood took us. Yet never was the fruit of our passion allowed to survive. Never did we feel anything more than lust. How could we? We were your gods. We were as far above you as the stars."

"Who was she?" Shani asked.

"She was different. Her people had made her a leader, which is how we met, and it didn't take me long to see why. I had never met a human before who saw herself as my equal. Not until I met her. She was intelligent and wise, and filled with new ideas. She was beautiful, and I took her to my bed.

"Yet even as I did so, I knew it was only with her permission. She would have rather died than give in to anyone who sought to control her by intimidation or force. My feelings crept up on me. I thought I was ruled by my passion, but it was more. I was in love.

"Suddenly I felt that I could see for the first time. With her to open my eyes, I came to realize that my brothers had lowered the cost of human life to nothing. You were worth more to us dead than alive. The slightest provocation and you were killed—one more body for the vats. I felt sick. What we were doing was wrong.

"I confronted my brothers, but they wouldn't give up their ways. They were disgusted that I had taken a human lover and tried to bring me back into the fold. We argued, and I left.

"You have to understand how hard this was for me. They were my brethren, and together we dreamt of wonders you cannot possibly imagine. Yet I loved her even more than I loved my brothers. I felt responsible for the humans in my dominion as well as for those in my brothers' dominions. I made my decision and chose a path I would never be able to turn away from."

The expression on Evrin's face told Ella how hard the decision had been.

"I gathered nine of the human loremasters to me. Looking at these men and women with my newly opened eyes, I saw that these were bright, intelligent people who deserved to be given the opportunity to be all they could be.

"I presented the loremasters with nine Lexicons, one for each school of lore. With these books, not only would the humans have the knowledge they needed, they would have a source of power that the Evermen would not be able to take away.

"I then told them the truth. My love was shocked beyond belief to discover we were no longer obtaining our essence from the lignite ore we found below the ground. The loremasters couldn't believe their gods had betrayed them. I showed them how the Evermen were slaughtering humans in ever greater numbers.

"I let them think. They needed to come to the conclusions that I had on their own. It is no easy thing, to rise up against your gods. The shock was replaced with rage, as I knew it would be.

"Yet the revelations did not stop there. When I next spoke with these ten humans—my lover and the nine loremasters—I had their full attention. This is when I told them.

"The Evermen planned a great project. My brothers wanted to open their first door to another world. For this they would need essence, always more essence. A great number of humans were to be harvested like wheat.

"The humans rose up, all of them. And so I, Evrin Evenstar, Lord of the Sky, led the revolt against the gods. The struggle was long and bitter, and in the process I was captured by my former brothers.

"They stripped my powers from me. I was rescued by my human allies, but my love was . . . killed . . . while I was held captive."

Ella looked at Miro and then at Amber with her babe in her arms. She saw Bartolo and Shani standing close together. Rogan had a far-off look in his eyes. Jehral had a wife back in the desert, Ella remembered. Ella shied away from looking at the prince.

"I'm sorry," Ella said.

"I won't say more, but against all odds we won. You . . . won. You cast off the shackles of your overlords.

"Yet even in victory, and even with the death of my love, I could not kill my brethren. I gave them a choice: to die or to flee through the portal into their new world. They left, but not before the Lord of the Night said his parting words. He said you humans would not be able to control your emotions; you are too filled with love and hate, ambition and aggression. You would not be able to rule yourselves, and if you called, the Evermen would return.

"I vowed not to rule the humans as my brothers had. Instead, I looked on and stayed silent as you fought among yourselves, though it pained me to see. I watched and did nothing as the nine loremasters formed nine separate houses. Each house took a land for their own, and a color, and then I watched in silence as builders fought enchanters, animators fought illusionists, and chaos took the land.

"With no lore of their own, the templars stayed neutral, and as they were the only ones who knew how to operate the machines in Stonewater, they enjoyed a special status, able to shape the events of the war of the houses and bide their time until a victor became clear.

"I stayed silent, deciding my role was to intervene only when the most dangerous lore came into your possession, such as the primate with his elixir, and the discovery of the portal inside the Sentinel.

"Eventually the Tingarans became dominant, leading to the formation of the Tingaran Empire and the banishment of the Akari—who were never one of the nine—to the north.

"The templars continued to occupy Stonewater, a sacred place even for the Evermen, and a distorted truth was put out, what you call the Evermen Cycles. Still, I did nothing as my brothers came to be worshipped, and the story of the brave humans who cast off their overlords was forgotten.

"At least . . ." Evrin said. "At least now some of those who will shape what the Tingaran Empire will become have heard this story. Perhaps this was my fault. Perhaps I should have let the truth be known earlier. But who would have listened? Would you believe me if you hadn't been here to witness what happened today?

"There are so many of you who revere the Evermen. If they ever return, you will not only face their incredible powers, unlike anything you have ever seen before, but you will face your own people, those who will mindlessly follow their god wherever he leads."

There was silence except for the sound of lapping waves as they each digested Evrin's words.

"If that ever happens," Miro finally said, "you will fight by our side, as you once did?"

"I will," Evrin said, "although with my powers taken from me, there is little I can do. I have my knowledge of the runes, but that is all."

"Your lover . . ." Amber said. "Did you ever have a child?"

All eyes were suddenly on the old man. Ella looked again at his piercing blue eyes and the flecks of ginger in his beard. When Evrin hung his head and a look of infinite sadness crossed his visage, Ella felt the blood drain from her face.

"Yes," Evrin said. "I never knew for sure, but yes, I believe we did have a child. And I think my child might have had a child of his own and that perhaps I have a descendant living today.

"I think I might have just sent him to his death."

EPILOGUE

Primate Melovar Aspen had one last surprise left in store for the world he had plunged into war and then abandoned with his death.

His veins had flowed with *raj nilas*, the substance he called elixir. Never had so much of essence's opposite taken residence in a man's body. Never had the two liquids been brought together in such concentration.

When the primate perished, the violent clash of *raj nilas* meeting *raj ichor* caused his body to disintegrate, a result not attributable to essence alone. His skin fell off in slabs, the limbs fell from his body, and his face came away from his skull.

Deep within the individual cells that joined to make up the rapidly dissolving tissues, the *raj nilas* bubbled and fizzed angrily. Each miniscule droplet struggled to retain its form, desperate to maintain an identity separate from the *raj ichor* around it. It was a fight with an inevitable outcome, as finally the two liquids met and combined.

The essence easily swallowed the elixir within its much greater volume, but nevertheless, the *raj ichor* was changed.

The primate's burning blood was now part of the pool.

The shift in the nature of the liquid that resided in the pool would have first been noticed by a new odor, tart and unpleasant. Yet the chamber within the Sentinel was empty and devoid of life.

As the sun passed over the Sentinel day after day, the composition of the fluid slowly altered. It retained most of the properties of essence, but it also developed some new properties.

Slowly, steadily, the liquid began to eat through the stone of the low wall around it.

Little by little, day by day, the fluid chipped at the stone, finding infinitely small cracks and dissolving the edges of the fissures until a seam opened up. When the seam tunneled through to the wall's outer edge, a single droplet of black liquid spilled out and onto the floor of the chamber with a hiss.

More time passed, and the steady steam of droplets became a trickle. The eating away of the wall now increased rapidly as the fluid hungrily found the path of escape, burrowing like a creature in the dirt, increasing the size of the opening with each moment that passed.

A watcher would have seen the level of the liquid decrease at a noticeable pace.

The unique liquid ran down the floor and found the spiral stairs. As it flowed down, it ate into the stone of the stairs until the stairway was gone, and the fluid ran down from above like a small waterfall.

And then the pool was dry.

The three seals on the portal faded first. They worked by draining the power from the pool. With no power left to drain, the seals ceased to function.

The shimmering silver surface of the portal shifted to burnt gold as it came to life.

The beacon sounded, shrill and overwhelming, rising and falling with each peal of its call.

The portal was open for a long instant before its innate power faded. In that brief window in time, a figure stepped out.

The portal closed behind him. The beacon stilled.

The man looked around the chamber.

He was tall and clad in rich black velvet, with diamonds set in silver on the cuffs of his long sleeves and a pendant of shining white crystal on a silver chain around his neck. His features were fine, almost delicate, and his eyes were a shade of intense blue, as light as the sky, yet as dead as the grave.

His lips were set with resolve, the lines of his forehead were cruel, and around his mouth there were only the marks of displeasure. This was not a man who smiled often.

His hair was severely pulled back from his forehead and it was a unique color, blood red, with the occasional lines of black at his temples.

Sentar Scythran, Lord of the Night, stood on the steps at the pool's center and turned, frowning and looking back at the portal behind him. Its color had shifted to silver to indicate it was no longer powered.

He took three steps down until he stood on the floor of what had once been a pool filled with essence. Squatting down, the Lord of the Night ran his fingertips over the dry floor and sighed. He straightened and looked around the chamber, remembering when he had last been in this place, on the day of his defeat.

He had always known he would one day return. The humans were weak, no doubt fighting among themselves as always, and ready to welcome him home.

The Lord of the Night inhaled deeply, breathing in the scent of a world he had left behind an eon ago. He was pleased to have returned, but the homecoming was tinged with sadness, for the way was now closed to his brothers.

A great weight had been placed on his shoulders. He would need an army, he knew, if he wanted to once more fill this pool with essence and open the way for his brethren. He would need to bring many of the humans under his dominion.

He walked forward, stepping over the low stone wall that rimmed the basin, now eaten away, until he stood at the summit of the opening where once there had been a stairway. The Lord of the Night knelt down again and touched his finger to a glistening spot, where the last trace of wetness remained.

He smiled. Essence.

A moment later Sentar Scythran, the Lord of the Night, floated down the empty stairwell.

He soon stood triumphantly in the open air, beside the great statue, gazing up at the stars, wondering on which one of the worlds above his brothers waited expectantly.

The Lord of the Night had returned.

ACKNOWLEDGMENTS

I wish to thank those whose combined efforts have made this novel into something no person could have made alone.

Huge thanks go to my editor, Emilie, and the team at 47North, for excellent guidance, support, and assistance with every aspect of development and publication.

Thanks go to Mike for (still more) tireless efforts with the editorial development of the manuscript, and for endless dedication and patience. I still feel I should insert an exclamation mark at the end of the last sentence.

I'd also like to thank all of the family, friends, and colleagues who over the years have provided me with constant support. In particular, I'd like to thank Marc F. for valuable input with too many things to mention, and Lyn W. for her editorial assistance.

Thanks to all of you who've reached out to me and taken the time to post reviews of my books.

Finally, thanks go to my wife, Alicia.

Without you there would be no dream to follow.

ABOUT THE AUTHOR

 James Maxwell found inspiration growing up in the lush forests of New Zealand, and later in rugged Australia where he was educated. Devouring fantasy and science fiction classics at an early age, his love for books translated to a passion for writing, which he began at age 11.

He relocated to London at age 25, but continued to seek inspiration wherever he could find it, in the grand cities of the old world and the monuments of fallen empires. His travels influenced his writing as he spent varying amounts of time in forty countries on six continents.

He wrote his first full-length novel, *Enchantress*, while living on an isle in Thailand and its sequel, *The Hidden Relic*, from a coastal town on the Yucatán peninsula in Mexico.

The third book in the Evermen Saga, *The Path of the Storm*, was written in the Austrian Alps, and he completed the fourth, *The Lore of the Evermen*, in Malta.

When he isn't writing or traveling, James enjoys sailing, snowboarding, classical guitar, and French cooking.